FOREVER TODAY

Book One

Katie J. Douglas

Forever Today
Copyright © 2019 Katie J. Douglas
Printed in the United States of America

This book is a work of fiction. Places, events, and situations
in this book are purely fictional and any resemblance to
actual persons, living or dead, is coincidental
* * * * *

Edited by Dr. Megan Hennessey-Croy

Cover design by Rachel Christmas

Photography by Ashley Elicio Photography

Formatted by Debora Lewis / Arena Publishing

ISBN-13: 9781798219966

For my husband and our three babies,
my whole heart.

I

"There is a crack in everything.
That's how the light gets in."
~Leonard Cohen

C harlotte was used to being new to places. In fact, it would've made her more uncomfortable to actually feel at home somewhere. She had been the new girl her whole life. Gypsies, that's how her mother referred to them. But sometimes homeless was a more accurate description. That life would be behind her now and Charlotte vowed to herself that she would never return. Aunt Rose was the only person she could turn to and she had no idea if that would even work. It was more than a leap of faith, it was a free-fall into the unknown.

When Charlotte showed up at her aunt's house in the middle of the night, Rose opened the door as if she expected her. She threw open her arms and embraced Charlotte in a tight, rocking hug.

"My baby niece is home at last!" she said, cackling loudly in Charlotte's ear. "It's about damn time you came to me, I've been waiting so long!" Rose ignored Charlotte's crumbled appearance and eyes that looked as if they hadn't slept for weeks. She likewise ignored the heavy bruising on Charlotte's biceps.

"Come, come. Inside with you," she said, pulling her through the small living room of her brick home. Rose chattered on and on about her home and Charlotte, who hadn't yet mumbled more than a brief hello, followed after her in a daze. Rose continued her rambling, aware that Charlotte didn't have an interest in telling her how and why she was there anyway. Rose pulled her around the house pointing out the bathroom, her room, and the guest room.

The house was clean and eclectic with art splattered over every possible surface. There were black and white pictures of wild horses covering one wall while another was seemingly dedicated to the religions of the world. Statues of the Virgin Mary and Buddha co-existed on the shelf while potted herbs and plants decorated the tables.

"Here's where you can come to chat with mother Mary, but careful, she's a straight shooter. Whoever else you need is here, too," she said, making a sweeping gesture over the wall.

"Aunt Rose," Charlotte finally got in. She hesitated, her voice hoarse from travel. "Can I- can I stay with you awhile?"

Charlotte felt her face flush through, ashamed to say the words aloud and to ask for the help that she knew she needed. She had spent her entire childhood in a state of relentless self-reliance, resisting the urge to ask help of anyone.

"Child," Rose stopped and turned to face Charlotte. "Has it been so hard for you that you've forgotten? You don't need to ask me that. This is your home for as long as you want it and I am your family. You're safe now, my love."

She pulled the girl to her and realized how much Charlotte had grown. The girl, who she'd not seen in at least 5 years, was now taller than her aunt. She was also striking, green eyes peeking out from behind her mess of blonde tangled hair.

Rose laughed loudly. "Shit, you've gotta know I love you because I'm not into this crying nonsense. See what you do to Aunt Rose? Makin' me soft!" Rose pulled away from her and quickly wiped the corners of her eyes as she turned away. "Oh now, let's get you settled. First thing's first though. We gotta clean your energy."

"My energy?" Charlotte said, amused. She had always known Aunt Rose was eccentric, but had forgotten that the woman, much like her mother, was full of surprises.

"Mmm hmm, yep. Gonna get you all cleaned up. Follow me."

Rose huddled into the bathroom and ran a bath in the claw foot tub. She opened a cupboard and took out small bottles of what looked like oils, tossing several drops into the bath. She lit candles all over the bathroom and turned on a small cassette player by the sink. Native American flutes playing an airy and soft melody came through the small speaker.

"Ok," Rose said. "That'll do us. Hop in here and I'll wash these clothes for you. I'm gonna get you some tea while you undress. Now, don't be shy, I'll wait for you to be back in the tub before I come back in. Christ though, if I had that body I don't know that I'd ever keep clothes on."

Rose blew out of the bathroom, leaving an exhausted Charlotte alone. She'd ridden four different Greyhounds to get there and didn't even know if Rose would be there when she did. She didn't have a plan B either. The anticipation of it all was overwhelming and she just wanted to sleep. But despite that, she didn't want to disobey her welcoming aunt, that strange woman so much like but unlike her mother at the same time. She unbuttoned her torn jeans and pulled them down her body with her underwear. Stripping off her shirt, she caught a glimpse of herself in the mirror. She didn't realize how bad the bruising was until she saw the blue and yellow circles popping off of her arm in the candlelight. Staring back at herself, she rubbed her hand over the sensitive bumps. To her surprise and horror, she thought she might cry. Instead, she jumped in the tub and immersed herself in the hot water, letting the oils and bubbles burn her face as she sank slowly under. When she came up, Rose was sitting next to the tub with a cup of tea that smelled of sage.

"Drink this, it'll fix you right up."

Charlotte put the tea to her lips and felt the warmth of it run down her throat. She tasted the rich honey and sage, soothing her mouth. At first she felt uncomfortable that her aunt was in the bathroom with her while she was naked as the day she was born, but the music and the candles and the calming scent of eucalyptus, coupled with the fact that she was just so tired, somehow made it ok. She relaxed, sipping her tea and listening to the sounds of the music coming from the cassette player. She felt peaceful. Like she could finally breathe again. She wanted to thank her aunt but didn't think that would be sufficient enough.

"Ok, now I'm going to teach you to clean your energy," Rose said, breaking the silence.

"Aren't I- I mean isn't that what I'm doing in the tub?" Charlotte asked, confused.

"No, that's for your spirit. You needed a little pampering," she said smiling at her sadly. "You clean your energy in your head, you see? It happens inside of you. Let me teach you," Rose said, scooting closer to the tub.

"This is all about intention and you can do this whenever you need to, but tonight we're gonna do it together and I'm going to clean your energy as well. Same time." Charlotte nodded in response, but she still didn't really understand just what the hell they were doing. Rose continued, "The purpose of this is to purge any negative energy or encounters you've had. To push that out and replace the bad energy with light. All you have to do is think it. Close your eyes lightly."

Charlotte obeyed and felt Rose reach for her hand in the soapy water. She put the other hand at the top of Charlotte's head, resting lightly above her forehead.

When she spoke, Rose's voice was melodic and soothing.

"We're going to start at the top of your head and work our way down the body. Again, all you have to do is think it. Envision a white, beautiful light traveling through your body, starting at your head and progressing down through your feet. This light is all-powerful, all-knowing, and Divine."

Charlotte concentrated, thinking of the light and the goodness that came from it. She felt a tingling in her fingers and toes, calming her in a way she had never felt before that.

"Charlotte, you are loved. Repeat that, say 'I am loved,'" Rose said. Her voice was completely different than how it was when Charlotte had first arrived.

"I am loved," Charlotte uttered.

"Again," Rose instructed.

"I am loved... I am loved...I am loved," Charlotte repeated over and over, feeling the new sensation pulsing through her body the more she believed it.

"Good," Rose whispered. "Very good. You are part of this world and you matter. You are loved."

Rose and Charlotte both sat silently listening to the flute music moving through the air. When Charlotte opened her eyes she felt like a different person. Despite her trek, she felt rested and content. She smiled at Rose who sat on her knees at the edge of the tub smiling back at her.

"Good shit, right?" Rose asked, eyes dancing.

Charlotte laughed, "Yeah, it's like magic." For an almost nineteen year old, Charlotte had seen a lot in this world but she had never seen or felt anything like that.

Rose waved a hand at her. "Nah, you ain't seen nothin yet. I'll teach you some real magic, my little spirit child. Now, here are some jammies. Why don't you put those on and we'll get into bed."

Later, they lay in Rose's colorful bed scattered with pillows, both of them eating ice cream out of the carton. Charlotte marveled at how close she felt to Rose despite the fact that they'd only met a couple of times before that. Charlotte's mom often referred to Rose as a witch, but Charlotte had never agreed. The few times she'd met her aunt they had formed an unbreakable bond, which Charlotte felt now more than ever.

"Ok, girl. You look exhausted. You'll sleep here with me tonight and tomorrow I'll get your bed all ready for you. That ok?" Charlotte nodded her head tiredly. She was back to being exhausted, but at least now she had clean energy, whatever that meant. Rose grabbed her hand and stroked the top of it with her painted thumbnail. "Good night, sweet girl," she said quietly.

"Thank you," Charlotte said and fell into an immediate and deep sleep.

Rose lay next to her holding onto her hand softly. She looked over her golden hair and the long black lashes that swept over the girl's cheeks. Her soft skin glowed in the lamplight of the bedroom. *Just a baby*, thought Rose. Rose considered herself one of the toughest people on the planet, but lying there next to her young beautiful niece she began to really cry for the first time in a very long time. She took care to stay quiet and not wake Charlotte. Her heart was sick with sadness and hot with anger at the same time. She stroked her niece's cheek softly.

"My baby niece," she said in a whisper. "How could she let that happen to you?"

Tears streamed down Rose's face and she prayed hard.

Please, God, let me help her. Please, God, allow her to thrive. Please, God, keep her safe. Please, God, make her strong.

⁓◦⊱0⊰◦⁓

Charlotte slept until 10 o'clock the next morning. A lifelong early riser, she was shocked when she woke to the bright sunlight coming through Rose's paisley bedroom curtains. She walked quietly into the kitchen to find her aunt, clad in overalls rolled up to the knee, making breakfast. Rose was a beautiful woman without having to try. What she lacked in height she more than made up for in curves that were obvious even in her overalls. She wore her brown hair piled on her head and her glasses at the tip of her nose. She had the look of both a woman who got things done and one you shouldn't mess with.

"Ah, Sleeping Beauty! How did you rest?" Rose said, continuing her cooking.

"Very good. Sorry, I never sleep in. I can't believe I didn't wake up when you did," Charlotte said, by way of explanation.

Rose waved her off. "You needed deep sleep, my dear. You certainly look better today, so does your aura!" She stopped, holding her spatula out to her side as she looked her up and down. "Dear lord- will you look at that? You're just, I mean, completely lit up! You'll be even better than me, I just know it," Rose said smiling broadly at Charlotte and turning back to fixing breakfast.

After handing Charlotte a plate of pancakes, crispy bacon, and scrambled eggs with green chili, she left the room and returned her clean clothes from the night before. Rose noted that Charlotte had but one duffle bag with her when she arrived and figured there couldn't be much in there.

"Now, I washed your clothes so after breakfast you get dressed and I'm going to show you around town. Then I thought we could zip over to Sierra Vista and do some shopping. We gotta get you a few things."

Rose's eyes danced with excitement as she looked at Charlotte for approval. Charlotte nodded politely with a full mouth of breakfast. She tried not to inhale the food as if she hadn't eaten, but she couldn't help herself. She knew she'd lost a few pounds in the last days of travel and the previous few months. After buying her bus ticket, she only had ten dollars and some change left for food the entire trip and she used it sparingly. The hearty breakfast in front of her was something she hadn't had in a very long time, but it embarrassed her to appear like an orphan child eating her first meal. She cleaned her plate and did not reach for more food, but sat quietly while Rose chattered on about their day.

"I think I'll take you to the taco stand in Sierra Vista for lunch. Do you like tacos?" She put another pancake on Charlotte's plate and shoveled more eggs and bacon onto the side. Charlotte nodded yes to the tacos and uttered a soft thank you for the second helping of breakfast.

"Well, that's good because that's what we have to offer here, summers as hot as the devil's asshole and Mexican food. Oh, Mexican men, too," she said, grinning. "Highly recommend those as well."

After dressing, Rose brought her through the side door of her house and into what she called her shop. It was a small, beautiful room with an antique wooden desk and a daybed covered in throw pillows. On the walls were tapestries of elephants and colorful designs. Charlotte was overwhelmed with a feeling of peace when she walked into the room and as Rose showed her around it, she noticed her aunt was watching her closely, a look of curiosity on her face.

"So, Aunt Rose?" Charlotte didn't quite know how to phrase the question. "What do you- I mean what is your business? What do you do?"

Rose laughed. "Didn't your mother ever tell you?" Charlotte flinched at the first mention of her mother but checked herself quickly. She shook her head but then reconsidered.

"Well, I guess she did, kinda," she hesitated briefly but Rose's friendly face urged her onward. "She said you were a witch."

Rose doubled over in laughter, cackling happily as she had to put her hand on the desk to support herself. She composed herself, wiping the corners of her eyes.

"That bitch'll never change will she?" she said to herself. She looked at Charlotte and tried to make herself be more serious. "Some people call me a witch, yes, but that's not really what I am. I prefer a white witch if people insist on that term since I work with light and not darkness." She assessed Charlotte's face but saw the girl was not intimidated nor uncomfortable, she looked more curious than anything. "I'm a lightworker, psychic, medium, clairvoyant, spiritual advisor- people all have their way of referring to me so it's- whatever. I basically utilize a sixth sense that we all have but most people don't develop. Understand?"

"Yes, I get it," Charlotte said.

"There's nothing really weird about it, you know. There are some maniacs who give us all a bad name but it really is just like a normal skill. Do you ever get a gut feeling about something, Charlotte? Or know something before it happens?"

Charlotte thought about all of the times her own mind had warned her of danger, how her constant voice inside of her guided her to higher ground when she needed it. She nodded and Rose beamed back at her.

"Yes, I bet you do. You've had the gift since you were small. That's why I tell you that you're my spirit baby. We've had many lives together, my sweet girl. And now you're back to me." Rose tried hard not to cry, but her eyes welled up. "It is my job to teach you and to take care of you. I'm only sorry it took this long for us to be together. You will be the most important work I will ever do and Charlotte, I promise to you that I will keep you safe." She looked the girl square in the eye and saw the doubt flash across Charlotte's face.

"I know, Charlotte. I know how you've been let down. I know it all and I swear to you I will prove it. I will not fail you." Charlotte shifted on her feet uncomfortably before Rose walked to her and embraced her again. She kissed her fiercely on the cheek before pulling away. "Oh damn it, Rose. I don't know what the hell is wrong with me. We don't have to talk about all of this now. I guess I just- I've been waiting for you and I-I want you to know you're safe."

Charlotte's voice was hardly above a whisper when she spoke. "I believe you, Aunt Rose."

Rose sighed heavily. "Well, shit, girl. Thank God. Lord knows you have no reason to trust anyone. Ok, enough of me being such a downer. Aunt Rose wants to spoil you today. Let's go shopping."

If Charlotte were to rank the days in her life up to that point, that first day with Rose might have been the best one. They drove the hour to Sierra Vista through the rolling hills of Arizona wine country, which consisted of three wineries. Rose fussed over Charlotte, insisting she get several new outfits, shoes, a swimsuit, and a new comforter for the guest bed. Rose oohed and awed over everything the girl tried on, going on about her perfect figure. Charlotte tried her hardest to be nonchalant but thankful. Most of all, she tried to act like this was not the very first time she got to buy clothes somewhere other than Goodwill. At lunch she excused herself to go to the bathroom where she sat on the toilet lid and sobbed.

It was sweltering that June day in Arizona. Even for a state used to droughts, that year seemed particularly bad. The air was dry and crisp among the rolling grass fields down south, so much so that it seemed every week there was a new prairie fire to put out. One careless cigarette out the window and 30 acres could be up in smoke before anything could be done. All the better, the local ranchers would say, the monsoons would be there soon and make everything green up after the earth was scorched. It was one of Mother Nature's most interesting metaphors- destruction, then beauty.

Wyatt parked his truck on a small dirt road that snaked back behind the lake, making accessible the quiet coves that few came to on days like this. The front of the lake was where most people went. Locals sat soaking in the warm water, doing anything but standing out in the oppressive heat. The lake was a social place and the people of Patagonia had enough solitude living in their tiny speck of a town that most saw no need to isolate themselves further. Plus, for the young people, that was where the other young people were, swimsuit clad and all. Wyatt, though, had no interest in that. Fishing and solitude were all he could ask for after the morning he had on the ranch.

So far he was enjoying his work on the ranch, but there was no getting around the fact that the work was almost unbearably difficult and he was forced to spend day and night with the other men who worked there. Sharing a bunkhouse with them made him miss even brief moments of solitude that were easily accessible at home. Plus, he was the most green among them and the only one who didn't speak Spanish fluently, making him the outsider. They would speak quick Spanish and Wyatt knew enough to know that he was sometimes the butt of their jokes. He wasn't fully part of their circle, which was an odd place for someone like him to be that summer.

He got out of his truck, taking his fishing pole and tackle box out of the back. He hadn't changed out of his work clothes, which he was now regretting. The long sleeve cotton shirt stuck to his back as his work boots kicked at the dust beneath him. The desert brush scraped against his jeans as he walked, oftentimes breaking for the weight of him. Wyatt, as his new boss described him, was a brick shithouse of a young man. He had filled out over the last year and his over 6-foot frame, which used to be lanky and sinuous, had transformed into a tower of lean muscle built for work. He was growing accustomed to his new physique but had to constantly think about his movements and actions, so as not to appear like a Labrador puppy.

As he wound around the rough path to the lake, the shore finally came into view. Water in southern Arizona was rare. Wyatt knew that back east and other places there were huge lakes stretching so far you might think they were an ocean. Not so in Arizona. Patagonia Lake was fairly small, but since it was set among rolling hills and rocky formations, there were places to hide, giving it the appearance of something larger. He was not uppity about the size of the lake though. When someone grows up in the dryness of Arizona, they are thankful for water in any capacity, no matter how small. The lake was calm and pristine that day with a clear open sky stretching above the reflection of it. Only the mesquite trees and brush near the shore looked green. From where Wyatt stood he could see the ring around the lake where the lushness of those trees stopped and continued into the crisp summer desert.

He approached the shore, choosing the biggest tree he could find to set up under for fishing. Plus, he thought, if the fish weren't biting, he could lean against the tree and shut his eyes. Truth be told, that was why he had come. He knew afternoons weren't the best for fishing, but why stay back in the ranch when the bunkhouse had no air conditioning anyway? Better to be there in the quiet, albeit hot as hell, stillness of nature than in the sweaty close quarters with the other men. He squatted next to the shore, opening his tackle box. He would have preferred a worm to fish with but had no energy to dig for them so he settled for salmon eggs. He baited his hook and tied the bobber on an arm's length away from the bait. Lazy fishing, he knew, but it would be easier to pop an eye open to check the bobber rather than fish off the bottom and have to hold his rod feeling for a bite.

After casting his line out far into the water, he stood on the sandy bank and unbuttoned his shirt, stripping it from his broad shoulders. He dunked it into the shallows of the lake and wrapped it around the top of his head like the Vaqueros at the ranch had taught him. He sat squatting there looking around the oasis. In the distance, he could hear the hum of a few small boats and the muffled distant voices of the people at the front. There was no one near him, and he was thankful. Quiet was what he needed. No one asking him to tie another fence post or dig another trench, just quiet. He secured his rod upright in the rocks and sat against the tree with the cool shirt pulled down over his eyes. Ranch work had completely worn him out and he was asleep within minutes.

Since he had arrived at the ranch almost all of his dreams were about the day's work. Constant fencing, digging, fixing equipment. He had classic anxiety dreams about not getting to work on time and about the other men making him build a fence but leaving him locked on the other side of it. Today, though, as he shut his eyes, he fell almost immediately into a dream about water. He was swimming in cool open water, sinking himself to the bottom as he watched the bubbles float above him. He could breathe just fine, so he kept inhaling and blowing out long streams of air. But he was not alone; there was someone else with him. She swam through his air bubbles so gracefully that he thought she was a mermaid. She must be, he thought to himself. She floated at the top of the water where the bubbles hit her back, rolling effortlessly as though she were part of them. He tried swimming toward her, but when he pushed through the water it was thick like slime and he couldn't move through.

"You're getting a bite," he heard a voice say through the fog of his sleep.

He struggled to a sitting position, unsure about where he was for a moment because of the shirt over his eyes. The sun blazed onto his face once he ripped it off. When his eyes adjusted, he saw her standing at the shore. Cutoff shorts, bikini top, and long blonde hair falling to the middle of her back. He thought he might still be dreaming at first. She was so achingly beautiful standing there that it was hard to believe she was real. She stood looking at him and it took him a moment to realize that her full mouth was smiling at him, on the verge of laughing.

"Sorry," she laughed. "I didn't realize you were sleeping. You've got a fish on your line," she said, gesturing toward the water.

Wyatt stared dumbly at her for a moment, still trying to get his bearings. He pushed himself to his feet, realizing how silly he must look in his work jeans, boots, and no shirt. He felt his face burning, self-conscious in the way only a young man who hasn't grown into himself can be. He retrieved his rod from the rocks and began reeling in the line, moving closer toward the shore and to her. Blissfully, she had stopped looking at him and was watching the line in the water as he reeled it in.

He could feel the tug in his hands and the fish biting on the other end. He hadn't planned on catching anything really- hadn't even brought a stringer with him. Afternoon summer days were the worst for catching fish, he had just wanted to nap for Christ sakes. As the fish came closer, the girl waded out into the water and grabbed the end of his line. She laughed heartily when she pulled it up out of the water, exposing a three-inch long bluegill fish. Wyatt smiled back at her again, feeling his face turn another shade deeper. He already looked like a jackass sleeping against a tree with a shirt around his head and now he had a goldfish at the end of his line in front of what might be the most beautiful girl he had ever seen.

"It's just a little bluegill!" she said amused.

"Oh," Wyatt stumbled over a speech. "I- I'm surprised I even caught anything really," he said, trying to sound casual.

"Yeah, so am I. Didn't think you could catch anything in this lake unless you fished off the bottom. But I guess that's what you catch when you don't," she said, chuckling to herself.

Wyatt wanted to defend himself. He wanted to tell her that he knew how to fish and he knew he should've been fishing off the bottom all along, really, but he had just wanted to nap. He wanted to tell her of all the fishing trips he'd been on, the bass that he had caught at lakes up north. How he was also a hunter and had taken his first whitetail at 300 yards. He wanted to pound on his chest and tell her he was a real man and knew how to fish so she shouldn't think he was a pansy. Instead, he just stood there with the rod in his hands looking at her with his mouth agape. She grabbed the bluegill and deftly removed the hook, pushing the line away from her.

"He's just a little guy. Look how cute he is." She held the fish out in her hands for Wyatt to see. "I'm assuming you don't want to keep him, right? You don't need him for dinner or anything, do you?" she asked sarcastically while appraising his sturdy frame from head to toe.

"No, I think I'll pass on him," he said.

She squatted down in the water and put the fish in. The bluegill lay on its side looking like it might die; it did not swim away. She moved farther down into the water until her jean shorts were completely soaked through. She took the fish into her hands and started running him back-and-forth, allowing water to go through the gills. Wyatt watched her, mesmerized. He had never seen a girl touch a fish like that without flinching, let alone a girl who looked like her. A smile came to the girl's face as the fish swim away.

"There he goes," she said more to herself than Wyatt. She stood up and turned to face him, letting her eyes roam down his bare chest to his dirty jeans and scuffed boots. He felt hot and anxious as she looked him over and stood frozen.

"Well, thank you," Wyatt stuttered. "I guess I just fell asleep for a while," he said, repeating himself nervously.

"Yeah you did. I saw your bobber going crazy the whole time I walked across the beach," she said pointing down the banks. "Looked like you had a big one on the line. Those little ones can be feisty." She looked directly into his face then, flashing him a toothy grin.

Wyatt thought he might fall over. He felt as though someone had punched him in the stomach, and hard. She wore no makeup, but had tanned, shiny skin, large and wide set green eyes, and the most beautiful mouth Wyatt had ever seen. Where in the hell had she come from?

"I'm Wyatt," he said, pulling himself together and pushing his hand out for her to shake.

"As in Earp?" she said, teasing him again.

"Yes, actually," he answered, smiling back at her. "My mom likes westerns."

"Ah, that explains it. Well, I'm Charlotte," she said, shaking his hand. The softness of her skin was in stark contrast to how firmly she touched him.

"As in the web?"

"No, as in Brontë," she said flashing him that grin again. "My mom likes literature."

Wyatt made a mental note to find out who the hell Charlotte Brontë was as he nodded to her.

"Well it's nice to meet you, Charlotte. What were you doing here today before you caught my own fish for me?" he asked, finally getting ahold of himself.

She shrugged. "Just swimming. There's a great hole down that bank and nobody's there," she said, stretching her arms out over her head yawning. "Such a beautiful day!"

Wyatt thought about telling her it was not a beautiful day, that it was hotter than hell, but looking at her standing in front of him, cutoff jeans hanging low off of her slender tanned waist, he could not argue the fact that this was maybe the best day ever.

"Yes," he smiled, "not the best for fishing, but definitely a great day." His blue eyes roamed the canvas of her face, fixating on her mouth.

She squinted at him, holding her hand over her eyes. "Are you from here? I feel like I've seen you somewhere."

Definitely not, he thought. He would've remembered meeting her.

"Well, I'm not from here but I'm working down here for a while. Over at the 87 Ranch. What about you? Are you from here?"

Wyatt already knew the answer. There was literally no way this girl was from Patagonia. She looked like nothing he had seen before in this town, let alone in the state. The way she moved, the way she talked, everything indicated to him that she was not native to her surroundings.

"Just moved here actually. My aunt lives here." She gave no further details other than that and Wyatt didn't ask. He wanted to ask several follow-ups like, where do you work? Where can I find you? Would you like to go out on a date? Will you marry me? He nodded at her instead. He could not think of anything else to say that wouldn't make him sound like a moron, a feeling he had experienced quite enough of for one day.

"Well, nice to meet you, Wyatt Earp," she said, smiling at him as she started away.

"Oh, yeah… you, too, Charlotte," Wyatt hesitated, taken off guard at her abrupt departure. "So, I'll see you around?" He tried to keep the hopefulness out of his voice and failed.

"Yep!" she said and then she started off down the path toward his truck. He couldn't keep himself from watching her go. She moved effortlessly through the desert brush even in flip-flops and shorts. Wyatt could not take his eyes off of her long muscular legs that moved quickly and quietly away from him through the desert. And then she was gone.

He squatted back down on the beach and looked around the lake again. It seemed empty without her there, but it also seemed as though he dreamed her all along. He sat trying to still his racing thoughts and the strange feeling in his gut that he couldn't shake. As a teenage boy he had experienced lust plenty of times, but this was not lust. He could not place it, but all he knew in that moment was he wanted more of it. More of Charlotte.

⁕

The next day at the ranch was the hardest day of work that Wyatt could remember. He felt like he was moving through molasses, partly because he hadn't slept and partly because he was counting the seconds until the day's work was finished. He had tossed and turned the night before trying to fall asleep to no avail. All he could think about was her. The way she talked, the easy way she laughed, her long unruly hair that framed her exquisite face.

He wanted to know absolutely everything about her and was desperate to see her again. Of course, the town was small but would she be back at the lake? Could he find her? Could he ask around until he knew where to look? But even then, what if he did ask and the other guys at the ranch got the jump on him? Before he knew it, he had worked himself up into a complete panic that he would never see her again.

That she was a figment of his imagination and probably didn't exist anyway.

He had no idea what was wrong with him, he was acting like this was the first girl he had ever seen. Since the second he met her there was burning in his chest that he could not contain. Even while he was busy digging trenches and doing the demanding physical work on the ranch, he simply could not think of anything else even if he tried.

"No, gringo!" Santiago yelled from across the yard. "This is the dirt you need to fill that ditch around back," he said shaking his head in annoyance, tapping himself on his own temple. "Donde?" he questioned. "Where's that smart white head of yours?"

Wyatt pulled himself back to the present moment, realizing he had checked out for a while and transferred the dirt he was shoveling into a random pile rather than into the waiting wheelbarrow. He squinted, looking up at Santiago who still had the irritated look on his face.

"Oh- I- I forgot," he said, exhausted.

"Yeah, forgetting all day long, gringo." He rolled his eyes before walking back into the barn to saddle his horse.

Wyatt couldn't even bring himself to get mad at Santiago's nagging for once. His head was someplace else. At the moment it was on Charlotte's plump lips and what they were capable of doing. Nevertheless, he finally pulled his head back to his chores and began filling the wheelbarrow. He started working systematically, shoveling a heaping pile into the barrow then bringing it in front of the barn.

Sometimes he felt like all he did on the ranch was move dirt from one pile to another. Busy work was his least favorite thing, but after weeks there he could see the progress that those worthless chores had made and it was significant. Wyatt did not complain either way, though; he did what was asked of him. He was one of four men working at the ranch that summer but he was the whipping boy since he was the newest.

When he heard about the job from a friend of his, Wyatt immediately knew he wanted it. High school was coming to an end and so was his parents' marriage. Wyatt being the only child, they had seemingly waited for him to graduate to officially divorce, living under the same roof but completely separate lives. The irony of them staying together for Wyatt was not lost on him. They made life at home painful and uncomfortable, hardly like the life he was used to growing up. He wanted to scream at them to just end it already, to put them all out of their misery, but that was simply not how things were handled in their family. Deal with it quietly and ignore the truth as much as possible. If you're lucky, it might just go away.

That was the force that drove him down to Patagonia from his Tucson home all of those months ago. When he came up the long winding driveway to Garrett's place, he felt a longing to be there in that solitude and away from the traffic and people of the city. Away from his home which no longer felt like home. He only needed the job until October when he would leave Arizona behind him for good. The ranch owner, Garrett Sturgeon, gave him the world's fastest interview that first day. He walked up to Wyatt's truck and shook his hand firmly while assessing his frame.

"Can you ride?" Garrett started.

"Yes, sir."

"Rope?"

"Yes, sir."

"You know how to work with irrigation?"

Wyatt hesitated, but then figured it couldn't be that hard. "Yes, sir."

"Alright, then. June first. Room and board- two meals a day- you gotta take care of your own dinner. Bring a bedroll."

"Yes, sir," Wyatt repeated.

"Well, come on then. I'll show you around."

Wyatt figured that Garrett was about 60, but he didn't seem his age. He walked quickly and efficiently and was sturdy on his booted feet. He walked Wyatt around the dilapidated but tidy barn and pointed out to the fields.

"I run the cattle here most of the year but I still have some out on the back pasture, too. You boys'll help me bring 'em in at the end of summer. The vaqueros will mostly be workin' with the cattle though. You'll have other work up around the barn and stables."

Wyatt nodded, trying not to show his disappointment. He had read enough Louis L'Amour over the years to know he wanted to be out working the cattle, not back at the ranch doing grunt work. The rest of the men, all migrant workers from Mexico, had vast experience in everything from construction to cattle and Garrett encouraged Wyatt to learn from them.

"Lotta folks treat them like they're less than, but that's not how it works here." They stood with their arms draped over the welded metal fence overlooking the horses, watching two of the men work with a young gelding. "They know this land better than I ever could and damn if they don't know how to do just about everything." He spit a long stream of tobacco out in front of him.

Wyatt believed him. Just by watching the way the men moved with the horses, he could tell they weren't very wet behind the ears. The gelding, clearly only green broke, hopped from side to side as an older man held him on a halter and the other moved to put a saddle blanket on him. The older man holding the horse moved with authority and grace, speaking Spanish in hushed tones to the animal. The younger man, who Wyatt would later learn was named Santiago, proved to be agile, moving out of the horse's way continuously, predicting his next moves. Santiago, or as the other vaqueros called him, Guapo, was enjoying the challenge. His profile set in intention, he couldn't keep the wide grin off of his face, white teeth sparkling in the sun. He was thoroughly enjoying the gelding playing hard to get.

Finally he slipped the blanket and saddle over the horse's back then pulled the cinch under him, skillfully buckling it with such ease that it made Wyatt envious. Santiago turned first to the old man holding the horses who smiled, then to Garrett who gave a brief nod of approval. Santiago puffed out his chest and took the lead-rope out of the older man's hands to walk the gelding in the round pen. The older man walked over to stand near Garrett and Wyatt.

"This is Luis. Luis, this here is Wyatt. He'll be our new hand this summer," Garrett said, introducing the two. Luis smiled all the way up to his kind eyes, his crow's feet scrunching up in the friendliest of manners.

"Muy grande!" he said gesturing to Wyatt's broad shoulders. "It's good," he laughed. "It's good for work."

Wyatt shook his hand firmly and smiled back at him, nodding in understanding. They started watching Santiago lead the horse around the round pen. Wyatt noticed that his way was not as gentle as Luis's and that every time the horse got out of line he used the tail end of the lead rope to roughly slap at the side of the him. Santiago made a point not to look at Wyatt and the other men and soon after he led the horse out of the round pen and into the barn. Wyatt never did meet him the first day he came to the ranch and when he showed up for work that summer he realized why. Santiago was what Wyatt's father would describe as a peacock. He had no use for someone like Wyatt since he wanted to be the youngest, strongest, fastest vaquero on the ranch. There certainly wasn't room for Wyatt or his biceps bulging out of his t-shirt. From the time Wyatt arrived that summer, Santiago took great joy in scolding Wyatt and making him look stupid whenever possible.

To make matters worse, Santiago's cousin Raul, a smaller, less good looking version of Santiago, was one of the other hands. He reveled in Wyatt's struggles and sat at Santiago's heel like a faithful ankle-biter, grinning as Santiago would admonish Wyatt. And old Luis, although kind to Wyatt, was family to them as well, though Wyatt couldn't ever figure out how. He had grown up with enough Mexicans and Mormons to know that the term "cousin" was used loosely, and families were so big that they were all basically cousins. So he was outnumbered and outranked that summer, but he had asked for it. He had left dozens of friends and faces he'd known his entire life to come here and do this. This was after all, a self-imposed isolation so there could be no complaining about it.

Wyatt wiped the sweat from his forehead with the sleeve of his dusty work shirt. He was starting to regret coming there all together but then he remembered there was Charlotte. There was the hope to see her again and that was enough to light a fire under his ass to finish digging that trench for the day.

⚬⚬⚬

It had been four days since he'd seen her, not that he was counting or anything. He had tried to go everywhere she might be. Back to the lake at the same time every day, then to three different restaurants in town- the one pizza place, ice cream shop, and local Mexican food joint. He drove around town slowly, casually looking for her. He was fairly ashamed of his desperation and wondered more than once if his behavior bordered on stalking. The town was not that big, he should have been able to find her. Granted, he had not asked anyone about her yet. Garrett was an old man and wouldn't know and if he told the other men on the ranch about her, God only knows what the repercussions might be. Other than that he knew no one in town, so he was on his own.

The days were getting oppressively hot, but Wyatt was used to this type of summer. June in Arizona is when residents earn the right to the winter and spring weather. He felt the anticipation of the impending monsoon season, which he knew would arrive within weeks. Until then, the talk would be about how this year must be the hottest on record and that last year never came close to being this dry. Then a period of denial invariably took hold, during which people would cast their doubts about whether the storms would come at all. But Wyatt knew, as sure as the sun rose each morning, the storms would come.

It was Friday afternoon and he found himself back at the lake. He told himself there was nothing else to do in the heat so even if she wasn't there again, it would be fine. But he did check his teeth in the rearview mirror and ran his hands through his thick black hair several times before getting out of his truck, just in case. That day he had the presence of mind to wear his swim trunks and a t-shirt so he would at least look like he belonged there. He left his fishing pole at the bunkhouse since it would be his luck to catch an even smaller fish that time. He felt like an ox lately- like nothing would go his way from everything work related to Charlotte. He simply couldn't catch a break.

He walked down to his tree and stripped off his t-shirt, hanging it on a nearby branch before diving in and swimming out into the lake. His lean muscles were sore from work on the ranch but the windmill motion of the swim coupled with the coolness of the water stretched him out nicely. He swam in a big loop back to shore, then sat in the shallows of the lake, shaking the water from his hair.

He sat looking over the lake and the distant mountaintops. As much as he thought he was ready to leave, Arizona was in his heart. He would miss it, heat and all. He knew it would always be home for him and he'd come back someday, but it was time for a new place. Her voice tore him from his self-reflection, back to the present moment and what he had come there for that day. Her. She came from the other side this time and just like the last, Wyatt did not hear her coming.

"Mr. Earp? Is that you?"

She spoke loudly, still walking up the shore, shielding her eyes from the sun with her hand. She wore the same simple blue bikini top and cutoff shorts. Her hair damp from swimming, she smiled brightly at Wyatt who still sat in the water. In all of these days trying to find her he hadn't thought of what he would say or how he would start to speak to her.

After a long pause he shouted back, "Yeah, hi Charlotte."

She was coming closer to him now and even though he didn't think it was possible, she was more stunning than he originally realized. Her tall thin figure was accented by rounded hips and breasts that reminded Wyatt of a Coke bottle.

"I was wondering if I'd see you here again. Anything biting today?" she said, raising her eyebrows in humor.

"No- I'm not fishing today. Thought I'd quit it for good after catching that bluegill the other day," he smiled at her. His wide mouth was full of perfect white teeth. *Braces*, Charlotte thought. *Definitely braces*. She threw her head back and laughed at him, mocking pity.

"Ah- no. That bluegill was a prized fish. You should've been proud."

She was standing next to him on the beach and before Wyatt could stand up, she started to unbutton her cutoffs and shimmy them down her hips and legs. Wyatt felt his face flush through as he looked up at her. He willed his thoughts away from the gutter with all of the mental fortitude he could muster.

"Mind if I join you?" she asked.

"No- I- yeah, have a seat," he said gesturing to the water next to him.

"I went for a swim at the front of the lake earlier." She made a cringing face. "Too busy up there."

"Yeah, nothing else to do in the heat I guess." *Damn*, he thought, the front of the lake was the one place he hadn't looked.

Charlotte nodded. "So are you from Arizona? You said not from this town but you look like an Arizona guy."

"Oh- do I?" he asked, amused. "I wasn't aware we had a 'look'."

"Well, it's the tan mostly. And the boots, I guess."

Wyatt grinned at her. "You've got me then. Born and raised in Tucson. Have you been up there yet?"

"Just passed through- looks nice though."

"Yeah, I like it. Most of my friends talk about wanting to leave, though, since there's nothing to do there."

Charlotte rolled her eyes. "Everyone says that. Literally everywhere I've lived. Everyone always wants out of their hometown. Except in Texas. People in Texas don't think there's any other place on earth."

"So is that where you're from then?"

She shook her head adamantly. "No- God, no. I've lived there though. We, um- my mom liked to move a lot so I'm not really from anywhere."

He wanted to ask where else she had lived, but she changed the subject quickly, asking him about his job on the ranch. She spoke to him so easily that he felt himself lulled into the conversation, his nerves floating away. He tried not to make direct eye contact with her, though, because when he did, it was jarring. Her green eyes were a dark shade he had never seen before and he lost his footing in the conversation when he looked in them.

She asked questions about his job, whether or not he'd been to the Grand Canyon, and if he'd gone to Tombstone to see where his namesake had become famous. He was surprised at the easy, open way she spoke to him and inwardly worried that maybe she was too comfortable in front of him. Usually girls were a little nervous in front of Wyatt. His friends literally used him as bait before they swooped in to do the real work since Wyatt never could close the deal the way they did. But Charlotte didn't seem intimidated by him or his appearance and he didn't know whether or not that was a good sign.

"So where are you living again? You said with your aunt, right?"

"Yes," she said. "She has a business here and she wants me to be her apprentice this summer," she said, a smile crossing her face.

"So what does she do? Is her business here in town?" Wyatt had learned his lesson, he would be able to find her this time.

"Well..." Charlotte paused. "She has a- it's like a counseling shop in town. Like a spiritual counseling place."

Wyatt didn't understand what that was exactly, but nodded his head at her.

"What's the name of it?"

"It's called Spirit's Soul," she said, appraising his reaction. "Have you heard of it?"

He shook his head. "I'm pretty new to the area, too. I basically only go here and the ranch. And the pizza place some nights," he added, hoping she might go also.

"Well, come by, anytime. My aunt is really nice and I'm sure she'd LOVE you."

Charlotte grinned thinking of Rose's reaction if she were to see Wyatt come in the shop. She'd lived with her just short of two weeks, but had fast discovered her aunt's affinity for good-looking men of all ages and races. Rose didn't discriminate.

"So will she, like, read my palm or something?" he teased.

Charlotte shrugged. "Among other things. She's magical, as she puts it."

Wyatt noticed the way her face became soft when she spoke of her aunt. Just like she couldn't hide her distaste for Texas, she couldn't hide her affection for her aunt. They sat chatting in the shallows of the water for what felt like a long time. Wyatt didn't want it to come to an end and kept thinking about what he would do the moment she said she had to go, when she would disappear through the desert again.

"Look, a little sunfish!" Charlotte said pointing out a fish swimming near their feet. "You need me to grab it for you? You know, for dinner?"

He felt like he would never live down that fish, and tried to keep his face from blushing, smiling good-naturedly.

"I swear I can fish. That was a fluke, an off day." He looked sideways at her and she pursed her lips at him.

"Alright," she said, "I believe you. Anyone with the name Wyatt should, in theory, be a skilled outdoorsman. Wyatt? Not Earp, but?"

"Sterling," he said, sticking his hand out of the water for her to shake. "Wyatt Sterling."

"Sterling? That might be a better cowboy name than Earp! Well nice to officially meet you, Mr. Sterling. Charlotte Holt."

He took her hand in his and shook it firmly, his large hand completely enveloping hers.

"Likewise."

The two kept their eyes locked briefly as they touched, both feeling the warm sturdy energy emanating from the other.

"Well, I better go," she said.

Wyatt was once again taken off guard at her quickness to leave, and inwardly scrambled for a way to get her to stay, if only for another moment.

"Oh- yeah- ok," he said. "So where did you park? Upfront?"

She stood and shook her head.

"Naw," she said, moving to retrieve her cut offs. "I walked over from town. It's actually not bad when you cut through here," she said, gesturing to the desert in the general direction of town.

Wyatt was indignant; it was at least a three-mile walk to town and it was over 100 degrees out. As far as he could see she had brought no water and not even proper shoes. The outdoorsman inside of him was floored that she had made that trek before.

"No, you can't do that. There are snakes everywhere this time of year, and that's far in this heat," he said, walking after her. "I have my truck right here, I can take you home."

Her entire demeanor changed once he said it. She looked down at the ground and swiftly pulled her shorts on over her wet swimsuit. He couldn't be sure, but it looked like she might be afraid.

"No, really. I'm fine, I've done it every day. It's no big deal and I know to watch for snakes, I've lived places with snakes before."

Wyatt didn't want to be pushy but was not to be deterred. It wasn't even about getting more time with her, it really was more about the fact what she was going to do was dangerous. The area was full of drug smugglers on top of the snakes, and the cowboy his parents raised could never let a girl, or anyone else, walk three miles through the desert alone. He put his shirt and baseball hat on and turned to her.

"No, really. I just can't let you do that- it's so dangerous. Please let me take you home. Plus, Wyatt Earp would never leave a lady helpless in the desert."

He smiled broadly at her and she couldn't help but smile back. She looked closely at his face and tried to read him like Rose had taught her. She felt for his energy and asked herself if he was safe. The softness of him came immediately through and there was a resounding *yes* from her intuition. She wanted to tell him that she wasn't helpless but he was just so sweet and so eager to be helpful she couldn't bring herself to do it.

"OK, Wyatt. Deal."

⁓⋙•❂•⋘⁓

He didn't know what he expected her to be like but whatever it was, he wouldn't have been right. She was funny, for one, self-deprecating, smart, interested in the world around her. Overall Wyatt could settle on the fact that she was different from any other girl he'd ever met. She marched to her own music in her head, that much was obvious.

On the drive home from the lake she continued her questions- if he played sports, about the horses at the ranch, whether or not he liked it there or missed home. She spoke in such a way that Wyatt knew she wasn't just trying to fill the silence, she truly listened to his answers. He certainly wasn't used to speaking to a girl the way he was speaking to her. Most of the girls he knew acted differently depending on who was around. But Wyatt got the feeling that he was getting the whole Charlotte, right then and there.

"So do you get to ride every day at work?" she was asking.

Wyatt wanted to be honest, but he could tell she was so interested in the horses he couldn't help but embellish a bit.

"Yes, most days, he's got some really great horses there."

"I *love* to ride. I mean, I haven't done that much of it but I'm jealous you get to ride all of the time." She glanced over at him across the cab of his truck. Her wavy hair had started to dry and was hanging long and unruly, below her breasts. He tried not to look but when he glanced at her, his eyes roamed down her body briefly before he tore them back to the road. *Please God do not let me crash this truck on the way to her house*, he thought.

She pointed down a small side street off of Main Street. "Right there, it's that one." She pointed out Rose's quaint brick home, yard impeccably mowed and potted flowers decorating the porch. To the side, he saw a smaller building attached to the home with the hand-painted sign labeled, "Spirit's Soul."

"So this is it, huh? Where all of the magic happens?"

"Oh, Aunt Rose would love that description," she said laughing.

He pulled up toward the front and put the truck in park.

"Well thank you so much for the ride, you really didn't have to do that."

"You're welcome," he said shyly. She locked eyes with him and smiled, not showing her teeth. There was a brief moment of silence between them.

"OK, I'll see you around," she said, climbing out of the truck. That did it for Wyatt. He wasn't about to let it end the same way it had all of those agonizing days ago. He opened the door to his truck and met her in front of the hood.

"Can I? I mean, would you want to, like, hang out sometime? Maybe go out for pizza or something?"

He could feel his face burning as he said it and for some reason his words sounded so ridiculous to him. Why pizza? Why not just hang out? He was second-guessing his every move with her, not wanting to appear as the boy he still felt like inside.

"Yes, of course. It's just that I don't know if that is, you know, all right with my aunt and everything. I don't know her rules and things like that."

Wyatt looked at the ground, feeling rejected. "Oh, OK then. Maybe one day."

She smiled brightly back at him, shaking her head. "No, I'm not bullshitting you, I would really like to go out. Maybe you could just meet my aunt first? She's just really protective over me."

"Oh good," he laughed. "I didn't take you for the bullshitting kind."

"Anything but that," she said smiling.

"Well, OK then. Just let me know when would be a good time."

"How about tomorrow? What time are you done with work?"

He had to contain his excitement and not appear like a complete idiot.

"I'm off early tomorrow since it's Saturday so I just have a couple of chores in the morning. I'll be done by noon so I could come by around four?"

"All right, then. Four it is. "

"Four it is," he repeated looking down at her.

"Thank you, again, Wyatt," she said walking up the steps.

"See you tomorrow." He stood with his hands in the pockets of his board shorts, watching her until she shut the door. When he climbed back in the truck her lavender smell was still in the cab. He inhaled her and a broad smile spread across his face. On the way back to the ranch he turned up the radio. George Strait was singing about his ex's in Texas and Charlotte was everywhere.

⚬⚬❦0❦⚬⚬

Rose's business was eccentric even by Charlotte's standards. The shop was just as Rose often described her work- magical. Each morning she and her aunt had English tea and a hearty breakfast together. After that they sat in the living room and meditated, sitting cross-legged across from each other on the floor. Meditation was one of the only things that Rose absolutely insisted Charlotte do. It was built into their routine and although at first Charlotte didn't quite understand the process, she was a quick study and worked hard to please Rose.

"It's simple. You sit quietly with your eyes closed," Rose told her a few days after she arrived.

"Ok- so just do nothing?" Charlotte didn't understand the point.

"Right. First you ground yourself. Imagine that you are rooted into the earth. Then imagine light coming down from God and through you. All the good stuff just pumping through your body."

"Ok, and what happens? How do I know if I'm doing it right?"

Rose laughed. "You must be the first Holt woman to be a good student! You know you're doing it right when you're done and you feel like you can run the world... or if you feel like you got a fabulous nap."

Charlotte understood and began to work at meditation the way she worked at everything. She had learned that she wasn't always the best at everything but no one could out-work her, and that was a talent in and of itself. It didn't happen right away but by the fourth or fifth day she started to feel clear-minded and alert after meditating. She could feel the energy running through and renewing her, just as Rose said she would. Her aunt watched her with a knowing smile each time they opened their eyes.

"Good shit, right?" she'd repeat every time.

Rose was a creature of habit and after her morning routine came time for work at the shop. Spirit's Soul was a two room addition to Rose's house that consisted of the beautiful office Charlotte had seen her first day there and a separate waiting room with a desk and merchandise for sale. Chakra candles, sage, crystals, books, religious statues, and other spiritual shit, as Rose called it, was scattered across the shelves. Rose wasn't big on peddling but her clients always wanted something to buy in addition to their reading, as if only words weren't enough. They needed a souvenir to prove it had really happened, so Rose obliged.

Charlotte's job was ringing up the customers after readings and keeping the shop in order. She kept her work space immaculate and Rose quickly noticed after Charlotte arrived that there wasn't a speck of dust to be found on the shelves or anywhere else in the waiting room. She chatted with clients and organized receipts and financials that had been crumbled in a drawer beforehand. After two weeks of having Charlotte around, Rose had no idea how she had made due without her for so long. Her business was transformed and running like a well-oiled machine compared with how it had been beforehand. And then of course there was the fact that she was crazy about the kid. Never having a child of her own, Rose treasured her niece and was happier than she'd ever been with her company.

Their days fell into a companionable routine that they both loved. The routine was therapeutic for Charlotte. Order was like medicine. So when she woke up on the day of her date with Wyatt, she felt more than a little thrown off her game. She had an almost frantic buzzing energy and a flip-flopping in her stomach she couldn't seem to calm. She had yet to mention Wyatt to her Aunt and she didn't like the idea of keeping yet another thing from her, not something like that anyway. As soon as they sat down for meditation together, Rose had her pegged.

"Whoa, who's the guy?" she asked, a conspiring grin on her face.

Charlotte's jaw dropped. "How the hell? How do you do that?"

Rose never tired of catching people in their own thoughts and surprising them.

"Well, it's only partly magical. First, he's all in your energy and I can feel it. But mostly, you took extra special care to brush your hair this morning and we both know that's not always on the priority list."

Charlotte laughed. Her hair was wild and with the monsoons coming, and the air was thick with humidity, making it even more wavy. She had tried to calm it by braiding it to one side, planning to let it down just before her date. She nodded her head in submission.

"Ok, yes," she said laughing. "He's the guy I met at the lake. The one who brought me home the other day."

"Yes, I remember. The cowboy." Rose hadn't seen Wyatt nor had Charlotte told her that he was a cowboy but little incidents like that were becoming more and more commonplace to Charlotte. Rose simply knew things.

"Yes," Charlotte started, "he wants to take me out tonight but I didn't know if that would be ok with you or not. I told him to come over and meet you today. Is that- is that ok?"

"What did your guides say about it?" Rose asked, referring to Charlotte's spirit guides, also known as her inner voice.

Charlotte was embarrassed to say what it felt like inside of her, plus, it was almost too much to describe. She felt like she knew him already. Her inner voice said his heart was pure and he was special. She found herself desperate to be around him and feel his eyes like water on her again.

"Well, I'm still second guessing what it says, but the first thing I got was that he is safe. Not just safe but good. A really nice guy. But I wanted your opinion and to see if it's, you know, ok with you."

Rose smiled softly at her. "Of course it's ok with me. And you should trust your voice. Your shit is pretty lined up already," she said, referring to her developing intuition. "Plus, I already checked him out," she said, tapping the side of her temple grinning. "And you're right. He's a gem."

Charlotte exhaled a small sigh, she hadn't realized she was holding her breath a bit. She also didn't realize how much that day mattered to her. It would technically be her first official date with someone. Either Rose was in her head or the look of it was all over Charlotte's face because Rose began laughing again.

"Oh, my girl. To be young and beautiful again with all of that hope inside of you! Come now, you've gotta calm the hell down. Let's meditate then we'll pick out your outfit."

Charlotte's heart warmed at her sweet aunt who had thrown herself into healing Charlotte, into making her feel the love she'd missed out on over the years. She'd never known how much she'd missed those small acts of love like someone making her breakfast or being invested in her day. She was shocked at how it felt to have her heart open the way it had for her and the side effect of tearing up on a regular basis, which she did in that moment.

"Thank you, Aunt Rose," she said softly.

Rose settled herself cross-legged across from her niece and winked at her.

"Namaste, baby," she said, as they closed their eyes together.

⚬⚬❦0❦⚬⚬

A couple of hours into his shift on Saturday, Wyatt contemplated telling Garrett to go to hell and quitting the job altogether. The day wasn't particularly hard but time was dragging on one second at a time. How could he be there tying fence posts when Charlotte was in town waiting for him to get off of work? Was it possible for time to slow down? Had he entered some kind of time warp? These were the questions that plagued his mind as he tied one fence post after the other.

The vaqueros all had Saturdays off and headed home to Mexico every Friday evening, so it was just him working that day. Garrett generally went easy on him on weekends, saying he only needed him until noon but sometimes he was done as early as 10 o'clock. That Saturday he was repairing some fence that was cut down, probably by drug smugglers or illegal immigrants. This was a weekly occurrence and part of Wyatt's regular chores. Any other day he might not have minded but that day he was doing it hurriedly which was unlike him.

Calm down, he thought to himself. She wasn't even expecting him until four anyway, no sense in rushing. But he could not calm down; more than that, all he could think about was her. This had never happened to him before. He'd had crushes on girls, he had dated girls, but it never felt like this. Never felt like there was nothing else in the world to think about other than one person. He thought about how her eyes had smiled at him once he had finally relaxed and could joke with her. How her face softened with love when she spoke of her aunt. He smiled thinking of how she told him she wasn't a bullshitter. The curse word out of her gorgeous lips seemed so out of place but so natural at the same time. He thought all day long about what it would be like to kiss her. To press his lips to that softness. He tried not to go too far into that fantasy, otherwise he had himself entirely too worked up. Too worked up for chores, anyway.

He knew himself, and he knew he would not kiss her that night. He knew no matter how much he liked her, that if it was difficult as it was to speak to her, he would not be kissing her, let alone putting his hands on her which he also imagined doing in great detail. And there had been that reaction, that strange way she looked when he offered to drive her home. She was afraid, there was no hiding that. For some reason, it made him genuinely concerned to think of why she had reacted that way. It also made him want to figure her out. To crack open her chest and see what was broken on the inside.

Garrett drove down the road near where Wyatt was repairing the fence and pulled his truck to a stop, tugging Wyatt out of his head and back to the present moment. He would often come by to chat with Wyatt while he was working which Wyatt had come to enjoy. It always made the time pass by faster. He was a man of few words but they were always important ones. Lessons were wrapped in what he said, even if they were in thick metaphors that Wyatt had to figure out much later. Wyatt nodded in greeting, sweat dripping from beneath his cowboy hat.

"Wyatt," he said nodding back to him. "Looks like you made a lot of progress here today."

"Yes, sir. I think I'm almost finished."

"And you're going to feed for me this afternoon?"

"Yes sir, I'll take care of that before I- before I head into town."

"Oh, away again are ya? You've been heading outta here a lot lately, huh? Whataya have a girlfriend or somethin'?" Garrett, grinned, his lip full of chewing tobacco.

Wyatt felt his face blushing and he looked back at the fencepost he was tying.

"Well, no sir. Not really. But I do have a date tonight," he smiled, beaming with pride as he said it.

"Well damn, boy, I should hope so. You're a good looking fella, oughta be out every night with a different girl!" he said, coughing a wheezing laugh.

"Well, I just got my eye on the one for now."

Garrett nodded knowingly. "Oh yeah, I know how that is. I married Millie when I wasn't much older than you. Didn't have much of a taste for a variety. No sir, find yourself a good one, you go ahead and lock her down right then and there. 'Course times were way different back then."

He looked off over the fields sadly. Wyatt had never heard the old man refer to his late wife and he was ashamed to admit that he wished he never had. The look in his eyes was so heartbreakingly sad, Wyatt almost couldn't bear it. Garrett took himself out of his reverie and remembered himself.

"So who's the lucky girl? Anyone I know?"

"Well, no. She's new to town but her aunt lives here. Owns that shop, the Spirit's Soul? You know her?"

"Rose!?" Garrett all but yelled. "Of course I know her! She's like a celebrity here!" Garrett laughed, wheezing again. "You haven't heard about her? No, of course you haven't, you're new here. Rose is kinda, well, some people call her a witch but damn, I think she's just a hell of a special lady who has a real gift. I mean it's a little strange but I can't get around the fact that she's just a real great lady."

Wyatt was floored. He knew for a fact that Garrett was a God-fearing man, he never missed cowboy church on Sundays and had a well-worn Bible on his dining room table where he sat each morning with his coffee. Now here he was telling Wyatt what a nice lady some fortuneteller was. It was shocking.

"Oh, wow," Wyatt said, not knowing how to respond. "She sounds... interesting."

"Oh yeah, that's one way of putting it. You hear about how she saved half the town's ass a few years back?"

Wyatt shook his head.

"No, of course not," he repeated. "You wouldn't have heard. Well it's like this, all the Mexicans in town just love her, call her the angel of the desert. About 20 years ago we had a huge monsoon season, storms everywhere rolling through town, you've heard of that right? Floods of '83? Well, the winter before it happened she told everyone living on the river to move their stuff, move all of their livestock out of any area with a floodplain around it. She was adamant," Garrett said shaking his head in amazement. "I still can't believe it after all of this time. Well, you know how people are, some people listened to her some people didn't. The ones who didn't, paid the price. Everything along the riverbed was taken out in that flood, all of the livestock, all of the houses, anything that was built too close was gone," Garrett said, shrugging. "So you know, ever since then, the town just kinda loves her. She's a fixture here. There's a pocket of Baptists here who can't stand her, say she's a witch and all of that, but she ain't. Damned if she just ain't a helluva good time. Funny as the dickens. She's a looker too, always has been. I imagine her niece is a pretty girl?"

"Yes," Wyatt said, a slight grin on his face. "Yes, I would say so."

"Well good for you, son. Why don't you knock off for the day so you can go back and get cleaned up then? Come on up to the house, I've got an iron for you. Can't be taking her out in your work clothes."

"Oh no sir, I'll finish this row, I have time. But I will take you up on that ironing, though."

"I said ironing board, I didn't say I'd iron that shit for you," Garrett laughed his wheezing laugh again walking to his truck.

"Yes sir!" Wyatt yelled after him. He finished his row as fast as possible then headed back to the ranch. He had cleaned out his truck that morning in preparation for the date. He kept the windows down on his ride back to the ranch so his sweaty stink didn't permeate the cab too much. Wyatt was always prepared as outdoorsmen should be, and a date was no exception. But no matter what he ironed, cleaned, or prepared, there was no calming the lightness of his stomach that he felt each time he thought of her. He was a goner.

⌘

Wyatt had played baseball since he was 4, he'd entered ropings with his dad for years, and he worked relentlessly to get straight A's despite major test anxiety. When added up, all of that pressure over the course of his entire life was a fraction of what he felt standing on Rose's front step late that Saturday afternoon. He was as prepared as he possibly could have been but he couldn't calm his nerves no matter how much he tried. He was sweating profusely under his pearl snapped shirt, the ironing job already starting to wear off for the heat and sweat.

When Rose answered the door, Wyatt had to look directly down at her since she was about half of his size. Not at all like her long-legged niece, but still, as Garrett had stated, a looker. She wore bright red lipstick and a friendly smile. Her overalls were in contrast to her made up face but somehow it worked for her. Her glasses were perched at the tip of her nose and she shamelessly appraised the young man from head to toe, beaming widely as she did it.

"Well, this must be the cowboy I've heard so much about," she said looking back into his eyes. Wyatt could feel himself blushing deeply at the thought of Charlotte talking about him.

"Hello, ma'am. I'm Wyatt," he said, sticking out his hand for her to shake.

"Ma'am?! No, that won't do it all. Makes me feel old is hell! Please, call me Rose and for God's sake give me a hug, we hug in this house." She unabashedly threw her hands around his waist and squeezed her face into his chest while he awkwardly patted her on the back.

"Well, it's very nice to meet you. Thank you for letting me stop by." She motioned for him to follow her into the living room, but Charlotte was nowhere to be seen.

"Please, please, sit down." She led him to the sofa with overstuffed colorful cushions. He felt like he might sink all the way down into it once he sat. He looked around the room, noting the eccentric decorations, the religious relics, and beautiful plants spilling out of their pots.

"She'll be out in just a minute, she's still getting ready. Not that she needs to, she's so beautiful she doesn't have to do a thing. Wouldn't you agree?"

Wyatt was taken off guard at the bluntness of her question but nodded tightly at her.

"Yes, and just about the sweetest, most hard-working girl you'd ever like to meet. Hell, I have no idea how I did it before she got here." Rose chattered on and walked into the kitchen, retrieving Wyatt an ice-cold Coke bottle from the refrigerator. She popped the lid and handed it to him, taking a seat opposite him on a rocking chair.

"This Coke is from Mexico so it's got the real sugar in it. Leave it to Mexicans to know how to indulge, they've got that figured out. Us stupid Americans are always depriving ourselves of the lovely things in life." She leveled her gaze at him and Wyatt imagined that she was reading his thoughts. With the Coke bottle in his hand he tried with all of his might not to think about Charlotte's curvy figure and the thoughts that came with that. Right on cue, Rose giggled at him.

"You seem like a nice young man, Wyatt. Charlotte wanted to make sure that I was OK with you going out with her, so why don't you tell me a little bit about yourself."

Parents generally loved Wyatt so he could not understand why he was so worked up about speaking with Rose. Maybe because he thought she could read his thoughts and for any teenage boy, that was a terrifying possibility.

"Well, I grew up in Tucson, born and raised and just graduated in May. I'm down here working on the 87 ranch this summer, with Mr. Garrett."

"Oh!" Rose said delightedly. "How is the beautiful son of a bitch? I haven't seen him lately, I need to make it a point to get out there and bring him some jelly soon. Just the sweetest man, isn't he?"

"Yes ma'am, I mean, Ms. Rose, he is a real good man. He's been real good to me."

"Well, if you're working for Garrett, I know you come from good stock. He's a solid judge of character."

Wyatt wanted to breathe a sigh of relief and he also wanted to hug Garrett next time he saw him. "What are your plans with my Charlotte?" He blushed again and Rose laughed out loud at him this time, hard.

"Oh child, not much of a poker face, have you? Well that's OK, I like a bad liar anyway. I mean what are your plans this evening?"

"Oh, I just thought that maybe we would go out for pizza tonight. Wherever she wants to go really. I won't have her out too late or anything."

Rose waved a hand at him, "Oh, I don't mind about that. Just as long as you keep her safe and you two are responsible and everything, I'm fine with you kids having a great time. What the hell is youth for anyway? I mean shit, one day you'll be my age and the most exciting thing you'll look forward to is your nap every afternoon!"

Rose's easy way was wearing Wyatt down and he was finally beginning to relax. He would think later that perhaps she did that by design because as soon as he felt himself becoming comfortable, Charlotte emerged from the side bedroom wearing a pair of torn tight jeans hanging low off of her hips and a black tank top accentuating her curves. He silently thanked God he had gotten ahold of himself by that point because he had the presence of mind to stand and greet her.

"Hi, Charlotte," he said, smiling at her from across the room.

"Mr. Sterling, I see Aunt Rose has been entertaining you?" She shot a glance over to Rose who threw up her hands in surrender.

"I promise, I went easy on him. No palm reading or spells. I kept it really Goddamn G-rated, I swear, but you know how it wears me out to be appropriate!"

They all laughed together, for Rose had a way of settling the atmosphere of a room, making everyone around her feel comfortable and be at ease. Some might say she did cast spells on others, but mostly it was her humor that cut the edge off. She eventually shooed them out the door, bidding them farewell on their way. Before Charlotte hit the door, though, Wyatt noticed that Rose grabbed the girl's face and kissed her fiercely on the cheek. It was such an intimate expression of their relationship that Wyatt felt the tug of his own family for the first time that summer.

When it was just the two of them in the truck, the conversation was easier than Wyatt had originally imagined. He asked what she would prefer for dinner or where they should go, but Charlotte was easy, she said anywhere was fine. They drove through town with the windows down and the hot air blowing through the cab. He looked over to see her blonde hair, usually wild and unruly, somewhat tamed and curly around her face.

"I'm sorry, do you want me to roll up the windows? I don't want to mess up your hair or anything."

Having a high maintenance mother had its perks; he knew how it irked a woman to have her hair messed up by the wind after spending time on it.

She laughed though. "Oh no, it's fine. Aunt Rose told me today that my hair isn't high up on my priority list and she's kinda right."

"I think your hair is beautiful." Wyatt could hardly believe the words that came out of his mouth. He imagined them in his head, but because he was so relaxed, they just fell out.

"Thank you," Charlotte said quietly and looked down at her feet, then out the window. She felt flustered and hot each time she felt his eyes on her and couldn't help but look away.

He hadn't prepared himself for the first time he would be seen in public with her. Up until now, it had just been Rose around them. When he held the door open for her to walk into the pizza place, every man in the restaurant turned to look at her. Those who were with their significant others or wives did it on the sly, but still, Wyatt saw them all glance at her. She might as well have been an alien for how they looked at her. He was both proud and disturbed by this. Like a boy with a shiny new toy that everyone wanted, he didn't want to share. He caught himself scowling at a table of young boys who sat gawking at her. He fought to ignore all of them and focus on her as they sat and ordered their drinks, two more Cokes from Mexico with the real, good sugar as Rose had called it, and a pizza with the works.

"I like everything," Charlotte had said, and so did he.

"So Charlotte," he started after they placed their order. "I feel like I've told you everything about me but you haven't told me anything about you."

"Sure I have," she smiled back at him over the table. "You know that I am a hell of a fisherman, first and foremost. That I'm new to Arizona, and that I have a crazy, psychic aunt who really loves men."

"Well, she did hug me today when I came in the house," he grinned at her and she laughed loudly.

"Oh my gosh, that woman. She can't help herself. Just can't pass up a handsome man." She smiled at him and he once again turned pink under her gaze.

"Well, I'm honored. She seems like a great lady. Really, tell me more about you. Where you're from first of all. Or did you just drop out of the sky?"

"Oh man, dropping out of the sky would be a much shorter explanation than where I'm from." She was smiling, but Wyatt could tell that this conversation made her uncomfortable.

"So, I think I told you my mom likes to move a lot. My mom is Aunt Rose's sister. Anyway, we've lived all over the place. The first place I ever remember living when I was about three was Florida. But my mom says that I was born up in Washington. I don't remember it there, though. So after Florida we moved to New York City, then we lived in Michigan really briefly, after that we moved to Georgia, to Texas, then Colorado with the hippies, Utah with the Mormons. And then the last place I lived, where I went to the last couple of years of high school, was back in Texas- San Antonio. And now I'm here." She exhaled after naming all of the places off of the list, as if relieved to get that information out and not have to repeat it again.

"Whoa," Wyatt said. "That really is a lot of places. What was your favorite?"

"Hmm," She said thinking. "I really liked Georgia. They have these big gorgeous trees that moss grows out of and the beach is close. I really love the ocean. So I liked it there. But I'll tell you, Arizona is really climbing the list."

"Yeah?" Wyatt said, popping out his chest a little, taking pride in his home state. "I'm glad you like it here."

"I do," she said. "It's beautiful and the people are nice. My aunt's been telling me about other places in the state where there are pine trees and lakes, so she's going to take me on some trips coming up." Wyatt was thrilled. This was something he was the expert on. Being a hunter and fisherman, he knew all of the mountain towns in the state and could speak as the expert on this topic.

"Whereabouts is she going to take you?"

"She said a place called Flagstaff because from there we can go to the Grand Canyon. Have you been up there?"

"Oh yeah, lots of times. My family hunts and fishes," he put his palms up toward her, "and I promise I'm good at both."

He chatted to her about all of the northern Arizona towns and what they had to offer.

"It's much cooler up there, that's the perk. After the monsoon season everything will be so green and the lakes will be high. Might be a good time to go."

Wyatt was starving, but he didn't want to stuff his face in front of her regardless of how much his body wanted to. He was shocked when the pizza came and Charlotte ate piece after piece, finishing almost half of it. So he reciprocated and didn't hold back.

Wyatt could not stop looking at her. She was looking around at the pizza place at the pictures on the wall while they chatted, but he could not tear his eyes away from her. He loved the way she set her head back on her shoulders when she laughed at him and the way that her eyes wrinkled up when she smiled. He was already dreading the moment the date would be over and cursing the fact that the town was so small there wasn't much else for them to do. Wyatt could think of plenty of other things they could do, but none of those were really appropriate for a first date.

When the bill came, Charlotte tried to argue with him about who would pay it. She took out her money insisting to pay for some if not all of it, but he refused. Never in all of the dates he had been on had a girl offered to pay. The suggestion of it was preposterous to him, but it also made her stand out that much more. She thanked him profusely for dinner and suggested they walk down to get an ice cream cone, which she insisted she would pay for herself. Wyatt obliged just to get more time with her.

They walked down Main Street side by side just as the sun was starting to set behind the mountains in the distance. Instead of shutting down, the town was just coming alive with people who had been avoiding the heat all day long. Shops were open, people were chatting, cars were passing through town. They both observed all of the different shops they weren't familiar with, mostly artist's co-ops, yoga places, and naturopathic stores. It reminded Charlotte of a miniature Denver.

"Arizona has it all over everywhere else as far as sunsets go. The best I've seen," she commented.

"They are good, aren't they? Wait until the monsoons come. Makes them even better."

"Ah, yes. I've heard all about this magical monsoon season," Charlotte said chuckling.

"I know, I know. Arizona people get really excited about the rain but you'll see why when they come. It's my favorite time of the year."

"Why?" she asked, a slight smile resting on her face.

"Well, it all cools down for one, but mostly it's the smell. It's like nothing you've ever smelled before. Once that rain hits the dried dirt and the creosote, I can't even describe what it's like but it's the best smell ever."

She nodded, looking up at him as they walked. "Well I'm excited, too, then. I do love the rain."

It killed him to allow her to buy the ice cream, but she was not to be deterred after the pizza place. They each got a cone with a scoop on top; she chose the salted caramel while he chose homemade strawberry. They walked until they found a bench in the grassy area of town where they could watch the cars go down Main Street and people walk among the shops.

They settled themselves down on the park bench close enough for their knees to touch. He wanted to hold her hand but thought that might be too much, so he didn't push his luck. They sat chatting with each other, eating their rapidly melting ice cream cones. He tried not to stare at her lips touching the cold ice cream, it was almost too much for him.

"Can I try yours?" she asked pointing to his cone.

"Yeah," he said, moving it toward her face. She leaned over and licked the side of the ice cream cone where his lips had just been. She held her mouth together, savoring the flavor.

"Mmm, that one is good. You want to try mine?" Wyatt didn't like caramel, let alone salted caramel, but his answer was yes. Hell yes he would like to lick the ice cream cone. She put it toward his face and he took a quick lick from the side.

"Good, right?" she said and Wyatt could only nod. The image of her licking his strawberry ice cream was still plaguing his mind. He was sure it would continue late into the evening, actually.

It couldn't have gone any better. She was easy to talk to just as her aunt was, and she had a way of putting him at ease. And likewise, the distrustful Charlotte found herself speaking and laughing easily with Wyatt, truly enjoying their time together. They sat and chatted on the park bench long after the ice cream was gone and Wyatt lamented that there wasn't much else to do in town.

"Maybe the next time we can go over to Sonoita or to Tucson. There's other things to do there."

"Next time?" she said teasingly and Wyatt looked at the ground a bit embarrassed.

"Oh yeah, I mean, if you want," he said.

"I do want," Charlotte said, leveling him with her green eyes.

"Ok, deal."

"Deal," she said back to him.

On the brief ride home, Johnny Cash's "Walk the Line" was blaring through the speakers and Charlotte reached over to turn it up. To his amazement, she sang every word and he couldn't help but sing along, albeit quietly. When he pulled up in front of the house he shut down his truck and looked over at her.

"Thank you for coming out tonight, Charlotte. That was way better than sitting at the bunkhouse all night."

"Thank you for asking me. I had a really good time." They sat in silence for a moment looking at each other, the air hot between them.

"When can I- I mean- can I see you again soon?" he asked.

"Well, I have mass in the morning with Aunt Rose but then she likes to nap and I was going to go to the lake for a swim. You want to join me?"

The jumbled images of Charlotte at Catholic Church and her bikini were almost laughable to him, but he kept a straight face.

"Yes, I'll be there. Our regular place?"

"Yes," she said. "Our place." The way she said it tugged at a feeling in Wyatt's gut that he was sure he would be stuck with for the rest of his life.

When he walked her to the door he wasn't sure what he should do. He wanted to kiss her, or maybe even just hug her, but he stood frozen in front of her with his hands in the pockets of his Levi's instead. The sky was still golden from the late setting sun and it lit her beautiful face a tinted orange color.

"OK," she said. "I'll see you tomorrow, Mr. Sterling."

"See you tomorrow," he repeated.

She looked at him standing with his hands in his pockets and his face red with the sunset and his usual embarrassment. He was a man, there was no doubt about it, strong forearms flexing out of the bottom of his short sleeved shirt and a physique any man would kill for. But his eyes gave him away. His eyes were those of a boy. They were a stunning blue color and his black lashes appeared to be wet all of the time. Charlotte couldn't help herself, she got up on her toes and leaned into Wyatt, placing her hands on his shoulders. She kissed his warm stubbly cheek swiftly before murmuring good night and going inside. He stood frozen with his hands still in his pockets and her warm kiss burning on his cheek.

"Good night," he said to the closed door.

For the first time in her life, Charlotte had a room that was her sanctuary. For most of her childhood, she had never even had a room of her own. But there she sat in that new place that Rose had deemed hers. Her aunt bought her a new ornate lamp and a yellow gingham bedspread that Charlotte picked out herself. She also insisted on buying Charlotte all new toiletries and the makeup that she would need. She told her to pick out anything she wanted to decorate her room and Charlotte settled on a couple of potted succulents which Aunt Rose said they could paint at home since they were too damn plain.

When she lay in her bed that night after her date, she could only think of Wyatt. She covered her face with embarrassment when she thought of her brazen act of kissing him on the cheek. She had kissed a couple of boys before, but had never been the first one to make the move and she was still shocked that she had. She lay in the quiet of her room thinking about what her aunt had taught her. She taught her the laws of the universe, that laughter breeds more laughter, hate breeds more hate, and love breeds more love. There was no other way to explain her behavior in front of Wyatt. Her aunt had nursed her back to health and opened her up to love. It was exciting and terrifying all at once, but there was Wyatt. There was his sweet, gentle way with her. She smiled thinking of the way he blushed in front of her, over almost everything. He was quite simply the nicest boy that she had ever met. Not to mention the best looking.

His beautiful appearance, tall, muscular structure, jet black hair, and bright blue eyes complemented by that gorgeous smile with all of those perfect teeth, were all secondary to his heart that Charlotte could already feel so clearly. She couldn't remember if she was able to read people in the same way before she had come to Aunt Rose. She knew she would get a sense for others, but never looked at it more deeply. Now, with the skills that Rose taught her, she was able to really look at him, really feel for his heart and his energy, and it was borderline overwhelming to experience.

Charlotte still had a small voice in the back of her head that asked why he would want anything to do with her. Her, just a little white trash, sometimes homeless, girl with no parents. No real family to speak of other than Aunt Rose. She tried to fight off her inner voice over and over again the way Aunt Rose had taught her, and sometimes she succeeded. But sometimes, when the night was quiet and she was alone with her thoughts, her mind would lose the battle, bringing her back to all of those times when she felt so inferior. So less than worthy. Make no mistake, outwardly she appeared like a soldier who had survived war, but her scars were deep on the inside and she didn't ever vocalize them or manifest them in any way. There was no way to sufficiently explain to somebody these things. The times she had started to talk to Aunt Rose about it she felt like she was trivializing her life. That speaking about it somehow made it less valid or not as real. But maybe it was too real for her and that was why she kept it inside.

Charlotte tossed from one side to the other trying to get comfortable, fighting her mind for the evening and pushing away her feeling of unworthiness. *No*, she told the voice. *He likes me and he says I have beautiful hair.* She thought again about his smile, about his perfect ocean blue eyes, and the warm stubble cheek she felt beneath her lips that night.

"Goodnight, Wyatt," she whispered to her pillow.

⚬⚬❍⚬⚬

"Well, well, well. It's about time you wake up and tell me about your date." Rose was already dressed for mass in a long flowing skirt with swirling colors complimented by a white peasant blouse. Her hair and makeup were impeccable and she smelled of her usual essential oils. She was cooking for Charlotte as she did every morning, waiting anxiously for the girl to wake so she could live vicariously through her, reliving the details of her date. Charlotte rubbed her puffy eyes and gave Rose a closed mouth smile, shrugging her shoulders.

"Umm, do I really have to tell you? I thought you were psychic, don't you already know?"

Rose waved her hand at her. "You know I wouldn't stick my nose where it doesn't belong, not even I'm that nosy!" Charlotte tilted her head, calling her bluff.

"OK, OK I just checked in to see if everything went well. I mean I didn't get details. That's what I have you for, so spill!"

Charlotte laughed and sat down at the table for breakfast, chorizo and eggs in a flour tortilla. Arizona definitely had the best food she'd ever tasted. Eating well was like a religion to Aunt Rose and Charlotte was fast converting.

"It was good. I mean, he's a really nice guy. We went to the pizza place then out for ice cream then he brought me home. That's about it."

Rose slumped herself down on the chair across from Charlotte. "That's it? I mean that's all you're going to give me?"

"Well?" Charlotte giggled nervously. "There's really not that much to tell! He's a cowboy, a hunter, a fisherman," she smiled slightly at their private joke. "Definitely a gentleman."

"Did you see the aura on him? I mean my God, he's like you, lit up entirely. Seventh chakra just shining out of him like a fucking beacon!" Rose made a wide-eyed face and took a bite of her breakfast taco smothered in hot sauce.

"Aunt Rose, I told you I can't see auras. I think you're wrong, I'm not magical like you are," she joked.

"Oh, please. You can't fool me. But fine, have it your way. If you didn't see his aura, did you see the ass on that kid?" Charlotte almost spit out her breakfast laughing.

"I mean it!" Aunt Rose said, laughing back. "It's a thing of beauty. I mean gravity hasn't touched it at all." She took her hands out in front of her and made a grabbing motion with each of them.

"Good lord, if I were 30 years younger," she lifted her fork in the air gesturing. "I'd give you a run for your money, princess."

Charlotte had tears collecting at the corner of her eyes, laughing at Rose. She finished the food in her mouth and finally spoke again. "Yes," she nodded, "I did see that... not bad."

"Not bad?! Christ, he's like a cowboy Adonis. Not a bad one to take for a spin, I'd say. Alright now, enough of you talking dirty. We've gotta make it to mass. Finish up."

Charlotte dressed in one of the church dresses her aunt had purchased for her. It was a long and flowing floral dress with spaghetti straps, so she had to wear a cotton button up shirt to cover her shoulders. Even Aunt Rose showed respect with her wardrobe and cursed the people who showed up to church in casual clothes. There wasn't much that offended the woman but sloppiness was one of the things that irked her.

When they walked into the church together they were greeted by so many patrons who hugged and kissed Rose and even Charlotte, who had been there several weeks in row. The mood was always friendly and chatty at that particular mass. But when the service started, a reverence fell over the beautiful old Catholic Church and Charlotte was shocked at how much she enjoyed it. She thought it would be something painful for her, but instead she felt a great peace and love when she sat down in the pew next to her aunt. She was a quick study and by her third time there, she was reciting the chants and responses with the congregation.

The church had character. There were long wooden pews and large stained glass windows depicting Jesus on the cross and mother Mary with praying hands. While the congregation prayed, Charlotte looked around at the relics and symbols that decorated the walls. Ornate, that was the word Rose had used to describe Catholics, particularly Hispanic Catholics. She liked all of the colors and pictures that told stories, it was way different than she imagined a church although she had nothing to compare it to, save for what she had read about in books.

Charlotte also looked at the faces of other people while they prayed. She noticed her aunt's closed eyes and concentrated brow as she knelt next to her. She felt a little left out when she looked at them, wondering how they got to that place. What they said to God when they prayed. She envied the fact that they could do this. Here they had been on Sundays, while she was elsewhere in all of those other places each Sunday of her life. What could she say to God? How did one even say it? She had no idea where to start. But regardless of that feeling, by the end of the service, Charlotte felt much the way she did at the end of meditation- rested and refreshed and with dozens of new questions about the world and her own spirituality.

She was still startled by the fact that Rose went to Catholic Church every Sunday like clockwork. Her mom had never taken her to church, but the religious people she had met over the years would never have associated with a psychic. Let alone a foul mouth, perverted sinner like her beautiful Aunt Rose.

"I still can't believe how nice they are to you," Charlotte said as they climbed into Rose's car after church. "I mean, all of the people I've ever met who go to church wouldn't, you know, they might not like..." she trailed off.

Rose fluffed her hair in the rear view mirror and reapplied her bright red lipstick. "Might not like me because I'm a witch?" she said, looking at Charlotte sideways.

"Well, yeah," Charlotte said, laughing. "Something like that."

"I told you, sweetie. Mexican Catholics have a freak flag, and they fly it," she grinned at Charlotte, her eyes dancing with mischief. "And I am their freak."

⚜

Without work Wyatt's morning passed even slower. He fed the horses and chickens, and the cattle were out to pasture so he drove out to check them and the water tanks. By the end of that it was only 9 o'clock so he still had 3 hours to burn. He contemplated going back to bed but knew he wouldn't sleep. He had enough trouble falling asleep after his date on account of the fact he needed to relive every detail. He had stopped being as embarrassed in front of her, so that was progress. But he really had to get himself under control in the blushing department.

He knew that she liked him. Her poker face, just like his own, was non-existent. She had alluded to him being good-looking and joked with him in a flirtatious way, but Wyatt knew that was not all he needed to impress a girl like Charlotte. Unlike other girls he had dated, she seemed to look a little deeper. This fact both excited and terrified him. Sure, most people thought he was a good guy, but what if she didn't? God forbid she could read his thoughts like Aunt Rose because he simply couldn't contain his imagination around her, bikini or not. His mind was hopelessly in the gutter when it came to her.

Wyatt leaned his arms over the fence that overlooked the horses. The vaqueros would be back that evening and his brief solitude would be long gone. Sunny, the oldest and most revered cutting horse on the ranch, came over toward him and commenced scratching his head against the fence and Wyatt. Wyatt laughed and obliged, rubbing Sunny down his face and neck.

"Good ol boy," he said patting him the way Sunny liked. He was hardly able to ride him since the vaqueros always used him in the pasture. Sunny was not to be overused or overridden unless it was for a cattle drive. Wyatt leaned in close and inhaled the musky scent of him. Rain and horses were his favorite smells, although Charlotte was rapidly climbing that list with her lavender scent. And that was the way of it. Wyatt could be smelling a horse when suddenly, he would be pulled back to thinking of her. He laughed at himself and shook his head. All roads led to Charlotte and he couldn't say that he minded one bit.

He passed the rest of the morning doing busy work, desperate as he was for noon to arrive. He showered off his work and horse smell even though he knew he would be swimming. He didn't want to be that grungy guy that she had met that first day, shirt around his face and all. Plus, he hoped that a cold shower would calm him down. Perhaps it would rid him of his foul thoughts. But there was no hope for him. He found himself naked in the shower immediately thinking of how she would have to be naked in the shower and all bets were off.

He arrived at the lake just before noon and it seemed quieter than usual. The front of the lake wasn't as busy as it was other days, or at least he couldn't hear it the way he normally could. As he walked on the dusty path, he was surprised to see her already sitting there on the beach cross-legged on an Indian blanket. She faced the water and did not turn to Wyatt but sat very very still. He stopped and watched her closely. He noticed that her hands were placed on top of her knees facing upward and her long neck stretched her face toward the sun. Her blonde hair was in curly tendrils that day and it fell down almost to her waistline. She looked like a portrait set among the blue sky and the trees, sitting perfectly still and not moving or making a sound. For the first time Wyatt thought he might walk right up to her and kiss her. Not even say a word but just put his face to hers and feel her lips like he had wanted to since the day he met her.

He would never know if he would actually have the guts to do that, though, because at that moment she turned and smiled at him. It was obvious he was standing watching her, his feet were not in motion but he couldn't bring himself to care or even pretend that he wasn't watching. He smiled broadly back at her.

"We meet again, Wyatt Earp." He nodded and finally got his feet moving toward her.

"Sister Holt, how was church?" Charlotte laughed then, a genuine belly laugh that caused her to throw her head back on her shoulders.

"Sister! No wonder Aunt Rose loves you."

"Ah, Aunt Rose. She is unique isn't she?" he said, grinning.

She stood to greet him but realized she didn't know what to do. It felt strange to just throw her arms around him and hug him or even kiss him on the cheek like she had the night before, so she put her hands on her hips and watched him come toward her. He wore his board shorts and a University of Arizona T-shirt and a baseball hat, his black hair creeping out from underneath it. His forearms were as deeply tanned as his face was which made his beautiful teeth seem even whiter. He brought a small backpack with him, which he carried over his shoulder.

"What's in the bag? What, still no fishing pole?"

"I tried explaining this to you. You killed my dreams forever with that bluegill nonsense the other day. I mean it, I think I quit fishing forever."

Charlotte shrugged. "Suit yourself, but I'm a great fisherman. I'm gonna have to get a pole in here and show you how it's done."

"Sounds like a challenge. Next time, I'll bring my pole and you can show me your angling skills." They were standing face-to-face now near the blanket, eyes locked and smiling at each other.

"Deal," she smiled, looking up at him.

"Deal," he said back. "I brought us some drinks since you're in the habit of walking through the desert without water," he teased.

"So you brought us some beers?"

Wyatt feigned a shocked face. "Don't tell me you drink beer. If that's true, you really might have been dropped out of the sky."

"Ha! Yes, Wyatt. Sister Charlotte does enjoy a beer from time to time."

"OK then, that's what I'll bring next time. This time I just brought us water and some Cokes. And some Mexican candy. I thought you might want to try it."

The Mexican candy was sweet and spicy all at once and came on a plastic spoon that was supposed to be sucked on slowly. He had loved it all his life even though most people didn't. Most white people, anyway. He might have had ulterior motives after the ice cream incident. When he stopped at the gas station he did think about watching her lick it but mostly, he just wanted to bring her something to be nice. He was not disappointed in her reaction either. She was thrilled.

"How nice! I'd love to try it, thank you!" She took one from him excitedly and placed it on her tongue, making a concentrated face when it first hit her taste buds.

"Uh-oh," he laughed. "You don't like it?"

She shook her head. "No, I do actually! It's so different. Spicy sweet, I think I like it." She commenced sucking on the spoon and Wyatt turned back to his backpack to pull himself together. They sat down on the blanket facing the lake, Charlotte cross-legged again and he with his long legs stretched out in front of him. Their thighs were touching and Wyatt could feel the heat coming off of her skin.

"Beautiful day," she commented in between licks of her candy.

He laughed. "I think you are the only person I've ever heard say that on a summer day before the rains."

"Well? It's beautiful though, right? Such a pretty lake. Plus I'd rather be hot than cold any day. If you've ever lived in Michigan during winter," she said, making a cringing face, "you'd think THAT was the gateway to hell."

"I thought hell was hot?"

She shrugged. "Ask Aunt Rose. I bet she'd tell you there isn't a hell."

He raised his eyebrows. "And she goes to Catholic Church? And has a niece who's a nun?" He nudged her knee with his and smiled sideways at her under the brim of his hat. She found herself laughing so easily with him and becoming more and more comfortable. They decided to get in the water, each eying the other discreetly as their excess clothing came off. Wyatt had a small patch of black hair on his chest and another small trail leading from his belly button down his board shorts. His torso was taut and tanned but not as dark as his forearms. *Farmer's tan*, she thought.

Charlotte wore the same blue swimsuit that sat low on her hips. The triangle top tied at her neck and back and, Wyatt noted, appeared to be easy to remove. Just one tug on a string. Tug. And that would be it. He dove out into the water and swam out a ways to cool off. She surprised him by following.

"You wanna swim to the other side?" she said loudly above the splashing.

"Really?" He hadn't considered it nor did he want to, but he wasn't going to say no to her. "Ok!"

They both swam freestyle steadily across the lake. As it goes with distance, it looked much shorter than it actually was. By the halfway point he thought about telling her they should maybe turn back, but she was still paddling strong and smiling at him each time he looked back at her, so he pushed forward.

When they arrived on the other side of the lake it was even more isolated. The beach wasn't sandy so he pulled himself up on one of the rocky ledges and waited for her, pulling her up to a standing position on the rock when she arrived. He did it with such ease that it made Charlotte's stomach flutter.

"Whoa," she said as she stood there dripping in front of him. "Strong after that swim. My arms are like Jell-O!" She shook out her arms and breathed heavily as she did.

"Yeah," he said in between deep breaths. "It didn't look that far before we swam it, did it?" He sat down on the rock looking back over the lake to their spot.

"Hope someone doesn't come and steal my truck keys, otherwise this day's going to get even more interesting."

"It's OK," she said breathing hard and sitting down next to him. "You can walk home with me if that happens."

He looked over at her with his mouth dropped open.

"You walked here again?" he asked disbelievingly.

She nodded, laughing at him. "Yeah, sorry. I'm not great at following directions."

He smiled back at her shaking his head. "I would've come and picked you up, you know."

"I know, but I didn't mind. Plus, you can take me home after. I won't fight you this time." She tilted her head and batted her eyes at him sarcastically.

"Ok, well... I guess that works out better for me anyway so I won't be too mad."

"Better for you?" she asked, raising her eyebrows.

He nodded looking back out at the lake. "Well, yeah. I have fun with you," he said quietly.

"Me, too," Charlotte said.

"And I like you." The words simply came out again and he proudly noticed that he wasn't blushing for once. He looked back at her sitting next to him, the sun on her wet face. She smiled.

"Me, too," she repeated. And there was quiet between them for a moment. Just the lake out in front of them and the sun beating down on their wet bodies.

"I like you even though I'm going to beat you back to shore." She stood and dove head first into the lake.

He laughed and got to his feet, but he decided to give her a head start. He liked the idea of losing to her. He was ready to wave the white flag on all fronts.

⸺⚬⚬⚬⸺

The rest of the afternoon passed quickly after their race, which she did in fact win. He wasn't upset with the view from behind, either. They sat and talked in the shallows, laughing and flirting, each becoming bolder with the other but never touching more than a brush of their legs or feet in the water. Wyatt could not take his eyes away from her when they were together and was fascinated with the magnetic feeling he felt in his gut. The weekend was coming to an end and he was already thinking of ways to see her again. It wasn't acceptable for him to have to wait until the next weekend.

All too soon they were headed back to town together and Merle Haggard blared through the speakers of his truck, lamenting about his love being taken away on silver wings. Wyatt could never relate more. He was just not ready to drop her off for the night. He turned off the engine in front of Rose's house and looked over at Charlotte in the passenger seat.

"I had a lot of fun, again, Charlotte."

"Same," she smiled, looking into his watery blue eyes.

"I have to work all week but I'd really like to see you again soon."

"Ok, well, I work in the mornings at the shop and then Aunt Rose usually naps. That's always when I go to the lake."

"Every day?" he asked

She nodded. "Aunt Rose said once the rains come I won't be able to anymore so I'm trying to get as much time there as I can."

"Ok, then. I'll bring my fishing pole and we can see those famous skills I've heard so much about." He flashed his white perfect teeth, teasing her.

"Oh, I will be ready," she teased back, climbing out of the truck. Once he got out she was already standing on the first step of the porch looking back at him. He walked toward her, looking her straight in the face.

"Look, I'm as tall as you standing on the step."

"Maybe a little taller," he said, moving closer and measuring with his hand.

Her hair was wild and dried wavy around her face flushed from the hot day. He was staring at her puffy lips, which were eye level with him on the step. There was another awkward silence and Wyatt took on his signature porch pose of his hands in his pockets. He felt his face flush through even though he willed it not to with all he had.

She smiled and laughed briefly. "Why do you act like you're afraid of me sometimes?"

"Do I?" he laughed. "Well I'm not."

"No? You act like I bite or something."

"Alright," he smiled. "You do make me a little nervous."

She still stood on the step above him and he had to tilt his head slightly to look up at her. He wanted to make a move but he felt frozen in place.

"You make me a little nervous, too, I guess," she said.

"Yeah? Well you don't show it."

Silence fell between them again and she put her hand on his shoulders as if to settle him. She cocked her head at him and smiled, crinkling up her green eyes. "Well, I don't bite so are you ever going to kiss me?"

He was somewhat surprised but laughed anyway, feeling his fear slip away slightly.

"Hmmm," he said. "I hadn't thought about it really."

"Oh no?" she said, smiling back. "Well, good night then." She turned to go in the house and he gently grabbed her arm spinning her back to him.

"No, no, no. Maybe I've thought about it a little bit," he said.

"And?"

"And I don't think it's a bad idea."

He paused only slightly before putting one hand around her slim waist and the other on the side of her cheek bringing her face toward him. She had to lean down off of the step into him. Her lips parted and yielded to the softness of his gentle kiss. He intended for it to be quick, polite even, but it wasn't. He gripped the base of her neck pulling her closer to him, pushing deeper against her. Her soft lips melted under the pressure of his. He pulled her off of the step so that her feet were hovering off the ground, feeling the weight of her on his chest. Finally she moved her head back to look at him. His mouth hung open and he felt that feeling again, the one where someone punched him. But this time it was worse and he knew for a fact he would never ever be the same. She smiled at him and kissed him once more as he set her gently back on the step. She turned to go in the front door as he stood with his hands at his sides looking dumbly back at her.

"Worth the wait, Mr. Earp." But he could not recover himself to say something witty back, he simply lifted his hand and waved at her.

"Tomorrow?" he mumbled.

She nodded and walked through the front door and into the house. His heart pounded in his chest even as he drove home. The sun was setting low in the sky making the town glow orange and he floated back to the bunkhouse in a daze, drunk on Charlotte.

⸙

Monday did not go according to plan for Wyatt. He nearly jumped out of bed in the morning to get moving on his chores, but it was a heavy day of work. Garrett was hell-bent on getting the irrigation in before the rains hit and since the vaqueros were busy working the cattle, the bulk of the work landed on Wyatt. Despite the ground being hard for lack of rain, he made quick work of the trenches. By lunchtime Garrett came and checked and was so encouraged with his progress that he decided to add even more rows of irrigation that Wyatt then had to dig.

He started to get panicked about the day passing and not being able to make it to the lake at all. What would she think if he stood her up entirely and didn't show? No, he simply had to get there to see her that day. He'd made so much progress with his nerves around her and had convinced himself the night before that he could and would kiss her this time without falling mute afterward. He was determined. She liked him. She had even asked him to kiss her outright. Even if it was after she told him that he seemed like he was afraid of her, he was still calling it a win.

Garrett came back out later in the afternoon and Wyatt silently prayed that he would tell him he was finished for the day. Garrett could go either way. Sometimes he felt like building Rome in a day and other times he would tell Wyatt to knock off at noon. Wyatt suspected that this corresponded to the time Garrett himself wanted to knock off and have his afternoon or evening whiskey.

"Alright then. Why don't you go ahead and head into town to pick up all of the pipes for this. Just head on over to the hardware store. I already told Smith what I needed," Garrett said.

Garrett was standing with his hands on his hips appraising Wyatt's work for the day. Wyatt assumed it was already about two if not three o'clock. He stood with the pickaxe in his hands with sweat dripping down his entire body. He crunched the time in his head. There would be no hope for a shower before seeing her if he wanted to make it in time.

"Yes, sir," he said back to Garrett. "Do you need me anymore after that?"

"No, no, you've done enough for today. We can get a jump on these pipes in the morning and by we I mean you," Garrett chuckled. "This is young man's work- gonna take you until nightfall for a few nights!"

Wyatt nodded good-naturedly and turned to put up his equipment.

"Oh, Wyatt. How was your date the other night?" Garrett grinned.

"It was good, sir. She's a nice girl."

Garrett nodded. "Well good! And did you meet Rose?"

"Yes, she said for me to tell you hello. Says she's going to make you some jelly or something."

"Oh that woman," Garrett said, sending himself into a wheezing laughing fit. "She makes prickly pear jelly and brings it to me. We've sort of got an inside joke about it."

Wyatt nodded, smiling. He noted the fact that he had never seen Garrett's eyes dance the way they did when he spoke of Rose.

"So, you gonna see her again?" Garrett asked.

"Yes, sir. I hope to."

"Well, alright then. You tell Rose I say hello now."

Wyatt nodded and Garrett walked back up toward the barn. Apparently, the Holt women had an effect on men. Wyatt figured if there wasn't any hope for the Bible-banging Garrett, there certainly wasn't any hope for a sinner like him.

It was physically painful to not drive directly to the lake, but to get the pipes instead. He dreaded walking in the hardware store since he knew Smith, the owner, loved to chat. Normally he would've been happy to nod along and listen to the old man's stories, but not that day. Time was running out and Wyatt was feeling the pressure. Why couldn't anyone else tell he had somewhere to be?

"Wyatt!" Smith exclaimed. "How are you, son?"

"Real good, sir. I'm here to pick up Mr. Garrett's order." Wyatt blew in the store, trying his hardest to exude an air of urgency.

"Oh, right, right. I've got it out back for ya. How bout this heat, huh? I'll tell ya, I don't know if the rains will come at all this year. Never seen it so dry."

Wyatt nodded and moved his body in the direction of where his order was allegedly sitting ready for him.

"Yes, sir. Pretty rough one."

"My arthritis isn't hurting a bit. I mean not a bit. If that ain't a bad sign I don't know what is."

Wyatt couldn't take anymore. "I'll go ahead and pull around back."

"Ok, alright then. I'll come help you load."

"No, no," Wyatt cut him off. "No worries, I've got it. You stay in here where it's cool," he grinned at him over his shoulder. "See ya, sir."

He charged out the front door and into his truck to load the pipes. They took up most of his truck bed and Wyatt thought he should head back to the ranch with them, but he looked at his clock and it was already 4:00. She could be leaving by now, so there would be no dropping off pipes, no changing, and worst of all, no shower.

When he finally got to the lake and walked through the desert he didn't see her at first. He looked all along the shoreline and his heart sank. But then he looked out in the water and saw her swimming. She was floating on her back paddling her arms slowly and leisurely. She looked just like the mermaid in his dream. She seemed completely one with the cool open water. He stood on the beach with his hand over his eyes looking out at her, but she didn't notice him for a long time.

"Charlotte!" he yelled out at her.

She flipped over and looked toward him, smiling broadly. She swam back toward the shore and when she was in the shallows she stood and walked to him, drenched in water. He was still dressed in his filthy work shirt, boots, and dirty Levis.

"I'm sorry I'm late. Work was crazy- I didn't even get a chance to change. Sorry I'm so dirty," he said gesturing to his outfit.

"That's OK. I figured you were busy."

She continued walking toward him through the water and he couldn't keep his eyes from roaming over her body even if he was obvious about it. Her bikini was starting to get worn by the sun and her skin was darker each time he saw her. A small strip of white skin showed itself below her navel where her swimsuit had slid down low. It took everything in his power to pull his eyes away from that untouched strip of white skin.

Charlotte walked directly up to him and hugged him tightly around the neck, her wet body pressing up against him. He hugged her back, moving his arms around her waist and locking them together behind her.

"Hi," she said.

"I'm sorry," he said into her neck. "I probably smell awful."

She turned her head and inhaled the place on his neck where his shirt had opened.

"I think you smell good. Like dirt. And sweat," she laughed.

He kept a hold on her and inhaled her deeply. "You smell good, too. Like you always do."

They stayed in the embrace a moment before he pulled his head away to look at her. "You feel good, too. Nice and cool." He leaned into her wet face and kissed her deeply. He was prepared this time and had given himself a pep talk all day while working. The night before left him feeling like he might die. He wanted more. He didn't want to be the scared little boy who blushed when she spoke to him. He opened his mouth, gently pushing his tongue against hers. His arms held her tighter around her waist the longer they kissed. She moved her hands to either side of his face, holding him while he pressed urgently on. When they stopped it was Charlotte who felt weak. She inhaled deeply, catching her breath and looking him in the eyes. His hands still rested on the small of her back and she noticed she was no longer cool from her swim; in fact, she was fairly certain she was sweating.

"I like you," Wyatt said after the silence.

She giggled nervously. "You told me that already."

"I know," he said seriously. "I just really mean it."

She kissed him lightly on the lips again. He had the widest, most perfect mouth and it thrilled her how he overtook her with it when they kissed.

"I mean it, too," she smiled. "You wanna swim? Did you bring your suit?" She finally pulled away from him but he grabbed her hand and held it gently in front of him.

He shook his head. "I didn't have time to grab that or even my fishing pole so we will have to fish another day, too."

She shrugged. "Just swim in your underwear."

Wyatt put his other hand to his heart feigning surprise.

"Sister Holt!" he said, acting scandalized.

She laughed, putting her head back on her shoulders the way he liked.

"I guess Aunt Rose is rubbing off on me."

"Well, you'll have to remind me to thank Aunt Rose again then. I just love that woman."

He unbuttoned his work shirt and stripped it off, exposing his sweaty tight torso. His filthy jeans sat low on his hips exposing the faint trail of black hair leading down from his belly button. His muscles were lean after a hard day's work and Charlotte noticed. She looked him over, unashamed.

"Speaking of Rose, she calls you the cowboy Adonis, you know."

Wyatt busted up laughing. "No, really? You can't tell me things like that. What if that goes to my head or something?"

She shook her head at him. "Never. You're too sweet."

"Me? Sweet?"

She nodded, smiling. "Oh yes, all gentleman."

Wyatt knew that she must not have the same mind reading abilities as Rose if she thought he was a gentleman. His thoughts about her were anything but chivalrous or gentlemanly. He looked at her standing in front of him with her hair dripping down her breasts as if to confirm that yes, he was a hopeless pig.

"Well, since I'm such a gentleman, I will ask this time. Can I kiss you again?"

"How come you didn't ask a couple of minutes ago?" she teased.

"YOU kissed me," he joked. "Right before you told me to take my clothes off, remember?"

She smiled and pushed at his arm, but he was too quick for her. He grabbed her arm and pulled her close against his naked chest. The feeling of her cold wet skin against his was almost too much for him, but he couldn't stop. She was like a drug. They kissed again, this time long and slow. He moved her wet hair down her back and held it out of the way with his large calloused hands. He saw her blanket laying under the tree and thought about pulling her on it. Thought about all of the things he could do to her to make her sigh again and have that dizzy look on her beautiful face. But he stopped himself and slowed completely before he couldn't stop anymore.

"I'm sorry," he said again into her neck. "I don't wanna get too- I mean, I didn't mean to go too far."

She kissed him on his collarbone before pulling away.

"Will you stop apologizing to me? See? A gentleman," she grinned. "Now, gentleman. Take off your pants and let's get in," she said grinning naughtily at him before running to jump back in the water.

Wyatt kicked off his boots and pulled his jeans down his body. He wore dark colored boxer briefs that exposed his white muscular thighs. He ran in the water after Charlotte, catching her around the waist and spinning her down with him. They tumbled down into the water, laughing and wrestling more before he caught her and held her close against him, not hesitating this time to kiss her again.

The lake was quiet that afternoon and the hot air persisted with the sun high in the sky. The moon would come out that evening just the way it did every night before. The world would continue spinning and all would be as it always was. It was just another June day in Arizona, but their worlds would never be the same.

II

"All good things are wild and free."
~Henry David Thoreau

Her life had never been so happy and, consequently, Charlotte found herself dreading the moment when all of the good things would go away. She tried to train her mind not to think that way, to push away the negative thoughts the moment they invaded her, but it was to no avail. There had been too many years. Too many things. Too many fleeting cheerful moments turned sad. Enjoying the love and excitement of the moment was more than difficult for her, but she was trying.

Still, there was Aunt Rose. There was her funny, unorthodox way of loving Charlotte. There was a roof over her head and food in her belly and the fact she didn't have to worry about what would happen tomorrow for once in her life. And of course, then there was Wyatt. The stunning, unexpected shooting star that came hurtling at her out of nowhere. No, she told herself, this was not pretend. It was real. The feeling in her stomach each time she thought of him told her it was.

When he dropped her off on Monday night the two had been inseparable, practically peeling away from each other on the front porch. When she stopped at the door to watch him leave, he jogged back from his truck and stood under the railing of the porch asking for one more kiss. She happily obliged, leaning all the way over the railing and into another goodnight kiss. She thought about that moment over and over for the rest of the week, smiling to herself as she did. She loved the way he blushed when he talked to her but she also loved this side, the side that was comfortable with her. The side that showed more of his true self and who he was when he wasn't trying.

As much as she enjoyed her work in the shop, the week was dragging on slowly. Wyatt had remorsefully told her Monday that he would be working long days for the remainder of the week and probably wouldn't be at the lake. He'd practically begged to take her out on Friday. Somewhere out of town he said, provided that was OK with Aunt Rose. So the days moved slowly for Charlotte. She reveled in her time with Rose, their meditation in the morning followed by their time at the shop, but Rose was busy with readings, so for most of the day Charlotte was out front ringing up the customers and keeping things in her usual meticulous order. By Thursday the shop was immaculately clean, not a speck of dust on the shelves, windows sparkling, and merchandise lined up in an almost obsessive manner.

Rose was on her second to the last reading of the day when the final client came through the door. It was obvious she wasn't a local or even one of the women who came across the border from Mexico to get a reading with the famous Rose. This woman did not have the look of someone who belonged in Patagonia.

"Hello," Charlotte smiled at her as she walked through the door.

The woman wore large dark sunglasses and long black slacks that fell over tall high-heeled shoes. She pursed her lips at Charlotte instead of greeting her and turned to sit in the waiting area. She flipped her short blonde bob off of her shoulder and sat perfectly still with her hands in her lap.

"Rose will be right with you," Charlotte said. The woman nodded back to her shortly, not removing her sunglasses.

There was an awkward silence in the shop so Charlotte busied herself doing anything but looking at the snobby patron. Mercifully, after about 10 minutes Rose emerged with her client, a very plain woman, middle-aged, dressed in jeans and a worn t-shirt. It seemed to Charlotte that she came to Rose for counseling more than anything. It was clear she had been crying, but now she was smiling, beaming really. She turned to embrace Rose in a warm hug before leaving the shop.

"Betty, clean that energy every damn day, you hear? If you can raise six boys you'd ought to be able find time for that," Rose said sternly to her.

"Thank you, Rose. I promise I will do it more," she smiled, appearing lighter than she did when she walked in. Charlotte paid close attention to the people who came in for appointments and their demeanor before and after. Rose was right to describe her work as magical because her results were nothing less than that.

"Patricia," Rose nodded at the woman in the waiting room.

"Hello, Rose. Shall we?" she stood walking toward Rose's office.

"Yes, let me just lock up the shop. My apprentice will be aiding me in the reading today," Rose said gesturing to Charlotte.

Charlotte tried to keep the look of shock off of her face since she wouldn't think of questioning Rose in front of a paying customer. Patricia was neither amused nor excited at the prospect of having Charlotte as part of the reading, which she made abundantly clear.

"Is that necessary?" she asked, looking down her nose at Charlotte. "She can't be more than 17."

"Almost 19, actually," Charlotte replied flatly. Patricia looked at Rose with her head cocked in annoyance.

Rose shrugged. "She's my apprentice and she's better than I am. But if you don't want the reading, we can cancel."

Patricia exhaled loudly. "No, you know I drove two hours to get here. Let's just do it already."

She let herself into the office as Charlotte dutifully locked the front door of the shop, shooting Rose a pleading glance while Patricia's back was turned. Rose grinned happily and walked back in her office. It was clearly not Patricia's first reading. She sat across the desk from Rose who pulled up another chair for Charlotte to sit near her. Rose took out a small plate of sand and shook it side to side gently, settling the grains.

"Alright," she said. "You know the drill."

Patricia placed her manicured hand in the sand and moved it back-and-forth several times. She pulled it back to her lap, resting her hands over her crossed legs.

"And please remove your sunglasses. This isn't a Goddamn fashion show," Rose said, looking at the sand.

Charlotte cracked a small smile but held in her laughter. Patricia obeyed, albeit with an attitude. She pulled off her sunglasses and tucked them away in her purse, exposing her eyes with deep circles under them although she tried to hide it with layers of makeup. This woman was tired. Charlotte felt for her energy as Rose had taught her. She felt sad, desperate, and angry. Strangely enough, the feeling Charlotte got from being around this woman was very similar to the one that she got being around her own mother. The thought of it made chills run down Charlotte's back.

Rose pulled the sand plate in front of her and began her reading, looking into the curves in the sand. She started off talking about finances and business opportunities. Patricia asked several follow-ups and ran a few names by Rose.

"Not him," Rose responded to one name. "Don't let your husband work with him unless you want jail time. Dirty business." Charlotte looked at Patricia to gauge her reaction and was surprised that the woman nodded, seeming to heed the warning.

"OK, who's this guy again? The one who died a while back. The sailor," Rose asked after a while.

"That's my father," Patricia said, rolling her eyes. "He comes through every time. What more could he possibly have to say?"

"Well, as I've explained to you, he's now your spirit guide, so he tries to come around and help you out," Rose said rolling her eyes at Patricia outwardly. "You want me to tell him to fuck off or should I see what he's got to say?" she said sarcastically.

"No, tell me, I guess," Patricia said, resigned.

"Alright so he's talking about this other man. This other love that awaits you. What's the connection to India?"

Patricia inhaled. "I know someone who was stationed there a long time ago. And he-he just told me."

Rose nodded. "Ok, so that's our guy. Your dad just wanted me to confirm." Rose was quiet for a moment, thoughtfully looking at the sand grains. "He's poor?" Rose sounded shocked.

"Yes." Patricia sounded almost ashamed.

"The connection between you is strong. You're in his immediate soul group."

"What's that again?" Patricia asked.

"Those are the people you keep coming back with in each life. They are the ones closest to you. Remember it's not always this soulmate bullshit we've been fed. Sometimes they are there to play a challenging role."

Patricia fought to keep a straight face, not wanting to give anything away. She sat waiting for more, but Rose simply looked at her.

"Well?" Patricia said impatiently.

"Well what? Do you have a question for your dad about this guy?"

Patricia rolled her eyes. "Yeah, what the fuck do I do?"

Rose looked over at Charlotte who sat close by, observing the scene.

"Charlotte, answer Patricia," Rose said. Charlotte's eyes widened and Patricia looked at her expectantly.

"Well?" Patricia demanded again.

Charlotte quieted her mind and waited for the information to come to her just as Rose had taught. She waited for the message to come, floating down like a feather. The room was quiet for a few minutes before Charlotte spoke.

"Where there is money there is no love and where there is love, there is no money. You- you have to pick one."

Patricia looked at Charlotte closely as if deciding if she should believe.

"But...that's it? What am I supposed to do?"

"Only you can decide. There is no set destiny in our life. We can choose from several. This is one of your choosing points," Rose interjected.

Patricia looked back at her anxiously, demanding an answer.

"Pick a street," Rose said simply.

"What the hell kind of reading is this?" she demanded. "THAT'S what I'm supposed to go off of? Christ, I could have gotten better advice asking a wall." Patricia pushed herself out of her seat, heading toward the door.

"You forgot to pay," Rose said without emotion. Patricia huffed, reaching into her bag. She took two one hundred dollar bills and threw them on the desk.

"Oh this is just perfect. I can have love but I've got to give up the money, huh? What a crock of shit, Rose."

Rose shrugged, picking up the money. "Being poor isn't so bad. Plus if you keep screwing him, you'll lose the money either way. It's time to choose. Choose wisely."

Patricia let out a sudden sob, holding onto her midsection.

"You don't understand. You can't understand how this feels. I can't lose him." Charlotte was confused who she was referring to, the husband or the lover, but her struggle was obvious and despite the woman's awful demeanor, Charlotte actually felt bad for her.

"So don't," Rose said, as if it were simple.

"I'm never coming back here. That's it." She blew out of the office and toward the door with Charlotte after her to let her out.

Charlotte caught up with her as she was pushing on the locked front door. She put her hand on her shoulder and moved the woman gently out of the way. Tears streamed down Patricia's face and she didn't try to hide it now. Charlotte put the key in the lock and stopped before turning it.

"Sometimes there's only one chance for the real thing. And once it passes it doesn't come again. I hope you make the right choice." The words came to her the same way they had in the reading. As if someone else said them for her. Patricia looked at her through swollen eyes and Charlotte released her through the door.

Charlotte walked back to Rose and found her waving a flaming sage bundled around her office.

"That bitch costs me a fortune in sage. Crack a window to get this shit outta here." Charlotte obliged, opening the large window behind Rose's desk.

"Aunt Rose, I'm sorry if I made her mad. I hope she comes back."

"Oh God," Rose said loudly. "I sure as hell don't. But she will. I'll never get rid of that one."

"She's so sad," Charlotte said.

Rose nodded. "It's like watching someone slam their hand in a door over and over again then be surprised when it hurts. She's fucking hopeless. But you, my little grasshopper. You were magnificent." She kissed her fingers and gestured them out from her face like an Italian.

Charlotte shrugged. "I don't even know what I said. I can't really remember it."

Rose nodded. "You told her what she needed and no more. It's not up to us to tell them what to do- only to show them choices."

Charlotte nodded back, looking thoughtful. She helped her aunt finish saging the room and started to shut down the shop for the night, all the while wondering if what she had said was true. If all of us only have one shot at the real thing.

⚜

Garrett was right. The work was hard and the days were long. After his regular chores feeding horses and cleaning stalls in the morning, he went right to the irrigation work. Garrett must've known that he exaggerated his irrigation experience since Luis was nominated to stay back with Wyatt to do the work. Wyatt was more than grateful for this. Not only was Luis one of the hardest workers he'd ever seen, but he was also patient and knowledgeable about seemingly everything. Plus, Wyatt didn't know anything about putting the pipes into the ground. He could dig the hell out of a trench but he would have been lost without Luis for the rest of the project.

Even the mornings were hot, but Luis, at least 40 years Wyatt's senior, didn't seem to notice. He worked relentlessly and Wyatt had to push himself to keep up. He didn't speak much English so he mostly showed Wyatt how to do things by actually doing it and then having Wyatt try.

"Here, you cut," Luis said, pointing to the pipe. He sawed through the pipe and held it out to show him. "See? Clean, yes? Cut fast so it's clean."

Wyatt nodded at him, watching the old man work. His hands were cracked and calloused, but Wyatt was constantly impressed with how efficient he was with them.

"Then glue, see?"

He wiped the adhesive around the pipe and showed Wyatt how to connect it to the next piece. Wyatt, ever the perfectionist, had the hang of it in no time. He started to work methodically, getting into a flow, and was rewarded by Luis's big grin and crinkled up eyes.

"Yes, good! It's good," he nodded, looking over Wyatt's work.

It was strange to work side-by-side with somebody who didn't speak the same language for the pure fact that there wasn't a lot of steady conversation. Just a few words here and there referencing the work. It was just as well, though, as Wyatt spent the majority of his day in his head reliving his time with Charlotte anyway.

After hours of thinking about it, he finally decided what it was that made her so different. It wasn't her beauty or the exotic nature of her having lived everywhere but here. It was that for the first time with a girl, he wanted to be her friend also. Wyatt was a man's man and had plenty of friends, none of them girls. But he found himself able to joke around with her, to relax around her to the point that he wasn't the Wyatt that he normally was around other girls. He was just Wyatt. Her beauty was the icing on the cake, though, and he was not immune to thinking about that, too. He thought about her long, lean body stretched out against him as he kissed her. Her perfect full lips and how the top one fit between his lips perfectly. He found himself craving her, anticipating all he wanted to do to her.

And so his agonizing week went on. He knew he wouldn't be able to see her with his long days unless he came to her house at eight every night just to kiss her on the porch then leave again. That was well worth it for Wyatt, but as comfortable as he was with her, he didn't feel right about asking for that just yet. But Friday was coming and the long agonizing workload was so exhausting that each night when he hit his pillow, he was dead to the world. He slept hard without dreaming and was always happy to jump up the next morning to do it over again since that would bring him a day closer to seeing her.

By Thursday, the irrigation was almost complete. Wyatt wouldn't be there next spring to see the orchard be planted but that part would be easy in comparison. At first he had resented the fact that he would be the one doing the irrigation instead of working the cattle, but once he looked around at what he and Luis had accomplished in all of those days, he was prideful. He kept looking over the project feeling accomplished that he had created something that would actually work. Something useful. And with Luis's supervision, the work was pristine and something to be proud of for them both. Close to nightfall on Thursday, Garrett came out to check the progress yet again.

"Well damn, fellas. Almost done!" he said grinning widely, spitting tobacco juice in front of him as he overlooked the work.

"Luis, was he fast enough for ya?" Garrett joked.

Luis laughed, waving his hand. "Es very fast! Learn fast!"

Wyatt stood with his hands on his hips smiling tiredly at Garrett and Luis.

"He's being nice. I could hardly keep up," he said.

Garrett nodded. "Luis is a freak of nature. My same age and makes me look like I belong in a Goddamn nursing home."

The men laughed together and Garrett went on talking with Luis about the logistics of the irrigation. Watching them communicate was comical to say the least. They both spoke in partial Spanish and partial English, but somehow they understood each other perfectly.

Wyatt's shirt was soaked through with sweat and dirt from the day's work and his back ached from bending over all day. He hustled around picking up the tools and trash, making sure the job site was clean. It would be finished tomorrow and finally he could see Charlotte.

"Well, Wyatt, what do ya think? This job will get you in shape for boot camp, won't it?" Garrett asked.

"Oh- yeah, I guess it will."

"You know, every man should have to go to boot camp. And I'll tell you it was the best thing for me when I was your age. This world would be a hell of a lot different if every young man had to do that."

Wyatt nodded back at him. He had heard the speech before from Garrett and tended to agree but he couldn't focus on what Garrett was saying. All he could think about was the fact that he had yet to tell Charlotte about the Marines. Granted, it hadn't come up but he still felt like he was keeping it from her somehow. He would tell her that next day, he decided. And plus, October was a long time away. It was still only June. It's not that he had forgotten about it, he just hadn't thought about it like he used to in the days before he met her. She'd changed everything for him that day at the lake and he was starting to realize the impact of it.

"Well all right then, boys. Get some good rest. This will be done tomorrow then it's onto the next one!" Garrett walked toward his truck, leaving Wyatt standing with the tools in his hands.

"Night, sir."

Wyatt finished his meticulous cleaning and walked to the bunkhouse with Luis for the night. Luis gave him a pat on the shoulder as they walked and Wyatt, once again, was thankful for the language barrier. He didn't feel like talking.

⚜

"Are you sure it's OK, Aunt Rose? I don't want you to feel like I'm ditching you again."

Charlotte was conflicted about spending more time with Wyatt. She loved it, truly enjoyed every second, but she couldn't forget that any time with Wyatt was time away from her aunt and she had a certain amount of guilt that came with that because of how wonderful Rose had been to her.

But Rose would hear none of it. "Will you stop that? Let me tell you, if he were coming here to pick me up for a date I would ditch you any day of the week," she said, raising her eyebrows at her.

"All right. Fine then, you go and I'll stay here," Charlotte joked.

"Oh don't you tempt me. But listen, if you're that worried about it, invite him for dinner over here tomorrow and we can all be together. But don't be jealous when he starts to like me more than he likes you," Rose winked at her.

"Ok, fine," Charlotte laughed. "I'll ask him if he's free."

"Oh please, he's gotta be eating out of the palm of your hand by now, right? Where's he taking you tonight anyway?"

Charlotte shrugged. "Somewhere out of town. He said if it's ok with you, that is."

Rose fanned herself with her hands. "So he was talking about me, was he? You might be out of luck, girl!" Rose cackled and turned to stir her dinner on the stove.

Charlotte sat at the kitchen counter dressed and waiting for him. Rose had insisted on a fashion show to pick her outfit although Charlotte could not have cared less. Rose picked a short jean skirt, brown sandals, and a white eyelet off the shoulder blouse. Charlotte had put on the tiniest bit of mascara and lip-gloss to finish off her look but kept her hair wavy and wild the way it always was. After all, she thought, he did say it was beautiful. She sat and watched Rose standing at the stove stirring with one hand and holding out a glass of wine in the other.

"So that client yesterday. Patricia?"

Rose rolled her eyes. "Oh yes, thinks she's Princess Di. What about her?"

Charlotte hesitated, unsure about how to phrase the question.

"She's not going to leave the guy with the money, is she?"

Rose shrugged. "She has the choice, but no, babe. It's not likely."

Charlotte furrowed her brow, thinking. "That immediate soul group thing. Is that why she feels so strongly about the other guy?" Charlotte asked.

Rose nodded, turning toward her niece. "Yes, that connection is strong. Difficult for her to fight but it's one of her challenges she's set herself up for this life. We all have soul groups like that. Guess who's in yours?" she said with a grin.

"You?"

"Damn right!" she laughed. "I'm sure you've got others but that's where that feeling comes from. The one you get right here." Rose's hand hovered over her gut showing Charlotte.

"So, why didn't you tell her that guy is, you know, better for her?"

Rose shook her head. "People have to work those things out for themselves. Plus, babe, sometimes in a reading, you'll figure out there are things that you can't tell a client," Rose hesitated. "Sometimes the whole truth is too much for people."

Charlotte nodded, thoughtful as she always was when Rose gave her these lessons.

Her aunt smiled. "You're a good student, my dear. I like the way you've got things rolling around in that head of yours."

Charlotte nodded, but her mind was back at the lake that first day she met Wyatt and reliving that stomach pang she got the second she saw him. Rose cocked her head, listening.

"I think Romeo just pulled up! Let me get the door!"

She all but tripped over herself going to the front door and opened it before he even had a chance to knock. Wyatt stood on the front porch in jeans, boots, and a short sleeved button up shirt exposing his muscular forearms. He held two large sunflowers in his hand. Rose squeaked when she saw him standing there.

"Look how handsome!" she said, standing on her toes to hug him.

"Hi, Miss Rose," Wyatt said, smiling broadly and hugging her back.

"Charlotte, will you look at this?" Charlotte stood by the kitchen giggling over her hopelessly perverted aunt.

"Hi, Wyatt," she smiled.

His jaw dropped a little when he saw her, but he checked himself quickly. Her tanned legs were shiny with lotion and her lips were even more pronounced than usual with the tiniest bit of color on them. He'd never seen her in a skirt before and the accessibility issues running through his mind were going to get him in trouble.

"You look pretty, Charlotte," he said, quietly. "I brought you each one of these," he said, holding out the sunflowers. "Garrett's got them growing like weeds all over the ranch. I thought you might like them."

"Be still my heart, Wyatt. You are just the sweetest!" Rose said, putting one hand on her chest and leading him inside.

"Yes," Charlotte grinned, locking eyes with him. "The sweetest. Thank you."

She walked toward him and took the flowers, brushing his hand with hers as she did. He wanted to grab her and kiss her but didn't want to be disrespectful in front of Rose. Charlotte busied herself finding mason jars for both flowers as Rose chatted up Wyatt. She asked him all about work and Garrett and finally, where he was taking Charlotte.

"Is it ok if we go over to Sonoita for dinner? I'll still have her home early but I heard the Ranch House is good."

"Of course! You two have fun. You're keeping me young watching you two. Now go on, get outta here." Rose hugged them both, cracking a few more jokes about her going with Wyatt instead of Charlotte then sent them on their way.

They were alone out front and Wyatt opened the passenger door for Charlotte to climb in the cab. She stood next to him, inhaling the shower fresh scent as he stood straight as a board holding the door tightly. His nerves, unfortunately, were back.

"Oh no, you're not back to being afraid of me are you?" she laughed.

"No- I. I didn't want to be weird around Rose."

She nodded hopping up in the truck. "Just messing with you, Sterling."

When he came around to the driver's side Charlotte opened the door for him, sitting in the middle of the cab. He got in next to her feeling the heat coming off of her body.

"Can I sit here?" she said smiling at him.

"Yes," he said. "Yes, please."

He rested his hand on her leg and leaned over to brush her lips with a brief kiss. It was Charlotte who leaned back in for a second, longer one, grabbing his hand to hold on her lap.

The drive to Sonoita was a little over 15 minutes through rolling fields and cattle country. It could have been five times that for all Wyatt cared. He liked the feeling of her sitting so close to him and felt proud when he saw people in passing cars look at them together. *Mine*, he thought. *She's mine*. Wyatt pointed out the 87 ranch and other places, telling her all he knew about the area. He showed her the spot there had been a wildfire the month before and how it had charred the fields black.

"But wait until you see how green it gets after the rains. All of this will look different," he said.

She nodded. "Kinda reminds me of Texas but Texas doesn't have mountains like you do here."

"But don't you hate Texas?" he asked.

She looked at him, surprised. "Did I tell you that?"

"Well, no, but the look on your face when you talk about it makes it pretty obvious."

"Yeah, Rose said I'm a bad liar."

"She told me that, too!" he said.

Charlotte giggled. "She thinks everyone is a bad liar since she can read their mind anyway."

"God, I hope not," he said without thinking.

"Why? What do you have going on in there?" she said brushing the side of his head with her hand.

He shook his head. "Nothing, I promise. Only pure thoughts," he grinned at her, tightening his hold on her hand.

"Sure. Me, too," she said, kissing him on the cheek.

"Sister Holt. I'm going to have to ask you to behave if you don't want me to crash the truck," he joked.

Sonoita was so small there wasn't even one stoplight. There were wineries and ranches scattered throughout the town, but the crossroads, as the locals called it, consisted of a gas station, local grocery store, and two restaurants including the Ranch House. It had been on Garrett's recommendation that Wyatt chose the restaurant. It was a small, old wood building with an entrance for the bar and one for the restaurant. The parking lot was full even though the sun had yet to go down.

They walked in and had to wait to be seated. While they stood in the lobby, Wyatt felt the eyes of the patrons, mostly older locals, on them. Mostly they were looking at Charlotte, but she seemed unfazed and pointed to the historic local pictures on the wall, showing Wyatt each one she liked. He loved the way she looked when she didn't realize he was looking. Her furrowed concentrated brow was adorable to him.

Soon they were seated across from each other in a corner booth. Wyatt would have rather had her next to him like in the truck, but when he saw how the candle on the table lit up her face so beautifully he decided he could tolerate that seating arrangement just as well.

"So I get to buy dinner this time, right?" she asked, looking at the menu.

"Yeah, right. I invited you out so I get to pay."

"Ok so if I invite you out next time I get to pay? That's how it works?" she smiled.

"Well- no. Not really," he grinned. "I always get to."

"Hmmmm this doesn't sound fair to me. But it does remind me, Rose wants you to come to dinner tomorrow."

"Yeah? Will it just be me and Rose or will you be there?" he joked.

"Oh, if it were up to her it would just be the two of you. But no, I'll be there."

"Ok, good. So you're not giving me away just yet."

She shook her head and looked him in the eye.

"No. Absolutely not." He wanted to lunge across the table and kiss her until she couldn't breathe, but he stayed put and smiled back at her.

Wyatt ordered steak and a baked potato and Charlotte opted for a salad. He gave her a hard time about ordering a salad at a steakhouse but once she looked at the prices on the menu she couldn't bring herself to order the steak dinner knowing he was going to pay for it.

Their conversation over dinner flowed nonstop. Each had the whole week of work to recount to the other. Wyatt told her about Luis and how he'd outworked him all week and about the animals and new batch of barn cats that were just born. Charlotte loved hearing about the ranch and all of the animals. He invited her to come over sometime although he hadn't worked out how that would go over with Garrett and the other men.

She told him about her week at the shop and about all of the people she'd seen Rose help. About all of the things she sold in the shop, special crystals, sage, portraits of Mother Mary and statues of the Archangel Michael. She left out the part about Patricia and her love triangle problems since it didn't seem right to discuss with anyone.

"So, has she done a reading for you?" he asked.

"Not really. She's big on people figuring things out for themselves. Especially me," she laughed.

"So she hasn't told you, like, what you're going to do with your life or anything?"

She shook her head. "No, but she wants me to go to college. She says that'll be good for my future. She didn't give me any more details though."

"What about you?" he asked. "Do you want to go to college?"

"Oh yeah, for sure. I just never thought it was an option for me. But now, I think maybe it is."

"Why wouldn't it be an option for you?" he asked, confused.

Charlotte shrugged and stopped making eye contact. "I don't know, Wyatt. Girls like me- like how I've been raised. We don't really do college or big things like that."

"What do you mean girls like you?"

She squirmed in her seat a bit before answering. "I don't know. You know, we moved all of the time so my grades were just ok and also, you know, the money thing. I just never thought it could be for me. That I could do it." She looked around the restaurant, anywhere but at him.

"I bet you could do anything." The words fell out of his mouth in complete frankness.

Charlotte smiled shyly. "You're being nice."

"No, really. You're like that. I just bet whatever you want to do, you'll do."

Charlotte blushed visibly. "Well what about you? What are you going to do with your life? Or do you need Rose to tell you?" she grinned.

He smiled back and sighed heavily. "It's funny, I can't believe we haven't talked about this yet," he paused. "I was supposed to go to college next year. I had a baseball scholarship to a small school up north but I- I decided not to."

"Why not?" she asked.

"I don't know actually. I think because it didn't feel like my idea. Felt like what everybody else wanted me to do. So, when I turned 18 in March I- I signed up for the Marine Corps. I didn't tell anyone. My parents or friends or anyone. That way they couldn't try and change my mind," he smiled sadly. "So, I start in October," he said, leveling his gaze at her to check her reaction. She couldn't hide the look of surprise from her face, but there was admiration there, too.

"Well. Sounds like you knew what you wanted. That's good," she said, falling quiet for a moment. "But aren't you too sweet to be a Marine? I mean, they're notoriously mean," she smiled.

"Hey, I'm tough, Charlotte," he said, eyes dancing. "You're the only person who thinks I'm sweet."

"Not true- Aunt Rose agrees."

"Ok, well, two people then."

They were quiet again looking at each other across the table. Both thinking about what all of this meant for them.

"So you're going to be a college girl, huh?" he said quietly.

"And you a Marine," he nodded and there was a brief silence between them.

"But not today," he said.

"Not today," she said as he reached for her hand over the table.

⚬⚬⚬

Dinner continued on and they didn't bring up the future again. Neither of them wanted to. They shared a slice of chocolate cake and ice cream for dessert, happily digging in with their spoons. By the time they left the restaurant the sun was just going down over the distant hills making a grapefruit glow over the open fields of grass.

"Oh my gosh," Charlotte said as they walked out. "Look how beautiful."

He came and stood next to her on the wood porch of the Ranch House, looking at the sunset. He looked down at her as she smelled the air.

He laughed. "What are you smelling?" he asked.

She inhaled deeply through her nose. "The dirt. Smells nice," she said turning to look at him. "And you. You smell nice, too."

"Well, I did shower this time. Just for you," he joked.

She shrugged. "I don't mind you sweaty, but I like you like this, too."

They stood alone in the quiet of the porch looking at each other. The restaurant was bustling on the inside with the noise of the patrons and dishes muffled for them to hear. The windows faced out to the porch and parking lot but Wyatt didn't care. He leaned down and put his hands around Charlotte's waist, pulling her toward him. He kissed her firmly on her soft lips, his hands roaming down the small of her back slipping down lower and lower. She looked dizzy again when he pulled back from her.

"I don't want to take you home yet," he said lowly.

"So don't."

"You want to go for a drive? There's some pretty places through wine country."

She nodded, taking hold of his bicep and walking toward the truck with him. She sat in the middle again, even closer now, and he put his hand on her thigh pulling her toward him.

They drove down a meandering road that took them by the wineries. Acres of grape vines stretched across the skyline, still visible with the slow setting sun.

"Look way out there," Wyatt said, pulling the truck to the side of the road. "Do you see that group of antelope out there? Just to the right of that barn," he pointed. It took Charlotte a long time to find them but finally she saw the horns peeking out of the grass.

"How on earth did you see that?" Charlotte could hardly find the little specks while the truck was stopped, she had no idea how he did it while driving.

He shrugged. "Lots of practice. Look, those two in the front are babies."

"Oh, I see! Oh look how cute they are."

He turned off the engine and rolled down his window so they could get a better look. The antelope, at least five that they could see, were bedded down in the grass so that only their heads were visible.

"They're so fast and they can see forever, too. Really good eyesight."

She cocked her head at him. "So you know more about wild game than fishing, huh?"

He put his arm around her and tickled her side roughly.

"I know about fishing and I'm still going to show you."

"Pfft. I'll believe it when I see it." She squirmed in his arms and he stopped tickling her. He looked down at her and let his eyes roam to her bare legs under her skirt.

"I like your skirt," he said dumbly.

"Rose picked it," she shrugged. "I'm not good at picking clothes."

"Once again, Aunt Rose is my favorite person," he grinned. "Let's sit on the tailgate," he suggested.

It was difficult for her to get on the tailgate with a skirt on and Wyatt, ever observant, noticed her dilemma. He lifted her from the waist and she hopped up to take a seat. Once she was there he didn't move, though. He stayed on the ground with his arms around her and hers around his shoulders.

"Hi," he smiled in her face.

"Hi," she smiled, back.

He stood on the ground turning to look out at the antelope with her. The night was quiet and it was a relief for both of them to be alone together once again.

"Why don't you ever talk about your family?" he asked abruptly.

Charlotte became immediately uncomfortable and made it a point not to look down at him, but kept her eyes on the horizon instead.

"I don't know, Wyatt. There's not much to tell," she sighed. "I'm the only child and I've never met my dad. No idea who he even is."

He was silent for a moment since he wasn't sure what he should say to that. "Sorry" just didn't seem to cut it.

"Well, what about your mom? Rose's sister, right?"

Charlotte was forced to think of her then. Her once beautiful, wild mother. She had plenty of canned responses she'd given to people over the years. My mom's a waitress, my mom works a lot, my mom is out of town on business. She'd spent her life making excuses for her and yet sitting there on that summer night with Wyatt, she couldn't bring herself to do it again.

Charlotte looked down at the dirt, gathering herself. "My mom is kind of a mess, Wyatt. You don't want to hear about her. She just- she just has a really tough time keeping herself together. Jobs, boyfriends, life in general. It just hasn't come easy to her."

Wyatt looked at her, thoughtful. "But- she had to do something right to have you as a daughter, right?"

Charlotte shrugged. "She doesn't think so. I'm not exactly her proudest accomplishment."

"What is then?"

Charlotte thought of her mother the drunk, her mother the adventurer, her mother the other woman, her mother the addict. She shook her head and found a smile, that one she could still dig out to fake it.

"Let's not talk about this, Wyatt. Come up and sit with me."

He decided he shouldn't pry further. Not yet, anyway. He couldn't keep himself from wanting to know more. Wanting to fix it in some way. But he would let her have her way for the night.

"I kinda like it down here," he said, moving in front of her and looking up in her face.

They locked eyes and everything else fell away. He pulled her head toward him and kissed her slowly and tenderly at first. Her skin was flushed from the warm night and she tasted like chocolate cake. Her arms wrapped around his neck pulling him toward her. He pushed his body between her legs, kissing her harder. His hands were tangled in her hair and their breathless kisses turned deeper and deeper. His hands roamed down her back and to the top of her bottom, pulling her closer to the edge of the tailgate.

"I'm sorry," he said into her mouth. "It's hard to stop."

She laughed at him pulling her face away a bit.

"Why do you always kiss me then apologize?"

"You're right," he said, moving in for more. "I'll stop."

He stopped and jumped on the tailgate and was on her immediately. He leaned into her pushing her back into the truck bed gently. She hugged him closer feeling his heavy breathing and pounding heart. He supported himself with his arms so as not to crush her, and kissed her relentlessly. His hands moved up and down the side of her firm body. He stopped, pushing himself up to look at her again. The sun was just behind the hills, leaving the softest rosy glow over her. Her hair was wild around her face and her lips pink and raw from kissing. Her blouse had slipped down lower on her shoulders and Wyatt couldn't resist. He lowered his head and kissed from one shoulder across her collarbone to the other. A brief sigh came out of her mouth and it was all Wyatt could do to not to rip the shirt off entirely. Instead he sat her up and pulled her close against him, exercising every bit of discipline in his body.

"Christ, Charlotte," he said breathing heavily. "You might be the death of me," he said into her hair.

She smiled and snuggled in closer toward him, but his words made the thought come unbidden into her mind the way she hated. *Yes*, she thought sadly. *Yes, I will.*

❦

Morning meditation turned into a question and answer session for Rose, who was more than happy about it. They were sitting in the living room across from each other as always, just having finished their brief meditation session. Rose held a hot cup of tea in both hands, sitting cross-legged and looking thoughtfully at her beautiful niece.

"You know sometimes when you just have a really strong feeling about something? You just know it for certain and it pops in your head out of nowhere? How do I know if that feeling is right or not?" Charlotte asked.

"Well," Rose started, "you can't ever really tell for sure, not in the state you're in right now. It just takes time to trust that voice. But how I know is when something just sort of floats in. Angels whisper, they don't shout. You know, it's sort of light as a feather but you can just tell it's true. It's hard to explain that feeling, though."

Charlotte nodded, looking thoughtful. She recalled all of the times when she was a kid when she knew things would happen before they actually did. It had become commonplace for her to know when a situation was bad or dangerous. She also remembered the many times when these feelings were linked to her mother. One time in particular in elementary school she was sitting at her desk in the middle of the day and knew, with every fiber of her being, that they would be moving again. She went so far as to say a heartfelt goodbye to her kind teacher that afternoon before ever being told they were going anywhere. Her mother had given her no indication beforehand, but sitting at her desk she had a vision of the packed car waiting for her in the parking lot. Sure enough when she left school that day, they were on the road and onto the next place.

Charlotte nodded. "Yeah, I know what you mean, but why is it always like, you know... Bad things? Seems like those are always the things I know about before they happen," she said avoiding eye contact.

Rose sighed. "It won't always be like that. I think it just seems that way because of how hard it's been for you, babe. One day, you'll get good thoughts and know those are for you, too. Now you probably get them but you dismiss them too quickly to notice. Like you don't get to have those nice things," she smiled sadly. "But you do. You can have good things, too, Char."

"It hasn't been that bad for me, Aunt Rose," she said quietly.

Rose put her head to the side. "Charlotte," she said, disbelievingly.

"No, really. I've seen people who had it much worse. It could have been worse. Really."

Rose nodded. "Yes, I'm sure. But you can feel sad about what it's been like. You don't have to be so brave all of the time. Not anymore."

"But I'm happy, Aunt Rose. I'm lucky. This," she gestured around her, "this is the most amazing life I've ever had right now, you know? So I don't want to feel sorry for myself when other people have so much less," she paused. "I'm really lucky."

Rose laughed. "Baby, listen, I know you've had it rough if you're talking about my shitty little house in Patagonia as if it's the Ritz!" she smiled, reaching her hands across to Charlotte. "But I'm happy, my sweet girl. And I'm the lucky one to have you here with me," she smiled at her. "And as far as those bad thoughts, all you can do is pray when you get those."

Charlotte fell quiet. "I can't really pray, though," she said, her voice low.

"Why not?" Rose asked, scrunching up her forehead.

"Well, because. I'm not baptized or anything. And I don't really know how to pray. I'd never been to church before I met you."

Rose shook her head. "Well, unfortunately, exclusion happens to be a big part of how people feel about religion," she rolled her eyes. "Listen, let me tell you a secret. There's no password. There's no secret handshake. God is for everyone and everyone is for God. Praying is just talking and I know you know how to talk," she smiled. "So all you have to do is talk to God. Ask for help when you need it, be thankful, which I'm pretty sure you're covering, and most of all, believe you deserve love from the Divine."

"But, I don't know anything about the Bible or God really. I'm just figuring it all out, you know? I don't know what I think of it all."

Rose waved her hand at Charlotte. "So you think you've gotta wait until you pass some God class to get to pray? That you've got to sign some contract before you deserve love?" she said, shaking her head vehemently. "You look for the divine and you will find it. You ask for help and you will get it. It's all very simple."

Charlotte looked skeptical and Rose knew she had to make her point hit home.

"How do you think you got here, to my place?" Rose asked looking at her intently.

"What do you mean? I saved my money and I came here. I made a choice."

Rose shook her head. "No, you prayed. You begged for something better. You prayed for a way out, you just didn't know it at the time."

Charlotte went back to that night in her mother's apartment. The air had been thick with cigarette smoke and the floor filthy with trash. She could hear them having violent sex in the next room where only hours ago they were arguing, throwing things around the room. She thought she had no more tears left in her, that she was as tough as she could be, but something snapped in her that night. Tears had dropped from the corners of her eyes onto her only pillow. *Please*, she thought, *please help me*. She didn't know who she was begging, but she repeated the words over and over into her pillow. *Please, please help me,* she cried.

Less than a week later, she finally left. She'd been saving her money, waiting for the right time to go, she just had no idea where. There was no one, she had nothing, but she would not stay a moment longer. Ready or not, the voice inside of her directed her where to go. It, just like her other thoughts, had dropped into her head out of nowhere.

Go to Rose, it said.

Charlotte's eyes widened and her jaw dropped, she looked at her aunt in shock.

Rose nodded knowingly. "You remember. God listened," she gripped her hands tighter. "God listened to both of us."

She was watering plants on the front porch wearing jeans and a pink tank top when he pulled up. Her skin was dark from summer and her hair even blonder from the sun. She smiled and waved at him, walking over to his truck as he got out.

"Hey!" she said, happily. "Always right on time."

He wore clean work jeans that were worn at the bottom with a blue t-shirt tight around his biceps. He didn't hesitate to pull her toward him in a solid embrace before kissing her firmly on the mouth.

"Why do you look so pretty? Aren't we just staying home?"

She laughed. "I'm wearing jeans, Wyatt, not a prom dress."

He grinned, keeping a hold on her waist. "Well I like them. A lot."

She smiled, kissing him again on the lips then on his stubbly cheek.

"Well, you look handsome. Just like always. I had fun last night," she said pulling back from him and holding his hand.

They both smiled at each other thinking about the night before. After getting tangled up in the truck bed, they headed back to Patagonia, Charlotte hugging tight to his side the whole way. Their front porch goodbye ended up taking them a half an hour and still ended too soon for both of them.

"Next time let's go there again," she said.

"Next time?"

"Yeah, next time," she laughed. "The time that I get to pay since it's my idea. Now come in. Rose won't let me keep you to myself for long."

Rose opted for an Italian dinner. She made homemade marinara that had simmered on the stove the whole day, permeating the house with the savory basil scent. She gave Wyatt her standard heavy petting greeting then sat him down at the breakfast bar so she could both talk and cook. Charlotte helped her aunt but would sometimes walk by him, brushing him with a hand and turning to give him a secret smile when Rose's back was turned.

The two created a beautiful dinner of pasta, salad, and garlic bread focusing on the smallest detail. It was the nicest meal Wyatt had in a long time since meals at the ranch generally consisted of meat and potatoes. Rose chatted on and on with Wyatt, asking him more about himself and where he was from in Tucson.

"So Wyatt, what about your folks? They live up in Tucson still?"

Wyatt nodded, trying to think of the best explanation. "Well, yeah, my dad does. My mom just moved though. She's in Salt Lake now," he said, looking down at his plate. "They split up this last year."

"That's too bad, dear. You have any siblings?"

"Nope. Just me. My parents had me later in life. I was kind of a surprise baby," he smiled shyly.

"Well, a damn good surprise, I'd say."

Charlotte was looking intently at him and he caught her eye and smiled as if to say, it's fine. It's not a big deal.

"I'll tell you though, that's why I never got married. I bet it's hard to share your life like that. But you know Wyatt, that was before I met you," she joked, reaching across the breakfast bar to put her hand on his.

"Um, hello, I'm right here," Charlotte said grinning.

"Oh, I'd almost forgotten. Well fine then, have it your way. Greedy, greedy. If only you had a brother, Wyatt. Or maybe a single, wayward uncle or something," she winked.

They sat down to eat, Rose in the middle of them, and they fell into a companionable conversation and steady laughter thanks to Rose. Somehow they got on the topic of the border town of Nogales and Rose launched into a long and detailed story about how she accidentally found herself in a strip club there one day in the middle of the week. She ended up giving readings to both the dancers and bartenders, all clad in their work attire. She detailed the story so perfectly and humorously that Wyatt and Charlotte barely got a word in through their laughter.

All three stood to clean the kitchen afterward, Wyatt making himself as useful as possible. He got sidetracked a couple of times watching the barefoot Charlotte washing dishes at the sink. If Rose weren't there Charlotte would have been up on the counter and in his arms and he could see that vision clearly in his head.

"Hey Romeo, get that dish for me, would ya," Rose slapped him on the arm, tearing him from his daydream. She grinned knowingly, patting his arm. "I don't blame you, kid. She's gorgeous."

Charlotte looked at them questioningly and Wyatt shook his head and smiling. He tried to keep from blushing but to no avail.

"Rose was reading my mind again," he explained.

Charlotte nodded. "Yeah, try living with her."

It was decided that Wyatt needed to see the shop and he was inwardly thrilled. His imagination had run wild with what might potentially happen there. He genuinely had no idea what to expect so when he walked into Rose's office, which was somewhat normal, it was a bit anticlimactic. Charlotte showed him out to the front waiting area to look at all of the merchandise and where she worked at the front desk.

"See how perfectly organized everything is? That's our girl's doing. Sales have gone through the roof since she's been here. Something about a beautiful girl that makes people want to buy shit," Rose said.

Wyatt was listening but his mind was hanging on the way Rose had called her "our" girl. He felt a swell of warmth and pride. He nodded, looking around at the different crystals and religious relics.

"So where do people get their readings? In your office then?"

Rose nodded smiling. "Yes, come back in here let me show you."

She walked around her desk and sat down comfortably, setting her glass of wine on the wooden countertop.

"So," she said, "shall we have a look?"

Charlotte stood near Wyatt with her arms crossed across her chest. She shrugged when he looked at her, not offering to bail him out.

"Um, I don't really know. Should we?" he laughed nervously.

"Well hell, just sit down, I'm not going to sacrifice a goat or anything, so just relax."

He sat down across from her and Charlotte pulled up a chair near them. He looked around at the colorful tapestries and inviting feel of the room. He didn't exactly feel nervous but had to admit to himself that it was sort of terrifying for Rose to look into his mind and heart, if she really could anyway. What if she didn't like what she saw? Rose brought up the tray of sand and set it out in front of him, shaking it back-and-forth to settle the grains.

"OK hot stuff, put your hand in there and move it around however you like."

Wyatt felt awkward doing it in front Charlotte but did it just the same. He moved his hand back-and-forth a couple of times and dusted it off before setting his hands back on his knees. Rose perched her glasses at the tip of her nose, brought the plate in front of her, and looked it over. She whistled beneath her breath after a couple of moments of silence.

"Oh my. Incredible energy as I thought," she looked up at him smiling. "You came here to do shit, did you? Quite the set up," she furrowed her brow together. "Are you planning on going into the military?"

Wyatt looked at Charlotte.

"Yeah, Charlotte told you?"

"Nope," Charlotte said giggling. He looked at her closely. "Really, I haven't mentioned it to her yet."

Wyatt nodded, still not buying it entirely. Surely Rose could've guessed he was going into the military. Young kid right out of high school. It was either college or the military, right?

Rose was quiet. She generally had a poker face when it came to readings but both Wyatt and Charlotte picked up the slight change in her demeanor. Her face had fallen and her eyes were no longer mischievous and happy as they generally were.

"OK, so that is going to be one of your life's greatest challenges and journeys," she paused, finding her words. "What you need to know is this: whatever happens, whatever challenges you face, just know that you have set yourself up for all of these. You decided what you would endure in this life so there's nothing that will come your way that you cannot handle. And I mean nothing," she shook her head disbelievingly. "I'm telling you. You're a fixer. You can basically do anything," she said, looking closer at the grains. "St. Michael is your archangel. Should you need anything, should you ever feel weak in heart or in spirit, you can call on him. He's very strong in your energy."

Wyatt nodded. He knew he was being ridiculous but he wanted her to tell him something more. Preferably that he could have Charlotte forever.

"You're good with numbers aren't you? Math comes easy to you."

He nodded.

"Ok well, that'll come in handy. In life, in the military. Everything."

Rose fell quiet again, looking closer at the sand.

"Can I see your hand?"

He held out a large calloused hand for her. She took it in both of her small manicured ones, holding it across the desk and in front of her face.

"Lots of hard work there, huh?" she said, running her hands over the callouses. She moved her thumb over the palm of his hands and all of the grooves and lines.

"You're still carrying a lot of things with you from some previous lifetimes. You'd be a great candidate for regression therapy, actually."

"What's that?" Charlotte piped in.

Rose lifted her head and looked at both of them over her glasses.

"So you know what it means to be hypnotized, right? Basically, regression is when someone is hypnotized into their past life. A lot of times they revisit that life and see that they might be carrying certain issues, phobias, or connections with them from previous lifetimes."

"Do you know how to do that?" Wyatt asked.

She nodded. "It's certainly not my specialty but I've done it before. We could do it sometime." She raised her wine glass in the air. "Perhaps a night Aunt Rose hasn't had a couple of glasses of wine, eh?"

"So what kinds of er- things- do you mean?" he asked.

Rose shrugged. "Nothing too extreme. Sometimes people have crazy phobias or things like that. I think yours is mostly just unfinished business. Cycles that you feel the need to complete." He nodded, still not understanding what she meant.

Rose smiled. "Is your best friend a very handsome young man? He's black, very funny?"

Wyatt shook his head, thinking of all of his friends. His closest friend from high school came from a large Mexican family. He knew other people that would fit the description, but they weren't close to his best friend.

She nodded, undeterred. "Must be someone you're going to meet. He's very important. Very difficult to find a true friend in this world. He will be that for you and in a time that you will need that." There was a touch of sadness in her voice.

"So," she said, shaking off the reading, "in a nutshell, you're amazing. Don't ever forget it, kid."

She moved the sand back in place, erasing his handprint and putting the box back in the drawer. She stood abruptly from the desk.

"And now, beautiful people, Aunt Rose has caught her limit for the day. Why don't you two run along and enjoy your evening. And don't do anything I wouldn't do."

"So what does that rule out?" Charlotte asked grinning.

"Murder," Rose said winking.

⸎

After Rose excused herself, Wyatt and Charlotte decided to walk down for an ice cream. They held hands walking in the glow of the streetlights with the hot night surrounding them.

"Well? What did you think?" she asked.

"About the reading or dinner?" he grinned.

She rolled her eyes. "The reading."

"Hmm, well dinner was delicious and the reading was... I don't know, weird?"

She nodded, looking ahead of them on the sidewalk.

"I seriously didn't tell her about the Marines. She just knows things like that."

He nodded, noncommittally. "Well, she's definitely a character, that's for sure. That past life stuff though? What's that all about?"

She shrugged. "No idea. I mean she has mentioned past lives to me before but never the whole regression thing. I'll have to ask more about it in class."

"Class?" he asked laughing. "You have class with Rose?"

"Yeah, she says I'll be her protégé someday except better. I don't know though. Seems far-fetched."

"So can you read my mind?" He stopped walking and stood next to her holding her hand. "Like right now, can you read it?" he said grinning down at her.

"Hmm, let me try." She closed her eyes and held his hand tightly.

She stood for several moments trying in earnest to do so, but it was no use. She smiled, on the verge of laughing.

"So naughty, Wyatt."

She stood up on her toes and kissed him standing in the middle of town, unfazed by people walking by them. She lingered near his face afterward, keeping her mouth in front of his.

"You wanted a kiss. Maybe more."

He grinned, tightening his hold on her. "Lucky guess."

"Mmhm," she said, kissing him again.

"You wanna go to the lake?" he said, holding her against him.

"But I thought you wanted ice cream?"

He nodded. "Let's do both."

"Was that what you were thinking then?" she laughed.

"Yep, but you were still right."

She beat him to the register for ice cream and he wasn't happy about it. He gave her a pat on her rump when she paraded by him with her cone, gloating. She asked for a lick of his again on the walk back home but this time after she licked it, he kissed her cold chocolate mouth, taking some of it back.

The lake was entirely empty for once, so they chose the front of the lake instead. Wyatt wanted to be at their more secluded spot but thought better of walking through the desert at night without a light. They got out of the truck and walked toward the shore hand in hand. The night was quiet and humid, the rains were on the way, and Wyatt could smell it faintly in the air as he could every year.

The moon reflected off of the surface of the lake, lighting the dark night just slightly. He spread an army blanket out just by the shore, sitting down with her directly next to him.

"How come you never told me about your parents?" she asked.

He shrugged. "I don't know. It's kinda a new situation so I don't even know what to think of it yet."

She nodded, and didn't push further. He was urged on by her silence.

"They should have divorced a long time ago really. I think they thought they needed to wait until I was out of the house to, you know, make it official. That's kind of why I'm here. I didn't even want to wait until October to go. It was pretty miserable there the last couple of years."

"I'm sorry," she said genuinely. "That must've been a big change since they were together your whole life and everything."

He nodded. "Yeah. It was a big shock to everyone once they finally announced it, but I've known for years, you know." He was quiet, deciding if he should tell her the whole truth. "My mom starting seeing someone else a few years back. That's why she's in Salt Lake now. That's where he lives. So she would leave a lot to go over there and, I don't know, we all just kind of ignored it. My family doesn't talk much."

She nodded, understanding. "My mom is like that, too. She doesn't like to talk about, you know, her issues or anything that's wrong," she laughed. "Not like Rose, obviously. She talks about everything."

"Yeah, I like that though. It's just all out there, you know? It's easier that way," he agreed.

She moved closer to him, nuzzling her head in his shoulder.

"Well what about your dad? Is he OK?"

Wyatt shrugged. "I don't know. He's not exactly an emotional guy. He's never even told me that he loved me before. Like my whole life. Isn't that weird? If I ever have a kid I'll tell him that I love him every day. I know that."

Charlotte nodded. "I'm sure he loves you, though."

He nodded slowly, looking out at the lake. "Anyway, we don't need to talk about this," he said lightheartedly. "Why don't you sit on my lap instead?" he said, pulling her onto his lap and hugging her tight from behind.

"I don't mind the front of the lake if we come at this time of day," he said into her ear.

"Mmm me either. So nice and quiet."

He pulled her hair to the side and kissed up her long neck from shoulder to ear. She squirmed the closer he got to her ear but he held tight to her.

"Tickle?" he said into her skin.

"Yes," she said, breathless.

"Sorry. Can't help it."

He rolled her off of his lap gently so she was lying on the blanket, her hair strewn out to both sides. He moved his torso on top of hers but kept his lower half respectfully to the side for various reasons. He kissed her slowly, wrapping his arms gently around her, caressing the small of her back.

"Why are you so soft?" he said in between kisses. "This part, right here," he said rubbing the place just above her low riding jeans.

"Am I?" she whispered quietly. "I think it's because your hands are so rough."

"I'm sorry," he said pulling them away.

"No, no," she said grabbing one and bringing it to her lips. "I like them." She kissed the callouses one by one and he thought he might explode.

"Ah, Charlotte," he said, pulling her on top of him. "What am I going to do with you?"

She held her face back from him, letting her hair spill on either side of him. She leaned in and resumed kissing him while his hands roamed her body finding their way from her back down to her bottom. He pulled her astride him and pushed against her, no longer embarrassed. He rolled her over again without losing his place between her legs.

"I wish you wore your skirt," he said, a smile in his voice.

"I thought you liked my jeans," she smirked.

"Oh I do, I do. I also like this shirt," he said, running his hand from her stomach and up to her breast. He gently gripped her, feeling the weight of her.

He kissed her feverishly and panted into her mouth. "Is this ok? Tell me to stop if you want to, ok?"

She giggled between kisses. "It's ok, Wyatt. It's ok."

He pulled at the bottom of her shirt exposing her flat stomach. His hand lingered by her bellybutton, then climbed higher and higher. He pulled her bra aside and let her breast fall out, rubbing the softness with his rough hand. She inhaled sharply and pulled at his biceps, bringing him closer. Her nails dug into his arms, urging him onward.

He sat up, bringing her with him, then pulled her shirt off over her head. She sat in her jeans and bra looking tousled and delicious in the moonlight. He thought to himself he might really die this time if he couldn't have her. He lowered his head and kissed the top of her breasts popping out of her bra, feeling her deep breathing and pounding heart as he did.

"Tell me to stop, Charlotte," he said against her skin.

"You want me to?" she breathed.

"No, but maybe you should."

He continued kissing her breasts, moving his hands hard down the sides of her stomach as he did. He sighed suddenly and sat up, taking her face in his hands. He kissed her hard on the mouth and drew back to look at her. They were quiet then, looking into each other's eyes.

"You're all I can think about," he said frankly. "All day at work. I can't think about anything else. I don't even know what to do with myself."

"Me too," she said looking back into his intense eyes.

They were silent then both thinking about what it meant for them now that there was no pretending that it wasn't as serious as it actually was.

"Charlotte. What are we going to do?"

She didn't have an answer for him so she kissed him instead and ignored the message that popped into her head, light as angel wings.

III

"We were together, I forget the rest."

~Walt Whitman

The new work week meant a new project on 87 ranch. The men had regular chores in the morning, Wyatt doing the grunt work of feeding and shit cleaning while the vaqueros checked the cattle. In the afternoons, though, they would all help to build corrals for the next shipment. Despite the fact that all Wyatt wanted to do was tangle himself up with Charlotte all day and all night, he was actually looking forward to the project. Luis had patiently taught him so much during the irrigation project that he was excited by the prospect of learning more about construction.

Luis was the foreman by default, his years on earth having taught him to do just about anything. Santiago and Raul even respected him enough to take orders without any backtalk. Wyatt noticed that Luis didn't speak to them as gently as he spoke to him, though, and he didn't know what to make of that exactly. He was determined to do precision work when it came to the corrals if for no other reason than he wanted Santiago to see how much he had learned. And of course, he didn't want to be scolded like a child by someone only two years his senior.

So Wyatt would try, he told himself, not to think of Charlotte all day long. He would try not to think of the day before at the lake when he finally pulled the string to her bikini top under the shaded trees. He wouldn't think about her laying under him in nothing but her swimsuit bottoms, kissing his neck and bare chest. He wouldn't think about how he'd almost ripped through his board shorts rubbing against her on the blanket in the sand. He wouldn't think about her perfect lips kissing down his stomach. No, he wouldn't think any of that. He would just work, pay attention, and not make an ass out of himself.

The days were getting humid which meant, finally, rain was coming. Wyatt knew the men would be racing the clock on this project. Once they started, the rains would come almost every afternoon, bringing to a halt much of the work done on the ranch. A fact that made Wyatt wonder about the places he could go with Charlotte on those rainy afternoons. Where he could take her that no one else would be. Being a planner, he wanted to figure that out before the rains actually hit. He shook his head angrily at himself for already breaking his rule of not thinking about her all day.

The men were gathering equipment to start the project. The first day would be dedicated to pouring the footers for the corral. The boys would need to be ready with the cement after Luis finished meticulously marking off the spots for each column. Wyatt walked with him as he measured and flagged each spot when he pointed to it. Santiago and Raul, having already prepped the rest of the equipment, lay down in the bed of a truck, lounging and waiting to start.

Luis, as always, explained what he was doing to the best of his ability in English. "Same. You must make these each the same, see?" he said, referencing the distance between the pillars.

Wyatt nodded, looking over the markers. He wondered how Luis had already known where to place each one. He hadn't seen him do any math that would aid him in this process like the math Wyatt had immediately done in his head. Wyatt saw things in pieces, he always had. Looking at the area where Garrett wanted the corrals, he knew instantly how it needed to be divided and Luis executed the vision in his head perfectly.

When they finished marking off each spot, Santiago and Raul rolled out of the bed and shuffled over. They were lethargic and both had uncharacteristically annoyed faces since they would have to do construction work instead of cowboying.

"Gringo, you know how to do this or do we have to babysit you again?" Santiago piped in.

"I know," Wyatt said without emotion.

Santiago rolled his eyes, looking at Raul. "Yeah, I'm sure gringo does Mexican work all of the time. Just let us do the important stuff," he said, grinning at Raul. "You just lift things."

Luis looked up at Santiago and shook his head. "Borracho. He just mad he got too drunk this weekend. No feel right," Luis said, gesturing to his stomach.

The men had come home late Sunday night and Santiago and Raul stumbled to their beds, collapsing into them immediately. Wyatt often wondered what it was the men did when they went home each weekend. They generally returned with fresh tortillas and a hangover so he was left to deduce the details for himself.

Each man grabbed a shovel and began digging holes for the footers, Wyatt making quick work of his. He purposely picked up his pace when he saw how he was lapping everyone but Luis, who was as efficient as ever.

Once they started to pour the footers they fell into a rhythm, Santiago and Raul mixing and pouring the cement while Luis and Wyatt planted and leveled the fence posts. He was proud that he was able to go all day without messing anything up, his work was precise and fast, mostly because he listened to everything Luis told him. Santiago couldn't even find anything to scold him about, much to his dismay. Toward the end of the day Garrett came out to look over the progress as always.

"Looks good, fellas. You're making quick work of it. Gonna have to. Rain'll be here by week's end." He spat out in front of him, looking over the new space.

"What do ya say, boys? Let's head into town and I'll buy you dinner."

The other men lit up at the prospect of not making their own dinner and having one they wouldn't have to pay for, but Wyatt's heart sank. He certainly couldn't say no to his boss, but he also knew that Charlotte would at that very moment be at the lake in her blue bikini, perhaps stretched out languidly on her blanket waiting for him. He would have rather skipped dinner for the entire week for that but he knew he couldn't. The men cleaned up the job site and headed toward Garrett's truck.

"Sir, I'm gonna take my truck if you don't mind. I have a-" he hesitated a moment. "I have a stop to make after dinner."

"Oh I get ya," Garrett grinned, "another date?"

Wyatt's face grew hot at the prospect of discussing her in front of the other men.

"Well, not exactly, no."

"Gringo has a girlfriend?" Raul piped in. "Didn't think you talked enough to get one," he laughed, looking at the grinning Santiago for reinforcement.

"You should bring her over sometime," Santiago said, flashing a sparkling smile. "I'd like to meet her," he winked and Raul laughed heartily.

"Si, guapo!" he laughed. "Santiago steals everyone's girlfriend. That's his favorite."

Wyatt told himself to laugh, to smile back, but it was not convincing. He grinned, but the smile didn't reach his eyes.

"Think I'll keep her to myself, fellas, but thanks," he said tightly, walking to his truck.

Garrett decided on La Casita, one of the only restaurants in town and one with Mexican food that wasn't "white people Mexican food", as he called it. Garrett, like most native Arizonans, wasn't snobby about much, but he held his Mexican food to a very high standard.

The restaurant was plain yet immaculate. There were no frills or decorations, just plastic tables and chairs, but the food, Garrett had assured Wyatt, was incredible. They chose one of the larger tables and all sat down still clad in their filthy work clothes. Santiago and Raul engaged in their own conversation in Spanish, leaving Wyatt out entirely, but Luis made a point to include him in his conversation with Garrett. The restaurant was crowded and the food took way too long to get there, or at least that's what it felt like for Wyatt.

"Luis, Wyatt's joining the Marines." Luis cocked his head indicating he didn't understand Garrett.

"War. He's going to go to war," Garrett said bluntly.

Wyatt didn't flinch but felt his stomach drop the slightest bit. Was that what he would be doing? He thought. Of course. There was a war on, had been since April, so yes, odds were that he would in fact be going. Suddenly he couldn't remember why he had thought that might be a good idea. Luis's face fell when he understood the word.

"No," he said looking at Wyatt, shocked. "Your parents know?"

"Yes, sir," he said, taking a long sip of his iced tea.

Luis made the sign of the cross, shaking his head, but Garrett waved his hand.

"He'll be fine. It's gonna be a fast war. We might even be out by the time he's ready. Not like Vietnam, that's for sure."

Wyatt knew that Garrett had been drafted into Vietnam and served four years in the Army, although he noted that Garrett never gave specifics about that time. He had, however, heard the same sentiment expressed by several people who had fought in that war the generation before. This would not be as bad, not as long, and certainly not as harsh.

"When do you leave again, Wyatt? October, right? That's good, definitely going to need you up until then. Then I don't know what the hell I'll do. You've done a real good job, son," he said, slapping him on the shoulder.

Wyatt nodded, thanking him modestly, but he was back in his head again as Luis and Garrett moved onto the next topic. War. A year from that very moment he could be at war in another country. He was still figuring out what that meant, on a lot of levels.

He ordered enchiladas, beans, and rice, which was delicious and filled him up, nourishing his body after the exertion of the day. He was thankful for dinner but when Garrett ordered coffee and dessert he thought he might cry actual tears. Where would she be at that moment? It was almost 6 o'clock, surely she was home from the lake by now, but he had to see her, there was no choice for him anymore.

When they finally left the restaurant, Wyatt's relief was palpable. He looked at the clock. 6:30. He worried she would be walking home again through the desert and he wouldn't be able to catch her at all. But maybe she was home? What then? He had never shown up uninvited before but he had to see her. He drove down Main Street and turned on the side road to their house, trotting up the front steps to knock before he changed his mind. Charlotte answered the door wearing jeans, a tank top, and an apron tight around her waist. Her face was surprised and happy when she saw him.

"Hey!" she said, throwing her arms around his neck. He held her tight against him, inhaling her scent.

"What are you wearing?" he asked quietly into her ear. "Are you trying to kill me?"

She pulled back and laughed. "An apron? You like it?" she said, giving him a brief twirl.

His eyes widened looking at her. "Yes, very much."

She giggled at him and grabbed his hand, pulling him inside. "Here, come in. We're getting everything ready to make jelly tomorrow."

He wiped his work boots on the front mat swiftly and followed her inside.

"Where's Rose?" he asked.

"She had to run down to the store. We need more sugar."

He followed her into the kitchen and looked around. There were baskets of prickly pear fruit sitting on the counter and the table was lined with brand new mason jars ready to be filled.

"Did you pick all of these?" he asked.

She nodded. "Yep. This afternoon. I was afraid you would try and find me at the lake and I wouldn't be there. Did you go?"

He shook his head, relieved she wasn't there without him.

"No, not today but I almost went to look for you," he smiled.

"Well I don't know if I can go to the lake for a couple of days. Rose is going to have me in her jelly sweatshop this week. You know she's serious when she skips nap for it," Charlotte smiled.

She turned to wash her hands in the sink then chatted on about her day, how she had to use tongs to pick the prickly pear fruit only getting stuck with cactus once all day. He was listening but he was also very focused on the ties of her apron right above her peach shaped bottom. And on her hair, which was piled on top of her head exposing her long neck.

"When did Rose leave to the store?" he asked, moving toward her.

"Just before you got here, why?"

He inched closer to her as she turned around to look at him. He was filthy and sweaty from work with dirt caked on his shirt and jeans. It was her favorite way he looked, hungry and messy after working all day.

"Because you didn't give me a kiss yet, you know."

"No?" she asked, his face closing in on her. "Did you want one or something?"

"I do, yes," he said, smiling.

"Ok then," she whispered before brushing her soft lips to his. Her arms went around his neck and his around her waist with the apron strings. He lifted her to sit on the sink so he was eye level with her.

"I missed you today," he said sweetly. "I missed the lake."

She smiled knowingly and hugged him to her, wrapping her legs around his sturdy core.

"Me too. I thought I wouldn't get to see you." She kissed from his neck up to his ear and his body instantly responded.

"Don't kiss me like that. Christ, I won't be able to sleep again tonight."

She giggled. "Like what? Like this?"

She took his bottom lip in both of hers sucking lightly on it then opening her mouth to kiss him deeper. He reciprocated, dipping her back against the sink even more, pulling her bottom toward him. He was out of breath when she pulled back again to look at him, an almost comical, pained look in his eye.

"Will you come see me again tomorrow?" she asked.

"Yes, please," he said kissing her again, using one hand to hold her bottom and the other to grip the base of her neck. They both heard the noise on the porch and pulled away from each other, Wyatt setting her roughly down and pulling up a chair at the kitchen table, trying his best to look nonchalant. Rose came through the front door already talking.

"Got all the damn sugar they had in town," she said, smiling, catching sight of him. "Well, Wyatt! What a nice surprise."

He was up and had the grocery bags out of her hands before she could close the door, mumbling a hello to her.

Charlotte busied herself at the sink trying her hardest not to look at her aunt while Rose launched into a tirade about the lack of supplies at the grocery store and the cashier lady who apparently had it out for her.

"Every damn time I go in there she acts like I'm buying things to cast a spell on someone or something. 'What are you doing with all the sugar?' She always has this face like she's just smelled shit, you know?" Rose rolled her eyes. "I had half a mind to tell her I was going to cook the intestines of my enemies with it but damn it, I behaved."

Wyatt and Charlotte laughed nervously. Rose put away the groceries and stood with her hands on her hips looking back-and-forth between the two of them.

"Good Lord Almighty, do you two smell that?" she asked.

"What? The prickly pear?" Charlotte asked.

"No," Rose grinned happily waving her hand in front of her face at the imaginary smell. "Hormones. Also," she sniffed the air again. "Love."

There was silence until Rose broke it, cackling giddily. "Charlotte, honey, however did you get all of that dirt on your apron?"

⚜

Between work at the shop and jelly making, the week was busy for Charlotte and Rose. The town's big Fourth of July celebration was coming and that meant big business for Spirit's Soul. Rose went on and on about how much help Charlotte had been, not knowing how the hell she had managed the years before. She had helped her aunt can close to 100 cans of jelly, most of which were sold at the shop during the celebrations.

Charlotte had delighted in learning something new and had the process of making jelly down after being shown once. That was her way. If she could put her hands on something and do it one time, she'd remember it forever. It was just one of the valuable tricks poverty had taught her. She learned to boil down the prickly pear fruit, which had a beautiful purplish red color. She'd never seen anything like them before coming to Arizona. She had to harvest them off of prickly pear cacti, which grew all over town, collecting them in baskets. Once she boiled them down, Rose taught her how to add the gelatins and sugar, mixing it quickly on the stove so that it jelled. When one batch didn't quite make it, Rose told her to save it for syrup instead. It could be used for everything from margaritas to pancake topping.

"The desert never stops giving. Never believe anyone who says it's trying to kill you. It's not a place for pussies, that's for sure, but it never stops giving," Rose had said.

Charlotte cut small pieces of gingham fabric to put over the lids of each jar, meticulously arranging them in boxes while Rose brewed afternoon coffee. She had held up rather well without her afternoon beauty rest but simply couldn't make it through the last part of the afternoon without caffeine and a bite of sweets. She was like a child, she admitted, if not fed and rested, tantrums would ensue immediately.

She set a cup of coffee and a cookie in front of Charlotte, chatting on about all they would have to get done in the next week. There was the parade which Rose was expected to participate in each year. Not just participate, but wow the townspeople with her costume and decorations of a saint, Goddess, mythological creature, anything that would get them talking.

"The year I was Athena, that was a hit. But this year I have you," she grinned. "I have the perfect idea. We're gonna knock 'em dead."

Charlotte smiled. "I have no doubt you will, but do I really have to be in a parade? People don't know me like they know you."

Rose laughed. "Oh please, don't act like this is the Academy Awards. It's Patagonia. There will be goats in this parade. No need to be nervous. Plus, everyone does know you, my dear. You can't exactly keep a low profile looking like that." She waved a hand at her and took a long sip of her coffee.

"You know there's a dance that night, right? After the parade there will be a barbecue, then dance, then fireworks. Big day in town."

Charlotte nodded. "You told me that. We need to be at the shop after the parade though, right?"

Rose shook her head. "Just during the barbecue, but I never miss the dance or fireworks. I wonder if there's a young man who'd like to go with you?" Rose grinned.

Charlotte shrugged, fighting a smile. "Don't know. He hasn't asked me."

"Well good then, means I've still got a chance," she said winking. "And on top of that, it's someone's birthday that day," she grinned.

Charlotte stopped moving and looked at her. "How'd you know?" she asked quietly.

Rose laughed as if it were obvious. "I remember when Lily had you. Plus, what other day could you have been born but on the Fourth of July, all fireworks and shine?"

Charlotte gave her a closed mouth smile but wanted desperately to talk about something else.

"Well, it's not a big deal or anything. Plus we have such a busy day so let's just focus on that."

Rose squinted her eyes at her niece, smiling. "Stop working a minute. Just sit and enjoy a break with me."

Charlotte obeyed, putting down the jar and sitting across from her aunt. She smiled at her graciously and picked up her coffee cup, inhaling the rich scent. Rose laughed.

"I don't know if I've ever seen someone so happy when they're working all day. You're a good girl," she said, patting her hand.

Charlotte shrugged. "It's fun work, though. Nothing not to be happy about."

She bit into the soft chewy ginger snap that she and Rose had baked the day before that. It had been a surprise to Charlotte to discover her love of cooking. She loved the feeling of making something delicious that could bring comfort to someone. It was an untapped talent that Charlotte had never explored. When someone is eating to survive, it doesn't cross their mind that cooking could actually be fun. She'd spent her life eating processed, cheap foods, foods that would make Rose cringe, but were covered under welfare. She'd eaten free lunch every day and learned how to make those stretch by never eating anything packaged at lunch. Instead, she'd slip it into her bag to bring home, often eating it for dinner on the nights her mom had nothing else for her. But those days were a million miles away from Rose's cozy kitchen, alive with the smell of sugar and prickly pear fruit.

"Alright, girl. We've been slacking on class for the week. Shall we discuss now while we have time?" Rose said, looking at the clock crunching the time for the day.

Rose's education for Charlotte was very much student directed. Charlotte, being the curious and unknowingly bright girl she was, had constant questions about how everything worked. It was these questions and thoughts that provoked conversations and lessons where Rose was simply the guide. Most of the time she asked, "Well, what do you think?" in response to Charlotte's lines of questioning, insisting that everyone had the answers inside of them but that the world had trained us not to believe.

"Ok," Charlotte started, "I'm curious about the whole regression thing."

Rose nodded. "Yes, interesting, right? It's basically a form of therapy for people. I've read about people who have cured themselves of anxiety, paranoia, things like that. The skeptics say it's not real of course, but shit, if something works and helps someone, who cares?" Charlotte nodded, digesting it.

"Ok, so is there a way to prove it's real?"

Rose nodded. "Good question. There's a couple of books I'll give you that discuss that. There have been cases of people getting regressed and they basically give details of times and places that there's no way they could know about. It's very fascinating."

Charlotte thought silently for a moment, finding a way to phrase her question without overstepping boundaries.

"So with Wyatt, why is it important for him?"

Rose smiled but broke eye contact, looking at her cup of coffee instead.

"Well, honey, I don't know exactly. He's truly an incredible young man. He's got some serious goals he wants to hit for this lifetime," she said falling quiet, cocking her head to the side thinking. "I think for him, regression therapy would be good down the line. So he can see why he connects with some things," she pursed her lips. "Both things beautiful and things dark."

Charlotte sighed. "I hate how you can do that."

"Do what?"

"Answer a question without really answering it," Charlotte smiled sadly.

"Occupational hazard, babe," Rose winked.

"But dark things? Doesn't seem like him at all," Charlotte replied.

Rose shook her head. "No, it doesn't. But this world has corners. No one gets out without getting scratched. You know that better than anyone."

Charlotte nodded, it was useless to argue again with Rose that her life actually hadn't been so bad.

"So what about for other people? Can it help with everything? I mean like therapy?"

"You mean your mom?" Rose asked, her face sympathetic.

"I also hate how you do that," Charlotte laughed.

"What?" Rose laughed.

"Read my mind when I don't want you to. But yes, my mom. Is there anything that could, you know, make her better?"

Rose shook her head. "Damn, girl. After everything, all that's happened. You've still got some hope left." Charlotte flushed and fidgeted with the jelly jars in the box, looking for a distraction.

"No, I didn't think I could have any hope left. I tried every way I knew how. But that was before I knew your way."

"The magical way," Rose said, smiling. "Do you want to tell me about her, my love? Are you ready for that?"

Charlotte had been with her aunt for just a month and they had yet to discuss her mother in depth, only in passing was she mentioned. Rose never once pushed her for answers and Charlotte figured that was because she already knew. Even if she weren't psychic, she grew up with her mother and knew enough to realize what it must have been like to be her daughter.

Charlotte shrugged. "I wouldn't even know where to start, Aunt Rose."

Rose nodded solemnly. "I get that."

Charlotte sighed heavily. "But it's bad this time. The worst I've seen it."

The guilt washed over her then when she said it out loud. Her mother could barely function with her daughter there, what would she do without her?

Rose didn't miss a beat. "It's not your fault and it's not your responsibility. You've got to know that. I want you to be kind to yourself about this, Charlotte, I'm serious. You did the right thing." Her face became grave, on the verge of tears. "You've got to believe me. It's important for you to detach from her entirely instead of feeling guilt. You were not the mother- she was."

There was silence between them. Charlotte had been quiet about it all for so long, kept her feelings locked so deep inside that she couldn't even find a way to say them. Every way she thought of didn't feel like it was enough. Rose exhaled deeply, trying to calm herself.

"She was supposed to protect you, Charlotte." Her voice cracked when she said her name and she looked fiercely into her niece's eyes. "It was her job to keep you safe. I don't want you ever feeling bad like you didn't do enough for her."

Charlotte nodded and reached for her aunt's hand across the table, comforting her. "I know, it's ok, though. I'm ok now," Charlotte said quietly.

That did it for Rose. She let the tears slip out of the corners of her eyes, losing her composure. She looked at the girl sitting in front of her, so full of hope, so resilient.

"No," she said. "No, it's not ok."

Wyatt was on a roll. Work at the ranch had never been better. He finally felt like he knew the routine and had hit his stride. Just the fact that Santiago had nothing to bitch to him about was success enough, but Garrett and Luis treating him like he was an important part of the team meant even more. Yes, he was still responsible for the majority of the grunt work but his jobs otherwise were giving him more and more responsibility.

By midweek it was Wyatt who Garrett asked to check the cattle in the back pastures instead of Santiago and Raul. For once those two had to stay and finish up the day's work on the corrals. Of course they wouldn't voice their disappointment to Garrett, but it was written all over their bitter faces. Wyatt loved the chance of getting away from the other men and doing something on his own. Not only did he enjoy the solitude, but it also made him feel more like a man rather than the boy he was always treated as there.

It was still about an hour from quitting time for all of them when he got in his truck and drove the small dirt road to the back pastures. The air was thicker and thicker with moisture each day and the talk now was whether or not they could make it through the Fourth of July celebrations without the rain hitting. The perfect time for it to rain would either be the day before or the day after, but many times the parade itself would be ruined by Mother Nature's ill and indifferent timing. For the first time in his life he found himself not looking forward to monsoon season. This was partly because that meant less time at the lake with Charlotte and partly because monsoon season's arrival would mean the date of his departure was coming closer. He tried not to think of it too much, but already the logistics of it were creeping into his mind.

When he arrived to check the pasture everything appeared to be normal, the tank was full and the cattle were bedded down to catch any coolness in the dirt. He noticed a repaired piece of barbed wire fencing that was starting to fall, though, so he retrieved his tools from his truck and began repairing it, this time better than the time before. It was clear that someone else had fixed the fence in a half-assed way, he imagined it was Raul. Certainly Luis would never fix anything in that manner but Raul tended to rush things, particularly when those things didn't involve him being on a horse.

It took him awhile to tear down the old section of fencing then string up more. The job was done better with two men but it could certainly be done with just one. He twisted and bound the barbed wire around the fence posts, taking care not to scrape himself with rusty thorns sticking out every couple of feet. He had no gloves and this work did nothing for his already cracked and calloused hands, but there was no choice. He smiled thinking of how much Charlotte loved his hands despite that. When they held hands she rubbed at the rough parts with her soft fingertips, making chills run down his spine.

The night before ran late at the ranch and he'd only been able to see her briefly. Showing up after dark he was afraid to even knock, but he didn't have to. As soon as he pulled up Charlotte flew out the front door and into his arms as he stepped out of the truck. Rose had already gone to sleep and Charlotte had been reading in the living room, waiting for him to come over like he said he would. She'd not said a word before kissing him hard on the mouth and hugging him tight against her. He had pushed her back against the truck, moving his hands down her back and around her bottom, gripping her against him. Afterward they'd sat on the porch and talked in hushed whispers about their days, stealing as many kisses as possible before they had to part.

Wyatt flinched, cutting his hand on the barbed wire. He cursed, angry at himself for getting back in his head again instead of doing what he should have been. He examined the wound, which was mostly superficial but bleeding profusely. He wiped it on the front of his shirt, finishing up the post and heading to his truck. He shook his head, laughing at himself for his stupid mistake. It was dangerous for him to think of her at work, there was no doubt.

When he arrived back at the barn he was surprised to see nobody working on the corrals. This made him hopeful that they might be done a bit earlier this evening since he wanted to take Charlotte fishing that night before the rains would come. He would tell her it would be so he could see her fishing skills, so she could finally prove it to him, but really he just wanted her alone by the water.

She was always so beautiful and peaceful there away from everyone and everything.

He parked his truck by the barn and walked around to the other side where he heard voices. He was surprised to see Rose standing there with her arm around Garrett's bicep talking to him intimately, laughing over some private joke. Garrett looked like a new man. He wore a huge grin on his face and his eyes were scrunched up and happy in a way that Wyatt had never seen before. He looked around for Charlotte and found her out in the field, mounted on Sunny. The sight of her made him stop in his tracks.

She always carried herself beautifully, head held high and posture perfect, but this was different. She sat on the horse like a queen, her spine straight and her chin level with the horizon. Her long hair flowed down her back, blowing slightly in the wind that Sunny made for her. She was riding in the opposite direction and couldn't see him, which he was thankful for because in the next moment, he saw Santiago walking to the side of her stirrup talking animatedly and smiling up at her. Raul, as always, walked on his left, practically drooling at her while Luis stood by the fence line watching them go.

Wyatt felt his face flush through with rage and his heart pound in his chest. His fists instinctively clenched together at his sides and he thought he might punch something, namely Santiago's face.

"Well hello, Romeo!" Rose called over to him. She still held tight to Garrett's arm but she was looking straight at him with a humorous smirk on her face. He forced a smile and stuck his shaking hands in his pockets as he walked toward them.

"Hello, Ms. Rose," he said formally.

She winked at him. "We brought you fellas some of our famous jelly. Ask Garrett, he can't get enough of it."

Garrett laughed himself into a coughing fit, covering his mouth with his fist. "Damn right. It's good stuff, I tell ya." Garrett glanced at him. "You get yourself hung up, boy?" he asked gesturing to his shirt.

Wyatt had forgotten about the blood he had wiped on his shirt. He looked down and shrugged, affecting nonchalance.

"Not bad. There was some fence down but I got it back up." He looked out at Charlotte and the boys again. They were moving farther out in the field making him feel wretched.

Garrett nodded. "Well, go on into the house and get that cleaned up with alcohol. Don't want it getting infected."

"Yes, sir," Wyatt said, moving quickly toward the house.

In the bathroom at Garrett's big house he found the rubbing alcohol and Band-Aids. He poured the clear liquid over the wound and found it disturbing that the alcohol didn't sting as it normally did. His anger numbed any external feelings. He tried to tell himself to calm down, that she was just riding a horse with him next to her, but he could not shake the image of her perched so beautifully on Sunny with Santiago next to her smiling. He splashed cold water on his face and sat on the toilet lid breathing deeply before heading back outside.

She was dismounting as he walked out the front door and Santiago took that opportunity to help her down, putting his hands on each side of her waist, supporting her to the ground. It was all Wyatt could do to not charge into the yard and tackle him right then. Charlotte turned and saw Wyatt standing by the barn and smiled brightly at him. She looked him up and down and her face became immediately concerned.

"Wyatt!" she said, jogging toward him. "Are you ok?" she asked, leaving Santiago holding the horse.

"You've got blood all over you, what happened?" She was standing in front of him looking him over for the wound.

Wyatt was uncharacteristically stone-faced. She looked into his eyes and furrowed her brow at his silence.

"Are you alright?"

He nodded, looking toward Rose and Garrett who were walking around the corral, indifferent to everyone else.

"Just cut my finger," he said holding it up.

"Oh, ok. You've got blood all over you and the look on your face," she said laughing. "What's wrong? Bad day?"

He shook his head, not looking at her.

"Charlotte!" Santiago called. "You wanna ride another one?" He flashed a sparkling grin at her and at Wyatt. For the first time Wyatt saw him as a girl might have, good looking, forward, confident. He was sure of it... he wanted to punch him.

"No thank you, Santiago. Thanks for letting me ride your horse though."

"It's not his horse," Wyatt said under his breath. "It's Garrett's."

Charlotte looked at him again, confused. "Are you- are you upset with me about something?"

He shook his head shortly. "No. Just- I don't know."

"Charlotte!" Raul called. "Come back and ride anytime," he grinned.

She waved a hand at him and walked toward the barn with Wyatt in step. "Alright, what's wrong with you?" she said.

They stopped, standing in front of an empty horse stall, Charlotte looking up into his face with her arms crossed.

"What did you guys talk about?" he asked.

"Who?" she said, confused.

"Santiago," he said a bit louder. "He had his hands all over you getting you off that horse."

Charlotte couldn't help it, she laughed. "Wyatt, you can't be serious. I just met him. I think he was just being nice."

"He's not fucking nice, Charlotte. Trust me."

She flinched, taken aback with his sudden anger.

"Well, it doesn't matter anyway, does it? I'm taken."

"Did you tell him that?"

She shook her head. "We didn't get that far in the conversation."

He nodded and they fell quiet.

"Geez, Wyatt. Remind me not to piss you off. I've never seen you like this."

He softened then, calming himself. "I just- I didn't expect that."

She nodded. "Ok. Well, just so you know, there's nothing to worry about."

He nodded, looking at the ground. He wasn't upset with her or really with Santiago because who could blame the bastard for falling all over himself for her?

He was more upset by his own reaction, shocked at how angry he got and how fast it happened. He had never experienced that hot of a temper before and had a reputation in sports for being cool under pressure. His tie to her was growing stronger and it scared him how he felt inside.

Rose called to her and they reluctantly left the shelter of the barn, walking out separately instead of holding hands like they usually did. Rose was standing by her car with all of the men passing out jars of jelly.

"And here, Wyatt. One for you, too. Charlotte made these herself." He reached out to grab it and thanked her, still a little red-faced from the embarrassment of the day. Rose kissed a giddy Garrett on the cheek and climbed in the car. Charlotte was standing next to Wyatt near the other men, and in that moment she made a decision.

"Thank you so much for letting me ride. It was so nice to meet you all," she said, looking at each of them.

"You come on back anytime, Charlotte. We'd love to have ya," Garrett said, smiling.

She looked square at Wyatt.

"Will I see you tonight?" she asked him loud enough for everyone to hear. He nodded, one hand in the pocket of his jeans and the other holding the jelly.

"Alright then. Tonight it is." She stood on her toes placing her hands on his shoulders and kissed him full on the mouth. He wore a look of surprise at first but by the time she made it into the car, a large grin spread across his face.

"Bye, Charlotte," he said, his voice full of the things he would only say in front of her.

⚜

"Now wait, this isn't fair. I've been baiting your hook all night so that's why you've caught more than me."

They were back at the front of the lake and it was after dark now. He had intended to spend more time kissing her than fishing but the fish literally refused to stay off the end of her line. She had six catches to his one and she was overjoyed about it.

"Don't be a poor sport- you're losing fair and square," she laughed, reeling in another fish.

She had tried to bait her own hook but he just couldn't allow her to do it. Each time she caught one, his manners got the better of him and he would pass off his rod and take hers over to bait again.

"Look at this one," she said holding him out for Wyatt to see. "Another bass or is that a catfish?"

"Hard to tell," Wyatt said, getting close. "I can hardly see."

"Well let's let him go either way. I won't have time to cook him."

"You sure? What about tomorrow?"

She shook her head. "Gotta run up to Tucson with Rose tomorrow. She needs more stock for the shop."

"So I won't see you tomorrow?"

"Probably not," she said, sighing.

He removed the fish from the hook for her, handing it over and allowing her to release it how she liked. She moved him back and forth in the water like he had seen her do that first day at the lake. Watching her brought him back to that day.

"I thought you were a mermaid the first day I saw you," he blurted.

She laughed, looking up at him from a crouched position. "What? Why?"

He shrugged. "I was having a dream that I was in the water and I could breathe. I was blowing bubbles and there was a mermaid in the water rolling around in my bubbles," he laughed. "Then you woke me up, so I thought it was you."

She was standing in front of him then, listening intently to his story.

"That's funny, Wyatt. A mermaid of all things," she said shaking her head. "You should tell Rose about that dream."

"No way, I'm sure she'll interpret it so I'm a pervert or something," he said joking.

"Well? She'd have a point. Plus, she's a bigger pervert than you anyway. If you don't feel violated around her you should."

"Oh yeah?" he laughed. "What about around you? Should I feel violated around you?"

He pulled her waist toward him, looking down at her large green eyes that stared back into his.

"Oh definitely. You definitely should." She stood on her toes to kiss him but he pulled away quickly after.

"I'm getting a bite!" he said, lunging for his rod. He set the hook and reeled it in swiftly. Blissfully, there was a decent sized fish on the line, redeeming him, if only a little, from his first day meeting her. He held up the line to show her the fish, grinning happily.

She laughed. "Alright, you can fish. I take it back. You gonna keep him?"

"Naw," he said, "catch and release tonight."

She nodded, sitting down on the blanket and watching him in the moonlight. He moved almost musically, his actions smooth and practiced. He washed his hands off in the lake and joined her on the blanket, sitting close at her side.

"All done fishing?" he said, putting an arm around her shoulders.

She nodded. "Yeah, I think I've caught enough to prove myself."

He laughed. "You are good, I'll give you that. Who taught you to fish?"

She hadn't expected that question even though it was a totally natural one. She hesitated, thinking about avoiding the truth then decided against it.

"Joe did," she said quietly. "He was one of my mom's boyfriends. One of the good ones," she smiled sadly. "Maybe the only good one."

He nodded. "Where was that? What state I mean?"

"Georgia, I was about 7. They were together a couple of years."

She had purposely avoided thinking of him for a long time, the ache in her chest growing even at the sound of his name. He was the closest she had ever come to having a father- patient, kind, hard-working, a cowboy of course, and maybe part of the reason she felt attached to Wyatt so quickly. Joe was everything that every other boyfriend her mother had was not, so of course it had to end. She knew then, even that young, that it would not be forever. He taught her to fish, how to ride, and how to shake hands firmly.

"You are my little girl," he'd told her one day on a fishing trip. "Don't ever let anyone tell you different." And she didn't. When her mom left him and twisted it to be his fault like she did every time, Charlotte never looked at her the same. It was then that she began to lose faith in her mother.

"I'm sorry," Wyatt said. "You don't have to talk about it if you don't want to."

She didn't realize that she had gone silent, retreating inward to think about Joe and forgetting where she was for the moment. She shook her head, giving him a brave smile.

"No, it's ok. I just haven't thought of him for a long time, you know? He was so good to me."

He nodded, not knowing what to say. His family might have had problems, but next to the fatherless and seemingly motherless Charlotte, his problems were G-rated at best.

"He taught me to ride, too," she smiled. "He told me I rode like a princess."

Wyatt nodded. "He was right, you do."

She turned and looked at him.

"I didn't think you even saw me riding, did you?"

He nodded. "Before I went into the house. Well, before I stomped into the house," he said good-naturedly.

She pretended to shudder. "Angry Wyatt is not someone to mess with."

"I'm sorry," he said pulling her across his lap. "I just got away from myself for a minute. It's never really happened before."

"It's ok, Wyatt. I get it. I hope I didn't embarrass you."

"How?"

"You know, when I kissed you in front of everyone."

He shook his head bringing his face close to hers. "No, not even a little bit."

He kissed her softly on the ear, then the cheek, then finally on her waiting lips, cradling her with his strong arms. He pulled back and smiled at her.

"So," he started, "are you going to the dance with me or what? Rose said I had to ask you."

"She what?" Charlotte laughed. "That woman and her meddling. I'm surprised she didn't ask you herself. Told me she thought she still had shot at you asking her."

"Oh she did. I'm taking both of you."

Charlotte's jaw dropped. "Seriously? You really are the sweetest ever."

"Were you gonna tell me it was your birthday, too?"

She stopped smiling then, breaking eye contact.

"She told you that too, huh?"

"Yeah, of course. Thank God, otherwise I would have been the jerk who didn't know about your birthday."

She shrugged. "It's seriously not a big deal. The Fourth is more fun to celebrate. Let's just do that."

He laughed, pulling her tighter.

"Why wouldn't we do both?"

"I don't know. I just don't like my birthday really."

"Why? What do you normally do?"

She shrugged. "We don't really have traditions for that exactly," she said, falling quiet.

He felt guilty then, thinking of his birthday parties each year. The homemade cake of his choice that his mother made without fail, presents, friends, and celebrations.

"Well, we'll start a new one. The parade, then the dance. It'll be fun." She nodded briefly, seeing her opening to change the subject.

"Speaking of which, did Rose tell you she's making me ride on a float in the parade?"

"Kind of, she told me to get a good seat so I could watch you ladies."

She covered her face with her hands. "Ahh- so embarrassing!"

He laughed, rocking her a bit. "Oh, it won't be bad. I'll be your biggest fan."

He leaned down again to kiss her lightly on the lips and she kissed him back harder, putting her arms around his neck. She slid off of his lap and pushed him gently to the ground and laid on top of him, kissing the side of his neck and up to his mouth again. His hands roamed her back and bottom pulling her closer to him. She put her forehead to his and looked into his eyes.

"You have the prettiest eyes," she said.

He laughed. "Pretty? No one's ever called them that before."

"Well they are. They're like this crystal we have at the shop." She leaned down and kissed his stubbly cheek again, working her way back to his mouth.

"Mmm," he said into her mouth. "I don't want to take you home."

"Me either," she said.

She kissed down his neck and into his open shirt collar, tasting the sweat on his skin. He breathed heavily, trying his hardest not to get carried away. He rolled her over onto the blanket and looked her over. She wore her cutoff shorts and a form fitting t-shirt tight around her breasts. Her hair was wild as always, spilling out in a curly mess to either side of her.

"You're the prettiest girl I've ever seen," he said, stroking up her smooth tanned thigh. He sighed, thinking of the day he met her. Was it only a month ago? Not even? He didn't remember what the world looked like before he knew she was in it.

They locked eyes again, hardly able to see except for the pale moonlight reflecting off of the lake. All of the words, uncertainties, and feelings hung thick between them, but neither wanted to talk about any of it. They ignored the indifferent clock, ticking away the summer.

⚬⚭❦⚮⚬

It took her a moment to remember what day it was when she woke up that morning. She was 19 years old. Where had she even been the year before? She knew Texas, of course, but couldn't remember what she'd even done on her birthday. Couldn't remember if her mother had even muttered a happy birthday to her or if that was one of the years she forgot entirely. Either way, she felt a long way from where she was then. She even felt different from where she was a month ago, really.

She stretched out luxuriously in her bed on her very own comforter, pointing her toes beneath her and stretching her arms above her. It would be a good day, an exciting day full of new things, traditions, Rose, and of course Wyatt. She smiled then, thinking of him and how he ran back from his truck over and over again a couple of nights before to give her one last kiss at the front door. She simply couldn't get enough of his sweet eager way, the way he always made sure she was ok, and how he constantly tried to put her needs before his own. Even when it meant her catching more fish than him.

The sun was shining through her curtains so she knew she had to get up. They would have to get all of the decorations on the float and the flags up around the shop before the parade even started. Then of course, she'd have to get into costume for the parade itself. She cringed with embarrassment even thinking of it, but she knew there was no way out of it. Rose was relentless and Charlotte simply couldn't say no to her.

When Charlotte walked into the kitchen it took her a moment to realize what was going on. Her eyes were still puffy with sleep and her hair was a mess. She wore pajama pants low on her hips and a tank top with no bra.

"Happy birthday!" Wyatt and Rose said in unison.

Charlotte jerked back, rubbing her eyes, then smiled at them. Rose was already dressed for the day in full makeup and a long flowing skirt. Wyatt likewise looked like he'd been up and ready for hours wearing his work jeans, boots, and a white t-shirt snug around his biceps. They stood in the kitchen next to a plate of waffles topped in whipped cream and strawberries. Rose had the candle stuck through the top and broke into song immediately, Wyatt following along.

Charlotte walked toward them looking at the beautiful breakfast and the two singing happy birthday to her. Her heart warmed and to her horror, tears came to the corners of her eyes. Wyatt stared at her as he sang, boring a hole through her with his crystal blue eyes. She sat in front of the plate as they finished, closing her eyes and wishing hard. She opened them, smiling, and blew out the candle to a round of applause.

"Thank you," Charlotte said, sincerely. "I told you guys not to do anything."

Rose rounded the table and leaned in to kiss her on the cheek.

"My baby. You're 19 and the world is yours. Happy Birthday." She squeezed her around the shoulders as Wyatt stood awkwardly looking on.

"Well go on, kid. Give her a birthday kiss already," Rose winked, moving toward the sink.

Charlotte stood, meeting him in the middle of the kitchen. He looked down at her smiling nervously.

"Happy Birthday," he said and brushed her lips with a gentle chaste kiss. She pulled him back to her and hugged him hard against her braless body, a fact not lost on Wyatt.

"When did you get here? You two are sneaky!"

"He's been here since 5- wanted to make sure we beat you waking up," Rose smiled. "He already put all of the flags out for us and helped with the decorations on the float. I'll tell you, he might be hired."

"Does that mean I'm fired?" Charlotte said joking.

Rose shrugged. "Well I'm sorry baby, on top of all of that he's also easy on the eyes."

"That he is," Charlotte said, reaching up to kiss him on the cheek.

They sat to eat, all digging in quickly due to the time crunch. The waffles were perfect and fluffy, the best Charlotte had ever had. She knew her aunt had made the whipped cream from scratch, too, and tasted the heavy vanilla flavoring with every bite.

"Alright, girl. I don't want to rush your breakfast but we better do presents before we don't have time," Rose said casually.

"Presents?" Charlotte said, genuinely confused. "No, I don't need presents, this is enough."

Rose sighed heavily. "Waffles? Waffles are enough? No, damn it, it's your birthday! Of course you get presents. I'll go first."

Rose took a small package wrapped in pink paper off of the chair next to her and handed it over the table. It was perfectly wrapped with a sheer white ribbon around it. Charlotte's eyes started to fill again as she looked across the table to her aunt. She willed herself not to cry.

"Thank you," she said quietly.

"Well, open it, my love," she said, smiling knowingly at her niece.

Charlotte pulled at the ribbon and gently unwrapped the gift, taking care not to tear the paper. There was a small white box inside and Charlotte was almost afraid of what was in it. She knew her aunt's tendency to go overboard. Inside the box there was a long silver chain and turquoise stone wrapped in what looked like silver twine.

"It's a stone of protection," Rose said, uncharacteristically serious. "It's for warriors. True warriors, like you."

Charlotte looked her in the eye and nodded, feeling the strength and love emanating from the stone and from Rose.

"Thank you, Aunt Rose. I love it." She took it out of the box and hung it around her neck. The stone dropped just between her breasts. She put her hand over it, cradling it against her body.

"I'll always wear it."

Wyatt and Rose beamed at her, alive with how happy she was, how genuinely thrilled she was over something so simple.

"Ok, we should get ready, I still have to-" Charlotte started.

"Wait," Wyatt interrupted. "What about me? I have a present for you."

"No, Wyatt. You shouldn't have done that."

He pulled a plain large gift bag out from under the table and handed it over.

"I can't wrap like Rose, though," he smiled.

She had to stand to get in the bag and pull out the large heavy box inside. She opened it and gasped. The most beautiful pair of boots she had ever seen rested inside. She looked at him with her mouth agape.

"No," she said disbelievingly as he grinned back at her happily.

"You can't ride in tennis shoes," he said.

She pulled one of the boots out of the box and held it up. They were brown with tooled leather at the top and a turquoise blue design woven in the sides. She had never owned a pair of boots and could hardly believe they were hers. He'd spent a week's pay on them but after seeing the look on her face he decided he would have paid a month's.

"Wyatt," she said, her mouth still hanging open. "This is- this is too much. You shouldn't have gotten these for me."

He shrugged. "You needed them. Garrett wants you to come back and ride again. But you have to go with me this time- that's the only rule."

"Thank you, Wyatt." She moved around the table and sat across his lap with her hands around his neck, unembarrassed in front of Rose. He hugged her against him and kissed the side of her head.

"Happy birthday, Charlotte," he whispered into her hair.

She put her hand out over Rose's shoulder, patting her at the same time.

"Thank you both," she said sincerely.

"Well girl, the magic is only just beginning! We've got a full day. Now go on and walk Romeo out so you can give him a proper kiss. You've gotta get dressed," she winked.

꧁◦◦꧂

Wyatt walked down Main Street through the crowds of people, a sea of red, white, and blue. Mexican music blared in the background and the smell of barbecue, smoke, and roasted green chilies floated through the air. The town was alive with excited children, noise, and friends warmly greeting one another.

Garrett had packed a lawn chair just for Wyatt that morning and told him he would save his seat at the "50 yard line", which Wyatt assumed was halfway through the parade route. Sure enough, when he walked through the crowds about halfway down Main Street, he spotted him sitting alone with a coffee thermos and an empty chair next to him. He was speaking with a gentleman about his age sitting to the side of him.

"Wyatt, my boy," Garrett stood. "Clay Scott, this is Wyatt Sterling. My new hand this summer."

Wyatt leaned down to shake Clay's hand. He was a large man, Wyatt assumed about 6'5 standing. He had gnarled working hands and friendly eyes under his cowboy hat.

"Good to meet ya," Clay said.

"Nice to meet you, sir," Wyatt said politely before taking his seat.

"Wyatt is going in the Marine Corps in a couple of months. Heads off to boot camp in October," Garrett said, sounding proud.

Clay looked at Wyatt, nodding in approval.

"Good for you, son. Makes me wish I wasn't too old to go," Clay said shaking his head. "I'd love to go fight those bastards."

Garrett laughed. "War is a young man's game though, Clay. We're past our prime."

"Yeah, but this one'll be fast. You better hope you get to even go at this point. Probably gonna be wrapped up here in a couple of months," Clay said, echoing Garrett's sentiments.

Garrett nodded. "They're no match for us, that's for sure. Our boys have been lighting them up."

Wyatt once again found himself silent in the exchange. He hadn't prepared himself for talks of war; he knew nothing of it except what he'd read in history books, some of which he would have liked to forget. When Garrett insisted on telling everyone about boot camp, Wyatt often felt like he was talking about someone else. Someone he hadn't met yet.

"Well, thank you for your service. Don't let Garrett work your ass into the ground before you get shipped off. Won't be any good to the Marines if this guy has anything to do with it," Clay shoved at Garrett's arm.

"Oh, now, believe me, he's had time for things other than work this summer. Even found himself a girlfriend in town."

"Well can you blame him? Handsome kid!" Clay said, smiling. "Don't squander that youth, son. It'll be gone like that," he said, snapping his fingers.

"Yes, sir." Wyatt nodded, but he was only thinking of her. And war. And the small space in between.

The parade began and it was everything Wyatt imagined it to be. Fire trucks and classic cars rolled down the route with smiling faces throwing candy for the kids. The small high school band played the star spangled banner and several mariachi groups performed out of the backs of trucks. There were 4H kids pulling goats on leashes and riding horses. Garrett and Clay laughed heartily when an eccentric shop owner in town drove through in a beat up car with a sign on the side that proclaimed himself "Citizen of the Year". The parade was longer than he thought it would be and Wyatt assumed that half the town was in it while only the other half was watching.

"Rose always comes at the end," Garrett told him over the noise.

He'd regretfully left Charlotte after breakfast so she could get dressed, although he told her she could've worn what she had on that morning. When she came out of her room, her face still puffy from sleep, he thought he might fall over. She was so soft and vulnerable looking that he had to restrain himself from taking her right back into her bedroom and nuzzling his face into her. She was quite simply delicious. Minus the time she had to work at the shop after the parade, he was going to spend the whole day with her. He was borderline giddy about it and kept thinking about the things he wanted to tell her.

"Here they come!" Garrett said, tapping Wyatt's shoulder.

Rose's neighbor was pulling their small float with his cherry red vintage ford truck. Wyatt had seen it that morning when he helped Rose put the finishing touches on it. There were large painted cardboard waves on each side surrounded by cut outs of sparkly seashells. Rose tied May flag ribbons on each corner of the float so that they would blow in the wind.

He saw Rose first as they came toward them. She was wearing a long flowing blue dress that made her look like the ocean itself. She was throwing something that looked like candy off of the float into a cheering crowd, shouting above the music to people along the route cackling and smiling brightly, alive with the energy of her town who loved her. She was once again a hit.

As they got closer he finally caught sight of Charlotte. She was sitting in a large ornate chair decorated with seashells and sparkles. She wore a shell crown around her head and her hair down long and wavy. She had on more makeup than usual, dark eyes and red lips making her beauty even more pronounced. Her breasts spilled from the top of a snug white sequined shirt and her legs were covered in a blue glittery skirt fashioned to look like a mermaid tail. She waved to the crowd, laughing at Rose and throwing the occasional item to the audience as well.

Wyatt could hardly believe that this was the girl he knew so well. The one he saw looking fresh from sleep only hours before. His mouth hung open and he stared at her passing by, the noise and the people around him falling away so that there was only Charlotte. Just as they were about to pass him by entirely she caught sight of him, her face lighting up with a smile he knew she only gave to him. They locked eyes then, connecting through the crowd. She brought her hand to her painted lips and blew him a kiss, waving goodbye. He grinned hungrily back at her, restraining himself from jumping out of his chair and running after her like a child, desperate for a longer look.

It wasn't until after she was out of sight that he realized Clay and Mr. Garrett were talking to him.

"That's her? That's the girlfriend?" Clay said, eyes wide.

"See?" Garrett coughed, laughing. "Didn't I tell you I hadn't been working him too hard?"

Wyatt smiled, his face blushing with embarrassment and pride.

"Yes, sir. That's her."

Clay whistled long and slow. "Good lord. They don't make 'em like that round here."

He wiped imaginary sweat from his brow and went on chatting with Garrett when Wyatt noticed something sitting near his feet. It was one of the items Rose had thrown from the float. It wasn't actually candy like he'd thought, but a small drawstring bag with a few polished crystals inside along with something that looked like a prayer card.

He opened it looking at the antiquated picture of a mermaid on one side and writing on the other. It read:

"*Atargatis- Goddess of the moon and waters, protector of her people. She became a mermaid after falling in love with a shepherd and begetting a child. Her divine lovemaking killed him and out of shame, she cast herself into a lake where she became immortal.*"

Wyatt laughed under his breath thinking of Charlotte, his mermaid even before today. He thought of her as Rose had called her, a warrior, strong and brave. He held the image of her sitting tall on the float the same way she'd sat on the horse, just like royalty. He thought about the shepherd and how that probably wasn't a bad way to go.

⚜

Rose had not exaggerated how busy the day would be. Charlotte had never seen so many people in and out of the shop. Along with jelly, patrons also bought crystals, religious candles, medallions, incense, sage, everything they had in the shop was selling and selling fast. On top of that, Rose gave half priced mini readings- first come first serve. There was a line of people waiting for their turn and Charlotte worried about getting them all through, although Rose assured her it would work out.

After the parade was over, Charlotte changed hastily out of her costume and into her standard jeans and a tank top which was much more comfortable for her. When she wasn't busy at the register, she walked around chatting with customers, answering questions and helping them find merchandise. She knew that this day was important for Rose and that the Fourth of July historically meant record numbers for the shop. She wanted to make it her best year yet so she sold the way Rose taught her- by never pushing people, just talking to them. They always ended up buying.

"This medallion is of the Archangel Uriel. You can call on him for anything, but he's really great for anything intellectual. Help with school, business."

Charlotte was talking to a patron clearly in from out of town. Although the man was dressed down, it was obvious to Charlotte that he came from money. He had silver, well-trimmed hair and wore Dockers and boat shoes, a sure sign of wealth. Her ability to size up people became an asset for the shop since she could point them in the right direction without fail.

"Interesting. An academic angel," he chuckled.

She nodded. "This book is all about the archangels and invoking their power. A very good read."

The man nodded at her and took the medallion off the shelf and book out of her hand to add to a pile of other things he needed. Charlotte flitted away, seeing to the needs of other customers. She rotated the next one in line to a mini reading with Rose, who gave Charlotte a quick thumbs up when she peeked in. The Holt girls were on a roll, no doubt.

She was so busy she didn't notice when the door opened yet again and Wyatt walked in with two covered plates of food. He sat them on the front counter and walked toward her slowly. He spoke over her shoulder in a low tone.

"Hello, miss. I'm, um, looking for a mermaid. You wouldn't have happened to have seen one, would you?" he said, a smile in his voice.

She turned and smiled up to him, makeup still thick on her face, the only reminder of the parade left on her.

"Oh no, sir. I haven't seen her at all," she grinned. "Maybe she's back at the lake?"

He smiled down at her. "Hmm. Well, have you heard she actually kills people with her divine lovemaking? That's the word on the street, you know."

She stifled a laugh, covering her mouth. "She sounds like a sorceress," she said seriously.

"Yes. A ruthless one," he said, eyes dancing.

"Why aren't you at the barbecue? I thought you were going to hang out with Garrett."

"I am- I was just bringing you girls a plate," he said gesturing to the register and the hot waiting plates.

"You're an angel, thank you," she said touching his arm. She wanted to kiss him, hug him, anything, but it felt unprofessional. He nodded to her smiling, as if reading her thoughts.

"I'll let you get back to work, Sister Holt. Be back at 5 to get you?"

She nodded, locking eyes with him in lieu of a kiss. "Yes, please."

"And miss? If you see that mermaid, tell her she was beautiful today."

He winked at her, turned and walked out of the shop, leaving her flustered and on the verge of laughing. The rest of the afternoon wore on in a blur. By the time Rose finished her final reading and they closed the doors to the shop, it was almost 4 o'clock. Charlotte proudly showed Rose the empty shelves from the day. Every bit of merchandise with Mother

Mary on it sold out entirely, as did the jelly, archangel books, and several types of incense and crystals. Rose was thrilled and threw a hundred dollar bill to Charlotte as a bonus even though she resisted taking it. Rose already paid her a ridiculous hourly rate, plus her unending generosity allowing Charlotte to live with her. It was more than Charlotte could handle. In addition to that, it was more money than she had ever had at once but Rose would not take no for an answer.

They recalled the day over a fast reheated dinner of barbecue, which they were endlessly thankful for after the long day. They would have to hustle into a quick shower to be ready for Wyatt to get them for the dance. Despite missing her nap again, Rose was on a high, excited and giddy as a schoolgirl.

"You go get in the shower, girl. But before you do, I have another present for you."

Charlotte sighed. "Aunt Rose, you've given me too much. I feel bad. First breakfast, then the necklace and money. It's too much."

She stood to clear their plates and Rose scoffed at her.

"The money was for work! A bonus! Know your worth, girl. You earned it." She flitted out of the room and returned with a garment bag, holding it up by the hanger.

"If you hate it you don't have to wear it, but I thought it might be good for tonight," Rose grinned. "Go on, damn it. We don't have all day."

Charlotte laughed and approached her to open the zipper. Inside there was a white dress trimmed in lace. It was short with spaghetti straps for sleeves and a light brown belt cinched around the middle.

"I couldn't pass by it without getting it for you. It's made for that figure of yours."

Charlotte ran her hand down the side of the dress, feeling the smooth fabric and beautiful lace. She had never owned a dress so grown up and new. Once again she was overwhelmed with gratitude. She hugged her aunt close to her, kissing her cheek sweetly.

"Thank you, Aunt Rose. Thank you so much."

Rose kissed her back. "Happy Birthday, my spirit baby. Now go get dressed. If you're late then I'll take him on my own," she winked.

⌘

Wyatt wished he had time to shower before picking her up, but being the prepared young man he was, he had the foresight to bring cologne, deodorant, and an ironed shirt hanging in his truck cab. He wasn't as fresh as he would have liked but it was an improvement from his sweaty t-shirt. When he came to the door he expected Rose to answer as usual, but she didn't.

Charlotte opened the door smiling a dazzling smile and it took him a moment to move. He looked her up and down unabashedly, practically drooling. She wore her new white dress, which came just above her knee exposing her lean thighs. The necklace Rose bought her hung between her breasts and to top it off, she wore the boots he bought her. Her hair was half up, pulled loosely behind her head, and she wore light makeup that made her lips glossy and kissable.

"You look perfect," he said flatly and continued to stare.

She laughed nervously. "I thought you might want the mermaid to go with you instead."

He moved in then, putting one arm around her waist and kissing her gently.

"I'll take you any way I can get you," he said into her lips. And she felt her stomach tighten immediately. Her face grew hot and she thought maybe they should skip the dance altogether, but then she remembered Rose.

"Rose is almost ready," she said, pulling gently away moving toward the kitchen.

He nodded, looking her over again.

"Your boots fit?"

She smiled happily. "Yes, seriously my favorite pair of shoes I've ever had, Wyatt. I owe you one."

He raised his eyebrows. "Yeah? I'll remember to cash that in. How long until she's ready?"

She shrugged. "Probably 10 minutes or so. You want something to drink?"

She walked toward the kitchen with him walking after her. He wore a blue plaid button up and jeans with his nicer boots. He held his cowboy hat in his hands, fidgeting with the brim. He shook his head and sat down at the kitchen table and she walked toward him.

"Have you had a good birthday?" he asked, putting his hand around her thigh.

"Best one yet," she grinned.

"And not over yet. You gonna dance with me tonight or is Rose gonna hog me all night?"

"She's lucky she's coming at all!" Rose said coming out of her bedroom. "She's been my own personal Cinderella all day so I have half a mind to keep her here lookin' like that."

Rose wore a long colorful skirt with a shiny black tank top exposing her hourglass figure. Wyatt stood to greet her and she stopped in her tracks.

"Jesus Christ, look at you two. Just beautiful. Come on outside, I need some pictures."

Rose used almost an entire roll of film taking pictures of them posing on the porch together. "Kiss in this one! Sit on his lap on the swing. Wyatt, put your arm around her! Don't act like you don't want to, I can read your mind, you know."

The photoshoot included several shots of Rose and Charlotte, and, best of all, some of Rose and Wyatt, her petite arms wrapped around his masculine waist. They decided to walk to the dance since parking would be a mess anyhow. The dance was held outside in the middle of town. Trees were strung with white Christmas lights and tables littered the grass around the wooden dance floor brought out just for the 4th. The Holt women flanked him, each linking an arm through his which made him feel both proud and self-conscious since they were definitely receiving some looks. Thankfully, once they looked around for a seat, Garrett flagged them down to a table he had saved by the dance floor.

Garrett and Rose immediately ditched them to dance, swinging around to "La Bamba" blasting loud through the speakers. Charlotte watched them laughing and smiling, taking in the sights and atmosphere of the celebration. She had been locked in the shop all day and unaware of anything happening after the parade. Wyatt watched her profile intently and noticed her sweeping black lashes and long neck only partly exposed because of her hair. She exuded happiness and he was sure she was the most beautiful girl he'd ever seen up close. She caught him looking and leveled her gaze at him.

"What?" she laughed uncomfortably.

He shook his head and gave her a tight lipped smiled. "Nothin'. You don't even notice everyone looking at you, do you?"

She waved him off. "They're not. Maybe they're looking at you," she said, bringing a hand to his cheek. "You look very handsome in your cowboy hat. Very Wyatt Earp."

They were sitting next to each other at the table then, people all around them, but he didn't care anymore. He leaned over and kissed her on the lips softly.

"This Wyatt wants to dance. You know how to two step?"

She nodded. "I do, yes."

"Of course you do," he said, laughing.

"What do you mean?"

"You seem like you know how to do everything," he said, smiling at her.

"Oh yeah," she said sarcastically. "Jack of all trades- master of none. I didn't say I was good so I'll let you lead." She stood up and grabbed his hand, pulling him from his seat.

His mom had taught him to dance when he was in elementary school. She taught him how a man always leads and can do it without overpowering or throwing his partner around. All he needed was a woman's hand and by touching it in the right way, he could show the partner where to go. He was never more thankful for that lesson than he was on that night.

When they hit the dance floor Waylon Jennings played through the speakers, singing about the only daddy that would walk the line. Charlotte was an exquisite partner and easy to direct. She spun when he spun her, dipped when he dipped her, and stepped when he stepped toward her. They slid across the dance floor, the hem of her dress spinning up with each turn. They laughed and smiled at each other, sweating on the hot summer's night and dancing until they were short of breath. When they sat down for a break, Rose and Garrett were at the table, clapping for their performance.

"Bravo!" Rose clapped, eyes scrunched up in happiness. "You showed us up- we had to quit after a couple of songs."

Rose and Garrett sipped on Coronas while they brought the youngsters Coke in bottles. They all sat chatting at the table as the sun set over the mountain tops, making the town glow orange and pink.

"Miss Charlotte? Would you do me the honor?" Garrett said formally, extending a hand.

She nodded and jumped out of her seat, heading to the dance floor. Garrett could dance just like any proper cowboy could and he looked like a young man with Charlotte in his arms spinning out in front of him. Wyatt watched intently as her dress spun up exposing more and more of her tanned thighs. He'd seen them plenty of times at the lake but for some reason seeing them under her dress was particularly thought provoking. He remembered he was sitting next to Rose, then, so he shook out his thoughts and tried his damnedest to be pure.

"She's beautiful, isn't she?" Rose said.

"She really is," he said, not taking his eyes off of her.

"You should see her heart. It's stunning."

He almost said that he had seen it, that he knew what she was talking about, but he caught himself.

"I believe it," he said instead and noticed Rose was looking at him.

"You're a doll, Wyatt. Don't ever forget who you are right now. You're a good soul."

He nodded, feeling unsure about what she meant.

"You wanna dance with an old lady?" she said, grinning.

"No, but I'd love to dance with you."

"Good answer, kid," she said getting up.

She grabbed his bicep and walked him to the dance floor where they danced several songs in a row, Rose getting handsy only a couple of times, laughing hysterically at the height difference between them. When the music slowed down, though, she pushed Wyatt toward Charlotte and grabbed Garrett back as her partner. "Blue Eyes Crying in the Rain" played and Wyatt held Charlotte close against him, swaying slowly to the lonesome sound.

"You're a good dancer, Wyatt," she said into his chest.

"You surprised?" he smiled.

"Naw, you like to do everything the right way. Doesn't surprise me."

"You think that?" he said, almost shocked.

"Oh yeah, you're the one who's good at everything."

"Well, I can't ride in a parade through a town of adoring fans."

She smiled shyly. "I'm glad it's over. Anything for Rose, though."

"A mermaid, just like my dream. Isn't that funny?"

She nodded, breaking eye contact. "Rose said there are no coincidences. Things like that happen all of the time if we pay attention."

He nodded, looking down at her. "Makes sense."

"So you're kinda psychic, too, I think."

He laughed at that, shaking his head. "I'll leave that to you, Atargatis. Goddess of her people," he grinned, leaning to kiss her on the lips.

When night fell they all sat at the table and watched the fireworks exploding over the little town. Wyatt sat with his arm slung over Charlotte's shoulder, holding her close to his side. Later, when the show was over, Rose and Garrett stood to leave.

"Time for the old people to head home. No, no," Rose said, holding an arm out to Charlotte. "You stay out as long as you want, birthday girl. Garrett is going to walk me home."

Charlotte stood and hugged a surprised Garrett then Rose.

"Happy Fourth of July," Charlotte said, kissing her on the cheek.

"Happy Birthday, sweetest girl. You stay out as late as you want. Make some bad decisions," she said, winking at her.

Rose hugged Wyatt close. "I won't be waiting up, young man." She slapped him on the shoulder and walked away without looking back, leaving them alone at the table.

The crowd was starting to clear out and the music had stopped. Wyatt and Charlotte sat and recapped the day, drinking Rose and Garrett's leftover beers discarded on the table.

Charlotte sighed. "Such a long day, but I don't want it to be over."

"It was a good day. I think I liked watching you wake up the best," he smiled.

She cringed. "I almost forgot about that part."

"Oh I didn't," he said, turning to face her, knee to knee. "Gonna keep that picture locked away," he said, tapping the side of his head.

"Yeah? Well, maybe I'll surprise you one morning when you first wake up."

"Promise?" he grinned.

"So where are you taking me now?"

"Anywhere but home," he said, eyes shooting through her. "Lake?"

She shook her head. "Why don't you show me the bunkhouse? All the guys are gone, right?"

Wyatt's face grew hot and his mouth felt dry. He knew what would happen if he took her there and he wanted it to happen, but he felt his stomach churning and felt his old nervousness returning.

"Yeah, ok. We could do that," he said, reddening despite his best efforts.

Charlotte laughed quietly, no doubt reading his thoughts. She stood and pulled him off of his chair.

"Alright then, to the bunkhouse," she smiled.

⌘

It was just as she imagined it to be, except cleaner. There were no frills about the place with a kitchen, sparsely decorated living room, two small bedrooms, and a bathroom. Charlotte walked around looking at the few pictures on the walls, mostly old oil paintings of the ranch itself.

"Garrett's mom painted those a long time ago, I guess," Wyatt said, watching her.

He had retrieved two Mexican beers from the fridge and stood nervously behind her as she walked around the living room.

"Pretty," she said, smiling.

"You wanna sit? You've got to be exhausted."

She nodded, taking a seat on the couch and a long sip from the beer he handed her. She exhaled loudly after as he sat down next to her.

"So good after a long day," she said.

Wyatt nodded, drinking almost half of his down. He hoped it would take the edge off since he could not seem to get his heart rate under control. He felt on the verge of panic and willed himself to calm down.

Charlotte snuggled in close to him and he put his arm around her.

"Rose wants you to come to movie night tomorrow at our house. You want to?"

"Just Rose wants me to come?" he said, pulling her tight against him.

"Both of us do," she grinned.

"Ok. What are we watching?"

Charlotte shrugged. "Don't know. Rose said I haven't watched any proper movies. I read all of the time so she's ok with that, but she gets annoyed when I don't know her movie references," she laughed.

"Oh, this ought to be interesting then. Rose is hilarious."

"She sure wanted to dance with you a lot tonight. I'm lucky I got to dance with you at all."

"She told me she won't be waiting up, you know," Wyatt said, mustering up as much bravery as he could.

"Yeah? Well good, then. What should we do?" She turned to him, getting on her knees on the couch next to him, her face closing in on his.

"No idea," he said quietly into her mouth.

"No?" She was close to him now but didn't kiss him, lingering just inches away. "How about a house tour?"

She stood off the couch and walked toward the two bedrooms. "Well, come on, Mr. Earp."

He pushed himself to a standing position and put his hands immediately in his pockets to keep himself from doing any harm.

"That one is Santiago and Raul's room," he said nodding to the door on the left. "And this is mine. And Luis's."

She walked in the room, her boots clicking on the hardwood floor. The bedroom was empty but for two full beds and a side table for each. One bed had a Mexican blanket stretched out on it, impeccably made, and the other was unmade with flannel sheets.

"I usually make my bed, swear. I was in a rush this morning, though." He smiled at her from the doorway as she walked toward his bed.

She smiled back, nodding. "Long day for you, too."

She sat on the edge of his bed and grabbed a book off of his bed stand. "Louis L'Amour, huh?" she said amused.

He grew hot with embarrassment. He knew she read all of the time and figured his silly cowboy books were beneath her.

"Yeah, we don't have a TV so I just read whatever," he said casually.

"I like his books. Haven't read this one before, though." She stroked the cover and looked at him. He stood in the doorway, hands out of pockets now and on the doorframe instead, seemingly restraining himself from coming closer.

"Wyatt, are you ok?" she asked.

He nodded, looking into her eyes. Her hair was down and messy now after the dancing, her face flushed from heat. Her dress rode up her thigh when she sat down, exposing that same place Wyatt had seen each time she turned on the dance floor. He wasn't sure he could handle stepping into the room.

"Why are you way over there? You afraid of me again?" she said, smiling.

He grinned back, looking at the floor.

"Not at all. I just- I just don't know what'll happen if I come over there, Charlotte. I don't want to push too far."

She laughed. "You don't think I'd tell you if you did? It's me, Wyatt. Don't be afraid of me again."

She stood off the bed waiting for him to come to her. And he did. He stood in front of her next to the bed but didn't touch her. He looked down into her eyes and held her in his gaze. It was Charlotte who raised her hands and put them on his chest to calm him. She stood on her toes and kissed him gently, softly, until he put his arms tight around her and kissed back more urgently.

He moved his hands down her back and around her bottom, pulling her against him. His hands dared to roam even lower, pulling up the back of her dress. She stopped kissing him then and he was afraid he'd done something wrong. His hands shook at his sides as she unhooked the belt cinched tight around her midsection. It dropped to the floor with a soft clang and she pulled her sundress over her head, leaving her necklace dangling between her breasts.

Her swimsuit showed more skin than her small cotton panties and strapless bra, but Wyatt was beside himself to see her the way she looked in that moment. She stared back at him and smiled shyly.

"Guess I'd better take off my boots," she grinned.

Wyatt wanted to argue and tell her that boots and her bra and panties were perhaps the best thing he'd ever seen her wear, but he was having difficulties finding words. She slid off her boots and socks, pushing them aside and putting her hands back on his chest. She unbuttoned his shirt slowly, then helped him push it off. She'd never forget that first day meeting him in his filthy jeans and no shirt. He was so sweet, so embarrassed. He had the same look on his face in that moment in the bunkhouse that he had that first day.

She ran her hands down his smooth muscular chest to the top of his jeans. She hooked her fingers just inside his waistband and pulled him toward her. He put his hands on either side of her face and kissed her deeply, trying hard to forget how nervous he was. He turned and sat on the edge of the bed, her face still in his hands. She tried to follow him but he kept her standing between his legs. She stood up and he pulled her stomach in front of his face. He kissed from just below her breasts to just under her belly button, Charlotte shivering the whole time.

"Will you turn around?" he said into her stomach, slowly spinning her around. "This part of your back, right here," he breathed. "It's my favorite."

Her soft skin stretched over her lean muscles, making a small perfect dip in her back that he had practically dreamed about every night. He kissed lightly just inside the crevice. Touching her there, kissing that hidden place, was thrilling. He felt a pit in his stomach and the familiar ache of wanting her. She reached her hands back and unclipped her bra, letting it, too, fall to the ground and he was sure he couldn't stop this time.

He spun her back around slowly and pulled her down on the bed as he looked her over. The sight of her on his rumpled bed wearing only her underwear was almost too much. He felt his heart beating and his hands shaking despite how much he fought it.

"Just kiss me, Wyatt," she said pulling him toward her.

And he did. He made them both dizzy with kissing, moving from her face to her neck and down to her perfect breasts. He kissed her breasts one at a time and thought he might finish entirely when he heard her heavy breathing and panted whispers. He kissed down her stomach and to the very top of her lace trimmed panties, moving his soft plump lips down as far as he dared. He was breathing heavily and still shaking with anticipation.

"Charlotte, you have to tell me to stop if you want," he said, moving back up to kiss her mouth.

She moved her hands from his neck down his muscular shoulders and arms where his hands supported his weight over her. "I'm not going to tell you to stop, Wyatt."

His shaking started to worsen then, and she could feel his lips tremble as he pushed back against her.

"Are you scared?" she whispered.

He nodded back to her, smiling shyly. "I can't stop shaking," he laughed quietly.

She sat up then and so did he. She grabbed his face in both of her hands.

"You're the sweetest boy I've ever met." She kissed him gently and stood up, pulling him with her. She unbuttoned his pants slowly and he quickly pulled off his boots and socks and removed his pants, leaving them both standing in front of each other in only underwear. She lay back on the bed looking up at him.

"You should see yourself right now with your hair covering you. You really are a mermaid."

He came down on the bed, moving himself between her legs. She could feel his hardness pushing against her as they kissed and she was sure of what she wanted to do.

"There are-" he hesitated, kissing her again. "There are condoms in the bathroom," he said embarrassed.

She nodded, kissing him back and running her hands down his chest.

"Should I- should I get one?" he asked, voice barely above a whisper.

"Yes," she replied quietly.

He moved quickly out of the room and to the bathroom. He knew Santiago kept a box of condoms under the sink although he had no idea when he used them. He grabbed one and hurried back to her where the room had gone dark except for the light spilling in from the hallway. He could still see her in the dim light. She was completely naked standing by the bed waiting for him. He went to her as if in a trance and ran his hands over the curves of her body.

"You're perfect. Like a Coke bottle," he said without thinking.

She laughed quietly. "A Coke bottle?" she said, smiling.

She hooked her fingers under the elastic in his boxer briefs and pulled downward. He tried not to be embarrassed as his erection popped offensively out of them.

They came together then, kissing deeply and feeling each other's full nakedness against their skin. They tumbled back on the bed and Wyatt positioned himself back between her legs, now skin to skin with her. He started trembling as he slipped on the condom, thankful he had indeed practiced before that night.

"Are you sure?" he said, on the verge of panting.

She nodded, pulling him back to her. He guided himself toward her, pushing slowly inside. She inhaled sharply and he stopped.

"Is it- are you ok?"

"Yes, it's ok," she said leaning up to kiss him.

He pushed slowly into the tightness of her, taking care to be gentle although it took everything in his power to be slow. He could feel her wincing beneath him and knew he must be hurting her but she kept begging him to continue, kissing his neck and chest, any part she could reach from her vantage point.

Once he was fully inside of her he moved slowly back and forth with her moving with him. He supported himself on his forearms plunging into her over and over again. He kissed her deeply on the mouth, breathing hard in between kisses. Like anything, making love was not what he imagined. It was more than he could ever have realized. She was like a dream. She held onto him, her hips rising to meet him time after time, fully surrendering to him.

"Wyatt," she breathed. "Oh my God."

He couldn't take anymore. He finished inside of her with a loud groan coming out of his mouth that he hardly recognized. He collapsed on top of her, struggling to catch his breath.

"Charlotte. Jesus!" he laughed breathing hard. "I thought I might die."

He kissed her lips hard before rolling off of her and lying close by her side. She turned over and put her face on his chest.

"Why did you think you'd die?" she said, catching her own breath.

"If I couldn't have you this time. I thought I might die," he grinned.

"You're the one who tried to talk me out of it," she laughed.

"No," he said, biting his bottom lip. "No, I just wanted you to be sure."

"I was sure," she said, brushing his lips with a soft kiss.

"Me, too. Very sure," he said exhaling deeply. He felt fatigue take over almost immediately.

They snuggled together, pulling the blanket over them, speaking in hushed whispers, and holding each other close. The day being as long and eventful as it was, they both dozed off to sleep with their arms tangled around each other.

Wyatt woke with a start what he thought must be hours later, but the dark night sky coming through the window assured him he'd not slept through his chores. It took him a moment to remember where he was until he felt Charlotte's naked body laying up against him. Her head was in the crook of his shoulder and her hair spilled out of the pillow. He'd never seen her sleep before, so he took care not to move her before he could get a good long look. Her plump lips were gently parted and her eyes softly closed. Her black lashes were pronounced with mascara and her skin still flushed from lovemaking. She was exquisite lying there. Perfect and soft, just as he had seen her wake up that morning.

"Excuse me. Goddess of Patagonia Lake?" he said quietly, kissing up her neck. He saw her mouth curve up in a smile but she didn't open her eyes or move.

"Please, you've got to help me. I think I'm going to die since I made love to you. Can we do it again before I do?"

He hovered over top of her now, kissing down her body until she squirmed and giggled awake. This time when they came together he didn't shake, he didn't tremble. Like anything he did, Wyatt did it even better the second time around. He pulled her on top of him, reveling in the sight of her naked body sitting astride him. She moved slowly, unsure of what to do at first, just as he had been. She moved with him rhythmically until she released herself, crying out and falling on top of him. It surprised and triggered him to finish as well, wrapped in Charlotte.

When they fell to the bed this time they weren't tired anymore but almost giddy, laughing and giggling over their shared heavy breathing.

"Charlotte, seriously," he said. "This might be my favorite day ever."

"Oh it's definitely mine," she said grinning. She cuddled up into his armpit moving her body into his side.

"Will Rose be mad I don't have you home yet?"

She shrugged. "Doesn't sound like it if she told you she wouldn't be waiting up. She did tell me to make some bad decisions tonight, too. Although this seems like a good one."

He kissed her cheek and held her close. "Can I ask you something?" he said.

Charlotte tensed up only slightly, anticipating the question. She nodded.

"Was it- I don't know if this is ok to ask but was this- have you ever done that before?"

She sighed. "I was afraid you'd ask that. It's complicated but yeah, I've done it before. Just not like that."

"What do you mean, not like that?"

She shifted in his arms, thinking of a way to put it.

"Just not how I wanted it to be. Not like that was with you."

He nodded and tried not to be disappointed. He had enough friends to know what happened when you took a girl's virginity and that didn't happen with Charlotte. Not all of it anyway.

"Have you done it before this?" she asked.

He laughed. "It's not obvious? No, never. You're my first."

They fell quiet then, Wyatt stroking her arm and rolling her words over in his head. He couldn't drop it.

"What do you mean it wasn't like you wanted?" he asked.

She felt her stomach start to churn and a lump form in her throat. She didn't want to tell him, specifically not now but she didn't see any other way. Not with him being so kind, so giving, so absolutely pure of heart. No, she couldn't lie to him like she had to other people. She sat up next to him and wrapped the sheet around her chest, gazing down at him.

"Wyatt, listen, I don't know if you want to know about this."

He sat up with her and put his hand on hers gently.

"Of course I do. I just don't understand what you mean."

She broke eye contact, looking at the floor and shaking her head.

"I haven't told anyone this before," she whispered.

He was silent, stunned at what he thought might be true. He felt the blood rush from his face then but tried to keep his reaction even.

"He- one of my mom's boyfriends-" She stopped, hesitating. "He made me. I didn't want to. It was a long time ago."

His hands started to tingle and he was shocked to feel hot tears form in the corners of his eyes. His heart pounded in his chest and he widened his blue eyes at her, but she wouldn't look back.

"You mean he raped you?"

Charlotte flinched at the word and recoiled a bit. Then she nodded and looked bravely up at him.

"I didn't want to tell you, especially now but- I," she struggled to find the words. "I just didn't want you to think there had been anyone else like you. Because there hasn't, Wyatt. There's been no one else like you and nothing like that. What we just did."

"How old were you?" he whispered, gutted.

"Twelve."

She put a hand to the side of his face, trying to comfort him. His mouth hung open in shock and he felt rage, a murderous rage he'd never felt before. He clenched his fists angrily and shook his head, trying not to let the tears fall.

"You should have told me," he said quietly.

"I'm- I'm sorry. Would you not have wanted to?" she said, looking ashamed.

He shook his head, reaching out for her. "No, no. I just- what if I wasn't gentle enough? I should have known, I'm worried I should have handled it different."

She laughed quietly, leaning her head against him.

"You were so gentle. That was perfect. You're my first, Wyatt. You're my real first. Now I have that instead of what I had before."

She kissed his lips lightly, smiling at him as she pulled away a few inches and looked into his face.

"I've given him so many days. I don't want to do that today. Today is ours, ok?"

He nodded, pulling her back down into the bed where he tucked her protectively into his arm. He willed himself to think of the day instead of what she had just told him. He closed his eyes and took a deep breath, fighting the rage that popped up so fiercely inside of him. She was his. To think of anyone doing that to her against her will caused him physical pain in his heart.

"Ok, Charlotte. I understand."

He kissed the side of her head and pulled her in closer and closer. They lay in the quiet bed knowing that the night would finally have to be over and she'd have to go home. He didn't want it to end at all and certainly not on that horrific note. He decided he would be brave like her and tell her his own secret. One he'd kept from her since he met her.

"Charlotte?" he said quietly.

"Hmm?" she mumbled into his chest.

"I love you," he said flatly. "I'm in love with you." And there was silence. "A lot," he pushed.

She turned herself over so she was on top of him and eye level. She was smiling brightly and he smiled back, taking that as a good sign.

"You do?"

He nodded trying to find the words.

"You're just." There was too much to name. "You're everything."

She leaned in to kiss him briefly and pulled back to look into his crystal eyes.

"I love you, back, Wyatt."

IV

"Lovers don't finally meet somewhere.
They're in each other all along."

~Rumi

"I t's absolutely unacceptable that you two haven't seen this movie," Rose lectured.

They were sitting in the living room after eating pizza for dinner. Rose rarely ate out but was so exhausted from the day before and the whole week without a nap that she not only ordered pizza, but even missed mass that morning.

"What's it called again?" Charlotte asked. "*Moonstruck?*"

Rose exhaled loudly. "Yes! For God's sake it's a classic, Cher at her absolute best." She fumbled with the VHS tape, pressing buttons on the TV.

Charlotte positioned herself on the couch next to Wyatt with her bare feet curled up beside her. He had stretched his arm out behind her, keeping a respectful distance despite how difficult that was for him. He felt like doing anything but watching an old movie, but he would take whatever he could. When he dropped Charlotte off that morning the sun was barely rising and he still felt like it came too soon. He'd gone back to the ranch and directly to his chores, feeding and watering quickly before finding his way back to the bunkhouse to take a long restful nap on his sheets that still smelled like her.

He'd relived last night over and over again countless times that day. It almost didn't feel real to him it was so perfect. She was everywhere and all he could think of no matter what he was doing. He felt like a man; in part because yes, they had made love, but more so because of what she told him- she loved him back. Only a man could be loved back by someone like her.

"Goddamn weather man said we'd have rain by now." Rose shook her head glancing out the window. "Mother Nature is sure taking her sweet ass time this year."

Charlotte had started to speculate aloud that there wasn't really a monsoon season since nothing had happened. It was all every Arizonan she'd met talked about since she'd moved here and she just wasn't buying it.

"Just wait," Wyatt had said to her. He acted like it was a big surprise. Something miraculous. But Charlotte still didn't get what the big deal was. When it came, it'd just be rain, right?

"Alright, there we go," Rose muttered when she finally got the movie to work. "Now, pay attention.

Don't get so busy playing grab ass that you don't watch."

Charlotte laughed and Wyatt smiled but blushed deeply. His inability to keep his thoughts pure in front of Rose was becoming a problem.

Rose settled herself into an armchair across from them while Wyatt sat stiffly on the couch with Charlotte snuggling into his side. He put his arm around her shoulders and rubbed her arm gently, feeling her soft skin, but he tried hard not to think about the skin on all of the other parts of her body. Charlotte's head rested in the crook of his shoulder and several times throughout the movie he caught her inhaling his scent.

He tried his damnedest to follow the movie, afraid the formidable Rose would have a test afterward. Or worse yet, tell him what he was actually thinking about rather than watching. It was difficult to focus with Charlotte next to him in her cutoff shorts, which came up high as she curled up next to him. He wanted to touch her so badly, his hands itching to move up and down her legs and the curves of her body.

Despite the distractions, the movie was actually pretty entertaining. Based on a large Italian family, it was about a wayward bride who chose the groom's brother rather than the actual groom. The overall theme was about the power of love and what it can do to people. How it can drive someone absolutely mad.

"See? This is why I love Italian people. Crazy as hell, always eating. Those are my people," Rose said.

"Rose, I'm disappointed. I thought this was about magical things," Charlotte joked.

Rose scoffed. "It is! What's more magical than love?"

"True," Charlotte said and looked sideways at Wyatt.

He felt his face flush again even though he tried to keep his cool. Rose started dozing in her chair toward the end of the movie and Wyatt took that opportunity to steal a few quick kisses from Charlotte, keeping them as chaste as possible so he didn't lose his mind entirely. When the movie was over, Charlotte roused Rose who excused herself to bed soon after.

"Damn it, I don't have it like I used to," she laughed, shuffling to her bedroom. "You kids have fun. Charlotte, I'll be back to my rested self in the morning and we'll get back in our routine." She patted them both on her way to bed then shut the door after her.

Charlotte suggested they sit on the porch so they didn't wake Rose. She poured them both a glass of sweet tea and sat next to Wyatt on the front porch steps, looking out at the night sky.

"You can see so many stars out here," she said. "Not like the city at all."

He nodded, taking a drink of his iced tea.

"It's like that up north, too. Whenever we go on hunting trips up there and sleep outside, you can see so many stars. Lots of shooting stars, too. It's like you're closer to them up there."

"Pretty," she said smiling.

He moved closer to her side and put an arm around her waist, rubbing the bare skin on her back. She turned her head toward him and smiled shyly, remembering the night before.

"Wyatt, thank you for yesterday. And last night."

He laughed. "You're thanking *me?*"

"Well, yeah. It was just- it was the best day."

He nodded, looking at her perfect profile. "It really was."

"And- I don't wanna talk about this again or anything but I- I just want to say thank you for not being upset about that thing I told you. I've been feeling bad for telling you that. I probably shouldn't have."

Wyatt was dumbfounded. "Why would you feel bad about that? I'm glad you told me. I just- I hope I didn't do anything wrong."

She shook her head smiling. "No. No, I meant what I said. You were so- you're just amazing." She leaned her head on his shoulder and pulled his bicep closer to her. He wanted to ask her so many questions. Who was the guy? Did he go to jail? What's his address so I can kill him? But he wanted to respect her and not force her to discuss it.

"You can tell me anything, Charlotte. Nothing will make me feel any differently about you. Just so you know."

She nodded, wanting to change the subject. "Lake tomorrow? What time do you think you'll be done?"

He shrugged. "Hopefully by 4? Is that too late?"

She shook her head. "I'll wait for you." She leaned and kissed him on the side of the neck, sending a chill through him.

"Will you be wearing your mermaid tail?" he said, putting a hand on her thigh.

She threw her head back and laughed. "That depends. Will you be wearing your jeans shirtless with a shirt wrapped around your face?"

He blushed, smiling. "Oh you remember that, do you?" He pulled her leg closer to him, digging his fingers in to tickle her.

She nodded, trying not to squirm. "I'll never forget it. That poor napping cowboy who couldn't fish worth a damn."

He dug his fingers in then and tickled her until she laid back on the porch laughing hysterically with him on top of her.

"Shhhh. You don't wanna wake Rose!" he said in a loud whisper into her face.

"Better kiss me to keep me quiet then," she grinned.

He lowered his head and kissed her softly, barely brushing his lips against hers. He held back, teasing her several times before opening his mouth and overtaking her with long deep kisses. His torso was on top of hers but his lower half still to the side. He moved his hands down over the front of her shirt feeling her breasts, stomach, then smooth legs. He sat her up next to him and put a hand behind her head, tangled in her hair as he kissed her.

Charlotte's hands roamed his body, climbing up his shirt to his hard, warm stomach. He breathed heavily into her mouth and moved a hand down to her legs. He ran it up the inside of her thigh to the bottom of her cutoffs, inching closer and closer to her. She started breathing heavier, panting a bit between kisses, and he could hardly take it.

"I want," she panted. "Please," she breathed.

"What Charlotte? What do you want?" he asked earnestly. Whatever she wanted he would give.

She pulled his hand up her thigh even more, urging him onward. He hesitated but then moved his large fingers over the seam of her shorts and she responded by moving against him. He slipped his fingers up her shorts, pushing her underwear to the side. Charlotte inhaled loudly as his fingers entered her. He moved them inside of her feeling how ready she was, how warm and soft she was. He kissed her hard and continued moving, determined to give her everything she wanted. He put his other hand around her waist gripping her tightly until she tensed up and sighed into his mouth.

"Oh God. We're in trouble," she laughed.

"Why?" he said, removing his hand and kissing her again.

"I just- I just want you so much. It's like I can't control it or something."

The way she said it, the honesty in her voice, gave him that punch in the gut again. It wasn't just about the sex- it was more. Bigger than that and way more frightening.

"Me, too," he said quietly, putting his forehead against hers.

Her large green eyes looked up into his. No matter how she looked her eyes always carried a hint of sadness in them. It made her vulnerable, childlike almost. He felt his heart tighten to think of her life-what she'd been through. He didn't even know the half of it but the parts he knew would break most people. Yet there she was, sitting on a porch with him, giving herself over to him in every way. It made him love her even more.

"Charlotte," he whispered into her mouth. "Charlotte, are you mine?"

She smiled, her eyes scrunching, staring back at him. "Yes, Wyatt. I'm yours," she said and wrapped her arms around his neck.

⚬⚬⚬❉⚬⚬⚬

"I'm born again!" Rose shouted from the kitchen. "Hallelujah!"

She was chipper and raring to go after 10 hours of sleep. Charlotte was also rested even though she had fewer hours than Rose. Wyatt stayed on the front porch with her for over an hour and then of course she couldn't fall asleep, thinking only of him.

Charlotte smiled at her from over her breakfast. "So what's on the agenda? Readings today?"

Rose nodded her head. "We've got one newcomer then Betty'll be back. I want you to sit in on that one. Less of a reading, more of a counseling session."

Charlotte nodded. "I'd like to see that. She gonna be ok with it though?"

"Oh yes," Rose waved a hand. "She's not like Patricia. And by not like her I mean she's not an asshole," she winked.

Charlotte laughed nodding. "Ok then. Inventory is down low again, too. Do we need to go back to Tucson?"

Rose shook her head. "No, I'm going to have to run up to Phoenix this time. I'll go this weekend."

"Ok, do you want me to get us a hotel? I can handle booking-"

"You're not coming, dearest. I need you to stay here to hold down the fort," Rose said, cutting her off.

"But- are you sure?" Charlotte asked, confused.

"Oh yes, I'm sure. Aunt Rose has a social engagement to attend to up there as well," she grinned.

"Really?" Charlotte said, drawing out the word. "As in a man?"

"Don't sound so shocked, my dear. You're not the only one who gets a little arm candy. Hell, I've got several!" she said slapping her hand on the table and cackling loudly.

Charlotte giggled. "Oh I have no doubt. Just don't tell Garrett. I don't know if he'll ever get over it."

Rose waved a hand. "Naw, he's just my friend."

Charlotte cocked her head at her, calling her bluff.

"Ok, ok. I gave him a spin once but that was in the name of therapy, I swear. I didn't charge so it doesn't count as prostitution."

Charlotte threw her head back and laughed uncontrollably.

"Aunt Rose!" she mock scolded. "You sorceress, you!"

"Only that one time," she said, holding her hand up beside her. "Scout's honor."

"Ok, I believe you," Charlotte giggled. "So who's this guy? Is he your boyfriend?"

"No- hell no," Rose shivered. "He's a lawyer in Scottsdale. Older, divorced, devilishly handsome, and a good time. But relationships are not for me."

Charlotte nodded. "You're not like your sister at all then," she said humorlessly.

Rose shook her head. "No, Lily came out of the womb with a boyfriend, I think. What about you, my love? Lots of boyfriends?"

Charlotte shook her head. "Not really."

Rose nodded. "Until now, that is," she winked.

"Well, just the one, but yes," Charlotte smiled a bit embarrassed.

"Speaking of Romeo, I'm sure he'd be happy to keep you company while I'm gone, right?"

Charlotte shrugged, fighting a smile. "He works a lot so I don't really know."

"You're a shitty liar, my dear. An excellent trait."

After meditation they opened up the shop, anticipating a much slower day than the crazy weekend before that. Charlotte reorganized what was left of the merchandise and took care to make it seem like the shelves weren't as bare as they actually were. While Rose took her first reading, a middle-aged Hispanic woman from Nogales, Charlotte logged all of the receipts and the sales from the 4th, which were impressive to be sure. She made quick work of all of it then decided to sweep and dust everything she could since there were no other patrons in the shop.

She edged near Rose's door and could hear the client crying softly, then Rose comforting her. She noticed the stark contrast between how Rose spoke to Patricia and how she spoke to this woman.

"It's closed, my dear," Rose said sadly. "That fortune is closed. You must move on to someone else."

The woman whimpered and Rose continued.

"Not this life, babe. Maybe another but not this one. Hold him in your heart instead. Send him light and prayers. You can still love him, you just can't have him."

Charlotte pulled herself away from the door in part because she felt bad eavesdropping and also because what she heard made her stomach ache. *Not this life.* It echoed in her ears until she physically shook her head, willing it to get out.

"Hello, Charlotte!" Betty said, coming through the front door. She wore overalls and a sun hat, her face scrubbed of makeup as usual. Charlotte thought Betty was more and more beautiful as she got to know her better. She was kind and unassuming, always putting herself last. Hence why she needed Rose.

"Hello, Betty," Charlotte smiled. "Rose is almost ready for you. She wants me to sit in today, is that ok with you?"

"Oh sure, honey. Rose said you're real talented," she smiled warmly at her.

"Well, I don't know about that, but she's taught me a lot."

Betty nodded. "You're learning from the best. Rose has been helping me for a long time. She's been there at my worst. She's like an angel."

Charlotte smiled thinking of her aunt. Foul mouthed and horny, but it was true. She was an angel nonetheless.

"Yes," Charlotte said. "She really is."

When Rose came out of her office she had her arm around the client's shoulders. The woman had gotten ahold of herself and gave a brave smile when she saw Charlotte and Betty waiting.

"Thank you, Miss Rose. I will be back again." She shook Rose's hand then moved swiftly out of the shop.

"Betty!" Rose said fondly. "What do you say, you ready for some magical shit or what?"

Betty blushed and giggled at Rose, following her into the office. Charlotte followed and pulled a chair up next to Rose.

Rose started by asking Betty about her progress, whether or not she'd been cleaning her energy or meditating, and how she'd been feeling. There was no doubt that Betty looked better than the last time she left the shop, tear-streaked cheeks and all.

"I've been really working on it, Rose, I promise. And I feel good. I- I just seem to have a problem shaking the whole guilt thing."

Rose nodded patiently. "I know that's hard for you. What are you feeling guilty about this time?"

Betty shifted uncomfortably in her chair. "Well, you know. The divorce. You know, in the Bible it says, you know, that nothing can really separate the bonds of marriage. So I keep thinking, maybe that means we aren't really divorced. And if we aren't really divorced, I shouldn't be thinking or looking at other men." She looked down into her lap shamefully.

"Ah, there it is," Rose said. "Another man? It's about damn time! Listen, Betty. You've been divorced five years. He left you, and, by the way, I'm glad he did. The guy was a first class asshole. Put the Bible aside for a minute and ask yourself, would God want you to be happy? Have you wronged so badly that our all-knowing God would have you be miserable for the rest of your life?"

Betty exhaled, shaking her head. "I just don't know, Rose."

"You do. Look into your heart and use logic. God did not create us to be guilty. He created us to love and be loved in return. We were made to be free thinkers, to be triumphant. Your ex was a test- nothing more. It's how you move forward that matters."

Betty nodded, mulling it over. "Ok, I understand. I just- sometimes, I know I shouldn't, but I'm just ashamed, you know?"

Rose nodded sympathetically. "I know, my friend, but you are a good soul. You're always helping others, you've raised some fine children, you contribute to your community, and you spread love to those around you. Why the hell should you be ashamed?"

Rose stared at her across the table and Charlotte sat silently by her side. She could feel Betty's energy, the precariousness of her poor spirit, always teetering on the edge of self-doubt.

"I want you to add this to your affirmations- I want you to say to yourself, 'I deserve love, too'." Rose said, and Charlotte knew she wasn't only talking to Betty. "I want you to treat your spirit like you would treat another person. You would never in your life be rude to another person, but you have no problem being an asshole to your own spirit. That stops now. Be kind to your spirit. Treat it like you would treat a friend. Speak nicely to it. When you catch yourself in your own head fighting with it, stop yourself. Don't allow anyone to talk to your friend that way," Rose winked.

Betty nodded, taking note of her words. "I like how you put that. Ok, yes. I'm going to work hard on that."

Rose nodded. "Atta girl," she smiled. "And Betty? Is it Pete the mailman?"

Betty's face flushed through and her mouth dropped open. "How did you- oh you're good. I haven't told anyone," she laughed, looking at Charlotte to confirm the magic.

Rose smiled, nodding her head. "I think your spirit would really like it if you banged his brains out," she grinned, then cackled at Betty's scandalized face.

⌒⌒⊰❦⊱⌒⌒

"I think it's gonna rain," Wyatt said, looking at the horizon.

They sat in the shallows next to each other and Wyatt smelled the air.

"You smell it?" he asked, inhaling deeply.

Charlotte closed her eyes and breathed in through her nose. "I think so, barely."

"Like wet dirt. And creosote. That's that bush over there," he pointed. "Smells so good when rain hits it."

She nodded, looking around the lake. "Well it's about time. I was starting to think you made monsoon season up," she teased.

"It's worth the hype, believe me."

"Yeah, but it'll ruin our lake days. Now what are we going to do?" she said.

"We can think of something, I'm sure," he said, flashing her a toothy smile.

It'd seemed like too long since they'd been there together alone. All of their meetings ran together now in a blur of laughter and flirtation and love. Each day with each other felt like the best one yet.

Charlotte smelled the air again and sighed. "I love it here," she said quietly.

"The lake?"

"Well yeah, but Arizona in general. I think it's officially my favorite state," she smiled. "Why do you want to leave here so bad anyway?"

They'd avoided talking about the Marine Corps or future in general, both dancing around it masterfully as if it didn't exist, so he was surprised when it came up. His stomach pitted out again and he felt his heart tighten.

"Well, I don't really want to leave," he said, letting his words hang. "I just- it felt like the right thing to do, you know?"

"Joining the Marines?" she asked, looking into his face. His blue eyes squinted, looking out at the lake instead of at her.

He nodded. "I wanted to- I mean, I want to serve my country. My grandpa fought in World War Two and I guess I thought it was my turn. My war."

They were quiet then, letting the words settle between them.

He laughed lightheartedly. "Seemed like a good idea at the time."

"I think it's brave," she said honestly. "I just can't imagine you making that choice when you had so many others, you know?"

He nodded. "I didn't want to do what everyone expected me to do, I guess. For once."

"I get that," she said evenly. "What do you think it's going to be like? The Marines?"

He shook his head. "Don't know really. Hard, I guess. A challenge."

"And you like a challenge," she said, smiling at him.

"You think?" he said, grinning sideways at her.

"Oh yeah. And you heard Rose, there's nothing you can't handle."

He squinted into her eyes, his lashes coming together.

"Hope that's true," he said quietly.

She reached for his hand in the water then, moving closer to him. She wanted to tell him that she already knew the man he would be one day, that somehow she already felt it. That she knew what he was capable of doing. But there was no way to tell him how she knew that. How she knew his heart already and seemingly had even long before they'd met.

"Come on, I brought something for you," she said.

She stood in the water pulling him upward, and he followed her to shore. He wore only board shorts, his muscles pronounced after working the corrals all day. Charlotte, as always, wore her blue bikini riding low on her hips. Now when he saw her in it he became even more aroused since he knew exactly what was underneath. He knew the curves of her body with nothing else distracting from it. It was like a secret he shared only with her.

They sat under their tree by the shore, wet from swimming. The sky was dark and ominous in the distance and the air thick with humidity. Charlotte sat cross-legged next to him, pulling something out of her bag.

He grinned at her, shaking water from his hair. "What did you bring?" he asked looking down at the bag.

"Cookies. Rose and I made them this afternoon." She handed a large, soft gingersnap cookie over and took one for herself. He bit into his and nodded approvingly.

"This is good. You're like a little housewife," he teased.

"Very domesticated," she grinned at him. They looked back out to the black sky and Wyatt pointed out the lightning, guessing aloud where the storm was.

"Looks like it's over by Sonoita right now. Might go right around us."

Charlotte shrugged. "At least we can keep swimming today, then."

She hugged up close to his side, her cool body connecting with him, making his imagination start up again. He turned and kissed her shoulder, then neck, moving her hair out of his way. She giggled and squirmed.

"So ticklish," he said, kissing around to the other side of her neck. He wrapped his arm around her waist and placed his palm over her stomach.

"You know this is what you were wearing when we met. Have I ever told you I drove all over town looking for you after that?"

"What?" she laughed. "Where did you go?"

"Name it," he said laughing. "And I went there."

"Really? That is so funny. You know that's why I came back that day, right? I didn't see you at the front of the lake, so I came back here."

"Well good. That means you won't turn me in for stalking," he said kissing her shoulder. "But wait! You almost didn't let me take you home that day. Then where would we be?"

"No, I was just being careful. I asked my intuition though and you checked out," she smiled.

"Yeah, what did your intuition say about me?"

Charlotte didn't miss a beat. "It said you hopelessly have your mind in the gutter but that you're an ok guy."

Wyatt flushed, despite himself. It was so accurate a description he wondered if she really did have a gift. He grinned at her and she laughed as he dug his hands into her sides, tickling her gently.

"Ok, maybe you are psychic then," he laughed. "I'm glad you came looking for me."

"Me, too," she said, smiling into his eyes.

"When do I get to see you again?" he said, his face moving closer.

"Tomorrow? Come over when you're done."

He nodded and brushed his lips against hers softly. "I'll be there."

"Rose is leaving town this weekend, you know," she said abruptly.

Wyatt moved his head back and raised his eyebrows at her.

"Is that so? What will you do with yourself?" he grinned.

She shrugged. "Don't know. Housewife stuff, I guess," she said, trying to keep a straight face. He pulled her across his lap, burying his face in her neck. "Maybe I could make you dinner Friday," she said, stroking the back of his head.

He moved his face closer against her and mumbled into her neck. "Will you be wearing that apron?"

She giggled. "I suppose."

"I will be there, then. Wouldn't miss that."

"Ok, it's a date," she said and snuggled him closer, his ear pressed tight against her beating heart.

⟡

Charlotte felt at home in every library she'd ever set foot in for many reasons. First because she loved books of all kinds but also because in each town she'd lived in, libraries had been her refuge. They were free to use and librarians were almost always friendly and thrilled to have a young person like Charlotte utilize their resources so thoroughly. She never understood why more people didn't come to libraries. On top of having free books, they had clean restrooms, comfortable chairs, and free workshops and classes available to anyone. Charlotte learned at an early age to use all of these resources to her advantage. Instead of going home, she could always go there.

Patagonia's library was small, but not the smallest she'd seen. It was located on the opposite side of town from the shop but still walking distance for Charlotte. That day Rose finished her readings early and closed the shop because, she insisted, today would be the day the rain finally arrived and that meant she needed to make spaghetti sauce. The first monsoon of the year wouldn't be complete without it simmering on the stove, she'd said.

So, Charlotte had time for the library that afternoon. Time to lose herself in the rows of beautiful books all there for the taking and time to be back in the only place she'd felt at home before moving there. She sat in an armchair tucked in the back corner of the quiet library, reading one of her selections from the day. She'd decided to research several topics including past life regression and war, although it seemed she'd already read several books about the latter. She settled on a nonfiction book about the Marine Corps and Hemingway's *A Farewell to Arms* in addition to the spiritual books about regressions.

She sat flipping through the book about the Marine Corps, looking at the faces of the young Marines in uniform. For the life of her, she couldn't picture her Wyatt that way- straight faced and a crew cut, eyes like stone. No, it just couldn't be. She read several sections of the book including the history and traditions in the Marine Corps. The emphasis on discipline and honor was almost overwhelming for her. Just the section about boot camp alone was enough to make her want to beg him not to go and boot camp wouldn't be the worst of it, she knew. She read on until her stomach started to ache with anxiety for Wyatt and she had to close it.

She looked out the window of the library and saw, finally, the clouds rolling directly toward town. Rose was right, today would be the day. She figured she had only a few more minutes before she should start home, so she cracked her book about regressions and began reading.

The book gripped her from the start, detailing an account of a well-respected psychologist and hypnotist who went rogue and decided to begin regressing patients into past lives. The author detailed his background first, affirming his legitimacy, then started in on different case studies he'd completed over the years. She was about halfway into the first one when she felt him. It had happened before at the lake when he arrived and was watching her through the desert. She had simply known that he was there and felt him before she saw him, just as she did in that moment. She knew he was close.

She looked up from her book and saw Wyatt standing against a bookcase, watching her in the silent library. He was still in his work clothes although he wasn't as dirty as he normally was. She smiled at him then but he didn't move, he stood where he was and stared intently at her, a half smile on his face. She wanted to run to him and feel his arms around her. She wanted to tell him that he couldn't join the Marines, that she couldn't take seeing his perfect face set like those other boys. But she just sat and stared back at him, waiting for him to come to her. He crossed the room and sat in the chair next to her, leaning in close.

"Miss," he whispered. "You are not permitted to look this beautiful in a library."

She giggled, her face blushing uncharacteristically.

"Why are you off work so soon?" she whispered back.

"Done with the corrals. Plus, it's finally gonna rain," he grinned.

"I think you're finally right," she smiled back at him. "How'd you know I was here?"

"Little psychic birdie told me. She wanted me to fetch you for dinner- didn't want you to walk home in the rain."

Charlotte nodded. "I got sidetracked reading, I guess."

He nodded, looking her up and down. She wore jeans and the same shirt she wore on their first date, exposing the top of her shoulders. He thought about getting on his knees in front of her chair and suffocating her with kisses but he figured the librarian might take issue with that.

"What are you reading?" he asked, picking up one of her books.

She cringed inwardly when he picked up the book with the large gold letters spelling out "American

Marine" across the cover. He looked at it in his hands then looked up at her, smiling sadly.

"What's this for?" he asked quietly.

She shrugged. "Just research."

He nodded, looking into her sad eyes.

"What's it about so far?"

She shrugged. "Basically how badass the Marines are."

"Yeah? What else?"

She looked at him with her fierce green eyes. "Nothing you can't handle," she said steadily.

He nodded, placing the book back on the stack.

"Can I take you home?" he said.

She nodded and stood with him as he picked up her books, walking them to the front for her. The librarian wrapped them in a plastic bag, talking excitedly about the impending rain. It truly was finally the day.

When they walked out the front doors of the library, the storm was right overhead. They both looked up at the dark sky and she could smell it then, really smell it. It was a mixture of dust and moisture and some other unknown scent that was fresh and wild. The wind blew her hair around her face as they hustled toward his truck. She jumped in through the driver's side and sat in the middle, Wyatt climbing in next to her.

"Finally!" she laughed.

He grinned at her and rolled down his window. They sat quietly, watching the wind blow the clouds in, darkening the entire town.

"Look," he said, pointing to the windshield. Small drops of rain started to hit the window, slowly at first then coming down harder and harder. Wyatt put his hand out the driver's side window and felt the cool rain hit his palm. She leaned across him and did the same, looking out the window and watching the rain come down, hitting the dry desert landscape, desperate for a drink.

"Oh my God," she sighed. "It really does smell amazing." She inhaled deeply and moved her hand around feeling the rain.

He watched her, his face only inches from hers, and felt a deep sadness wash over him. Where would they be next year when the first rains came? What would happen to them? He didn't know, but he knew it would not be here, not like this. He watched her beautiful face smile into the storm until she realized he was watching her and turned to look at him. He didn't smile or say anything, he just watched her. His blue eyes made him look more boyish and wounded than ever.

"What?" she questioned quietly. "What's wrong?"

He brought his wet hand up to her face and pushed her hair back over her shoulder. He slowly shook his head, not having the words. She moved herself closer to him turning around to face him on her knees.

"It's raining," she said quietly. "Be happy."

He grabbed her face with both hands now and brought her lips in front of his.

"I love you, Charlotte." The rain beat against the truck, softly surrounding them with the steady rhythm.

"I love you," she said back quietly. And he kissed her softly and slowly, holding her close against him, willing time to stop.

<hr/>

They sat in the truck for several minutes like that before driving back through town with the rain coming down harder and stronger. Charlotte knew he wasn't his normal self- she didn't know if it was the book or the rain that triggered it but she worked hard to pull him out of it, snuggling up against his side and kissing his neck on the drive home. She promised him dinner with the apron the next day until he couldn't help but laugh and smile, softening his edge.

When they arrived at Rose's, the sky opened up and began pouring down rain in streams of water that fell from the heavens. The dark clouds cracked above them and the sound of the water hitting the ground roared around them. They jogged out of the truck and up to the porch but were soaked regardless. Wyatt widened his eyes at her white shirt soaked through with rain. It was hopeless, no matter what she wore all he could think about was ripping it off.

"It's coming down so hard!" she said over the sound of the rain on the porch roof.

They removed their shoes before Charlotte opened the front door. Rose was sitting on the couch with glass of wine in her hands. All of the windows of the house were open making it smell of rain and faintly of the sauce simmering on the stove. Rose's eyes were red-rimmed and clearly wet from tears even though she feigned normalcy. It was obvious she was crying.

"What's wrong?" Charlotte said immediately to her. Rose waved a hand and took a sip of her wine.

"Nothing. The first rain always makes me emotional. It's so beautiful."

Charlotte squinted her eyes scrutinizing her but didn't want to push hard in front of Wyatt.

"Can I help with dinner?" Charlotte asked, changing the subject.

"Well yes, as a matter of fact. You got busy at the library did you? Little bookworm, this one." Rose stood off the couch and moved toward the kitchen, working hard to shake her mood. "Romeo, will you be joining us for dinner? Charlotte has to join us, too, so she'll be the third wheel but still."

Wyatt grinned at her. "I'd love to but I have to get back to the ranch. Luis is making pozole for everyone. I wouldn't want to be rude and miss it."

"Pozole!" Rose clapped her hands together. "Oh, Charlotte, we need to make that next week. Mexican soup- just delicious."

Rose chatted up Wyatt as always, asking him about his week and Garrett while Charlotte busied herself in the kitchen stirring the sauce and putting the water on for pasta. She poured more wine for Rose and looked for another task, still put off by Rose's unorthodox crying. She knew it was not the rain.

"Well, ladies. I'd better get going," Wyatt said, leveling his eyes at Charlotte. He wanted to ask about their plans for the next day but it felt strange in front of Rose. His conscience was already guilty for what he knew dinner would turn into when Rose was gone.

"Oh now wait, Wyatt. I need you to do something for me," Rose said, stopping him.

"Oh sure," he said squaring his shoulders to her, readying himself to lift or move something.

"I need you to come and stay here with Charlotte this weekend. I'm headed out of town and I don't want her staying alone."

Wyatt felt his face flush through entirely. He hadn't prepared himself for anything like that coming out of her mouth and the logistics of it all running through his head was just too much. Charlotte was standing at the sink behind Rose, a mischievous smile spreading across her face. He tried to ignore her and looked at Rose instead.

"Oh, ok. I-" he stuttered. "I can do that. I'll tell Garrett I'll come back to feed and everything." He tried hard to keep from seeming uncomfortable to no avail. Rose, as always, ate it up. She grinned, looking up at him.

"Thank you, Wyatt. Such a good boy." She raised her hand up and patted him on the red cheek.

"Well- ok," he said nervously, "I'd better go."

Rose sat at the kitchen table and put her hand under her chin looking at him. She sighed.

"If you must. Charlotte, is he not the dreamiest thing you've ever seen?"

Charlotte crossed the kitchen and put her hand on his arm to calm him, before kissing him gently on the cheek.

"He's not bad."

He was nervous again. There was no way around it. He drove to her house with his duffle bag in the passenger seat and the music off. His palms were sweating on the wheel and he could feel his stomach churning. He'd taken a cold shower after work to prepare himself, to calm his racing heart, but it was no use.

The night before he'd gone back to the ranch in a daze to eat dinner with the other men. Garrett had joined them and made several comments to Wyatt about him being even more quiet than usual. Santiago and Raul ignored him as always, and Luis just smiled at him, looking at him the same way Rose did. Like he knew what was going on in his head without asking.

Dinner was delicious, the best pozole he'd ever had by a landslide. Luis made the soup with roasted green chiles, black beans, pork, and hominy. The seemingly simple recipe was alive with flavors Wyatt hadn't had the other times he'd tried the soup.

"A man of many talents!" Garrett had said, slapping Luis on the shoulder. "This is why he has such a pretty wife."

Luis smiled shyly and looked down, avoiding eye contact. Wyatt had no idea that Luis was even married. He spent the week at the ranch and only the weekends back in Mexico so it didn't seem like enough time to have a wife.

When the meal was over the other men left the dirty kitchen, all but for Wyatt and Luis. Wyatt helped clear the table and wash the dishes, his manners kicking in as always.

"Good kid," Luis said, patting his large shoulder as Wyatt cleaned.

Ever since the day Garrett had told him about the Marine Corps, Luis became even kinder to Wyatt. He looked at him in a new way and exhibited a somewhat fatherly protection over him at times. The two cleaned the kitchen in the same way they did projects together, efficiently and with teamwork, Wyatt following his lead. When they finished cleaning, Luis stopped Wyatt before he headed to the shower.

"Wait," he said, getting into a high cupboard. He removed a mason jar filled with a gold colored liquid in it and handed it to Wyatt.

"Es for you. Tequila. My brother make it," he grinned.

Wyatt had heard about homemade Mexican tequila. Mexican moonshine is what his friends back home called it, although Wyatt had never tried it. He knew it was a big deal for Luis to give such a gift so he didn't take it lightly.

"Really?" he said, surprised. "Thank you, Luis. Muchas gracias," he smiled to him looking at the jar. Luis beamed back at him.

"Only little bit," he said, holding his fingers out to indicate an inch. "Not too much!" he warned.

Wyatt nodded, smiling. "Ok, just a little."

He rolled the jar over in his hands watching the liquid move. He removed the lid and inhaled the strong scent, Luis laughing at his scrunched up face.

"See?" he laughed. "Not too much!" he repeated.

So Wyatt drove to her house that day with the liquid courage in his duffle bag, just in case. The sun was headed down over the mountains and a storm brewed in the distance. The smell of wet dirt still hung in the air from the storm the day before and the temperature had finally dropped out of the 100s to the low 90s. Blissful in comparison.

When he pulled up to her house he thought about taking a shot of tequila before entering, but he decided against it. It was his Charlotte and there was no reason to be nervous around her anymore. At least that's what he told himself. He threw his duffle bag over his shoulder and held the sunflowers he'd picked for her in the other hand. He climbed the steps to the house, knocking on the front door. He heard music coming from the inside and the sound of footsteps.

She opened the door wearing, as promised, her apron tied tight around her waist. Underneath she wore jeans and a white tank top with her hair piled in a messy bun at the top of her head.

"Hey!" she said smiling at him. "You moving in?" she said, eyeing the duffle bag.

He put his free arm around her waist and pulled her against him, inhaling her lavender scent.

"I'm here strictly to work security for Rose so don't get any ideas," he said into her neck. She giggled and pulled her face back to kiss him firmly on the lips.

"Do security guards bring flowers? Or is that a Marine thing?"

"Maybe more of a Wyatt Earp thing," he said, still holding her close.

She shook her head, taking the flowers. "Naw, it's a Wyatt Sterling thing."

She kissed his cheek and moved quickly back into the kitchen leaving him to follow. He dropped his bag by the couch and watched her at the stove.

"How was work?" she asked.

He shrugged. "Good I guess, humid."

She nodded, stirring something on the stove. "I think it's going to rain again. You were right by the way, it's as good as you said it would be." She looked over his shoulder and shot him a glance.

"What, the monsoons?"

She nodded. "I slept with my window open last night just to smell it."

He thought about her sleeping alone in a bed he would be in that evening and he got nervous all over again. When she offered him a drink he figured that was his opening to show her the tequila. He hoped it would take his nervousness away and allow him to be normal. She was thrilled about it and asked how it was made and where it was from to the point that Wyatt knew she'd be researching tequila the next week at the library.

She mixed the tequila with some prickly pear syrup and lemonade, pouring them each a glass over ice. He sat at the table watching her work since she'd refused any help.

"You like it?" she asked after he took a sip.

He felt the tequila shoot through his veins and warm his toes and finger tips although he could hardly taste it.

He nodded. "You?"

She grinned. "Yeah, it's good. Could be dangerous though. I can't even taste the tequila."

He laughed. "Well, Luis warned me to only drink a little bit. What do you mean dangerous, though? What happens if I feed you too much tequila?" he asked, raising his brows at her.

"Me? I'm more worried about you. You might be dancing on the table for all I know." She moved back to the stove and continued cooking until Wyatt came up behind her.

"What are you making? Pasta?"

She nodded. "Shrimp and veggies over pasta. Do you like that?"

"I do," he said, leaning to kiss the back of her bare neck. "And you wore this for me, I see." He put his hand around her waist and touched the apron, following it from her bellybutton to the ties on the back.

"I told you I would," she said, smiling. "I didn't know if you'd show though."

"What?" he said moving his head back to look at her. "Why wouldn't I show?"

"Well, I don't know. You looked a little unsure when Rose asked."

He laughed. "Can you blame me? I try to keep my thoughts pure in front of Rose and it's difficult when she asks something like that."

"So you do think she's magical for real, huh?"

He shook his head, not committing. "I don't know, but I'm not going to risk it."

She turned off the burner and spun to face him. Hank Williams played through the radio speaker but there was silence other than that. She looked up at him.

"What about now?"

"What?" he said, confused.

"Are your thoughts pure now?" she smiled.

"Oh definitely. For sure. I told you I'm just here to work security," he said trying to keep a straight face.

"You sure?" she said, moving her face in front his. Her soft lips were slightly stained with the prickly pear syrup and looked delicious. He moved his hand down the side of her body and over her hips and shook his head.

"No, I'm not." He kissed her gently, barely brushing her lips, restraining himself from pushing further.

"Good then," she said, patting him on the bottom. "Sit and let me feed you."

She tossed the pasta in butter and Parmesan along with the shrimp and sautéed zucchini, separating it out into two bowls. It killed him to sit while she worked but he wasn't upset with the view at all. Her apron strings and bare feet were enough to bring him to his knees. She chatted on about the shop and Rose while she worked and he sipped his drink, savoring the sweet and sharp mix of prickly pear and Mexican moonshine. When she sat his plate down in front of him, he restrained himself from reaching out and pulling her apron-clad body on his lap. Patience was a virtue, but he had less and less of it when it came to her. The meal was simple and delicious and he told her so over and over again.

"Why do you sound surprised?" she laughed.

"I don't know, it's just impressive. My mom doesn't cook that much. She likes to bake but not cook."

"Mine either. Rose has been teaching me, though."

"Well, you're a fast learner then," he smiled over at her, taking another bite. "Have you talked to her?" he asked.

"Rose?"

"No, your mom." He knew she didn't like to talk about it but the tequila made him forget his manners for a moment.

She sighed. "No, I haven't. She was kind of a mess when I left. Who knows how long it took her to realize I was gone, anyway."

"So, you just left?" The drink was already going to his head, he felt like the questions came out of his mouth easier. He was thinking about what he was going to say less than before which was rare for him. She leveled her green eyes at him and took a long sip of her drink, which was likewise beginning to go to her head.

"Yeah, I left one night. Took a bus here," she smiled. "I don't recommend Greyhound as a travel method if you can avoid it."

His mouth dropped open a bit. He had never thought about how she got there, he only knew that one day there she was, waiting for him to wake from a dream.

"You took a Greyhound? By yourself?" he asked, shocked.

She nodded. "Yeah, it wasn't so bad. Just slow. I had to change buses a couple of times but I got here so..."

He shook his head slowly. "You're brave," he said bluntly. He'd seen a few Greyhound stations before and knew enough to know that those were not the places for a beautiful girl like her.

She shook her head, breaking eye contact.

"Naw, it was just..." she paused. "It was just time for me to go," she smiled sadly.

"I'm glad you did," he said quietly. "I hate that you had to come here like that, though," he said shaking his head. "I don't even want to think about it."

She smiled at him, and sighed again. "Well, I got here safe so it's ok."

"Just don't do that again, please?"

"What, ride a Greyhound?"

"Any of it," he said, his eyes intense.

She nodded and looked down at their drinks. "You want another? I'll make another." She stood abruptly from the table, taking their drinks to make more. Wyatt cleared their empty plates and positioned himself at the sink to clean the dishes. She laughed at him from her place at the counter.

"You look so funny doing dishes," she said, mixing the drinks.

"Why?" he said grinning over his shoulder.

"I don't know, you in your boots and jeans. You look like you should be driving cattle but you're in my kitchen instead," she smiled. "I like it."

He scrubbed the plates one after the other until all of them were done. Charlotte dried each one and put them away. They moved to the porch to watch the storm come in, bringing with them their newly mixed tequila drinks. They sat on the front porch swing, Charlotte stretching her bare feet out in his lap. He put a hand on her leg, watching the horizon.

"It's coming. Out over Sonoita right now for sure," he said, looking out.

She looked at him, admiring his profile. His face was tanned and his mouth was always set in the same way, he always looked ready to smile.

"You're so handsome, Wyatt." The drink was definitely getting to her. Her head felt warm and she felt her guard being dropped entirely but it didn't scare her like it normally did.

He looked over at her and smiled broadly. "Is this the tequila talking?" he teased.

"No!" she laughed. "I was just thinking. You know, why you didn't have a girlfriend. Like, I'm- I don't know. I'm surprised you were-" she fumbled for the words.

"A virgin you mean?" he said, bailing her out.

"Yes," she laughed. "I just don't know how that was possible."

He shrugged, looking back out at the storm. "I don't know, Charlotte. I had the option for sure. I just never wanted to before- you know- before I met you," he smiled sideways at her.

She took her feet off of his lap and scooted close to his side, linking her arm under his bicep.

"Same," she said simply.

He pulled her closer, moving his arm around her. "But there you were one day. Just fell out of the sky right in front of me," he grinned down at her. "Hell bent on making me feel like a shitty fisherman. I was a goner."

She threw her head back and laughed loudly, sounding like Rose.

"I just love you," she said it so normal. Like breathing. It made the feeling in his gut pang intensely.

They sat there like that for a long time, waiting for the storm to blow their way. And it did. Just as the sun went down they heard the first drops of rain on the porch roof. They both inhaled the scent and sat in companionable silence listening to the rainfall and the thunder rolling in the distance.

"I think I'm done with the tequila for the night," she laughed. "Feeling a little dizzy."

"Me, too. I don't know what the hell Luis put in this," he said, taking a last sip.

"What time do you have to go do chores in the morning?" she asked.

"Early. I won't wake you, though," he said, rubbing her shoulder.

"No, do. I wanna come with you."

He pulled his body back to look at her. "You do? On your day to sleep in?"

"I don't ever sleep in. I like the mornings," she smiled.

"Ok then, farm girl. I'll wake you." He leaned in and kissed her, putting his hand on her cheek, pulling her closer.

"Are you ready for bed?" she asked quietly.

He nodded. "Am I- I mean, Rose doesn't mind if I sleep in your bed?"

She laughed. "Wyatt, it's not like she thought you'd sleep on the couch."

He nodded, pulling her face back toward him for a brief kiss.

"Ok," he whispered.

"I need to shower. You wanna come inside and wait or sit out here?" she asked.

His palms started to sweat thinking of her in the shower, but he kept his voice level.

"I'll come in. I'll get ready- for bed," he said, fumbling over his words.

They walked inside hand in hand and she showed him to her bedroom. He'd never seen it before and he smiled when he walked in. It looked like her somehow with the bright colored comforter, plants, and books piled high on the dresser. There weren't many personal items in the room, which was to be expected now that he knew how she came here- like a refugee through the night.

"Ok, make yourself at home, I'll be back. Oh, those are the pictures from the 4th," she said pointing to an envelope on the bedside table. "Those are your copies Rose made for you." She turned and removed clothing from the dresser before leaving the room. Wyatt sat down on the edge of the bed and took out the pictures.

He smiled flipping through them all remembering the night. She was stunning of course- happy, smiling brightly by his side, then on his lap, even grinning into his mouth in the one picture Rose had them kiss.

It was only a week ago but for some reason he already had an aching for that day. It was one he'd never forget.

He retrieved his duffle bag and put the pictures protectively inside before changing into a white t-shirt and basketball shorts. He felt self-conscious thinking of her seeing him in his pajamas even though technically she'd seen him in a lot less than that. He sat on the bed and waited, picking up one of the books from the stack titled *Through Time: Regression Therapy*. It was what Rose had told him he should get, regressed into a past life. He still didn't understand the concept but it was thought-provoking to be sure.

He'd wondered about it several times since Rose had mentioned it to him, rolling the idea around in his head to get his bearings on it. He settled on it being a possible concept but a little out there for sure. He was reading the back cover when she walked back into the room- wet hair, pajama pants low on her hips and a tank top with no bra.

"You reading?" she smiled at him.

He looked up at her and tried to keep his face even and not stare at her wet hair hanging over her perfect breasts.

"Yeah," he said, nodding. "Interesting stuff."

She nodded and sat down next to him on the bed. "It really is. I was reading some of it today. It was talking about how we come back with the same people in life after life. The same groups, we just all play different roles."

"Yeah? So last time I could have been, what? The girl? And you could have been the guy?" he grinned at her.

"Maybe," she smiled back at him. "Although hopefully you looked different. You'd make a hideous girl."

He laughed, putting the book back on the stack. "You think?"

"Oh yeah. You're all man."

Wyatt smiled, looking down into her face. He was quite aware of the fact that he was a man, a hopeless one at that. He could think of nothing but laying himself on top of her and kissing her entire body. He was torn, though. He didn't want her thinking that was all he wanted each time he saw her, but every time without fail he couldn't control himself. He told himself to wait. Just wait and be sure that was what she wanted. She stood and pulled the covers back from the bed, scooting toward the far side. She looked up at him and laughed at the nervous look on his face.

"Come on, I still don't bite," she said.

He grinned and climbed in next to her as she snuggled into his chest. She moved her hand up and down his flat stomach and inhaled his scent.

"I love how you smell," she said, breathing in again.

"Yeah?" he smiled. "Even after work?"

"Especially after work. You have this very distinct smell."

He laughed. "Distinct? You do, too. You smell like some kind of oil. Is it lavender?"

She nodded. "I guess. It's what my shampoo is."

He leaned his head over and smelled her wet hair. She was still stroking his stomach but he restrained himself from touching more than her shoulder. They were quiet laying in the bed and listening to the rain that was still coming down.

"Oh wait," she said, climbing out of bed. "I wanna keep the window open to hear the rain."

She crossed the room and moved the curtains apart, pushing open the large window, the sound of the rain coming through even louder. She came by his side of the bed and stood next to him, looking down. She clicked the lamp off but didn't move back into bed. She stood and removed her pajama pants, slowly dropping them to the ground. He could see her in the dim light, perfect and smooth.

"What are you doing?" he asked, sitting up.

"I can't sleep in pants," she said quietly.

She moved standing between his legs as he ran his hands up the sides of her hips, feeling the curve of her.

"I'm ok with that," he said back lowly. He moved his hands up to the bottom of her shirt and pulled it upwards. She helped him remove it over her head so she stood in just her panties in front of him.

"You don't need this either," he whispered, throwing the shirt on the floor. She leaned down to kiss him, starting off sweetly and slowly before pushing him back on the bed and climbing on top of him. He moved his hands all over her body, kissing her hard. He told himself to go slower this time so he wouldn't finish so quickly. He was determined to take his time this time around.

He rolled her over on the bed so he was on top of her, pausing to remove his shirt. Her legs were wrapped around him as he kissed her, losing himself in the warmth of her. He slowed himself and moved down over her body, kissing her breasts and stomach, slowly putting his tongue over her belly button. She breathed heavily, squirming her body around and moving against him.

"Is this ok?" he whispered, pulling down her underwear.

"Yes," she breathed, moving her body so he could take them off.

He sat back on his feet and looked her over, savoring the image of her naked on the bed and nothing in his way. He leaned down again and resumed kissing her body, trailing down her stomach slowly, down under her navel.

"Is this ok?" he asked again, breathing against her soft skin.

"Mmhmm," she panted, as he gently nudged her legs apart.

He kissed down lower, slowly, taking his time until he was all the way down. He placed his lips on her and she responded, sucking in a sharp breath. He kissed her and moved his tongue around the softness of her, acting in tune with her responses. Whatever she liked, he did more of. Ever the perfectionist, he wanted to do it right. She moaned and breathed in ways he hadn't heard before and it was more than he could handle. Finally, he could take no more. He stood abruptly and took a condom from his bag, removing his shorts and putting it on swiftly. She lay still panting on the bed when he came down on top of her, easing her legs apart with his calloused hands.

"I can't wait anymore," he said breathing hard.

He pushed inside of her and groaned, kissing her and holding the back of her head tight.

"Charlotte," he breathed. "Oh my God."

Her fingers dug into his back and she kissed the side of his neck, getting him as close to her as he could. He moved in and out of her, pushing deeper and deeper inside until she cried out.

"Are you alright?" he said, slowing.

"Yes," she panted.

He kissed her, pushing his tongue into her mouth that still moaned quietly for him to keep going, but he couldn't. Her pleading for more of him made him finish entirely and he fell on top of her, struggling for a breath. He moved off of her to the side and pulled her close. He felt drunk with her and it wasn't because of the tequila.

"Oh no, Charlotte," he said, breathing. "What did you do to me?"

⁓⊶❦⊷⁓

He'd loved her two more times before they finally fell asleep late in the evening, exhausted and content with an uninterrupted night of each other. Between work at the ranch and drowning himself in her all night, Wyatt could have slept all day to recover. He felt like he'd only slept ten minutes when she woke him that morning, dressed and ready for chores.

"Wake up, cowboy," she whispered, kissing up his bare back.

Wyatt lay on his stomach, face down into the pillow with only the sheet covering his lower half. He stirred, getting his bearings before rolling over to look at her. She wore jeans and boots with a plaid button up shirt over a black tank top. Her hair was braided down her back and she looked way more well rested than he felt. She smiled down at him, wrinkling up her eyes happily.

"You just gonna sleep all day? We've gotta go do chores."

He smiled, his eyes still half closed. "It's not my fault. The Goddess of Patagonia wouldn't let me sleep all night." He pulled her down into an embrace and she laughed. He was warm from sleep and felt incredible against her but she wasn't to be redirected.

"Oh and you weren't willing, huh? Come on, get dressed. Can't have you getting fired."

She stood and left him to get ready which he did quickly, once he located his clothing strewn about the room. He came out tucking his button down into his work jeans and moved quickly to the bathroom to brush his teeth.

"I made you some coffee and breakfast to go," she said when he came out.

"Really? How long have you been up?"

She shrugged. "About an hour. Wanted to let you sleep as long as you could," she smiled.

He was shocked he hadn't woken since he was generally a light sleeper. His exhaustion was definitely real.

"Thanks," he smiled, taking a to go cup of coffee from her. "You're already the best ranch hand I've ever worked with. For sure the prettiest," he said leaning down to kiss her softly on the lips. "And good morning," he whispered into her face, holding her around the waist.

"Good morning," she said back quietly.

She'd made bagels and cream cheese sandwiched together for each of them. On the drive to the ranch she sat close by his side and handed him one with a napkin wrapped around the bottom half, chewing on her own.

"Are you always this prepared?" he asked appreciatively.

"Only when I can be," she smiled at him. "So what do we need to do? Fix fences or what?"

He laughed. "It does feel like that's all I do, doesn't it? Naw, we just need to feed the horses and chickens. Then maybe check the cattle."

She nodded, looking out the window. "Then what?"

"After chores? I don't know, a nap?" he laughed.

She grinned over at him. "Tired Mr. Earp? Wonder why."

He smiled at her with tight lips, fighting the urge to blush. "I'm having fun with you. Might need to ask Rose if I can move in. Plus, you're a way better cook than I am."

She laughed. "Oh Rose would love that! You'd have to quit work on the ranch though. She'd have you as her pool boy in no time."

"But she doesn't have a pool," he said.

"Exactly," Charlotte winked.

The ranch was quiet on weekend mornings without the other ranch hands there. Wyatt relished those times alone but having her with him was even better. The storm the night before had washed clean the land and left, as always, the incredible fresh scent that Wyatt, Rose, and every other Arizona local had tried to describe to Charlotte. They were right, it was worth the hype. When they parked the truck by the barn, Wyatt got out and assessed the wet land around them.

"We definitely have to go check the cattle after this storm. See where the washes ran and washed out those big crevices?" he said, pointing out to the fields in the distance. "I need to check and make sure it didn't wash out any fences."

Charlotte nodded. "Do these only run during monsoon season?"

"Basically. They can really get moving and be dangerous, too. Don't ever try and cross one in a car or anything. People get swept away constantly doing that."

He brought her around to each horse stall and showed her the process for feeding. Each horse was to get a flake of hay and a cup of oats. She jumped in as soon as she knew the way, and helped him make quick work of feeding all ten horses, stopping to scratch each one on the head and even leaning to kiss a few on the nose. While Wyatt cleaned out the stalls she filled all of the water troughs without being asked, taking time to put fly masks on each horse, gently wrapping the mesh fabric around their faces.

He watched her a stall over, scratching Sunny gently behind the ears. Sunny pushed his large head into her, rubbing against her and she laughed, patting the side of his neck.

"He loves you," Wyatt said, smiling.

"He's my favorite," she said, smiling back at him. "Such a good boy," she said into Sunny's face before kissing his thick neck.

She insisted on helping with another chore but he refused to allow her to shovel manure. He settled on her feeding the chickens and sent her across the yard with instructions. She came back ten minutes later with Garrett walking in step with her, smiling over at her and chatting like a young man.

"Wyatt, why is this beautiful girl doing chores? Damn boy, this is not the best idea for a date!" Garrett said, laughing.

Wyatt grinned. "She insisted, I swear. I didn't let her muck the stalls, though."

Garrett smiled over at Charlotte. "You wanna ride while you're here? Wyatt'll need to check the cattle anyhow- y'all can ride back and check."

Charlotte was overjoyed and walked with Garrett into the barn followed by Wyatt who had finished his stall cleaning.

"Wyatt, I want her on Sunny, ok? He's bomb-proof, that guy. Always steady."

Wyatt smiled thinking of how infrequently he'd been able to use Sunny, who was practically royalty on the ranch. But Garrett was right, she should be on the safest horse. Wyatt took Sunny and Doc out of their stalls and tied them to the hitching post. Garrett handed Charlotte a brush and showed her how to brush down the hair on the horse's back, checking for burrs or anything else that could get stuck under the saddle blanket. She tried to help carry the saddles over but Wyatt would have none of it, only allowing her to carry the saddle blankets over for each horse while he easily hefted the leather saddles onto each of them.

Garrett fussed over her, helping her into her stirrup and up on the horse. Wyatt grinned to himself as he pulled himself up on Doc easily. Charlotte had a way of making everyone want to help her, even if she didn't need it. Garrett even insisted they come back to the house after riding to get a bite to eat after they were done, then he sent them off on their ride.

The two rode off side by side toward the pasture, Wyatt wearing his straw working cowboy hat and Charlotte in his U of A baseball hat that had been on the dash of his truck. He looked over at her perched on Sunny, and was amazed that no matter what she wore or what she was doing, she always looked more beautiful than the time before.

"That hat suits you. Maybe you should go to U of A," he smiled.

"Yeah? I don't know, Rose wants me to look at NAU. Wants to take me up there next weekend," she said, offhandedly. "But Tucson is closer. Maybe I should."

He immediately felt the stabbing pain in his stomach, an empty pit, although he couldn't understand why. He'd be leaving anyway, he reminded himself. It didn't matter if she was in

Flagstaff or Tucson. Wherever she'd be, it would be far from him. He was quiet thinking of it all for a minute and then he nodded, remembering himself.

"It's a good school. You'll like Flagstaff," he said, looking out ahead of where they were riding.

She smiled sideways at him, sensing his true feelings. "I can't go anytime soon, though. I don't even know if I'd be able to get in."

"Of course you would, you're smart. All you do is read," he grinned.

"Well, that's not *all* I do," she said, grinning back. "So show me how far the ranch goes that way. Is all of this Garrett's?"

She succeeded in changing the subject and asked him questions about everything as they rode to the pasture. Wyatt was a natural teacher and liked the idea of showing her things she didn't know about already. The rain had come through the washes hard and it showed. The water beat paths through the desert brush and prairie grass alike.

"See where the fire came through?" he said, pointing to the charred grass. "That'll be so green by next week. It'll be even prettier than the other grass."

He looked over at her and smiled. "I just love how you look on a horse." He brought Doc right alongside Sunny and leaned out of his saddle toward her, tilting his head to get their hats out of the way. He kissed her swiftly since the bumpy ride made it difficult and she smiled back at him.

"Thank you for bringing me here. Garrett's wrong. This is a good date," she smiled.

"Even if you had to do chores?" he laughed.

"Oh yeah," she nodded. "Chores and all."

"I thought your favorite date was your birthday," he said, smiling shyly.

She sighed, looking out around her. "I don't know, Wyatt. I think they're all my favorite. You're my favorite," she said, smiling sweetly at him.

He was surprised to feel his face flush through, but he smiled back anyway. "Same," he said, looking into her eyes.

They let the silence of the morning take them over then, feeling the steady rhythm of the horses' hooves moving them through the grassy landscape. The morning was clean after the rains, creating a renewed energy that Charlotte could feel as plain as day. They rode the fence line of the pasture, checking for any breaches, but they found none. The cattle, too, were enjoying the fresh green morning, grazing the new sprigs of grass already popping up.

"Look," Wyatt pointed, "that wash is still running."

They pulled the horses over to the small wash running through the prairie, both looking down into the water. The wash had run hard the night before, washing out a five foot wide path that left behind debris and smoothed over sand. The small trickling still carried sticks and pieces of cactus floating down it. Charlotte looked toward the other side and squinted at something on the side of the wash.

"What is that?" she pointed. "Is that a rat?"

A small gray fur ball was seemingly clinging to the wash wall, hardly visible, but Wyatt saw it immediately.

"Let's go see," he said, leading Doc to cross the wash. Doc hopped to the side a bit, skittish about the water, but Wyatt controlled him beautifully, kicking firmly and keeping a tight rein on his neck. Sunny, true to Garrett's description, was bomb proof and crossed without complaint. They both dismounted on the other side, Charlotte holding the horses while Wyatt went to investigate. He crouched down to see if the animal was alive and it was, he could see its small stomach rise and fall.

"It's a baby rabbit," he said, surprised. "Must have been washed out of his nest in the storm."

He gently scooped the bunny into his large hands and walked back toward Charlotte. The animal did not look good, its eyes hardly open and its demeanor listless. Charlotte all but squealed when she saw it resting in his hands.

"Awe! Poor little thing. Can we help it?"

Wyatt shrugged. "I don't know. I don't know much about rabbits. He doesn't look so hot."

"He's gotta be warm," she said. "I remember that."

He looked at her and grinned. "Let me guess, you've read about wild rabbits before?"

She laughed. "No, actually. I- I had a few when I was little once. At Joe's house," she said looking down at the bunny to break eye contact with him. "I remember when they're little they have to be really warm."

She reached her hands out and placed them over his, cradling the tiny fuzzy ball. He looked at her face set with intention and concern and he smiled.

"Here, you hold him. We can head back and ask Garrett what he thinks we can do."

She carefully took the bunny from him and put it between her breasts, cradling it close. Wyatt knew that Garrett was a ranch man and had no time for saving the lives of wild animals displaced in a storm, especially a baby bunny. He also knew, though, that his boss was a sucker for Charlotte and would probably do anything he could to help the bunny because of that.

They rode back to the barn side by side, Charlotte with one hand on the reins and the other holding the bunny against her. She tucked it just under her shirt between her breasts and held it tight. Wyatt widened his eyes under his cowboy hat.

"That is a very lucky bunny," he smiled.

She threw her head back, laughing. "You jealous?"

"Very," he said.

They rode back to the barn where Wyatt helped Charlotte off of Sunny so she could continue cradling the little fur ball. He insisted that he could unsaddle alone while she went to find Garrett, so she reluctantly set off to find him, leaving Wyatt in the quiet barn to take care of the horses. He unsaddled each of them then took them to the yard to spray them off with the hose, taking care to brush the sweaty places the saddle sat. He'd smell like wet horse when he was done but he had no choice. He'd have to shower at her place.

When he was finished he found her on the front porch of the main house, sitting close to Garrett. They were hunched over the bunny wrapped in a dish towel, feeding it milk from an eyedropper.

"That's right," Garrett was saying, "just little drops right in his mouth. They only need to eat about twice a day. If you can keep him alive he can eat hay and grain in another couple of weeks."

Charlotte was holding the bundle with one hand and feeding it with the other while listening intently to Garrett.

"Where should I keep him? Where should he sleep?" she asked.

"They like a tight place like their nest, so something small and cozy for them."

Wyatt looked at Garrett, the tobacco-chewing cattle rancher he knew so well. He could have laughed out loud to see him fussing over a baby bunny, but he held his tongue. Charlotte looked up and saw him standing at the bottom of the steps and smiled.

"Garrett thinks he might make it. We need to take him home and get him all better."

Wyatt nodded. "I had no idea you knew so much about bunnies, Mr. Garrett."

"Well," Garrett smiled, "you're here on earth long enough and you learn how to do just about everything," he beamed over at Charlotte. "Can't say no to this sweet girl, either. Come on, let me feed you. Least I can do after Wyatt made you do chores on a date."

They sat in Garrett's kitchen and ate turkey sandwiches and chips, Garrett's standard lunch. Wyatt volunteered his cowboy hat as a nest for the rabbit who slept wrapped in a dish towel snug in the hat, its full belly looking like it might burst. Charlotte asked Garrett endless questions about the ranch and his life, listening to all of the answers which Garrett ate up, of course. Life on the ranch was often lonely. He loved having company, especially Charlotte who lit up his dreary kitchen with her laughter and interest.

"How long have you lived here, Mr. Garrett?" she asked, pouring him a glass of tea.

"All my life, really. Grew up in Elgin, right next to Sonoita," he said.

"That's where we saw the antelope," Wyatt said.

Charlotte smiled back and nodded. "Real pretty over there. And have you always been a cattle rancher? Your family I mean."

"You bet. Family business. Only, that ends with me I guess. My boys want no part of it. One's in real estate, other's a lawyer," he shook his head. "Much easier to make money that way, I guess."

Charlotte shrugged. "Well, that means you raised successful kids, though. Bet they learned a lot of important things growing up here."

Garrett beamed at her, then looked to Wyatt. "You realize what a catch you got here? Beautiful and smart?"

Wyatt blushed briefly but looked at her anyway. "Yes, sir. I do."

Charlotte chatted on with Garrett, listening closely to his responses and laughing at his jokes. It was afternoon by the time they left back to the house with Charlotte holding her new pet on her lap, tucked in Wyatt's hat. He looked over at her petting the bunny gently and smiled. She could hardly take her eyes off of it, her concern for its survival obvious.

"I think we should name her Bailey," she said when they were almost home.

"Bailey?" he asked.

She nodded. "After your hat. I love that name."

He laughed. "Ok, Bailey it is. Maybe we could find Bailey a new nest when we get home so she doesn't pee in that one," he grinned.

When they arrived home, Charlotte put Bailey in a shoebox lined with towels and set the box in a warm place near the kitchen window. The bunny slept deeply, still worn out from the death-defying activities of the day. Charlotte and Wyatt were likewise exhausted from the morning chores and lack of sleep from the night before. They agreed that Bailey had the right idea, a nap would be in their best interest.

Wyatt sat at the kitchen table watching Charlotte remove her boots and socks. He pulled his off as well and smelled his filthy work stench. He couldn't get in her bed like that.

"Is it ok if I shower?" he asked almost shyly.

"Of course," she said. "I need one, too." She cut her eyes at him just slightly and he smiled.

"You wanna-" he faltered for the words, "you wanna get in with me?"

She nodded, locking eyes with him.

He swallowed hard and tried not to look nervous to no avail. They were quiet walking to the bathroom together, the anticipation thick between them. They stood in front of each other outside of the shower curtain and Charlotte smiled up at him after turning on the shower. She stood on her toes and kissed him softly on the lips and moved her hands to unbutton his work shirt. She pulled it off of his shoulders and ran her hands over his chest and down to his waistline.

"Cowboy Adonis," she grinned. "Rose is right."

He blushed but pulled her in for a slow kiss before she could realize he was red, yet again. He pulled her tank top off over her head, discarding it on the floor as she unhooked her bra and let it drop. He moved his hands over her breasts, looking down over her body.

"You're so perfect," he said quietly before kissing her again. "Sorry, I know I smell like a horse."

She giggled in his mouth. "So do I. Let's get in."

She dropped her pants and underwear so quickly and unashamed that he followed suit and climbed in the shower after her. He watched the water drip down her hair and over her curvy bottom and had to work to catch his breath. Clearly, there would be no hiding his feelings about how she looked. She turned to face him, pulling him under the stream of water with her, and kissed him deeply as the water washed over them.

"Here, you get under. I'm hogging the water."

They maneuvered around each other so Wyatt was completely under the water and she stood outside of it to wash her hair. He scrubbed himself clean quickly since he knew he might get sidetracked again.

"Let me smell that." He grabbed the shampoo bottle out of her hands and smelled the top. "I love that smell," he grinned. "Smells like you."

She smiled, scrubbing her hair clean. "Let me wash your hair with it."

He put his head down in front of her so his eyes looked right down to her naked body. He put his hands on the sides of her hips and pulled her closer.

"You better close your eyes," she laughed. "You're gonna get soap in them."

"Worth it," he mumbled, but closed them anyway and let her work her fingers through his thick black hair, the sensation almost lulling him to sleep.

"Ok, rinse," she said.

He put his hair back into the water washing it clean, and moved so she could do the same. He watched her with her eyes closed and her hands above her head scrubbing out the shampoo and he almost couldn't believe how beautiful she was. He was sometimes taken off guard at how intense his feelings for her were. He had a hard time remembering what life was like before his nights were spent loving her and his days were spent thinking of her. She opened her eyes and caught him staring.

"You wanna take a nap now?" she asked.

"No," he said. "No, I don't."

They got out of the shower and dried themselves off, staying wrapped in their towels. Charlotte hastily brushed through her tangled hair before Wyatt grabbed her hand and walked her down the hallway to her bedroom. He stood in front of her and leaned down to kiss her, wrapping his arms tightly around her waist, kissing her harder and harder until she could hardly breathe.

"Charlotte," he panted. "Can I have you? Please?"

She answered him by dropping her towel down to her feet and pulling his from his waist and letting it, too, drop. He eased her down on the bed and kissed the length of her body, exploring her in the daylight of the room. He worked his way down her, moving her legs apart again and kissing her the same way he had the night before, only better this time. She breathed heavily and moaned until she shook with release and he was satisfied with a job well done. When he entered her this time he went slow, moving his face in front of hers and looking into her eyes as he moved rhythmically in and out of her.

"Wyatt," she said, her face pleading. "More," she panted, pulling him closer.

He moved his legs under hers so he could push deeper inside and she responded, moaning louder.

"Charlotte," he panted into her mouth. "I don't want to stop."

He loved her like that for a long time, stopping to look at her gorgeous flushed face and brow furrowed in pleasure before finally releasing himself.

"I thought you wanted to nap? You trying to kill me?" he panted looking sideways at her.

She giggled and snuggled close to his side. "You can nap now," she said kissing the side of his cheek. There was quiet between them, the exhaustion setting in. They moved in closer, both falling fast asleep wrapped in each other.

He woke to dusk falling through the curtains of the room and it took him several moments to get his bearings on the time. He finally realized it was evening and they'd not yet had dinner but seemingly slept the afternoon away. He was alone in the bed, naked and covered in only a sheet. He rose quickly and pulled his jeans over his naked body, retrieving a fresh t-shirt from his duffle bag. He walked out of her room and saw her then, but stayed quiet. She was sitting on the front porch with the door wide open so he could only see her profile. She had Bailey in her hands wrapped in a small towel, feeding her with the dropper.

The evening sun shone through her wild blonde hair, making her look like an angel. She wore a flowered sundress and no shoes, sitting with her legs tucked under her, looking down at the bunny in her hands. She turned to look at him and he smiled shyly.

"Sorry I slept so long. How long have you been up?" he asked.

"Just a little while," she smiled up at him. "Had to feed the baby."

He nodded and crouched down next to her, reaching out to pet it.

"She looks better," he said, scrutinizing the bunny.

"You think it's a she now?" she smiled.

He shrugged. "Bailey is a good girl's name. So yeah."

She looked him up and down settling back on his sleepy face.

"You were tired. You slept a long time, Mr. Earp."

He shook his head, feigning concern. "You're just wearing me out, babe."

He moved to sit next to her on the porch and took the bunny out of her hands and held it, looking it over.

"She looks stronger. And fatter," he laughed. "She's eating well."

He stroked the top of her with his large finger and Charlotte watched him closely. His t-shirt was tight around his biceps and for once he had bare feet under the hem of his jeans. His hair was messy from sleep and his eyes still sensitive to the light. He was beautiful fresh from sleep like that and she wanted to tell him so, but she stopped herself.

"What time is it?" he asked, confused.

She shrugged. "I think around 6."

He shook his head, laughing. "You should have woken me up. I almost slept through dinner."

"You hungry? What can I make you?" she asked.

He looked up at her, still stroking the bunny slowly. She was scrubbed clean of any makeup and he was fairly certain she wasn't wearing a bra or underwear under her thin sundress. Yes, he was hungry.

"Let me take you out to dinner. I don't want you to have to cook. You've been busy doing chores for me and taking care of the baby, after all," he smiled at her, scrunching up his eyes.

"Ok," she smiled. "Let me just go get changed."

He shook his head sternly. "No, no. I want you to wear that," he said, looking her over again. "Please," he grinned.

She laughed and pulled the fabric from her body. "Wyatt, it's like a house dress. I at least need to put on a bra."

"Yes, do that," he grinned. "I can see right through it." He reached out a hand and brushed the side of her

266

stomach and ribs, confirming that it was all her underneath.

They settled on staying in town for dinner since it was already so late. After getting Bailey cozy back in her nest, Wyatt pulled his boots back on and waited for Charlotte to finish dressing. She did in fact put a bra on and although he wasn't sure about the panties, he certainly planned on finding out. She'd pulled her hair up in a messy bun on top of her head and put on a touch of makeup. She looked like a flower child in her dress, as wild and unruly as the desert. He grinned up at her from his place on the couch.

"On second thought," he said, his white teeth sparkling. "I don't know if we need to eat, do we?"

He pulled her toward him so that she was standing with her stomach in his face.

"Yes!" she laughed. "I'm actually starving, so yeah, we need dinner."

He shook his head and pulled her down on top of him so that she straddled him on the couch. He moved his hands over her bottom feeling his way around.

"Knew it," he mumbled, kissing her neck.

"What?" she said, squirming.

"How can you expect me to go to dinner when you're not wearing panties?" he said, kissing her hard.

She giggled into his mouth. "Consider it motivation to get home. Now let's go before I change my mind."

She pulled a reluctant Wyatt off of the couch and they walked through town to dinner. There would be no storm that day, but the temperature was still much nicer than it had been before the rains started. They held hands and walked down the sidewalk, talking about their day. About Bailey and about Garrett being so sweet about a bunny of all things.

"That's what you do to people. They can't say no to you," he smiled, looking down at her.

She laughed. "Oh believe me, plenty of people have told me no before. Garrett's just a sweetheart."

"Careful," Wyatt said, joking. "I might get jealous again."

"Of Garrett?" she said laughing.

"Oh yeah. Anyone. I'm even jealous of that bunny. Snuggled all in your chest like that. Not fair."

She hugged up close to his side, pulling his bicep against her. "Well, I already told you that you're my favorite so don't worry. Remember, I'm not a bullshitter," she said, pulling at his arm.

They decided on The Velvet Elvis for pizza again, mostly because the Mexican restaurant looked crowded. They hadn't been back there since their first date and Wyatt marveled at how far they'd come since then. Was it just over a month ago? Was that all the time that she'd had to root her way so firmly into the corners of his heart?

"I'll sit on the same side as you this time," she said, thinking of the last time they'd been there also. "You know, since you're not afraid of me anymore or anything."

He let her in the booth first and reached his hand out to slap her rump discreetly as she moved by him. They were both ravenous and ordered a large pizza with the works, knowing full well they could finish it.

While they waited they chatted quietly, their heads together laughing and smiling, oblivious to anything else but what was happening at their table.

"Wyatt," she said as they were finishing. "I really want to pay, ok?"

He laughed and waved her off. "You know the rules!" he grinned. "I invited you so I get to pay. Fair and square."

She shook her head and her face looked more serious. "No, really. I don't like how you pay for everything. And you got me those boots. I saw them at the feed store, Wyatt. Those were expensive." Her brow was furrowed together in concern, but he couldn't help but laugh.

"Babe, really. It's not a big deal. I just can't let you pay for things. Why does it bother you so much?"

She shrugged and looked away from him. "I just know about money. You know, how hard you have to work to make it. I just don't want you to waste it."

"Well, I'm not wasting it. I like doing it, ok?" She sat quietly and still wouldn't look at him, but she nodded. "Plus, I don't need this money anyway. Soon I'll be living rent-free. Three squares a day," he said, exhaling.

"Sure, rent-free. You just had to sign your life away." She said it so quickly that she didn't realize how it could have come out until she saw him look down at the table, avoiding her gaze.

"Wyatt, I'm sorry. That came out wrong. I just meant that- I don't know what I meant actually. I'm sorry."

He shook his head and mustered a smile. "Naw, it's ok. I know what you meant. I guess it's not really rent free," he smiled sadly. "But either way, I'm buying dinner."

"Ok," she smiled up at him. "I won't fight you anymore," she said, kissing his cheek softly. "Can I buy you ice cream?"

He nodded, looking down into her eyes. "Yeah, but what about you wasting your money? You need it, college girl."

She laughed. "You'd be surprised how little I can live off of."

He shook his head. "It wouldn't surprise me. You're pretty tough, Charlotte," he said seriously. "Tell me how you got here. How'd you get the money I mean?"

She turned red then, her face completely flushed through, embarrassed for him to see that part of her. That poor girl, who scraped and saved just for a bus ticket. It made her feel dirty, pathetic.

She sighed. "Alright then," she smiled at him. "Since I've told you so much already." She took a deep breath and looked away again. "I used to go to the library every day after school and I made friends with the librarian. She- she was like an angel to me. Just wanted to help me for no reason. One day she just offered me a job out of the blue. I think because I was always there helping anyway. So I worked at the library every day when I was done with school. And I did any odd jobs I could find, too. Weed pulling- babysitting. I cleaned a couple of houses. I collected recycling to cash in," she shrugged. "Just basically everything. I saved and saved. Kept my money on me at all times so no one could- you know, so no one could take it."

He was quiet listening to her, his face stoic thinking of what it must have been for her.

Charlotte paused, thinking of telling him the whole truth, but decided against it. "Rose said it was because I prayed. I prayed for a way to leave and then those opportunities just found me."

"Did you?" he asked, interested.

She shrugged. "I don't know. I know I begged for help. Just didn't know who I was begging at the time," she smiled up at him. "But it happened, and here I am."

Her face was drawn and serious as she spoke about it, even though she smiled. He felt an ache in his gut and a fierce need to protect her, thinking of her alone and begging for help. There was a physical pain in his chest just hearing it. He had no words for her. There was no way to take away what had happened to her. No way to fix it now, as much as he wanted to.

"Here you are," he said quietly, kissing the side of her head and pulling her close.

⚬⟡⚬

They walked home with the ice cream cones melting under the setting sun. The next day Rose would be home and he'd have to go back to the ranch. They'd go back to stealing minutes together, ducking into corners to find places to love each other. The weekend had brought them even closer, more in love and connected than ever and they both felt it.

She sighed heavily as they walked home. "I don't want the weekend to be over," she said sadly.

"Me either. But we still have tonight," he smiled shyly. "What do you want to do? You want to go anywhere?"

She shook her head. "No. I kinda like it just us. At home. Oh, Bailey, too," she smiled.

"You're a good mama," he said, putting an arm around her shoulders. "Do you ever wanna have kids?"

She looked at him with her eyebrows raised and he laughed at her expression.

"I don't mean now!" he said. "I mean, one day. You want to have a family?"

She shrugged. "I don't know actually. It's kinda scary for me. I don't know if I'd be good at that."

"You?" he said shocked. "You'd be a great mom. You're doing a hell of a job with that bunny," he smiled.

She laughed but still looked uncomfortable. "Yeah, I just don't know if I'm nurturing enough."

She thought of her mom then, how detached she was from Charlotte her whole life. Would that be her? She'd read about nature versus nurture and she was worried, always had been, that she'd turn out just like her mother. Distant, cold, jealous of her own daughter. No, she didn't think it would be worth the risk. Wyatt was being kind as always, but she couldn't be shaken from what she knew would be true, so she changed the subject instead.

"What about you?" she asked. "You want a family?"

He shrugged. "I guess. That's what I've always thought I'd have someday, anyway."

He wanted to tell her he wanted all of that with her. That if he could have his way, he'd marry her before boot camp even started, but he knew it would scare her. He knew it wasn't time. They were kids, he knew that, but that couldn't keep him from dreaming of it any chance he got. He knew, even then, there would be no one else he'd ever feel the way he felt about her. He didn't remember begging for it, or praying for it, but yes, there she was. Everything.

When they got home Bailey was squirming around her shoebox, looking much more agile than she did that morning. Charlotte cooed at her.

"Look at you! You're doing such a good job. Such a strong girl," she said, bringing her to her lips and kissing the gray fur.

Wyatt watched her smiling, wanting to remind her of what kind of mother she would make, but he thought better of it. She'd looked truly terrified when he'd brought it up before and he didn't want to scare her again.

There was no rain to watch that evening so they decided on a movie instead, browsing Rose's shelves until they found one vaguely familiar. Neither of them had ever seen *Gone with the Wind*, although Charlotte had read it several times before and knew the storyline by heart.

"Scarlett O'Hara. That's in a Waylon Jennings' song," he said when the movie started.

"It is? Which one?"

"Belle of the ball," he said. "It goes, 'like Scarlett O'Hara loved no one but wanted them all.'"

Charlotte laughed. "Oh my gosh, Waylon knew his stuff. That's her. See? You know poetry, Wyatt."

He laughed. "I don't know about that. I do know a lot of songs though."

"Same thing," she said and snuggled into him on the couch, cradling Bailey against her neck as she did.

He made a deal with himself that he would watch the entire movie without gluing himself to her. It was a minute-by-minute struggle but somehow, he succeeded. This was in part due to the fact that the movie really was fascinating and had everything from war to love involved. He was floored at the ending though.

"That's it? They don't end up together?" he said, disappointed.

"I know. Every time I read the book I hope it'll end up different somehow. It never does. Obviously."

"How many times have you read it?" he asked.

She shrugged. "I don't know. Probably five? I always want her to end up with Rhett, though."

"Yeah?" he said grinning. "Not an Ashley fan?"

She made a face. "Yuck, no. He's so girly."

Wyatt really laughed then, in love with her honesty and her inability to hide her real feelings about anything.

"Well, I hope I'm more Rhett then," he said grinning.

Charlotte got up to put Bailey back in her nest but kept talking even as she walked away.

"No, you're not Rhett. I mean, certainly way more Rhett than Ashley. Definitely manly but way sweeter than Rhett," she smiled over her shoulder.

"You're starting to give me a complex, Charlotte," he joked. "I can't be sweet in the Marine Corps, you know."

She finished tucking Bailey in for the night and crossed the room back to him. She still wore her sundress and bare feet, her hair back down wild around her face.

"You can be tough and sweet at the same time, Wyatt."

He nodded, looking her up and down. "Like you?"

She looked down at him and smiled shyly. "I'm not that tough. Or sweet," she laughed as he pulled her toward him, holding both of her hands.

"You are," he whispered. "Will you come here, please?" he asked, pulling her on top of him on the couch again.

He hugged her tight against him and buried his face in her chest, inhaling her. She wrapped her arms around his neck and tangled her hands in his thick black hair, thinking of how they would shave it all off in boot camp. His thick, slightly curly, beautiful head of hair would be gone.

"I don't want you to go," she whispered in his ear.

"What, tomorrow?" he asked.

She pulled back and looked him in the face, shaking her head. "No, I don't want you to leave at all," she said, looking at him sadly.

He locked eyes with her then and realized what it must have looked like to her. All this time he'd felt bad for himself for having to leave her. He hadn't thought about Charlotte. Charlotte who never had anyone she could count on. Charlotte who scraped together coins to escape her life. Charlotte who had to stare the devil down at 12 years old but still gave all of herself to Wyatt, loving him despite it all. Charlotte who would once again be losing something she loved. He felt selfish for never having considered it before she put it right in front of him, showing him with her bottomless green eyes just how much it would hurt her. He stared back at her and said the only thing he could say.

"I'm sorry, Charlotte. I'm sorry."

He grabbed her face with both of his hands and kissed her softly, slowly, until she moved her arms around him again and kissed him deeper, pushing herself closer to him all the time. He moved his hands back over her bottom and held her as he stood with her wrapped around him. He walked to the bedroom with her clinging to him.

He laid her down gently and stood at the foot of the bed to undress himself. She watched him in the dim light of the room, aching for his touch. She sat up and pulled her sundress over her head and discarded her bra. He would have made a joke about her not wearing underwear but he didn't feel happy. He felt desperate for her, gutted at what he knew was coming, and he knew she felt the same. He moved on top of her and brushed her hair out of her face, studying her perfect plump lips and sad green eyes looking up at him.

"It's like it's getting worse," he said seriously.

"What's getting worse?" she asked sadly.

"It hurts, Charlotte. I'm serious. My heart. It's like it hurts. I know that sounds dumb."

She shook her head, stroking his face. "No. No, it doesn't," she leaned up to kiss his lips. "I hurt, too," she whispered.

He smiled. "That means you really do love me, then, huh?"

"How could I not love you?" she asked earnestly.

When she kissed him she moved her legs apart and pulled him toward her, reaching her hand down to guide him inside. The both exhaled, relieved when they were joined. He loved her slow and steady, not stopping until she released herself several times and was entirely spent. He finally finished and rolled to the side of her, completely exhausted. Her breathing started to deepen in no time and he could tell she was already falling asleep.

"Thank you," he whispered.

"Hmm?" she said groggily. "For what?"

"For loving me back," he said and she moved in closer, not having the words to tell him what he was to her.

V

*"It is not in the stars to hold our destiny
but in ourselves."*
~William Shakespeare

Flagstaff was not as she imagined it would be. Rose had told her it was in the forest, high in the pines, but somehow she was still shocked to see a place like that. High mountain peaks canvassed the sky creating a stunning backdrop for the town, and the smell of pine trees hung thick in the air. Charlotte marveled at the temperature which hovered around 80 degrees, a stark contrast from the oppressive summer heat at Rose's.

The town itself was small, much bigger than Patagonia but certainly not like some of the cities she'd lived in. It was packed with people, tourists there enjoying the summer weather ready to tour the Grand Canyon, only an hour's drive away. Shops and restaurants lined the streets and pedestrians were everywhere. It, like Patagonia, reminded her of a miniature Denver. The people were all dressed casually, "outdoorsy hippies", as Rose called them. She fell in love with the town immediately but as always, tried not to get her hopes up about moving there.

They'd left the house before the sun came up that Friday morning, wanting to make it to town before the admissions office closed for the weekend. Rose insisted they stay a couple of nights and see the sights and Charlotte was excited, but disappointed to leave Wyatt back in Patagonia, which suddenly seemed so far away. Rose invited him, even offered to call Garrett to get him out of work, but there was no way since the new shipment of cattle would be there that very day and there would be hours of work to do- sorting, branding, feeding. No, as much as he wanted to go, he couldn't.

The week before had gone quickly once Rose got home from Phoenix and Charlotte and Wyatt had gone back to meeting at the lake in the afternoons, loving under the shaded trees, the cab of his truck, wherever they could. They'd been spoiled by a weekend uninterrupted by anyone or anything and instead of quenching their desires, it only made it worse. Wyatt was out of his head with her, able to only think of her and her perfect soft body against his. Charlotte felt the same, finding herself distracted at the shop, thinking of him and worrying about the war. She'd continued her reading about the Marine Corps and she liked nothing about what she learned. Marines, devil dogs, leathernecks, jarheads, no matter what they were called, they didn't describe her Wyatt.

What was worse were the dreams that began as soon as she started the book. Wyatt in water, yelling for help where she couldn't reach him. Wyatt sitting alone and ignoring her when she talked to him, his eyes cold as stone like the boys in the pictures. And, worst of all, Wyatt at war, filthy with the dusty desert and looking for something he couldn't find. She'd woken up several times that week disturbed by what she saw and each time she did as Rose taught her, she prayed. She prayed for him to have strength, for him to have faith, and most of all, for him to come home safe. She didn't tell him about the dreams but instead clung to him even more when they saw each other. She knew he needed her in some way, her dreams told her as much, but she didn't want to worry him.

She tried to forget about her dreams, and stop her incessant thinking of Wyatt so she could focus on Flagstaff, focus on college, although she knew she didn't belong there. There would be no college that would take her, surely. Her grades were just ok, she had no special talents, and most importantly she was Lily Holt's daughter. No, a girl like her was not good enough for college, but she would humor her aunt.

They made it to town just around noon and went directly to campus, even though Rose was dangerously hungry and starting to border on cranky. The walk through campus was beautiful. The old brick buildings with large white pillars were flanked with aspen trees blowing softly in the summer breeze.

Rose and Charlotte walked side by side as Rose pointed out different buildings.

"I can't believe you didn't come here, Aunt Rose," Charlotte said looking around her. "How do you know where everything is?"

"Life experience, my dear! No, really, I took a couple of yoga courses here but I never enrolled officially. Not like you will," she said, smiling over at her.

Charlotte remained quiet and avoided eye contact. How could she tell her sweet aunt that she was wrong? That now that she was here, on the beautiful campus alive with things she knew nothing about, that she knew she stood no chance. She expected someone to pop out of the bushes at any moment and tell her she wasn't even smart enough to even be there. College, as her mother had told her over and over again, was not for a girl like her.

The admissions building was smaller than she imagined, but intimidating nonetheless. Charlotte and Rose walked through the white pillars and into an empty lobby. The secretary desk was vacant, as were the chairs in the waiting room. The room echoed with emptiness and made it even scarier for Charlotte. She tried to slow her breathing and repeat her mantra in her head.

I am loved. Let me have peace. I am loved.

It didn't work. Her hands were sweating and she felt like turning to run out of the building, especially when they couldn't find anyone working. But Rose was nothing if not persistent. She walked several hallways, throwing her hands up in cranky impatience when she finally found someone. A middle-aged woman sat at her desk with glasses perched at the end of her nose. She had long gray hair braided down her back and her tanned wrinkled face was free of any makeup at all. She wore Tiva Sandals and cropped jeans rolled to just below her knee, exuding the common casual theme they'd seen around town.

"Can I help you?" she said looking up from her desk over her glasses, assessing the women head to toe.

"God, I hope so," Rose said, exacerbated. "We're looking to speak to someone about my niece attending school here."

The woman looked to Charlotte noting the exposed inches of her tanned stomach and her jeans tight on her curved hips. She didn't move her head or change her posture, only her eyes moved assessing the girl.

"Have you graduated high school?" she asked.

Charlotte nodded.

"What's your GPA?"

"I don't know exactly," Charlotte replied.

"Have you taken your SATs?" she said shortly.

"No ma'am," Charlotte said quietly.

The woman looked back at the papers on her desk and continued highlighting.

"You can't come here if you haven't taken your SATs or if your GPA is too low. Try the community college."

Charlotte looked down at her feet, her cheeks hot with embarrassment and shame. It was just as she thought it would be, this was not the place for someone like her. Rose, though, was indignant.

"Really?" she said, drawing out the word. "That's the only way to attend this school? There's no other way?" she said putting her hands on her hips and cocking her head.

The woman shrugged. "Plenty of other ways- just not something we deal with here. Again, that's a community college issue. Not really a division one thing."

"It's ok, Aunt Rose. Let's just go. We can check there instead," Charlotte said, turning to leave.

Rose put her hand out and on Charlotte's shoulder, stopping her. "We most certainly will not. Do you know the dumbasses I know who have college degrees? I'm not buying it. There are other ways."

That got the woman's attention. She rotated her chair to face Rose and looked up at her with an annoyed smirk on her face.

"Again, there are other ways. Community college," she said, staring Rose in the face.

"I'm going to need to speak to someone else," Rose said sternly.

"Why is that?" the woman replied.

"Because I don't think you're smart enough to help my brilliant niece here. I also don't like the shitty look on your face." Rose turned on her heel grabbing Charlotte's arm and walked farther down the hallway, ignoring the woman's annoyed response behind her.

"Now this is a good spiritual lesson, my dear. If some asshole says no, there's always another asshole to try after that one. And another after that."

Charlotte couldn't even bring herself to laugh, she looked down at her feet as her aunt shuffled her down the hallway. Rose looked sideways at her.

"And another lesson. Don't ever let anyone fuck with you. Get your chin up where it belongs."

Charlotte obeyed, putting her chin level with the ground. She mustered a smile and Rose reached out and squeezed her hand. They walked up a flight of stairs to more empty offices and a waiting room until they heard soft music coming from an office toward the end of a long hallway. Rose hustled Charlotte toward the noise and stood just outside the door. The woman at the desk was younger than the other woman, somewhere in her mid-30's. She was plain, yet beautiful, with a loose brown bun tied at the base of her neck. She smiled up from her desk when she saw the women in the hallway.

"Hello," she said warmly. "Can I help you ladies find something?"

"Yes, please," Rose said, her demeanor completely changed from the previous encounter. "My niece would like to talk to someone about her options for attending NAU. Maybe in the spring semester?"

The woman looked to Charlotte and smiled, nodding her head. "I can help! Come on in and sit down, let's chat. I'm Flower, by the way."

Rose laughed. "Beautiful name. I'm Rose, another flower, and this is my Charlotte."

Charlotte stuck her hand out and shook Flower's hand firmly but could hardly look her in the eye. Flower smiled at Charlotte, scrunching up her eyes.

"Nice to meet you both," she said, conscious of Charlotte's nerves.

She pulled out a notepad and spun her chair around to face the women. She settled herself in her chair and crossed her legs casually.

"Ok Charlotte, tell me about you. What do you like to study, where did you attend high school? Extracurricular activities. Anything and everything."

Charlotte swallowed hard and looked at her Aunt. She could feel her heart beating in her chest and the embarrassment from earlier creeping back in. *Let me have peace. Let me have peace.* She repeated in her head.

"Well I- I graduated in San Antonio, Texas in May. And I- I really like books. Literature. I read a lot."

Flower smiled warmly. "Me, too," she said. "I'm getting my masters in English here right now actually."

She'd meant it to be relatable, but it made Charlotte feel even more intimidated.

"So what about extracurricular things? What else did you do in high school?"

Charlotte thought about the times she had sat outside the school watching other kids go to their respective groups- sports, clubs, activities. All things which required money. Also things you had to know how to do, years of practice already under those other kids' belts. Nothing. She had nothing to offer.

Charlotte raised her head and looked in Flower's face. She decided to be truthful.

"I didn't do anything. I worked a lot. My mom and I moved around and she needed my help so I couldn't really- I wasn't able to join anything else. I worked at a library before I left so I know how to categorize books and things but I- I don't really have any special talents or anything. I've never played any sports or been part of any clubs."

Rose sat quietly by her side, allowing Charlotte to own her truth, but Charlotte could feel her wanting to reach out and hold her. Still, she remained quiet. Flower looked at Charlotte and nodded sympathetically.

"I'm sure you have talents," she said quietly. "In fact, I think it counts for more than extracurricular activities if you were helping your family out," she said smiling at Charlotte and then looking over at Rose. "Tell me, Charlotte, are you the first person in your family to attend college?"

"Yes, ma'am. I think so."

Flower nodded and spun her chair around. She grabbed a thick packet off of her desk and turned back to face the women.

"Charlotte, there are some great opportunities for you here. Scholarships and grants available to you because you'd be the first to go to college. You'll need to take some placement tests and we'd have to do a lot of paperwork. It's a difficult process to navigate but I'd love to help you," she smiled at Charlotte looking her in the eye. "I have a feeling you would really love it here."

Charlotte smiled shyly at Flower and nodded her head, working hard to keep her emotions in check. Rose beamed over at her from the chair next to her and Charlotte's mind went back to their meditation from the day before, Rose's lesson echoing in her mind.

Rose had sat across from her before closing her eyes to meditate. She looked thoughtfully at her niece and sighed heavily.

"Grace is everywhere. Love is everywhere. Good is everywhere. Sometimes we just have to dig a little deeper to find it."

✿

It was hours later that Charlotte emerged from the building. Rose had excused herself to find food since she could not be trusted if she grew any hungrier. Charlotte saw her sitting under a large pine tree in the lawn in front of the admissions building, a smile stretching across her face when she saw her niece.

"Well, well, well," she said, sitting cross-legged and looking up at her. "If it isn't Miss Brontë. How did it go?"

Charlotte grinned back at her and sat down facing her under the shaded tree.

"She thinks I'll be able to get in for spring," Charlotte said, trying to keep the giddiness she felt out of her voice.

Rose slapped her hands together. "Hot damn! What did I tell you? Turns out old grumpy pants was wrong, huh?"

Charlotte shook her head briefly but kept smiling. "Not entirely, no. I do need to take a couple of classes at a community college this semester. But Flower said I'll be able to test out of several."

Rose waved a hand. "Piece of cake! Here, eat. I brought you a sandwich. Thought I might snap if I didn't find food. Now tell me everything!"

Charlotte went on to recount her hours in Flower's office. She had filled out packets of paperwork to submit for grants and scholarships, Flower contacted her previous high school for transcripts, and even had her unofficially take placement tests, just to get an idea of her academic level.

"It's as I thought," Flower had said after Charlotte finished. "You're brilliant."

The whole encounter was surreal for Charlotte. Flower was so gentle, so supportive that she quickly put her at ease, making the unreachable seem doable for once in her life. Charlotte could see the steps now in her head, her way to attend college. It was within reach and the possibilities connected with that excited and scared her, giving her a feeling she'd seldom felt in her life: hope.

"Why do you look so surprised, my spirit baby? Why can't you see how incredible you are?" she beamed over at Charlotte who smiled back at her.

"I just- I just didn't think it could happen for me. It never seemed like something I could do."

"And now? Look around this place. What does your heart tell you?"

Charlotte looked around the campus full of pine trees and rolling fields of green grass. The summer breeze floated through the tree above them and the sun shone down on them from a cloudless sky. She inhaled deeply and closed her eyes. She listened to hear her heart the way Rose had taught her, letting the quiet settle her into the earth.

"It says I can grow here," she said quietly and she opened her eyes to look at Rose.

"Plant yourself then, my dear," she said, and leaned over to kiss her softly on the forehead.

⁕

Wyatt couldn't shake the empty feeling in his stomach. He'd told himself several times that she was only gone for the weekend, that he was being ridiculous, but he couldn't make himself be happy. He couldn't find a reason to laugh, even at the banter of the men on the ranch. He'd spent her first night gone tossing and turning in his bed, thinking of her without him. College, NAU, a whole new life for her that he knew she wanted, he knew she deserved, but he couldn't bring himself to be excited or happy about for some reason. He knew he should, but he just couldn't. She'd be there without him. It was a fact.

He caught himself thinking about what would have happened if he hadn't joined the Marines and played baseball instead, at a college an hour from hers. Would it have all been different? Or would he have met her at all? He talked himself in circles in his head, torturing himself with the different possibilities. *But what if you never went to the lake that day?* He'd always end up asking himself. The possibility was unfathomable to him, but that didn't stop him from thinking of it.

He was thankful for the workload, which, as promised, was the toughest he'd seen, but it got him out of his head as much as anything possibly could. The new shipment of cattle had arrived and he never imagined what all that entailed. They sorted them, rounding them up into one of the large corrals they'd built weeks beforehand. The work was stressful and hot, no storm clouds in sight to alleviate the relentless sun beating down on them. All of the men were on edge except Luis, who Wyatt decided must be a saint of some kind. No matter the workload, the yelling, the difficult situation, Luis couldn't be ruffled. But the rest of them, Garrett included, were frustrated with the heat and the hours of work stretched out in front of them.

Garrett made an executive decision to brand the cattle right away, which made Santiago and Raul look like they might cry. Wyatt, though, had never branded more than a couple of cattle at a time and had no idea how much work it would be to finish all of them.

"Luis, I want you on Sunny roping the calves since you're the best shot. Then you boys flank 'em down and I'll do the branding," Garrett ordered.

It was only around 10 am and the temperature was already hovering around 100 degrees. Wyatt felt the sweat drip from under his cowboy hat down the back of his neck and found himself wishing he had wrapped a wet towel around his shirt collar like the other men. He helped Garrett set up the branding equipment and stoke the fire Garrett had lit in a metal barrel. There was newer, better equipment to use rather than a fire and the branding iron, Wyatt knew, but Garrett liked his old ways.

"If it ain't broke, don't fuck with it," he muttered, sticking the iron in the fire to heat.

Santiago was in a fouler mood than normal, partly because of the work ahead of him and partly because he didn't get to be the one roping. It was true, Santiago was a talented roper and almost never missed a calf, but Luis was steady and wasn't in the business of making mistakes of any kind. Wyatt knew Garrett had done this hundreds of times and put each man where they should be, so he wasn't disappointed and wouldn't kick rocks like Santiago.

"Gringo, you just hold the head and we'll pin down the legs so Garrett can brand them. Don't let up too soon and get me burned," Santiago said to him, his face already annoyed.

Wyatt nodded, looking at the brand in the fire rather than at Santiago. He hated that even when Garrett gave specific instructions that Santiago still felt the need to give his own to Wyatt. Most days he could deal with it but between Charlotte being gone and getting his ass handed to him by ranch work, Wyatt felt his patience beginning to thin.

It took awhile for the men to find their rhythm, but after a couple of calves, they did. Luis would rope the calf around the neck, letting it circle around and look for a way out while he held tight, the rope dallied around his horn. That's when the boys would move in and flank it to the ground, Wyatt normally doing the heavy lifting of getting it down before the others would jump on the lower end.

The day wore on with the sun rising higher in the sky and Wyatt wondered inwardly if they were going to work through lunch. He was starving and thirsty, but he certainly wouldn't be the one to ask about it like a child would. He continued working systematically, but he was getting fatigued from hefting the calves to the ground each time. His back ached, as did his shoulders, and his shirt was drenched in sweat and dirt.

He didn't like watching the brand hit the hide, so he generally didn't watch that part. The smell of burning hair and cowhide was strong in the air and the noise of each cow bawling in his ear was almost as bad as watching the hot iron melt against them.

"Hold him longer, gringo!" Santiago snapped at Wyatt. "You let him up too soon, I wasn't ready."

Wyatt removed his hat and wiped his hand over his sweaty brow in frustration. "Well, be ready next time," he quipped back at him.

Santiago rolled his eyes at him, looking at Raul for reinforcement. Raul didn't respond but looked at the remaining cattle instead, no doubt calculating how long it would be before he could eat. Luis still sat perched on Sunny, his rope looped and ready in his hand, while Garrett likewise worked like he was a young man, always standing ready with the branding iron.

It was way past lunch when Luis found a large, somewhat feisty calf huddled in the corner of the corral. He promptly roped it and dallied the rope around his horn, but the calf was not going down easy. It ran back and forth in the corral, moving Luis and Sunny with it. The boys had to each close in on a side of him before painstakingly wrestling him to the ground. Wyatt could feel the fatigue in his muscles and he knew he needed food to fuel himself. He was lightheaded when he hit the ground with the calf and waited to hear the singe of the brand.

As soon as Wyatt heard the hot brand connect with the hide, he felt the calf jerk underneath him. Still being lightheaded, it caught him off guard when the calf struggled out of his reach, jumping up quickly. There was commotion and cursing among the men as the calf ran off to the other cattle. Santiago hopped on one foot cursing in Spanish.

"The fuck, Gringo?" he yelled. "He stepped on my foot!"

"You were supposed to be holding him, too, Santiago. I can't do it all myself!" Wyatt could feel his heart beating in his chest and the exhaustion of the day closing in on him.

"You think you been doing it by yourself?" Santiago said, his voice raising. "We gotta babysit you with everything! You never know how to do shit!"

Wyatt fought to keep his anger under control to no avail. "I've been the one taking each one to the ground!" he shouted, indignant. "It's not my fault you're not strong enough."

Santiago puffed out his chest, his face growing angrier. "I am strong enough, you just don't pay attention! Head always in the fucking sky!"

"Shut up, Santiago," Wyatt said, turning away from him to cool off.

"Just dreaming of that white girl pussy all day long so you keep fucking up!" Santiago shouted to his back.

That did it for Wyatt. He turned and made a run for Santiago, lowering his shoulder and wrapping his arms around the other man's waist. He easily took him to the ground and he could hear the other men shouting in the background, but he couldn't stop himself. He outweighed Santiago by at least 50 pounds but Santiago had what Wyatt did not, years of practice fighting. He punched Wyatt in the side of the face, ribs, and anywhere else he could make contact with from his place beneath him. The two rolled over each other and Wyatt reciprocated by punching him hard across the jaw. His vision was cloudy with rage when the men pulled them apart, Luis taking a firm hold on Wyatt and pushing him back.

"Don't ever fucking talk about her!" Wyatt shouted over Luis's head.

Santiago spit blood and saliva out in front of him and grinned at Wyatt's angry face. "Don't talk like she's your wife, gringo. Girls like that are not wives!"

Wyatt went to charge him again but was stopped by Luis holding him tight and speaking firmly into his face.

"No! I said no more. You stop!" he said to both boys.

Garrett was unimpressed. "Goddamn it. This bullshit," he said throwing up his hands. "We gotta have a dick measuring contest now? Goddamn." He threw down the branding iron and wiped the sweat from his forehead. "Alright fine. Y'all need an hour to cool off. Santiago go to the bunkhouse, Wyatt you come to the big house with me. And God dammit Santiago not another word. I mean it!"

Luis walked with Santiago and Raul back to the bunkhouse. The boys hung their head as Luis ripped into them in Spanish, speaking louder and harsher than Wyatt had ever heard him. Wyatt and Garrett walked to the house in silence, neither of them speaking until they entered his kitchen.

"Sit down," Garrett said shortly to him. He opened the freezer and retrieved a bag of frozen vegetables. "Put this on your eye. Gonna have a shiner."

Wyatt put the cold bag on his eye even though he couldn't feel anything wrong with it. He actually liked the dull feeling on his face and wondered why he thought being punched in the face would be so bad. It was actually somewhat refreshing next to the tortured feeling he'd carried in his stomach lately.

Garrett made him a sandwich and put a cold Corona in front of him silently, sitting down across from him to eat. Wyatt remembered his manners suddenly and felt shame wash over him.

"Sir, I'm really sorry. I didn't mean to do that. I shouldn't have acted that way," Wyatt said and took a long drink of his beer.

Garrett shrugged. "It was bound to happen. I've seen him push your buttons all summer. Surprised it's taken this long, actually."

Garrett took a bite of his sandwich and looked at Wyatt thoughtfully. "He's got your number though. Don't let him get to you."

Wyatt shook his head. "It won't happen again, sir."

"What's going on with you, son? You're not yourself. Is it Miss Charlotte?"

Wyatt flushed and looked down at his plate. "No- I mean, maybe," he hesitated but Garrett waited patiently. "I'm just distracted I guess."

Garrett nodded his head, eating his sandwich.

"You've got some big changes coming up, I know. It's a lot for a young man like you."

Wyatt nodded, still avoiding eye contact. He did not want to talk about the Marines, not with Garrett. He couldn't hear again about how it's a man's rite of passage to go through boot camp, or how great the war was going. He simply couldn't think of it any longer. Garrett looked up and smiled faintly at him.

"Son, I know it all feels like a lot right now, but you'll find your way. You've got a good head on your shoulders."

Wyatt nodded and thought about staying silent, but decided against it. He was tired of hearing about how great he was when he didn't feel like that at all.

"Yeah? What if I don't, though? What if I don't have it together like everyone thinks I do?" he asked miserably. "What if I made the wrong choice?"

It felt strange to be so honest with Garrett, to let him see so clearly into his heart and head, but he had no energy to hide it. Garrett took a swig of his beer and looked across the table at Wyatt, smiling sadly.

"There are no wrong choices, son. Only your choices that send you one way or another. Never lose faith that God will always put you right where he needs you and when. The rest isn't up for us to know."

Wyatt didn't respond but nodded, letting his words settle. He felt a little better after eating but he was disappointed in himself and ashamed for acting the way he had. Although it had felt good to hit Santiago. The two continued eating in silence, both gathering their strength for the work ahead of them.

After lunch, Wyatt excused himself to go to the bathroom and pull himself together. He stood with his hands on the sink looking back at the reflection in the mirror. His face was covered in grime and he could see the bruise starting to form around his eye. He looked at himself straight faced in the mirror and was struck by how different he looked. His face was drawn and serious, making him look less and less like the young boy he started out as that summer. He felt the pang hit his stomach again and the hollowed out lonely feeling that had plagued him since she left town. His blue eyes stared back at the changing person in front of him.

⚬⚬⚬

Saturday in Flagstaff was a perfect day. The weather was just as it was the day before, mild and breezy, like heaven compared to what she'd experienced in southern Arizona that summer. Rose wanted to show her the whole town so she could get the full experience. Charlotte, who still wasn't accustomed to vacations of any kind, was floored at all of the beautiful shops, restaurants, and grassy parks the town had to offer.

Rose took shopping very seriously and wanted to look in each store they passed. Antique shops, clothing stores, and bath and beauty spots were her favorites. A couple of hours into shopping she had several bags over each arm, many of them containing clothes and items she insisted on buying for Charlotte. She wouldn't take no for an answer.

"Now, we simply MUST go in here," Rose said, grinning at Charlotte.

The sign read "Buddha's Closet" and there were religious relics and colorful tapestries hung in the shop window. The inside smelled like sage and patchouli and the sound of meditative flute music floated through the air. Rose walked around looking at the merchandise, pointing things out to Charlotte. There were tarot cards, and angel cards flanked with books about witchcraft and spells. Rose picked one up and looked at the back, reading and chuckling to herself.

"What a crock," she said under her breath. She set it down and looked to Charlotte. "Get your shield up, my dear."

Charlotte nodded and did as Rose had consistently asked her to practice. She envisioned an invisible shield of light surrounding her, protecting her from negative energy and people. The first time she'd done it, it felt silly to her but the more she and Rose worked, the more she utilized her shield to protect herself and keep her energy clean. Once she realized how effective it was, how much more energy she had rather than being drained, she believed.

"Thoughts are things," Rose told her, and she was right.

The shop was empty but for them and it took several minutes for any employees to be seen. Finally, a young woman came out of the back room. She was beautiful in the Flagstaff, hippie way. She wore a tank top falling off of her shoulders and a long flowing skirt with a psychedelic purple print. She had long, brown, messy hair that fell almost to her waist and an intense gaze that Charlotte disliked immediately.

"Greetings," she said mildly to Rose and Charlotte. "Can I be of any assistance?"

Charlotte looked at the woman and tried to read her as Rose had taught. The first thing she thought was that this person was pretending to be something she was not.

"Oh no, thank you," Rose waved her hand. "Fascinating place you have here," she said continuing to look at the books and items on the shelves.

"Are you two interested in the metaphysical world?" the woman asked, looking Rose and Charlotte up and down, noting the copious amount of shopping bags.

"Oh, not really," Rose said, waving her hand. "We don't know much about it."

Charlotte turned away to look at the merchandise so she could grin to herself. Rose smelled the bullshit, just as clear as she did.

"Would you be interested in a psychic reading? We never have openings but we just had a cancellation. I could take you right now."

Rose put her hand to her heart and feigned surprise. "My dear, did you hear that? A psychic reading!" she said looking at Charlotte who fought to keep a straight face. "How exciting! I want you to do it!"

Charlotte looked back at her wide-eyed and shook her head slightly.

"Oh no, don't be silly, Charlotte. My treat!"

Rose's eyes danced with mischief as the woman led them back through a small door and into a dark office. Charlotte doubled down on her shield when she entered. She didn't like the look of the tarot cards and dark candles burning on the desk. Pictures of Buddha hung on the walls but they seemed out of place to Charlotte who equated him to gardens and fresh air, not a dingy back room. The woman sat and shuffled the cards, looking across the table at Rose and Charlotte. She appraised Charlotte for awhile, her dark eyes connecting with hers through long tendrils of brown tangled hair. She flipped over several cards lining them up in front of her. She pointed at the first one that looked like a picture of someone being hung. She tapped on it and looked up at Charlotte.

"There's something you need to compromise about. Your stubbornness is going to get the better of you. You must bend."

Charlotte looked to Rose who winked when the woman wasn't looking. *Not even close,* Charlotte thought. The woman moved her hand over the love card and looked back at Charlotte deciding how she should spin it. The card had a heart with a knife through it.

"You will fall in love one day but you won't find one that lasts for a long time. You're a free spirit. You haven't known real love yet. "

Wrong again. Charlotte thought.

She moved to the next card with a sword pushing through a stone.

"This represents what you need to be. This is a reminder to grow stronger. To be tough," she said, cocking her head at Charlotte's non-expressive face. Charlotte wanted to turn to Rose and tell her she was wrong about her warrior spirit, that apparently she wasn't tough after all.

The woman went through several more cards and it took everything in Charlotte not to yawn in her face. It was tedious listening to her overgeneralize and reach for answers that weren't even there. Rose, though, was in full actor mode, oohing and awing at the woman's assessments and always looking to Charlotte with a conspiring look written all over her face. When the reading was over, Rose paid the woman the $50 fee, thanking her profusely for such a transcendent experience. Once they were outside and out of earshot, Rose cackled loudly at Charlotte's unamused face.

"Aunt Rose! That was a lot of money for that ridiculous reading! Why did you make me do that?" she asked miserably, walking down the busy sidewalk.

Rose was still in her laughing fit, carrying her shopping bags and reaching up to wipe the corner of her eyes which had teared up. She was clearly very pleased with herself.

"I'm sorry, baby. It's just so damn funny!" she said laughing. "Listen, come sit. I'll tell you why."

They had reached the square at the center of town that was full of people watching live musicians play. The city was alive with people and a relaxed energy Charlotte attributed to the fact that everyone there was stoned. They found an empty bench and sat, Rose moving her bags to the other side of her so she could scoot close to Charlotte.

"All right, listen. I didn't just do it to be an asshole, I swear. Although I'm aware it looks that way," she busted up laughing again and Charlotte joined despite herself.

"Ok, tell me. But it better not be a lesson on how to read those creepy cards. I don't like them," Charlotte said, cleaning the energy off of her again for good measure.

Rose shook her head. "No, no. You are not a novice. Tarot cards are not for you. Why give you glasses when you have 20/20 vision already?" she said, finally calming her laughing fit. "I had you do that so you know the difference. So you understand people's distaste for this kind of thing. I'm sure you picked up on the fact that was bullshit, right?"

"Immediately," Charlotte confirmed.

Rose nodded. "Good girl. It's important for you to see the fringe weirdos like that. Unfortunately, they give us all a bad name. Witchcraft books and black candles? Total nonsense and not what we do but we will always be associated with that. Understand? People can't bring themselves to believe in something unbelievable, something magical, so they associate us with that instead. There will always be people who treat us like witches at the Salem Trials and that's why," she pointed back to the shop. "You've gotta be ready to deal with it if you do this line of work."

Charlotte nodded and looked out at the musicians playing reggae in the square. She squinted her eyes, thinking.

"But am I, Aunt Rose? Is that what I'm supposed to do?" Charlotte asked, looking at Rose. Her aunt smiled back and put an arm around her shoulders.

"You go where your heart tells you, Charlotte. I can't tell you anything other than that."

"But why? Why won't you ever read me?" Charlotte asked earnestly.

Rose sighed, looking around the square. "In life you come to crossroads. Sometimes people need help knowing where to turn, how to get somewhere. You don't need that. You know. You know in your heart where to go and you always will. You have a plan for your life. Even if you don't realize it right now."

Charlotte looked back at her aunt and exhaled loudly, clearly frustrated.

"I don't want to spoil the ending for you, babe. Don't you see? What is it that you need to know?"

Charlotte could think of a hundred questions about Wyatt, school, her future, her mother, but she knew that Rose wouldn't give her the answers to the test that she was meant to take herself. As much as Rose enjoyed breaking rules, this was not one of them.

"Maybe I'll go back to tarot lady for a better answer. She seems to have her shit together," she sighed, exasperated. Rose cackled loudly above the music, hugging her niece close to her side.

⚬⚬⚬

It had been a miserable weekend without her. Saturday after lunch all of the men had gone back to work and acted as if nothing was wrong. Wyatt had cooled down and avoided Santiago and Raul just like normal. Luis gave him a pat on the arm to let him know everything was ok, just as he always did. Wyatt worked mechanically for the rest of the day and when the work was done, he went to feed all of the animals and clean stalls, even though Garrett didn't expect him to do that until Monday. It was like therapy for him, the ache in his back and arms distracting him from the tension and from thinking of her. He'd finally come to the bunkhouse after dark, going directly to the shower then crawling into bed without eating while the men sat speaking Spanish in the kitchen. He lay looking at the ceiling, wondering what in the hell had happened to him. For the first time in his life he felt like he wasn't doing the right things and he proceeded to drown himself in self-loathing because of it.

Waking up on a Sunday with them in the bunkhouse was worse than he thought. He wasn't used to all of them being there on the weekend and missed his time alone. They had all decided to stay since cattle work took through Saturday evening. So Sunday, their day off, the men lounged around the house cooking, napping, laughing with one another. It was more than Wyatt could take to once again be the outsider, him and Santiago avoiding even looking at one and other. After feeding in the morning he put on his board shorts and headed to the lake. He hated the thought of being there without her, knowing that she wouldn't be home until much later that day. They hadn't planned to see each other until Monday evening, but there was literally nowhere else for him to go. He wondered just what in the hell he would've done that entire summer if not for Charlotte. Would he have even made it this far or would he have quit and gone home, spending his summer doing the same thing he always did- swimming and hiking with friends, playing baseball, avoiding his parents? He didn't even know who that person was anymore and to think of it made him feel empty and lost all over again. It was that person who had signed him up for the Marine Corps, not him.

A storm brewed in the distance as he pulled up to the lake, but he figured he would at least have a couple of hours. He went to their spot as he always did and sat down under the trees, looking around the lake. She would say it was a beautiful day, even though it was muggy and nasty out. But the lake was clear and still and he could hear the sound of quail calling in the distance. Yes, he thought, a beautiful day.

He swam for awhile, letting the cool water soothe his sore muscles before lying on his stomach in the shallows, feeling the grainy sand underneath him and the sun beating down on his back. He was annoyed with himself for being so miserable even though he tried like hell to be happy. He simply could not get himself out of his head, rolling over everything that had happened that summer and what was to come.

He drug himself out of the water to lay down under the shade of the trees on top of his army blanket that smelled faintly of her. It was pushing late afternoon and the clouds were still gathering. He knew it was probably time to get back, but he couldn't bear the thought of being in the house with the men, Santiago and Raul pretending he didn't exist and Luis taking pity on him as always. He didn't know which was worse.

He stretched himself out and put a shirt underneath his head and his baseball hat over his face. He was hungry, probably because he hadn't eaten the day before, not enough for the amount of work he put in, anyway. He missed her again, then, thinking of the food she made him, and how she was always concerned if he had eaten enough. He closed his eyes and tried hard to fall asleep and finally did, fading into the blackness without dreaming, giving way to his exhaustion.

He woke to her soft hand on his chest, startling him out of sleep. He jumped, his hat flying off of his face as he sat up. She was kneeling next to him, her hair falling around her shoulders and a grin spreading across her face. She wore the sundress he loved, her tan skin pronounced in the summer sun. She stopped smiling suddenly, a look of concern taking over.

"What happened to your eye?" she said, touching it lightly.

He was so taken off guard, his relief upon seeing her was palpable. He smiled and laughed, pulling her on his lap and hugging her tight against him.

"Wyatt, really. Are you ok?"

She leaned back from the hug to get a better look at his eye. Her brows were scrunched together and her mouth set in a thin line. She was so distraught and it only reminded him of how much he loved her.

He pulled her face into his and kissed her over and over again without saying a word, moving to kiss her cheek, neck, and shoulder until she gave way to giggling.

"Well I guess you're ok, but what happened?"

He shrugged, finally allowing her to pull back to look at him, keeping his arms wrapped around her.

"Santiago and I had a disagreement, that's all."

"About what?" she asked, shocked.

"Everything," he said, grinning.

Her eyes widened and she laughed. "Two days. I leave you alone for two days and this happens?" She leaned in and kissed him on the cheek, moving up to his black eye. She pressed her lips lightly against the swelling.

"I'm better now," he said quietly, looking into her eyes. He wanted to tell her how desperately he'd missed her. How horrible it had been without her there, but he didn't want her to see how pathetic he was. She moved her hand to his hair and brushed it off of his forehead.

"I missed you," she said quietly.

He sighed heavily, relieved that she still felt the same, even though it had only been two days. "Babe, I- I'm so glad you're back," he said simply.

He remembered then where she'd been. That this weekend had been important to her and just as he'd rehearsed in his head, he would be excited for her.

"Tell me about it. How did it go? Do you like Flag?"

She moved to sit down next to him on the blanket, holding his hand in her lap. "You were right. I love it there. The town, the pine trees," she smiled sideways at him. "Just like you said it would be."

He nodded, smiling. "I can see you there," he said quietly. "It would be a perfect place for you." He couldn't keep the sadness from his voice, as much as he tried. She picked up on it and squeezed his hand tightly.

"Thank you, Wyatt," she said quietly.

"What about NAU? How did that go?"

Charlotte told him about the entire encounter, laughing with him about Rose's formidable, no-nonsense ways with the stonewalling employee they'd met. She told him about the admissions woman whose kindness and willingness to help had changed everything for her.

"I think maybe I can get in for the spring," she said, shaking her head. "Isn't that crazy?"

"Not really," he said, laughing. "I had zero doubt you'd get in. I don't know why you don't realize how smart you are."

"You're just saying that," she said, pushing his arm.

"Why would I just say that?" he asked seriously.

"I don't know," she said grinning. "Because you love me?" she smiled shyly at him.

"Well, I do love you. A lot. But I wouldn't bullshit you, babe," he grinned at her, moving in closer to her face.

"No?" she said quietly into his face.

"No," he said, laying her down to the ground and moving on top of her.

She moved her legs apart and wrapped them around his sturdy center. He kissed her softly but pulled back suddenly.

"Wait, how did you get here? Why are you home so early?" he said, remembering. "And how did you know I'd be here?"

Charlotte laughed, moving her hands up and down his muscular arms.

"We just got home and Rose is beat. I had her bring me here on our way home."

"Yeah, but how did you know I'd be here?"

Charlotte shrugged. "Lucky guess."

"Uh-huh. Sure. So you really did miss me then?"

"I did. Did you miss me or were you busy fighting the whole time?"

He laughed, thinking of how miserable he had been only minutes ago.

"I missed you," he said, locking eyes with her. "Bad."

He kissed her slowly, taking his time savoring her before moving down to kiss her neck, pulling down the spaghetti straps on her dress. He moved the dress down lower, pulling her hard nipple out and sucking on it lightly. Her breathing started to quicken immediately and she pulled him tighter against her. She moved his face back to hers and kissed him deeply, pushing her tongue breathlessly into his mouth and moving against him.

"I don't," he said, panting. "I don't have anything with me," he said, trying to slow down.

"I don't care, Wyatt. Please."

She was already pulling at his board shorts and breathing the way he loved, so desperate for him that couldn't make himself stop. She pulled him out of his shorts and toward her, moving her underwear to the side. The feel of her without a condom was like nothing he'd ever felt before and he couldn't stop himself, even though he knew he should.

"Babe, I shouldn't," he breathed, still moving in and out of her.

But Charlotte was insatiable. She simply couldn't stop herself from having him right then and there. She sucked on his lower lip, begging him not to stop, raising her hips to meet him each time. She stopped him to move on top, Wyatt sitting up against the tree and kissing her neck as she rocked back and forth, releasing herself over and over, crying out into the quiet desert. He held tight to her, thrusting forcefully from under her. He moaned and breathed heavily trying hard not to finish.

"I can't. I shouldn't, babe."

"Wyatt. It's ok. Please," she whispered into his ear, and that was all it took.

He finished with her on top of him, his naked chest heaving into her breasts still hanging from her dress. He was dizzy, feeling like it had been months since he'd had her, even though it had only been a couple of days. How? He wondered. How the hell would he live without her?

⌁◦❦◦⌁

It was well into August. The change of month both excited and terrified her for the first time in her life. It would be the month she began her college journey, and one month closer to him leaving. The conflicted feelings trapped her so much in her own head that Rose made her start meditating in the backyard each morning instead of inside.

"Shit, girl. Roll in the dirt if you have to. You've got to stay grounded and out of that head of yours," Rose had said, admonishing her.

Charlotte listened to her, as always. She sat out in the grass with her hot tea each morning, listening to the sound of the town coming awake and Bailey hopping around in the pen Wyatt built for her. She tried each day to center herself, to do as Rose taught her and connect herself with the earth, and some days she did. Some days she could feel a light, a connection to the world around her blossoming inside. But other days it was gone, and all that remained was the worry. Worry for Wyatt, for her mother, for her uncertain future, and for the other shoe which she knew would drop without fail.

She'd continued making time to see Wyatt each day, often having him to dinner with Rose since she knew he didn't want to be around the bunkhouse, the blow up with Santiago making life at the ranch tense. He'd find her each day, at the lake, at home, at the library, sometimes not bothering to shower if he didn't have the time. They'd become woven into each other's lives, both living for the day and ignoring his impending departure, save for the misery they felt in their own hearts.

They'd both kept busy with work and Charlotte with studying. She'd been pouring through the various competency notebooks that Flower had sent with her from NAU, studying anytime she had the chance. She knew, because Flower had told her, that she could test out of several classes that were prerequisites for being admitted to NAU. And the others could be completed via independent study. It had all seemed too easy for Charlotte, who thought of college as so untouchable for so long that it was difficult to believe that she could actually get classes under her belt so easily.

"The classes are hard but it's almost like a puzzle to piece together a degree. I'm just giving you the map to make it easier," Flower had told her. Charlotte wanted to believe her, but she wouldn't. Not until it actually happened. She couldn't get her hopes up.

It was midweek when Charlotte and Rose left for Tucson early in the morning for her tests at the local community college. Charlotte sat in the passenger seat chewing on the inside of her cheek nervously. She'd worn her old jeans and a tight fitting t-shirt, snug across her breasts. Her hair was down and wild around her face, Charlotte not even having the presence of mind to brush it out that morning. Rose reached out to pat her shoulder.

"Wish we would've had time to meditate this morning," Rose said regretfully. "Try to close your eyes and ground yourself. I swear it'll help."

Charlotte tried then, closing her eyes and setting her intention.

Please God, don't let me mess this up. Please give me confidence. Let me have peace.

She kept her eyes closed for 20 minutes of the drive, working hard to put her skills into practice. When she finally opened her eyes she felt much better, although still a little nervous. Rose chatted to her to relax her as much as possible, pointing out landmarks on the way to Tucson and telling her about all the stores she'd go to while Charlotte was testing.

"And if you're a good little girl," she said joking, "Aunt Rose has a surprise for you after your tests."

"Really?" Charlotte said dully. "Is it a waitressing job that I'll need since I won't be able to get into college?"

Rose laughed. "Smart ass. You stop bashing yourself. Not a good color on you," she turned and winked at her. "Hey, remember that pain in the ass client?"

"The lady with all the money? Patricia?" Charlotte asked.

"Yep. Do you know she graduated college?"

Charlotte shrugged. "Doesn't surprise me. Why are you telling me that?"

"You read her, Char. She's an absolute shit show. Does anything about her strike you as particularly brilliant?"

Charlotte thought hard about her encounter with her, feeling for her energy. It had all felt so shallow. Not a thinker, that Patricia, that was for sure. Truth be told it did make her feel a little better to think of her.

"Not really," Charlotte conceded.

"Ok then, I could name you 100 more schmucks like that who got through college. Stop acting like it's not for you and it's for them. You're smarter than that. I demand you walk in there like you own it."

So that's how Charlotte walked into the community college that day. Like she owned it. As if she belonged there even though every fiber of her being still told her she didn't. The plus side was that the community college was not half as intimidating as NAU. The people there were more like the people she was used to. Working class people, struggling people, trying to pull their lives together. Single moms back to school after years away, rougher looking kids around her age like the ones in the neighborhoods where she'd once lived. There were more misfits than she saw in Flagstaff and it gave her comfort since that meant she was not alone.

The campus was large and functional, set among the rocky hills just outside of Tucson. The fall semester was just beginning and Charlotte could feel the newness of it all, which also made her feel like she belonged since she wasn't the only one finding her way. Rose helped her find the right building then left her there after one last pep talk and a firm hug.

Charlotte took one test after another, the first one for reading comprehension, which was ridiculously easy for her, then onto writing, which was more challenging. The essay exam was still in her wheelhouse, though, and she felt solid in her answers, going back to edit them time and time again until she could submit something she was happy with. The most challenging of the tests was math and she caught herself wishing Wyatt was there to help. He'd come to the library looking for her the week before when she was about to throw her math booklet out the window in frustration. She smiled to think of him then. He'd so patiently pulled up a chair next to her and gone over the algebra problems with her, reviewing things she had forgotten.

"It's just steps. Just take one little step at a time and it makes it easier," he'd whispered in the quiet of the library. He'd put it so simply to her, teaching her in a way no one else had.

So she held him with her that day. She pretended he was there helping her, easing her into each problem. She imagined his steady deep voice explaining each step, putting it in a way she could understand, and it worked. It calmed her and allowed her to see it as he did, as pieces of a puzzle.

When she emerged from the building and walked out to find Rose, she held her shoulders back and her chin straight, a slight smile on her face. Rose was in the car with the AC blasting, leaning back in the driver's seat for her afternoon nap. Charlotte tapped lightly on the window until Rose stirred, smiling through the glass at her. She rolled down her window and looked up at Charlotte.

"Well? Was I right or was I right?" she asked, grinning.

"Well, jury is still out on my writing, but," she said pulling out two pieces of paper and holding them in front of her, "I tested out of all of the reading classes and tested into college algebra."

"So what does that mean?" Rose said, grabbing the papers.

"It means, you're right. Maybe any schmuck can get into college," Charlotte grinned, her eyes sparkling.

Rose jumped out of the car and held her tight against her small frame, the hot summer sun beating down on them. She kissed the side of her face, standing on her toes to do so.

"This calls for a celebration. A magical one," Rose said, giddy.

She refused to tell Charlotte where they were going, only that it was a surprise. As far as Charlotte could tell they were headed back to Patagonia, Rose getting back on the freeway and heading south. She exited just on the outskirts of Tucson, pulling off to an area that looked like much of the desert that time of year, just starting to green up after the monsoons. Charlotte looked out the window and saw it then, her mouth hanging open.

The building was massive and white, jutting out of the desert landscape like an oasis. It reminded Charlotte of a castle but not one she'd ever seen before that. There were towers with church bells at the top of it and ornate rock work in the middle, decorating the white adobe walls. She could see the cross perched at the top and gardens surrounding it, gated in by rusted wrought iron and adobe fencing.

She knew the place was special. The feeling in her stomach was much like the one she got when she saw Wyatt for the first time. It was a pang of recognition, an acknowledgment of something unexplainable. Rose said nothing as she pulled in the almost empty parking lot. Charlotte stared out the window, her mouth still agape. They sat like that for several minutes and Charlotte felt herself completely overwhelmed and on the verge of tears. Rose sighed heavily.

"I've been waiting a long time to take you here, babe," she said looking out at the building. "This is San Xavier Mission. It's been here since the 1700s and it's very special to me." Rose wiped the corner of her eye and looked back to Charlotte. "Do you feel it?"

"Yes," she whispered, although she didn't know what "it" was. But it was certainly something.

They walked in together, sticking close to each other's side. The whole mission was surrounded with a thick adobe fence with elaborate wrought iron woven between, creating a beautiful fortress. The brick walkway wound around the building and into smaller chapels and gardens. The balconies were trimmed in tattered stained wood and the archways exposed the thick walls, chipped here and there and showing the bricks underneath. The architecture itself was stunning in its simplicity and Charlotte immediately felt the urge to reach out and touch the chapel before walking into it. She felt the hot, pure energy enter her through her palm and imagined herself as the mission, rooted to the earth.

Rose smiled knowingly at her. "Follow me," she said quietly.

The mission was mostly empty since it was a summer afternoon and the tourist season wouldn't pick up for another couple of months. Inside the chapel it was unbearably hot, but Charlotte hardly noticed. She looked up at the ceilings clad with thick wood beams and Saguaro bones. On the walls there were statues of angels and mosaic tile portraits of Jesus and Mother Mary. The colors of gold and red blended effortlessly with the white backdrop of the walls. Charlotte looked up at two angels painted on the ceiling and almost fell to her knees before finding a seat. Rose touched her arm gently and guided her to a pew toward the front of the empty church.

Candles lit in front of a statue of St. Francis glowed from the corner and in the silence there was the same reverence she'd felt in the Catholic Church in Patagonia. Rose sat next to her not speaking, but looking around just like her, experiencing the place anew through Charlotte's eyes. She knelt in the pew and Charlotte followed suit, placing her hands together and closing her eyes.

She felt like it was the first time she'd ever really prayed. Closing her eyes, she thought of God and tried, as always, to just talk. She held the people she loved in her heart and lifted them, praying humbly for their protection. Rose, Wyatt, and finally, her mother. She felt something wash over her then although she didn't know what it was. Something pure, something beautiful, something grounding her to that place.

Pray for yourself. She heard the voice inside of her say.

So she did. She prayed that she could be something-do something important with her life. She prayed to be able to love herself. And to be a good person. She felt the tears well up in her eyes and fall down her cheeks, but she didn't even try to stop it.

Thank you, God. Thank you for saving me.

She said it over and over and for the first time, she felt heard. She was overwhelmed with gratitude for being where she was rather than where she'd been. They sat in the chapel for a long time that way before Rose stood up and gently pulled Charlotte up after her. She walked her around the grounds showing her the cactus garden, fountains, and museum. The place had a rich history and now sat on the Indian Reservation, bringing together a spectacularly eclectic combination of the Spanish and Tohono O'odham cultures. Rose could have been a tour guide for all of her knowledge and Charlotte was a captive audience. She showed Charlotte outside to all of the candles lit in front of paintings of Mary. She lit three and closed her eyes for a brief prayer before looking back to Charlotte.

"Are you ready for your surprise?" she asked, grinning.

Charlotte smiled and laughed. "Isn't this it?" she said, putting her hands out around her.

Rose shook her head and crooked her finger at her, telling her to follow. She walked down a long empty corridor toward the back of the building that led to a large shaded porch. There were empty vendor tables along with only a few full ones with flustered looking native people sitting behind them. Charlotte browsed the merchandise of turquoise rings and necklaces along with dream catchers and other religious relics like crosses and medallions. Rose kept walking toward the end of the porch where a rotund native woman sat doing needlepoint. She looked up when

Rose got close, a huge smile stretching across her face.

Rose knelt down next to her, taking the woman's hands in hers. Rose smiled, looking like she was on the verge of tears and uncharacteristically in awe. The woman must have been in her 70s and wore a large traditional Mexican skirt embroidered with flowers along the hem. Her long gray hair lay braided down her back with ribbons intertwined. She held Rose's hands and gazed in her face.

"There you are," she said, happily. "I've been waiting." She pulled Rose's forehead to her for a kiss then pulled back to look at her again, hands on either side of her face. Rose looked up at Charlotte and beamed.

"She came," she said to the woman. "She came like you said she would."

Charlotte looked down at them, confused but polite as ever. She stuck her hand out to shake as Rose finally introduced them.

"Charlotte, this is Nova. My teacher, my friend," Rose said.

"Family," Nova said smiling. "We all family."

She pulled Charlotte down for a hug, cooing to her.

"Es a strong girl," she said, patting her. "I knew you could do it."

Charlotte was still confused when Rose pulled two chairs up to Nova and went on chatting about their day. About college and the shop, the weather. The two talked like the best of friends as Charlotte sat quietly nodding and answering when she was spoken to.

"Nova, my dear niece needs something. Something I can't give to her. Would you mind?" Rose said.

"To read?" Nova chuckled. "She not need me tell her anything! She know more than us!"

Rose chuckled back to her in agreement. "I know that and you know that, but she doesn't know that yet."

"Ok, ok. I understand." Nova smiled and beckoned Charlotte to move closer to her.

She did, scooting her chair in front of her and sitting nervously knee to knee with Nova. Nova held Charlotte's hands in hers and closed her eyes, her faint smile fading from her lips and a look of concentration taking over. When she opened them she looked like a different person.

"You know, we been waiting. We been waiting for you to come. I told Rose last year- soon," she smiled.

Charlotte shifted uncomfortably in her seat and looked back into Nova's deep brown eyes framed in crow's feet.

"You had to walk through fire to get here. I know. We prayed for you. Right here in this chapel, we pray for you."

Charlotte fought the tears forming in the corners of her eyes and nodded. "Thank you," she whispered.

"You have to walk through fire again someday. All of us have to. When you're like us," she said gesturing at herself and Rose. "But you will always prevail. Light always wins. Understand?"

Charlotte nodded her head, although she didn't understand at all.

"You must believe you deserve God's love. No more questioning. Darkness will always seek you because you shine," she shook her head. "You always win. The light is never lost. You feel it in you?"

Charlotte nodded shyly, not having the words to tell her what the light inside of her felt like. Only that it was there, and alive, part of her now more than ever, especially there.

"You will be more than you've ever dreamed. More than you can see right now," she shook her head in amazement. "Business. You have mind for it," she tapped the side of her head, looking thoughtfully at Charlotte. "Everything you need already there. All inside of you just waiting to come out."

Nova sighed, looking up at Rose concerned. Rose nodded her head, almost giving permission.

"Your mother. You must pray for her. Pray for God's will to be done. Just pray. Have her here," she said tapping her chest lightly.

Nova closed her eyes again, her brow furrowed. Charlotte thought for awhile that she might be done, that her unexpected reading was over, until her eyes popped open again.

"This love you have. You know each other- many lives together," she shook her head smiling. "Great love. Pure. True." She sat silently for a minute thinking of how to continue. "Both of you has one heart, yes?" she said, bringing her hands together to illustrate her point.

Nova fell silent again, wrinkling her brow together in concern. She looked back at Rose who nodded again, just barely.

"You have one heart but two destinies," Nova said finishing the reading, her truth echoing heartbreakingly in Charlotte's bones.

✦

It was another rainy night, probably one of the last big monsoons they could expect for the summer. Once September hit, there would be a couple of storms but nothing like the fierce ones of summer, cracking open the sky and turning on a faucet from the heavens. They sat next to each other at the Ranch House restaurant again, this time seated at the front where they could look out the window at the lightning striking across the open sky and the wind blowing the rain sideways.

They'd long since finished their meal but decided to stay for dessert and coffee since there would be no driving in a storm like that. At least not with her in the car. Wyatt sat comfortably with his arm slung around her shoulder, drinking coffee with the other hand. He watched her watching the rain, her perfect mouth open slightly and accentuating her plump lips.

"I have to ask you something," Wyatt said seriously to her.

"What?" she asked, curiously.

"Who is Charlotte Brontë?"

Charlotte laughed, throwing her head back like he loved. "She was a writer, why?"

He shrugged. "You told me you were named after her the first day I met you. I didn't want to tell you I didn't know who that was."

"Ah- I see. Yeah, she's a writer my mom likes- or used to like when she read books," Charlotte said, looking away.

"She doesn't read anymore?"

"No. Not for years," Charlotte replied and fell quiet again.

She wanted to tell him everything. How afraid she was for her mother, how she dreamed of her every night without fail, and most of all, how she knew that her mother needed her. But there was no way to tell him what she knew in her heart. No way to make him realize the thread between them that stood strong regardless of how she'd tried to cut it.

He squeezed her against him. "Well, it's a good name for you. It suits you."

"Yeah?" she smiled. "I always thought it was a little fancy for me. My-" She stopped and hesitated before going on. "My mom actually calls me Charlie."

"Charlie?" he laughed. "Not like you at all. You're too pretty to be called a boy's name."

She smiled shyly. "Well, she's the only one who calls me that. But it's funny, when I was falling asleep last night I heard someone say that to me."

"Like in a dream?" he asked.

"Yeah, kinda. That place where you're just falling asleep, you know. Between dreaming and awake? But it was just weird."

Wyatt didn't know how to respond to that, and truth be told some of the psychic stuff creeped him out a bit. He couldn't deny that Charlotte did have a way of reading situations though.

"Do you ever just get a feeling about something? Like your intuition? Do you ever just know things?" she asked abruptly.

"Not really," he laughed, "no." He sat and thought a moment. "Ok, well- yes I guess so. When I- well it sounds stupid now but when I played baseball, a lot of times I could tell where the batter would hit the ball. I mean, you watch for signals for that but I just sometimes knew where they'd hit it so I'd move to catch it when I could- you know?"

"Yes exactly- just something that kinda comes to you. So you're psychic, too, then," Charlotte grinned.

Wyatt laughed. "Oh, I doubt that. Why, though?"

Charlotte shrugged, not wanting to tell him the whole truth just yet. "I don't know. Rose tells me everyone's got that voice inside of them if we listen- mine is just more pronounced than other people's. And I've just- I'm just worried about my mom all of the sudden. Like more than normal," she looked back out the window. "I hope she's ok," she said more to herself than to him.

Wyatt rubbed her shoulder, holding her close against him since there were no words to make her feel better. He knew there was no easy fix or one-liner that could ease her pain so he just sat by her instead. She turned and looked up at him and smiled with her lips closed, looking into his blue eyes. He moved his face in close to hers and kissed her lightly, lingering in front of her face afterward.

"You taste like peaches," he said quietly.

"So do you," she smiled, kissing him back again. "Let's go home."

Wyatt was disappointed. He wasn't ready to end the evening just yet, he wanted more time with her as always.

"Ok. Looks like it's letting up so I can take you home."

"To the bunkhouse," she corrected.

He turned and widened his eyes at her. "Miss Brontë. That's quite forward of you," he grinned.

"How forward is it of me to ask to spend the night?" she said, kissing the side of his neck briefly. "Rose has a date so I offered to stay with you. She didn't object."

Charlotte took one last drink of her coffee and stood to leave. She wore a new dress from Flagstaff that was a blue paisley print and came to just above her knee. The fabric moved easily and when Wyatt touched her, it felt like she wasn't wearing a thing. He stood after her, putting a hand on the small of her back.

"After you, sorceress," he said and Charlotte giggled under her breath leaving the restaurant.

The ride home was slow since the rain was still falling down steadily. Wyatt drove cautiously on the small highway with Charlotte sitting close to his side as always. He'd noticed she'd brought a purse that evening which was rare for her, but he didn't imagine she'd brought it to spend the night. He was thrilled thinking of her in his bed all night and it wasn't just because of the sex. He loved feeling her sleep next to him. Hearing her steady breathing comforted him in a way he couldn't explain.

"I love you," he said suddenly in the quiet of the car ride.

Charlotte turned to him and smiled, leaning in to kiss his neck. She worked her way up to his ear, whispering back to him. "I love you, Wyatt Earp."

She continued kissing him and he fought to keep his eyes on the road. He gripped the wheel and blinked his eyes trying to focus. Charlotte unclipped her seatbelt and leaned over him to kiss the other side of his neck, keeping her head below his so he could see the road.

"Babe," he whispered. "This is a bad idea."

Charlotte giggled. "I think it's a great idea."

She moved a leg over his lap and straddled him, keeping her head to the side so he could see. She continued kissing him, unbuttoning his collar to kiss the crevice in his chest bone. Wyatt's breathing started to deepen. He dropped one hand from the wheel to grip her perfect bottom, seated on his lap. She moved her face up to kiss his, tilting her head to the side so he could still see the road. She licked his lips lightly, kissing him with an open mouth. He kept his eyes open and on the road but barely.

"Babe, I'm gonna crash. Jesus," he whispered.

When he pulled on the road to the ranch he threw the truck in park and put both hands around her, kissing her hard and moving her against his hardness. He ripped at the straps on her dress, kissing her shoulders and chest as she panted on top of him.

"Take me home," she said between kisses.

She didn't move off of him but let up enough to let him drive down the long dirt to the ranch. When they pulled up in front of the bunkhouse he put the truck in park and kissed her again, pulling her tight to him. He opened his door and carried her out, holding her under her bottom with her legs wrapped around him.

When they entered the bedroom they both thought of that first night together. How shy they'd been, how unsure. It was far from where they were now. Now that they knew each other's bodies so well. He took her dress over off over her head and unclipped her bra before laying her on the bed. He pulled off her panties roughly and Charlotte giggled.

"You still have all of your clothes on," she laughed.

He hadn't noticed, he'd only been thinking of her sprawled out in her bed. Her long mess of blonde hair strewn out over his pillow. He grinned at her, moving over her body with slow kisses before standing to undress himself. He moved on top of her, fully naked, pausing only for a moment to put on a condom.

He pushed into her urgently and she cried out in pleasure. He kissed her hard, moving with her, doing everything he knew she liked. He couldn't get enough of her, pulling her on top of him and watching her move, her head back and her blonde hair long enough to cover her breasts. She was perfect, wild and free like that, and he had to concentrate so as to not lose himself. When he finally did, it was with her, both of them colliding together and kissing each other with trembling lips.

They lay in the bed together cuddled close, listening to the thunder which had started back up again. His bed was so full with her in it that he forgot what it was like when he was there alone thinking of her, listening to the rhythmic sound of Luis's snoring instead.

"I got you a present," she said shyly into his chest.

"That wasn't it?" he grinned.

She laughed and stood, pulling her sundress over her naked body.

"No, since that's a present for me, too," she said smiling over her shoulder. She left the room and walked out to the truck to retrieve her purse. When she walked back in she came and sat on the edge of the bed and he sat up, a sheet covering his lower half. His chest was tanned and smooth, shining in the glow of the lamplight. She rifled through the bag and he saw that it indeed had clothes in it; she'd been prepared to stay.

"So you knew you'd spend the night and waited that whole time to tell me?" he said smiling. "You brought pajamas?"

"Wyatt, please. You know I don't like wearing clothes to bed. I brought my suit so we can go to the lake tomorrow," she said, eyeing him.

"Good idea," he whispered.

Charlotte pulled a small fabric bag out of her purse and held it in her hand. She looked at him and something crossed her face that he couldn't place but it seemed a little sad, maybe embarrassed.

"So, I got this the other day when I went to the mission. I don't know, you might think it's silly, so you don't have to wear it all of the time. I just- I wanted you to have it."

She handed the bag over and he held it in hands, smiling at her with his eyes.

"Thank you," he said quietly, opening the flap. He poured the contents out into his hand.

A silver chain with a small medallion attached fell into his large palm. A picture of a male angel with huge wings and a sword was etched on it. He had a shield in the other hand and had a formidable yet angelic look about him. Wyatt turned it over and read the engraving: "St. Michael Protect Us."

"It's the Archangel Michael. He's the one Rose said is your angel," she smiled. "He's- he's the patron saint of warriors."

He looked at it, rolling it over in his palm, his heart swelling.

"Thank you," he whispered.

She smiled at him, tight lipped and hesitant before speaking again.

"I want you to wear it. I want you to wear it if you ever- you know, if you ever have to go over there."

"To war, you mean," he smiled sadly back.

She nodded. "Will you?"

He looked at her sitting perfectly by his side, rumpled from lovemaking. Her eyes were large and sad looking back at him, two pools of green that he'd learned to read so easily.

"Of course."

He put it on then and let it hang down his bare chest. She was overwhelmed to see it on him and put her hand out to feel it, pressing it close to his beating heart. She looked at him straight in the eye and she knew then that he would have to go, she saw him there in her mind plain as day. She continued holding her hand over him until he reached out and put his hand over hers.

"What's wrong, babe?" he asked quietly.

But she couldn't tell him. Wouldn't tell him what she knew to be true: that he would go there. He would go and feel as if he was pushed to the edge of hell. And she was powerless to stop it. He, too, would walk through fire, as Nova had said. She held her hand there and asked for Michael's protection in her head and the words came out without her thinking about it, like someone else said them for her.

"Don't ever give up. Don't ever lose faith," she said quietly.

⟶⟵❂⟶⟵

The backyard was shaded for the first morning hours each day, which allowed Charlotte and Rose to meditate there before heading to the shop. Rose had been insistent since she wanted Charlotte to imagine herself like a tree, sprouting from the earth. The exercise was incredibly effective and Charlotte felt that more and more with each practice.

The morning was fresh and new after the rains the weekend before. Bailey the bunny was growing bigger each day and hopped around her cage, distracting Charlotte. She wanted to hold her but Garrett warned her that if Bailey were to be set free again, Charlotte had better not. Bailey would need to be wild. So Charlotte would watch her in her cage instead, trying hard to forget how it had felt to feed her from a dropper, her little warm body expanding in her hands.

"When are you going to let her go?" Rose asked her after meditation.

Charlotte shrugged, looking over at the bunny. "I don't know. Couple weeks I guess," she said sadly. "I want her to be fast enough. Strong enough."

Rose nodded, smiling. "Rough being a bunny mama."

Charlotte nodded, thinking to herself. The two sat in the grass on a quilt, facing each other as always. She loved her mornings with Rose. Meditation had become a way of coming home for her, going back to a place of peace that was always inside of her. Plus, Rose answered all of her questions, never making her feel silly or insecure about what she asked.

"Aunt Rose, what did Nova mean about walking through fire?" she asked, looking to her aunt thoughtfully.

"You mean before you came here?"

"No, no. I know what she meant with that. How she said I'd have to do it again. How we all have to when you're like us."

Rose sighed, thinking of a way to explain. "Well, babe. It's not like it sounds. I mean, the things that happened to you, it doesn't mean those things will happen again. Is that what you're worried about?"

Charlotte nodded. Just barely. She didn't want to admit how much it scared her for those things to happen again. The freedom she'd felt from it after that summer had shown her a new light. No, she didn't want to go back.

"When Nova says walk through fire she means the dark night," Rose said. She sat up straighter, trying like hell to get her bearings. This was Rose's least favorite topic. Charlotte listened intently.

"What's the dark night?" Charlotte asked.

"It's hard to explain," she said, falling quiet a moment. "Actually, Char. I hate explaining it," she laughed humorlessly. "The dark night of the soul is something Nova thinks all lightworkers have to experience. But I'd like to think it can be negated, or at least diminished with our skills. It's basically your soul being ripped bare, plunged into darkness. Your spirit guides give the ok for this if it's in your plans. They just kinda step back and let the darkness take you for awhile. And it's up to you to fight back."

"But... why?" Charlotte asked simply.

Rose laughed. "Shit, I wish I knew, believe me. I think mostly because you can't ever really know the light without knowing darkness. You can never really know God until you've been tested that way. It's awful, but I'll tell you, it's like a damn badge of honor. Only the strongest can survive it."

Rose was quiet, allowing Charlotte to digest her words. Her face was thoughtful, thinking about what it really meant.

"Have you gone through it?" Charlotte asked.

Rose nodded solemnly. "Yes, babe. When I was young. Some people- some people have more than one, also."

"Like me?" Charlotte asked.

"Like you," Rose said. "You've had one already. Do you want to discuss it with me yet?"

Charlotte fell quiet, looking down at the grass. Suddenly she was that little girl again. That broken little girl with a drunken mother passed out in the other room. She could hear his thick breathing in her ear and feel the heavy weight of him on her chest. Her eyes brimmed with tears and she tried to shake the feeling off of her to no avail.

Charlotte felt her stomach turn and the anger build up in her again. She thought about how everything had changed after that. How she had indeed been pushed into darkness alone with nobody to help her, no one to pray to, no safety net like she had now.

"I can't, Aunt Rose," she whispered, a tear falling from the corner of one eye.

Rose reached out for her hands in front of her and held her in her gaze.

"You don't have to, babe. I know. I know your heart," Rose said comfortingly.

Charlotte nodded, squeezing her hand, and tried to clean her energy free of him for the thousandth time. She tried to detach but she never could completely. Charlotte wiped her eye and exhaled loudly.

"How do you know what happened to me?" Charlotte asked.

She'd never told Rose the whole story, mostly because deep inside, she knew that Rose already saw it. Probably that first night she walked into the house. Rose closed her eyes, shaking her head slowly.

"There are some things I just know, babe. Sometimes through my dreams. Sometimes through a random vision. Sometimes things I don't want to know. And Nova. She's told me you'd come to me for a long time now. She knew that you'd- that you'd had hard times," Rose smiled at her niece sadly. "All I could do was wait. I never knew where you were. Your mom stopped talking to me after the last time I saw you guys. You must've been about 10, right?"

Charlotte nodded, remembering her aunt's brief visit. How she'd bought her little gifts and clothes in her short time there, seeing her need for it immediately.

"That's when I just fell in love with you. So young and full of promise. You shined just like you do now," she paused, thinking. "It was hard to leave, knowing what you were up against but I- there was no choice."

"I know, Aunt Rose. Don't feel bad," Charlotte said quietly.

Rose sighed. "Nova told me how close we are, you know, our souls. She told me what we'd do together one day. How you'd be the most important work I'd ever do. And I- I just had to wait. But here you are. Walked right through the flames and back to me," Rose said, sadly.

Charlotte smiled back at her, squeezing her hand. "That fire. Can I handle it again?"

"My dear, you can handle anything," she said as if it should be obvious.

"And Wyatt. He's got to walk through fire, also," Charlotte said surely.

Rose nodded. "You saw that, did you?"

She thought about his perfect smiling profile, his blue eyes still boyish with joy each time they were together. It was a stark contrast from the Marine of her dreams, eyes empty with anger, heart completely changed.

Charlotte nodded sadly. "You're right. Sometimes there are things you just don't wanna know."

⁃⁃⁃❦⁃⁃⁃

The Santa Cruz County Fair was always the last week in August, which generally meant the rains could be avoided. It would hold true that year, the sun blazing high in the sky and not a cloud in sight. Wyatt and Charlotte pulled up to a crowded parking lot just before dusk, dressed for the dance after the fair, Wyatt in the same button down as the fourth of July and Charlotte in a black simple sundress and the boots Wyatt had given her. Aunt Rose had decided to sit out the fair entirely though.

"Too many people," she'd said. "Too much energy for me to be around."

She'd given Charlotte a brief lecture about keeping her shield up and protecting her energy, which Charlotte had agreed to do. When they pulled up to the crossroads in Sonoita she'd imagined her shield all around her, reflecting any bad energy. She could already feel the overwhelming sense of the crowd and took a few deep breaths to steady herself.

"You alright?" Wyatt asked her as they parked.

"Yeah, fine," she smiled. "Sometimes big crowds are hard for me."

Wyatt nodded. "I get that. Especially after living in Patagonia all summer."

It was true, the quiet of their little town had changed them both that summer, allowing them to detach from their respective problems and live in the silence of nature and each other. They held hands walking into the fair, sticking close to each other's side. Neither had any interest in the carnival rides, Wyatt because his nearly 6'3 frame didn't fit on them and Charlotte because she hated the feeling of not being in control of her own movement.

They walked through the crowd to the 4H tent and strolled through the livestock pens. Country kids from all over the county were dressed in their Sunday best to show their animals- calves, pigs, rabbits, even chickens. It warmed Wyatt's heart to see them standing proudly in their clean stalls, showing off their hard work. A 4H kid himself, he remembered the pride that came along with showing an animal. The fair was the grand finale, what they'd worked toward for months and he could feel their excitement.

He explained the process to Charlotte, who, as usual, asked several follow up questions and listened to his stories. He loved the way she watched his mouth when he talked, holding tight to his hand and acting as if they were the only people for miles around. They stopped in front of the show bunnies and Charlotte asked a proud little girl about her long-hair lop-eared one.

Charlotte squatted down and rested her bottom on the heels of her boots, bringing her hand down to pet the bunny gently. She smiled up at the little girl who was about 7 with long blonde hair braided in pigtails on either side of her face.

"And what is your bunny's name?" she asked.

"George," the little girl said shyly.

"What a good name for a bunny," Charlotte said encouragingly. "And he's beautiful. You've kept his coat so nice," she said stroking it.

The little girl stood up straighter, smiling back.

"I gave him vitamins. And I washed him with coconut oil."

Charlotte kept a straight face, nodding intently. "Well I'll have to keep that in mind for my bunny," she grinned at her. "Good luck to you and George," she winked at her before standing back up and grabbing Wyatt's hand.

"You think Bailey would stand a chance at this show?" he said smiling down at her.

She sighed. "Naw, poor Bailey. Just a plain country bumpkin. It would be like me trying to run for Miss America or something," she laughed.

"And what would be wrong with that? You're way prettier than any Miss America I've ever seen," he said honestly.

Charlotte laughed. "Sure Wyatt. Can you imagine me giving one of those pageant speeches?" she said making a cringing face. "Probably wouldn't go over well."

"Hmm..." he said thoughtfully. "You're right. You're way too honest for that. I think you have to be a bullshitter to do that and as we know, you aren't one."

"Nope!" she said smiling up at him.

Her hair was down and wild around her face and she wore a touch of makeup, accentuating her beauty. He stared at her lips, fluffy and pink with lip-gloss. He stopped walking in front of the calf stalls and leaned down to kiss her briefly. She kissed him back, pulling him back for one more when he moved away.

Once the sun was down the music started, and Charlotte could hear the mariachi guitars and trumpets floating out of the tent where the dance would be held. They had to fight the crowds to get dinner, Charlotte sitting and saving part of a picnic table just outside of the tent while Wyatt waited in line for their dinner- Indian fry bread with beans and pulled pork on top, a local delicacy. He knew she'd love it since she'd never been picky about anything they'd eaten, always gladly trying new things. He found his way back to her and they ate, savoring the food that she did in fact love.

Charlotte had to remind herself several times to put her shield up, working hard not to get overwhelmed with the people and the energy around her. She kept reaching out to touch Wyatt, anchoring herself to him instead of allowing herself to become lost in the loudness of her surroundings. Her face gave her away as always, her furrowed brow and deep breathing making him worried for her. He'd continuously asked her if she was ok, doing all he could to make sure she was comfortable, but she assured him she was fine. When they finished the Navajo tacos, they sat watching the band play. Couples both young and old took to the dance floor to dance to the rapid Mexican music, feet moving quickly to the upbeat sound.

"Now this is a dance I can't do," he said, laughing. "My friends have tried to teach me but I'm no good at it."

She was sitting next to him on the picnic bench, her hand on his thigh. She looked out at the dance floor, then back at him.

"Don't believe you," she said shortly. "You're good at everything."

"Why do you always say that?" he asked.

She shrugged. "Just everything you do. You just do it, I don't know, you do it perfect. And I mean everything," she grinned naughtily.

Wyatt blushed despite himself and Charlotte laughed.

"Awe, I didn't know I could still make you blush, Mr. Earp." She leaned in to kiss the side of his neck.

They sat for a long time watching the band play and people dancing. He liked the feel of her next to him. He'd even gotten used to men gawking at her, some more discreet than others. It didn't matter to him when he knew she didn't look back; in fact, she seemed oblivious to it, clinging close to him as always.

When the band went on break, country music finally started blaring through the speakers. Wyatt pulled her from the picnic table, not saying a word but shooting her a white toothed grin. He led her to the dance floor, hand on the small of her back, and spun her around the floor for several songs in a row. It was packed with people and they had to take care not to run into anyone. They were even more in step than they'd been the last time they'd danced, better practiced and in tune with one another.

He held her close to him for the slow songs, her warm sweaty body pressed tight against his. When they decided to stop for a break they noticed how busy it had gotten; all of the tables were taken and a new batch of people had shown up, mostly young people, dressed to the nines and ready for the dance. Charlotte found herself immediately overwhelmed when they walked off of the dance floor, Wyatt searching for a place to sit. He led her to a retaining wall toward the edge of the tent, already full of people perched on the top of it laughing, drinking, and socializing. Charlotte hopped up and sat on the wall with Wyatt standing in front of her. The night was hot and muggy and Wyatt could feel his shirt sticking to his back. He pulled at his collar, unbuttoning the top button and letting air in.

"Hot," he said to her over the noise. "You thirsty?"

She nodded back to him, looking around at the large crowd.

"Ok, save our place here," he said. "I'll go get us some drinks."

He touched her leg briefly before leaving her to wait in the long line at the bar. She sat and watched him go, taking a deep breath again and centering herself. She was surprised at how much the large group of people was overwhelming her, but Rose had warned her that the more her skills developed, the more she would feel uncomfortable in situations such as this. So she tried to use her tools to fight through it, finding Wyatt through the crowd and shooting him a smile toward the other side of the tent where he stood. She looked back around the dance at the couples dancing and continued her steady breathing.

"Hey."

He'd appeared in front of her seemingly out of nowhere. He was tall, almost as tall as Wyatt, but way skinnier. He had shaggy blonde hair and snaggly teeth that grinned at her. He wore a white t-shirt and dirty jeans and Charlotte could smell the booze on him immediately. She once again put up her shield.

"Hello," she said back coolly.

"I'm Colter," he said, sticking out his hand. Charlotte reluctantly put her hand out and shook it, retracting it directly afterward, a feeling of dread spreading through her as she touched him.

"Charlotte," she said shortly. She looked to Wyatt but he wasn't looking back, his head turned and waiting in line.

"You wanna dance?" he said, smirking out of the side of his mouth. He swayed side to side, hardly able to keep his wits about him.

"No, thank you," she said, looking away from him.

Colter laughed coldly, putting his hand on the wall next to her to steady himself.

"So you think you're too good, huh?" he spit, his eyes narrowing at her.

She could feel her heart pounding in her chest but remained outwardly calm.

"No. I'm here with my boyfriend," she said, hoping that would send him running.

"So?" he said, growing angrier. "I asked to dance with you. Not fuck you."

Charlotte took a deep breath and steadied herself. *Let me have peace*. She said inside her head.

"Just leave me alone," she said firmly.

Colter was indignant in the way only a drunken person can be, completely justified with his own way of thinking.

"You know," he scoffed. "Why do you wear shit like that if you don't wanna be hit on?" he said, waving a hand at her dress. "You have your ass hanging out, you should expect people to notice." He stood, moving closer in front of her and Charlotte inhaled sharply, her inner alarm ringing of danger.

"Get away from me," she said, her voice not wavering, not giving away the fear she felt inside.

"It's a free country," he said, getting in her face. "I can do whatever the fuck I want."

Charlotte tried to put her shield up again, tried to ground herself, tried her peace mantra, and none of it worked. She could feel her hands starting to shake with a mixture of fear and rage.

"I'm gonna tell you one last time to leave me alone," she said steadily.

Colter laughed, his crooked teeth grinning back at her. "Or what? What the fuck are you gonna do? I told you, you don't want people to look don't have your ass hanging out. As a matter of fact," he slurred. "If you don't want people to touch, don't do it either."

He placed his hand on her bare thigh, grabbing her hard and Charlotte didn't hesitate. She raised both legs into her stomach and kicked him in the chest with all of her might. There was commotion around her as he flew to the ground with Charlotte after him. He was on the ground gasping for breath when she came down on top of him, her vision completely red. She put a knee over his throat, indifferent to her dress flying up around her. She could feel people closing in around her, which made her panic even more. Colter squirmed under her but she didn't let up, keeping her knee over his throat.

"Don't ever fucking touch me!" she yelled, hardly able to recognizing her own screeching voice.

Wyatt pushed through the crowd then, his face panicked and angry. He leaned down and grabbed Charlotte under the arms. She jerked violently away from him, bringing her knee back down on Colter's choking throat.

"Charlotte," Wyatt said. "Charlotte, it's me. What happened?"

She looked up at him and Wyatt was taken aback with the look in her eye. She didn't even look like herself- her eyes had the look of a cornered animal. She stood, pushing her way through the crowd without saying a word, people clapping at her and laughing at Colter writhing on the ground. Wyatt had no idea what had happened and wanted to smash Colter's face in for good measure, but Charlotte didn't give him the chance, moving quickly out of the tent. He caught up to her just by the exit, jogging up behind her to keep pace.

"Charlotte, are you ok?" he said worriedly. She didn't respond but kept walking faster toward the truck. "Babe, what happened? Please, stop and tell me." He reached out to her, touching her shoulder, and she shrugged him away roughly. She was breathing heavily, her face red with anger.

"Don't. Please. Just take me home," she snapped.

Wyatt walked in step with her trying to comfort her but it was no use. No matter what he said, she wouldn't look at him, only stare right out in front of her, a vacant, angry look in her eyes. When he opened the truck door for her she sat on the passenger side, not in the middle like she usually did. Wyatt fired up the truck and started driving home, giving her a moment to cool off before asking again if she was ok.

"I'm fine," she said, looking out the window. "Just mad, that's all."

Wyatt hesitated, not wanting to aggravate her more. She was acting like a different person and it scared him to see her so upset, so detached from him.

"What happened?" he asked again quietly.

"He touched me, Wyatt. He just grabbed my leg."

Wyatt tightened his hand on the wheel and thought about turning the truck around to find him.

"I just wanna go home," Charlotte said as if on cue, and Wyatt nodded back, not wanting to make her angrier.

"I'm sorry," he said into the silence of the truck.

She laughed coldly, crossing her arms across her chest and looking back out the window. "Why would you be sorry? You didn't do anything."

"I should have been over there. I shouldn't have left you alone over there," he said remorsefully.

"Please, Wyatt. Clearly I can take care of myself," she said shortly.

"I know that, Charlotte. Everyone knows you can handle yourself," he said, growing annoyed. "I just wanted to be there to help. I shouldn't have left you over there."

"Stop with the Jesus complex, Wyatt. You don't need to ride in and save me. I'm fine."

Wyatt could feel his blood pump through his veins harder and the right hook hit his heart as if it were a physical punch.

"Jesus complex? I just want to help, Charlotte."

She looked at him then across the cab, her eyes still blazing. She kept her arms tight across her chest and Wyatt could see that her hands were still in fists.

"Well just forget that. You're not going to be around to jump out and save me anytime I need it, remember? You're leaving. I've taken care of myself long enough, I don't need anyone to do it for me anyway."

Wyatt's jaw dropped open just a bit and he looked back at her wounded.

"So you're going to be mad at me now? I didn't do anything, Charlotte. You don't have to fight me like this. I just want to help you."

"Well I'm not a fucking charity case so don't bother," she said, raising her voice.

She felt completely out of control of herself and couldn't reel herself in as much as she tried. The anger had taken her and snowballed into something bigger, triggering something scary inside of her.

"So you're going to be mad at me because I want to help or because I'm leaving?" he said, his voice starting to rise.

"Would you just take me home? I don't want to talk about this," she said exasperated.

"You never want to talk about it!" he said, yelling now. "It's in a month, we can't just keep ignoring it!"

"What the fuck do you want me to say, Wyatt? You're leaving. What else is there to talk about? You're leaving so don't sit here and act like you're gonna be the fucking knight in shining armor who can come save me all of the time," she shouted. "It's bullshit!"

They were just on the outskirts of town and Wyatt pulled the truck over to the side of the road, throwing it in park. He rested his hands on the wheel, looking out through the windshield.

"I said take me home," she said after a moment of quiet.

"How many times do you want me to tell you I'm sorry?" he said quietly. "I'm sorry I'm leaving. If I had the choice I wouldn't go anymore."

She laughed again, looking out her passenger side and away from him. "Sure. I'm sure you'd change your life plans for a girl you met a couple of months ago."

He was mad now, he could feel himself starting to lose control like her. He ran a hand through his hair looking at her angrily.

"Yeah, I would. I'm not a liar, Charlotte. It's not my fault every man you've ever met is shit. I'm not them."

She wouldn't look at him. She turned her body to look out the window and he noticed her hands were quaking but she was trying to hide it. Remorse washed over him again and he felt bad for yelling. He knew something was severely wrong and he remembered then how it must have felt for her.

"Babe, I'm sorry. Are you scared? I'm sorry, just calm down. It's me."

"I'm not fucking scared," she said angrily, flipping her head to look at him.

He stared back at her, not breaking eye contact, trying to make her see that it was him. Trying to make her realize that place that they shared together so she would calm down, but she wouldn't budge.

"What do you want, Charlotte?" he asked quietly.

"Just take me home," she said and he didn't respond, but let quiet fall between them, hoping she would see how irrational she was being.

When she didn't speak again he threw the truck into gear and sped back on the highway. Neither of them said a word as he drove and he could feel her trying to detach from him. He pulled up in the drive and she moved to open her door and get out, but he reached a hand over to stop her.

"Charlotte, please. Please, stop," he said quietly.

She looked at him then and he saw a brief glimpse of her recognition of who he really was cross her face, but her eyes still had that scared look of an animal trying to survive.

"This is why you shouldn't want me, Wyatt," she said flatly. "I'm- I'm not- I just can't talk about this. I have to go."

He could feel the stabbing pain hit his chest and he was desperate for her to stay with him, but the more he pushed, the more she pulled back. He nodded slowly, a thousand things he wanted to say, dead on his lips.

Wyatt watched her get out of the truck and up the steps without looking back at him. He sat in his empty truck watching her go as she slammed the front door after her, his heart sinking to his stomach.

He didn't sleep all night. He lay in his bed in the empty bunkhouse waiting for exhaustion to take him over and drift off to sleep but it never came. The night had been completely silent, no storm to listen to, no TV to distract him, and, most notably, no Charlotte to wrap himself up in like he had every other Saturday night that summer. His stomach had a hollowed out feeling and he could feel the physical ache in his chest growing the more time that went on.

Since he was up all night, he had time to devise a plan to fix the problem, much like he always did. He just needed to talk to her, to comfort her, to make her realize who he was and that she was safe with him. He knew he could do it if she just gave him the chance. It was Sunday so she'd be at mass with Rose and maybe, if she had cooled off, she'd go to the lake and wait for him like she always did. But if she didn't, he would go to her house. He'd head to Rose's and knock on the door and insist on talking with her. He could even talk to Rose if that helped, since Rose loved him. Yes, he told himself in the wee hours of that Sunday morning, he could fix this.

He got up to do chores, going through the motions while his mind and heart stayed with her. He realized several times that day that he was working without even being aware of it, his body seemingly carrying out tasks that his mind didn't even agree to. He'd fed the horses and chickens and mucked out the stalls perfectly, afterward looking at it as if it had been someone else's work.

He loaded his fishing pole in the truck and headed to the lake soon after, even though he knew she'd probably still be at church. Secretly he hoped that when she did come and see him at their place with his fishing pole in hand, she'd remember who he was. She'd remember what they'd shared that summer and that he truly did love her. He'd plan to tell her that and to make her realize how serious he was.

She'd doubted him. Doubted the fact that he really would stay with her if he could. The fact that she didn't actually understand or believe his feelings for her was gutting. How many times had he thought about it? Thought about how different it could be if he didn't have to leave? He'd kept it all locked inside of him instead of telling her, but he would tell her now, even if it scared her. He would tell her how he really felt, how he would marry her right now if she wanted to. He was ready, in his sleepless haze, to put it all on the line.

There would be no storm again that day but he was fine with it. He wanted her to come there, to be in their place, and the rain would only get in the way. He set his pack and the army blanket under their tree and put a line far out into the water. The lake was calm again that morning, not a person in sight since school had started up again and summer fun had come to an end.

He sat there for hours in the heat of the day, catching a few bluegills and throwing them back in afterward, not even able to laugh about how little they were. The more time that passed, the more his heart ached. He looked at his watch constantly, timing when he knew she would have been done with mass. It was pushing two o'clock when he realized she wasn't going to show. She'd been done with church for hours by then and was nowhere in sight.

He decided to move onto his contingency plan of heading to the house. He loaded his truck and nervously drove there, his hands sweating on the wheel the whole way. He tried to keep himself calm and remind himself how she must have felt. She was scared, she was reacting. His poor Charlotte had been through things he had no idea about and some asshole triggered her, that was all. He could fix it.

When he arrived at Rose's he noticed her car wasn't in the carport, but he was not deterred. Maybe Charlotte being there by herself would be a good thing, he thought. They could talk alone and be in the place that they had shared together. He moved quickly up the steps and knocked on the door, wiping his sweaty hands on his work jeans. He cleared his throat and took a deep breath, preparing himself to talk to her. When no one came to the door he knocked again, waiting a long time before walking around to the backyard.

He knew she sat out back with Bailey frequently and thought she might not be able to hear the door. The back porch was empty, though, and Charlotte was nowhere to be seen. He walked around to the other side of the porch to see the cage wide open and Bailey gone. He felt his stomach drop again and the shot hit his heart. He felt panicked seeing the empty cage even though he knew she'd planned on letting Bailey go. Something about it unsettled him though.

He couldn't bring himself to go back to the empty bunkhouse even though he had no more plans. The library was closed on Sundays and there was nowhere else she could be unless she and Rose ran up to Tucson or another neighboring town. If that were the case he should wait for her. So he did. He sat on the front porch swing and waited for a solid two hours before finally calling it quits. He felt completely pathetic waiting for her for so long, wasting an entire day just trying to talk to her. It reminded him of when he searched the town looking for her all those months ago, but way less hopeful.

He'd head back to the ranch for evening chores, planning to try again at nightfall. Surely she'd be back by then, wherever she was. He didn't turn on the radio for the drive home but sat in his own silent misery. He missed her. Only yesterday she'd sat in his truck hugging tight against him on the way to the fair, but it felt like it had been ages since then. He was in trouble, no doubt.

He pulled his truck up to the barn and fed the horses their evening hay and grains, again working only from his physical body. His mind was still absent. He cringed when he saw Garrett come out of the big house and head toward the barn, knowing that he couldn't fake being happy and that he couldn't share anything with him, fiercely protective over

Charlotte's past and secrets. He kept working, not stopping when Garrett found his way to him.

"Hey, Wyatt. Been looking all over for you since this mornin'," he said, standing in front of him with his hands on his hips.

"Sorry sir, you need something?" He tried his best to fake normalcy but hardly recognized his own voice.

"Well," Garrett said, spitting out in front of him, "Rose called here for you, but you were gone."

Wyatt stopped working and squared his shoulders to Garrett, listening intently.

"She did? What did she- did she need something?"

He could feel the sweat forming under his hat and his heart beating in his chest. Rose didn't call for Wyatt, not ever, for anything. Something was wrong.

"Well, it's a bad deal really. Charlotte-" he stared, "her mama died."

Wyatt felt the earth had been pulled out from under him, his throat so thick he couldn't respond.

"They left to Texas this morning to go settle everything. Rose just didn't want you to be worried."

"But-" Wyatt fumbled. "Why- how did it happen?"

Garrett shrugged. "She didn't say," Garrett looked at Wyatt closely. "You alright son?"

"Yeah," he said, trying to get his bearings. "I just- I feel bad for her," he stumbled, his tortured feelings, his grief for her too much to explain.

Garrett shook his head. "I know it. Poor kid. Rose told me she hasn't had it easy. Just the sweetest girl, too," he said sadly.

"Are they going to come back?" Wyatt said stupidly. He didn't realize how pathetic it would sound before he thought it. "I mean, do you know when they'll be back?"

Garrett shrugged. "I'd imagine several days. It's a full day's drive each way."

Wyatt nodded, leaning his hand against the barn for support.

"Thanks for letting me know, sir."

Garrett nodded and slapped Wyatt on the shoulder before walking away, leaving him in the quiet of the barn by himself, his world tumbling uncontrollably away from him.

VI

"I said to my soul, be still and wait...
So the darkness shall be the light,
and the stillness the dancing."
~T.S. Elliot

Rose sat in the quiet of her car trying to focus only on the road in front of her. She felt completely out of control of herself and that was a foreign feeling for her. In an instant, she'd gone from being rooted to the earth to spinning, spiraling into darkness. Feeling as pathetic as one of her clients was not something she enjoyed and she inwardly battled herself to pull out of it, to be brave for Charlotte, but she felt like she was failing.

She hadn't been told how her sister had died but she didn't need to be. She'd known this was coming. In fact, when her skills started to emerge as a child, she knew even then. She woke from a horrific nightmare one night and shook her sister awake. She'd tearfully warned her then not ever to do drugs.

She made her promise that she would never touch anything more than a drink or two and Lily had agreed, at the time. Whether she had forgotten about Rose's warning or whether she just didn't care, Rose had no idea, but Lily didn't heed that warning. She'd started smoking pot in high school, drinking heavily, and eventually moving onto more exotic things like cocaine.

It was Rose's first lesson in futility. Sometimes, no matter what she saw, no matter what warnings she shouted from the rooftops, it flat out didn't matter. It had been the first of many times that she'd had to watch someone ruin themselves after she had specifically told them the right road to take. Yes, she'd known this was coming for a long time so she couldn't understand why it hurt so much, why she felt so empty inside.

She looked over at Charlotte in the passenger seat. The girl hadn't cried when Rose told her, but nodded her head slowly and walked promptly to the bathroom and vomited for the better part of an hour, not making a sound except her retching. She didn't cry after that, either, but calmly asked Rose if they could go to Texas to get her, to do something, even though it was too late. Charlotte, too, had been warned by her own dreams, by the whispering in her ear before she fell asleep, but she'd done nothing. Nothing but prayed. And clearly, that wasn't enough.

Rose had tried to talk to Charlotte but it was like running into a brick wall. They'd left the house early and were all the way to El Paso and she'd only responded briefly when Rose asked her something. So she let the girl have her silence and sat supportively by her side, even though it broke her heart to watch her sweet, normally vivacious niece stare vacantly out the window. She prayed in her head, she said her mantras, she even tried to clean Charlotte's energy, but she felt completely bogged down by the sludge and grief hanging thick in the air between them.

Please, God. Let me help her. Please God, don't let me lose her.

Rose wasn't one for making deals with God. Usually she prayed and trusted, knowing the divine would not steer her wrong. But this was different, she couldn't leave it to someone else this time, no, not with her Charlotte.

Please God, don't let her give up now. Rose pleaded as she drove on toward Texas to bring Lily home.

❧❦❧

September. The month had changed and she'd still been gone. The next month he'd be gone, away from her and everything they had together. Wyatt had never hated September more. He counted the days in his head constantly. The days she'd been gone, the days since he'd kissed her, the days since he'd loved her in his bed, the days since she'd turned and run up the steps toward her house, not looking back. Most of all, he counted the days he had left before he had to go. Every day she stayed gone ripped him open since he knew that was a day wasted.

Five days. She'd been gone five days and he had no word from her or Rose. Not that he expected to, he hoped though. Every time Garrett came out to check work in the barn or in the fields, Wyatt looked at him hopefully, willing him to tell him some news, but there was nothing. The days dragged painfully on and nothing helped, nothing made him stop thinking of her as much as he tried.

He went to the lake every afternoon without fail, each time hoping she'd appear magically as she'd done that first day and days after, a mermaid in the middle of the desert. She never did, though, and it always felt empty there without her. Even emptier when he pulled away alone without her sitting close to his side. He got in the routine of leaving the lake and heading straight to her house, his heart falling each time he saw the empty carport and the shades still drawn. He'd watered Rose's plants and even mowed her lawn, the feeling of helplessness too much to bear to continue doing nothing.

He thought about going back to Tucson for a couple of days, of finally calling his dad and visiting home, but he couldn't bring himself to do it. He wasn't even the same person he'd been when he left, he was no longer able to fake it. To be the Wyatt they'd all known forever. Plus, what if he left and she finally came back? No, he had to stick it out and wait. Keep vigil until she returned and he could do something, although he had no idea what.

⌒⊶⊷⊶⌒

The lull of the car should have put her to sleep, but it didn't. She didn't know if she would ever be able to sleep peacefully again without a nightmare ripping her from darkness and sitting her up screaming for help. Rose had been there each time she'd woken, holding her and rocking her slowly until she could calm her breathing and try futilely to get the images from her mind. Images she'd never be rid of.

She swore the last time she left would be the last time she'd set foot in Texas, but she'd been wrong. Three was the number. Three. The months it had taken her to return. Three. The months it had taken for her mom to die without her there. Three. The days that her mom lay dead in her filthy apartment before anyone had noticed she'd been gone. Charlotte thought shamefully of the things she'd been doing while her mom was dead, with no one to help her. She'd gone about her new, beautiful life, laughing with Rose, loving Wyatt, all while her mother's heart was no longer beating. She was no longer of this earth and Charlotte had no idea.

How had she not known? Rose, even Nova, had told her over and over again how talented she was. How much she could see, and still, she'd seen nothing. Worse than that, she'd done nothing. She'd done nothing but listened to the whispers in her ear and ignored them. Said a prayer like Nova had told her and went bouncing back to her happy life in Patagonia.

Rose continued driving them back to Arizona, all the while looking from the road ahead of her and back to Charlotte. Charlotte knew she should try and fake it, muster a smile for her sweet aunt who'd done so much for her, but she couldn't. Even her tie to Rose was tainted now. She'd picked her aunt over her own mother and now, Lily was dead. Charlotte was filled with guilt and grief, going over her last moments with her mother.

I'm sorry, mom. I'm sorry. She said to herself over and over again.

But no one talked back. No message popped in her head, no angels whispered to her. The light inside of her that she had felt burning so brightly only days ago was gone.

I deserve this. This is my fault. She thought, hating herself for what she'd become. She had put her needs before anyone else's, and that's why she couldn't stand to be in her own body, why she couldn't stand the look of her own reflection in the mirror. For all of her fears of being just like her mother, she'd done it. She'd done it in a more brutal way than she could ever have imagined. Above all else, she was Lily's daughter. She was, as she feared, just like her mother.

⋯⋰⊹0⊹⋱⋯

Fridays were usually his favorite day of the week. That meant work was over and he would have more of Charlotte, the lake, and more Charlotte. But when he woke up that Friday morning he didn't feel his normal excitement for the day. He even had to tell himself not to get his hopes up about her finally being home. That way he wouldn't be so devastated when he went to the lake and didn't see her there. His heart wouldn't fall into his stomach when he once again saw the empty carport and the curtains over the windows. At least, that's what he told himself.

Garrett had them vaccinating the cattle that day, easy in comparison to branding, which was good because it was only Garrett and Wyatt working. All of the vaqueros left early for the weekend for a relative's wedding in Mexico, leaving the bunkhouse blissfully empty a whole day early.

"Family's so damn big, they've got a wedding or a party every weekend," Garrett laughed to himself, prepping the shots. "Just me and you, son. We can knock this out in no time though." He patted Wyatt on the shoulder as they walked to the barn to saddle Sunny.

Wyatt was stoic, uncharacteristically quiet but just as productive as always, maybe more so. The work was the only thing that made the minutes go by faster. The aching in his back and arms from the arduous chores of the week was the only thing that took away from the pain in his chest and the hollowed out feeling in his gut. He'd considered picking another fight with Santiago before he left, just to find a distraction from the pain, but ultimately decided he didn't even have the energy for that.

No matter how many times he tried to talk himself out of it, he couldn't shake the feeling that she was gone for good. That she was never returning and he'd have no way to reach her again, no way to find her. Just like after the first day he'd met her, he'd have no idea where to start. Plus this time, he'd be gone, too. With just over a month until he left for basic training, he was running out of time.

Wyatt hefted a saddle onto Sunny's back and pulled the cinch tight around his center. He patted the side of his front haunch, moving his other arm around his neck and releasing his halter. He gently slipped the bridle around his nose and clipped it behind his ears. Sunny pushed his head into Wyatt, rubbing against him.

"Think he's gonna miss you," Garrett said, stopping to watch them.

Wyatt cracked a small smile. "He's a good horse," he said quietly, patting Sunny again. "You want me to push the cattle in, sir?"

Garrett nodded. "Only the ones in this front corral. We'll do the rest next week."

"You sure?" Wyatt asked, confused. It wasn't like Garrett to not want to finish it all in a day. He was, next to Luis, the most efficient man he'd ever met.

Garrett nodded back to him. "You've worked hard this week, son. You deserve to knock off a little early. I know it's been a hard week for you."

Wyatt flushed, he hated that he'd been so transparent and even more than that, he was embarrassed that Garrett was fussing over him the same way he'd fussed over Charlotte. He found himself once again thankful the other men were gone.

"Alright, then," Wyatt said and finished saddling Sunny.

"I bet she'll be back this weekend. I'd imagine that anyway. Unless they had the funeral there. But they don't have any kin there. Well, they don't have any here either, so hell, I don't know."

Wyatt avoided eye contact, checking the tightness of the cinch and being sure nothing was pinching

Sunny. He nodded at Garrett without responding but Garrett stayed put.

"I'm sure she'll be happy to see you," he persisted.

There was quiet between them until Wyatt sighed, trying to be as nonchalant as possible.

"I don't really know what I'll say to her, though," he said, looking at the ground.

Garrett nodded, looking back at Wyatt. "Not much you can say to someone when things like this happen. Most people just wanna be heard. Maybe just listen to her. You've got a gift for that," he said smiling then turned to walk toward the corrals.

Garrett had a way of saying so much in so few words. He also had a way of comforting him in the least coddling way possible. Wyatt felt his chest tighten again thinking of his life there that summer. Garrett, Rose, Luis, and, of course, Charlotte. He'd made a life there. He'd been there with them and soon he'd be gone, and maybe it would be like he'd never been there at all. It all made him feel empty.

Wyatt stood next to Sunny's side with his hand on the saddle horn and pulled himself easily up into the saddle. The day was hot but not as bad as usual, clouds hung thick in the sky casting a darkness over the fields but posed no threat of rain. He followed Garrett to the corals and set to work, pushing the cattle toward the shoot where Garrett would give each cow its shot, then release it into a neighboring corral. At first the work was tricky with only the two of them there, but, as always, Garrett had a plan and Wyatt had no doubt the old man could have actually done the whole thing on his own if he needed to.

Wyatt pushed all of the cows in line for the shoot, Sunny happily going after the few stragglers who wanted nothing to do with Wyatt or the large cutting horse coming at them over and over again. Wyatt loved being on Sunny. He rode smooth and steady, a dream compared to some of the skittish horses he'd grown up riding. Being on him was one of the only things that took his mind off of her, if only for a minute before he thought of her sitting on that very horse, perched with her chin high and shoulders set behind her. Then he was back in his spiral.

He and Garrett worked well together. After Wyatt pushed all of the cattle in the shoot, he dismounted and tied Sunny to the nearest post. He helped Garrett prep each shot and watched as he skillfully grabbed the skin off of the shoulder of each cow with one hand and quickly injected the shot with the other. Wyatt released each one after quickly opening the shoot, closing it again before the next one could escape.

"How come you don't have a vet do this, sir?" Wyatt asked as they worked.

"Used to. Got too damn expensive, though, so I started doin' it on my own," Garrett chuckled. "Plus vets always have an ego about them. Don't know what it is about a man with a bunch of schoolin' makes him think his shit don't stink."

Garrett was right, they knocked out the work in no time, finishing the entire corral before the day was up. Wyatt asked Garrett over and over again if he wanted to finish all of the cattle but the old man wouldn't budge, insisting Wyatt deserved the afternoon off, even inviting him in the big house for a sandwich once he unsaddled Sunny.

Wyatt, despite his dark mood, enjoyed the day with Garrett, valuing, once again, the man's quiet, steady way with him. They walked together to the big house, each of them washing up before lunch. Wyatt splashed water on his face, removing the grime and sweat from the day's work. When he walked in the kitchen, Garrett was making them sandwiches and had a Corona on the table for each of them. Wyatt stood next to him, wanting to help, but Garrett fixed his plate for him, telling him shortly to sit and drink his beer before setting a turkey sandwich in front of him.

"Eat up, son. You're wasting away," he said, slapping his solid arm.

"Thank you, sir," Wyatt said, digging in. The two sat in companionable silence until Wyatt broke it.

"Sir- I," he faltered for the right words. "I wanna say thank you for having me this summer," he looked down at the table. "It's been- it's been a really great experience and you've been real good to me. I just want you to know how much I appreciate it."

Garrett smiled at him. "Don't think I've ever had a hand say that before," he laughed heartily. "Usually they quit and don't say anything."

Wyatt smiled at him, taking a long drink of his beer.

"You shouldn't be the one thankin' me, Wyatt. You've done real well here. Gonna be sorry to lose ya," he smiled with his eyes looking closely at him. "But you've got bigger fish to fry, my boy. You've got some miles to put on those tires. But you can come back here anytime. You're always welcome."

Wyatt nodded to him, afraid if he spoke again he would get emotional. Garrett and his ranch had changed everything for him. It had brought him there, taught him so much, and, of course, led him to her.

They were in the middle of dishes when the phone rang. Wyatt's heart jumped in his chest but he tried to remain outwardly calm when Garrett crossed the kitchen to pick it up.

"Hello," he said gruffly. "Oh hi," he said, his tone softening. "Yes. Yes of course. Ok, I'll send him now," he said, shooting Wyatt a glance. "Ok. Ok, bye now."

Wyatt put down the dish he was washing and looked at Garrett, his hands to his sides already beginning to shake. It was her. He knew.

"That was Rose," Garrett said gently. "She said she needs your help at her place."

⚬⚬❍⚬⚬

He practically flew across the yard to his truck parked all the way by the bunkhouse. A million thoughts ran through his head. Garrett had said it was Rose, not Charlotte. What if she didn't come back? What if she had stayed in Texas? He was already devising a plan to drive to get her, going through the hypothetical scenarios in his head. His stomach churned and he immediately regretted the sandwich and beer he'd inhaled at lunch.

He pulled into Rose's drive in the late afternoon light, the clouds still making the day darker than normal. He thought he would be more relieved to see her car finally parked in the drive but he wasn't. He realized the only thing that would fix him would be her. Seeing her in front of him. Nothing else. He parked and walked briskly up the stairs and knocked on the door, praying Charlotte would be the one to answer.

Rose creaked the door open and Wyatt had to work to keep his reaction in check. He'd never seen her look like she did in that moment and it scared him to see her that way. Steady, formidable Rose stood in front of him and looked even smaller somehow. She had on no makeup and her eyes were red-rimmed from crying. Her hair was not in place as it normally was, but hung in a brown mess around her face. She wore overalls and an old t-shirt underneath. A far cry from the put together woman he was used to. She sighed when she saw him standing there and began to cry softly. Without thinking he stepped to her and hugged her gently against him, patting her back.

"I'm sorry about your sister," he said quietly.

Rose hugged him back tightly, patting his lower back where she could reach.

"Come in sweet boy. I need to talk to you."

Wyatt's heart sank at her words, his stomach knotting even more when he looked around and didn't see Charlotte. Rose walked to the kitchen and sat down at the table, motioning for him to sit, but he couldn't.

"Where is she?" he said, his voice catching on the last word.

Rose smiled sadly up at him. "You poor thing. You've been so worried. So sad." She looked down at the table then back at him. "Just sit for a minute. Let me talk to you."

Wyatt finally obliged, sitting opposite Rose with his shaking hands in his lap.

"She's back. She's here," she said, reading his fears. "She's at the lake. We- we spread Lily's ashes there. And I-" her voice trembled. "I couldn't get Charlotte to leave," she said, wiping the corner of her eye.

"What happened? What happened to your sister?" he said, his manners failing him.

"She overdosed, Wyatt. She was an addict." Her words hung on the air between them. He'd long since known Charlotte's mother wasn't right, wasn't a great parent, but he didn't expect that. He felt his heart burn thinking of how it must have felt for Charlotte. Suddenly he understood her so much more. That one piece of information unlocked a truth about her that he hadn't seen before that. His mouth hung open as he stared at Rose across the table.

"Wyatt, I just wanted to warn you. Charlotte's not herself. She's very broken right now. I've known this was coming and I tried to prepare her without telling her. Without warning her all of the way. I thought-" She said, a tear falling on her cheek. "I thought if I built her up... If I made her strong again that she'd be able to face it. But," she said sadly, "it just wasn't enough."

Wyatt wanted to say something to help her, to make her feel better, but he couldn't find the words.

"What do I do, Rose?" he asked quietly.

She smiled at him and reached to grab his hand across the table.

"Just love her, Wyatt. And don't ever give up on her," she whispered and Wyatt felt the chill run up his spine.

⸎

The lake was completely silent, almost eerily so. The clouds still hung thick in the sky, hazing over the sun behind them. He parked his truck in the regular spot and moved quickly through the desert. Usually he would have been upset about still being dirty and in his work clothes, but he didn't have the presence of mind to care. His boots scuffed through the desert brush on his now well-worn trail to their place. Where he knew she'd be.

He saw her as soon as the lake came into view, sitting on her knees in the shallows of the water with her messy blonde hair blowing around her. She wore the white dress she'd worn on her birthday, which was soaked from her bottom down. He stopped walking, struck by how heartbreakingly beautiful she was. By how alone she looked with nothing but nature around her.

Shaking himself from his trance, he walked toward the shore, coming closer and closer to her. She didn't turn around although he was sure she'd heard him. He stood just feet from her, his mouth dry and a pit in his stomach. For all of the time she'd been gone, he should have had something to say. Something to help her. But there was nothing. His helplessness overwhelming him into silence.

"I'm sorry for how I acted before I left," she said without turning around. "I shouldn't have treated you like that." Her words were flat, devoid of her usual emotion.

"Charlotte-I" Wyatt faltered. "Don't worry about that. I- I'm so sorry. I'm so sorry about your mom."

Charlotte's hands hung in the water to her sides. She continued looking out across the lake, not turning to look back at Wyatt.

"She's here now. I put her in the lake."

Wyatt was quiet, remembering what Garrett said. To just listen.

"The last thing I said to her was that I didn't love her anymore. That was the last thing I said. That day before I left. I meant it, too. I hated her."

Wyatt squatted down just feet behind Charlotte, moving as close as he could without touching the water. Without touching her even though he ached to.

"He came back. That's why I left. She let him back in our house and I- I couldn't take it. I thought I might kill him if I stayed."

"She let who back?" Wyatt asked, confused.

"Him," she said, and turned to look at Wyatt. Her eyes were still beautiful but they were haunted now, nothing like the softness she had before that. Or even the slight sadness she normally had. Wyatt looked back at her, trying to steady her with his gaze, but she looked away and he understood then who she meant.

"She said he was different. That he had changed and he was sorry. That she loved him and I had to understand," Charlotte went on, her voice almost robotic.

"And she knew?" he asked quietly. "She knew what happened?"

"She walked in on it," she said, her voice not faltering. "She knew."

Wyatt thought he might vomit to think of it then. To think of Charlotte as a little girl, helpless and violated that way.

"She left him that time," she said, shaking her head. "I thought I was rid of him for good." Charlotte slumped over, moving her hands around in the water slowly, absentmindedly.

"Then he was back. A couple of weeks before I left. I came home one day and there he was, on the couch with my mom. I thought it was one of my nightmares but it wasn't. It was really him."

She was silent again and Wyatt had to restrain himself from splashing into the lake and taking her in his arms. He knew she didn't want that. He knew she just needed to be heard.

"She was high that day. Like, higher than I've ever seen her. And different. I think heroin. She'd been clean for small stretches but I knew with him back that would be over. And it was."

She looked down at her hands in the water where hours ago she'd released her mother from them and into the lake. Her mother, no longer flesh and blood but dust, returned to the earth. It couldn't be real.

"I wasn't ready to go yet. I'd saved the money so many times and had to spend it to keep our electric on- pay bills. Or she took it for drugs. That happened a few times- before I started keeping it all in my bra. I wasn't ready to leave yet but I had to- I didn't have enough money. I hardly made it here. But I couldn't stay there with him."

She moved her hands around in the sand feeling the grains move through her fingers, imagining some of them as her mom.

"She passed out and he came home mad. He tried to wake her up, like, pushing at her and slapping her face and I just- I snapped. I started hitting him, scratching him. Fighting him. I wanted him to fight back so I could kill him. Or maybe so that he'd kill me. I didn't care."

Wyatt could feel the tears burning his eyes but he fought to keep himself in check. Of all of the times he wished she would talk to him, share more of herself, he never imagined he'd want to beg her to stop. But he did. He felt physical pain thinking about her so hopeless. His Charlotte, so alive, so free.

"He liked it though. He was laughing. He wouldn't hit me back, only held my arms real tight while I fought him. It just-" Her breath caught but she recovered herself. "It just made me even more mad. I went crazy."

Wyatt thought of her at the fair. Her scared but infuriated face. The face of someone trying to survive at all costs. She came into focus for him, even more than she had before. He was starting to understand that place in her, that shadow of darkness she'd kept hidden from him.

"She woke up when we were fighting. Finally. And she- she blamed me. She took his side. So I told her. I told her I fucking hated her. I told her I didn't love her anymore. And I took off. I just left to the library where I worked. I stayed until it closed then walked until I knew they'd be asleep and I could pack my bag. And then I left. I left and I told myself I'd never go back."

He reached for the right words but couldn't decide what he should say. What words could he possibly find to make a dent in her grief?

"She rotted in there three days before anyone found her. He left, who knows when. And she had no one. She had no one because I left. I left her and she died. Nobody even cared. No one even noticed."

She looked back at him again briefly with the same vacant stare before looking away again.

"I had to identify her body. She had bruises all over her. She was missing teeth." Charlotte shook her head, looking down into the water. "It didn't even look like her. She was beautiful when I was young. She would walk into a room and everyone noticed. She was just- she sparkled. But she hasn't. She hasn't for a long time. When I got older and- and people, men, started to look at me instead of her she- she started to hate me more. I mean, she was never loving like Rose but she started to get, you know- mean. Plus, I was the reason she had to leave him."

Wyatt inched closer to her, listening quietly.

"I wanted to get back at her for all of that. That's why I left. For me, but also because I wanted her to hurt," she sighed. "I guess I did it."

"You did the right thing, Charlotte," he whispered, trying to soothe her.

"I shouldn't have let her die," she said, ignoring what he said.

There was quiet between them. Wyatt knew her well enough to know when to say when. He didn't want to push her, he just wanted to help her. He had no idea how to do that though. He sat squatting still feet behind her and let her sit in silence without prompting her to speak again. The wind blew through the mesquite trees around the lake and Wyatt could smell the rain in the air, distant but still there floating toward them.

"Baby? Will you please come out of the lake? You're going to get sick if you stay in there."

Charlotte didn't respond but looked down into the sand under the water, moving her hands through it once again.

"Please, babe. Let me take you out of here."

His voice was pleading and so sad for her that she couldn't take it, his unwavering kindness too much to handle. She doubled over, grabbing her stomach and began to cry. Wyatt couldn't hold himself back any longer. He stepped into the lake with his boots still on and scooped her gently into his arms, cradling her against him. He kneeled down on the beach holding her while she sobbed into his chest, clinging tightly to him.

"Sweet girl," he whispered into her hair, kissing her head. "You're so brave. Just cry. It's ok."

He rocked her back and forth like a child and let her tears fall into his chest. She sobbed uncontrollably, bellowing into his chest in breaths that gasped for air. He patted her back and stroked her hair, letting her lose herself like he knew she needed. They sat like that for a long time, until her dress was done dripping water on his jeans. The sun was sinking behind the mountains and he knew he had to get her to Rose. He still held her as she caught her breath, her breathing unsteady like a crying child.

"Let me take you home," he said, kissing her head again.

She nodded, her face red from crying. Wyatt looked around for her shoes and saw her sandals nearby. He set her gently on the beach and brought the shoes to her, slipping them on her water pruned feet and helping her to stand. He led her to the truck quietly, opening the driver's side and helping her to the middle seat in the truck.

As he drove back to Rose's house, he kept one arm around her. She leaned into him, letting him keep her tight against him. He said nothing, but just sat steadily by her side. She fell asleep within minutes of the drive, her eyelids falling heavily closed in the warmth of his shoulder.

He pulled her close and listened to her breathing. It was the same rhythmic sound he treasured the few nights they'd spent together. When they arrived, he put the truck in park and shut off the engine carefully so he didn't wake her. He looked down at her face, tear streaked, eyes swollen and puffy, and he was still sure she was the most beautiful thing he'd ever seen. Her lips were gently parted and he wanted to kiss her, to feel her against him, but he knew he shouldn't. Instead, he opened his truck door and gently pulled her out and into his arms. He walked her to the house and she still didn't wake, but snuggled in closer to him, the fight entirely gone from her.

Rose pulled open the front door before he could knock, still looking as disheveled as before and sighing with relief upon seeing Charlotte in his arms. She motioned him toward Charlotte's room and he dutifully followed. She pulled back the blankets on the bed so he could lay her down. Once she was in the bed, Rose moved the covers around her, tucking her in. Wyatt stood, looking down at Charlotte, his arms empty without her in them. Rose looked at Charlotte's face then and gasped.

"Did she cry?" she whispered, looking at him with wide blue eyes.

He nodded, thinking that should have been obvious.

"She hasn't cried since I told her," she whispered, shocked.

Wyatt felt bad then, like it was something he did. He looked from Charlotte's poor tear stained face to the ground, moving his hands in his pockets.

"No, no," Rose said to him in hushed tones. "It's good," she said, wiping a tear from her own eye and smiling up at him. "She needed you. She needed you so she could let go," Rose's voice caught. "You did good," she said, patting his arm.

They stood looking down at Charlotte, her blonde hair stretched out on the pillow beside her the way he loved.

"Can I stay with her? Please?" he asked quietly.

Rose smiled and stood on her toes to kiss his cheek. "Of course you can."

She left him in the quiet of the room and he sat gently on the edge of the bed, removing his boots and laying down close to her side. She didn't wake but moved into him, nuzzling her head in the same place she'd fallen asleep, both of them drifting off to the place of dreams, where the world no longer existed.

⁂

Rose wanted to keep the shop closed another week, but Charlotte insisted that she open again on Monday. She knew the price of closing the shop for two weeks in a row would be catastrophic for Rose's finances and she refused to be the source of that burden. So Rose complied, thinking that the work might be good for Charlotte, the distraction helpful for her. Maybe then, Rose thought, she'd be able to pull her out of the spiral of grief she knew the girl couldn't escape on her own.

Charlotte had spent the weekend mostly sleeping. Once Wyatt brought her home and lay down next to her, she had finally rested. She slept until lunchtime the next day, giving Wyatt time to go home for chores and a shower before returning to be with her. He'd sat with Rose in the kitchen speaking quietly about what they could do to make her feel better. Maybe watching a movie, going out to dinner, or a trip up to Tucson would do her some good? But when she finally woke it was past noon, her face was still drawn and serious even after she walked out of her room and saw them sitting there. All they were able to do was coax her to eat some soup before she returned to her room, Wyatt coming silently behind her, laying down close by her side, all the while his heart breaking to see her that way.

So Monday morning Rose vowed that they would get back to normal. She'd nurse the girl back to her old self the same way she had when she arrived there. Yes, she told herself over and over, she'd be able to do it. They'd meditate, cook, laugh, and have fun in the shop just like always. But when she peeked at Charlotte during meditation and saw that the girl's eyes were not closed but open with that same blank stare, she knew she had a lot of work ahead of her.

Business at the shop would start to pick up again. It was September, which meant slightly cooler weather and birdwatchers, who practically invaded southern Arizona each fall and winter. A complete humdrum hobby in Rose's opinion, although she faked it well for the sake of her business. Within two hours of opening the shop they had several birders awaiting a reading, leaving Charlotte without Rose for most of the day. She didn't chat with the patrons as usual but busied herself cleaning obsessively, wiping the dust that had accumulated in every corner over the past week.

Her body executed the movements but she was not there. She was deep in her head in the darkness of her dreams, mulling over everything that had happened. She had worked with Rose all summer and had learned all about the symbolism of dreams, how they send messages, how they give warnings, so she knew things were only going to get worse. She'd lost her mother, but she'd not yet hit bottom. Her dark dreams of her mother's dead body, face rotting and teeth missing, coupled by her dreams of Wyatt, lost and hateful, haunted her waking minutes almost more than her sleep.

The only time she'd slept was with him lying close to her. She'd fallen into a dreamless sleep, resting more than she had in the entire week she was gone. When she'd woken with a start, he was immediately alert, pulling her close to him and hugging her tight, never saying a word but just there, his sturdy, warm body the only thing securing her to the earth. She'd seen him watch her, even though she'd tried to ignore it. He looked at her the same way some of her teachers would, or the librarian in Texas, the pity splashed so clearly on his face that it made her ashamed, just like it always had.

So she cleaned. She did anything she could at the shop to not interact with anyone. She couldn't fake it. Couldn't talk about angels or energy or God. None of it was in her anymore and she marveled at how quickly it was gone, like it was never there at all.

"Charlotte? Charlotte?" Rose called to her, pulling her from her reverie.

She was behind the front desk on her hands and knees, wiping the corner of the floor and vigorously trying to get all of the dust out of the shop. She looked up at her aunt and saw her brows drawn together in concern. Rose had pulled herself back together that workday but not entirely. She wore a white peasant blouse and dark jeans cuffed at the bottom. She looked classy as always but Charlotte knew she still wasn't right. Her makeup wasn't completely done and she wore no jewelry, a rarity for Rose.

"I have one more reading then we're done. You want to sit in on it?" Rose asked eagerly.

Charlotte shook her head. "No thanks. I have more to do out here."

"You sure? You wanna go home for a nap instead?"

Charlotte shook her head again. "No, I'm ok," she said, managing a small, unconvincing smile.

"Ok, doll baby. I'll be done soon," Rose smiled back, walking her final client into her office.

Charlotte was relieved to be by herself again. She stood from the floor and walked to the shelves to check the inventory, stopping at the display of archangel merchandise. She picked up a book with St. Michael on the cover, sword in hand held high in the sky above him and his foot covering the devil's head below him. She studied his angelic, masculine face trying to find the strength she'd found in it before. Searching herself for that place of comfort that had emerged that summer, somewhere deep inside of her. But she found nothing. She came up empty and hollow each place she looked.

"Can you even hear me?" she whispered. "Are you even real?"

She waited to hear back like she had before, but there was only quiet that surrounded her.

⚜

Wyatt was a fixer, even Rose had told him that. If there was a problem, he always had a way to remedy it. His mathematical mind allowed him to troubleshoot anything in life. Except now. He had no solution for Charlotte and the light gone entirely from her eyes. No way to make her happy since he'd not seen her smile since she returned. Most of all, he had no solution for the fact that he was weeks from leaving her. Leaving her far away to a place where he couldn't even speak to her over the phone. He was at a complete loss as to what to do, twisting his stomach in knots that wouldn't untangle.

He'd gone to her after work each day without fail. But she was never at the lake, sitting waiting for him like a flower in the middle of the desert. She was never at the library, reading quietly. Never sitting on the front porch waiting for him, her face lighting as soon as she saw his truck. Instead, she'd be at Rose's, usually in her room when he arrived. Sometimes she'd be sleeping and others she'd just be laying on the bed silently, staring at the wall. She'd been home almost a week and he hadn't yet succeeded in pulling her out of her dark mood, as much as he tried.

So that Friday, a day that had always been their day, he was determined to make her feel better. If only for a little while. He'd talked with Rose about it and she, willing to try anything at that point, gave him the go ahead to take her. So Wyatt planned. He finished work on Friday and tidied the empty bunkhouse, the vaqueros having left for the weekend and leaving him the quiet he loved.

He showered, changing into his dress jeans and his nicest button down, the same one he wore on her birthday. He stopped in the yard to pick a bundle of sunflowers which he knew wouldn't be around much longer. He tried not to think of them and the fact that in one more month they'd be gone, just like him. He shook his head, trying to rid himself of the thought before filling a mason jar with water and placing the flowers inside, leaving them in the middle of the kitchen table.

Before heading to Rose's, he stopped at the local grocery and picked up steaks, potatoes, and salad. He'd watched Luis cook all summer long, in awe of his talents, but a steak dinner was still all he felt comfortable cooking on his own. He didn't want to mess it up but even if he did, maybe it would make her smile. Maybe she would crack, if only a little bit, at his pathetic attempt to cook for her. When he showed up at her door, Rose answered as she had all week. She still didn't look like her normal self. Her eyes were puffy and red-rimmed and she didn't have as much makeup on as normal. She smiled at Wyatt as she opened the door.

"Ah, Romeo," she said, quietly. "Steady as the sun."

Wyatt smiled shyly and followed her into the kitchen, looking around for her as always.

"How was she today?" he asked quietly.

Rose shook her head, opening the fridge to retrieve a Coke for him.

"The same. Maybe quieter," she replied setting the Coke down on the table beckoning him to sit.

"It's been almost two weeks. I just thought she'd be feeling better by now," she said, sitting across from him.

Wyatt nodded, feeling once again at a loss for words. He'd never known anyone his age to experience that type of personal tragedy. He had no playbook for what to do or how to provide comfort.

"I wish I knew how to help her. I mean, this is what I do. I help people, push them through times like these but- she's just- she's so lost."

Wyatt wished Rose would stop talking. He wished they hadn't gotten so close and she would go back to only exchanging pleasantries with him instead of being so honest. It scared him to hear those things come out of her mouth. Rose, so strong, no nonsense; it was truly awful to see her that way.

"Well, hopefully getting out of the house'll be good for her," he said, trying to be supportive.

Rose nodded, looking up at him.

"Thank you, Wyatt. It's worth a shot," she said, scrunching up her eyes in a smile.

Charlotte came out of the room then and he was a little encouraged. She wore his favorite sundress and had put on a little makeup, her hair piled on her head in a messy bun. She was always beautiful but she still had that sad, empty look in her eyes even when she tried to muster a smile.

"Hi," she said, walking toward the kitchen.

"Hi," he said, shooting through her with his eyes. "You look nice."

He could tell she'd lost weight already, her collar bone more pronounced above her breasts and her cheeks ever so slightly thinner, making her appear older than when he'd met her.

"Wyatt's taking you somewhere tonight, doll. You need out of this house with your lame Aunt Rose. Go be a kid, cause some trouble. Light something on fire, shit, I don't care."

Wyatt laughed and Charlotte smiled, but not like she normally did. Rose was working hard to make her laugh but hadn't yet succeeded.

Rose bid them farewell, pouring herself a glass of wine and sitting on the porch to watch them go.

"What's all this?" Charlotte said when she got in the truck.

"I'm cooking you dinner," he said, grinning over at her. He'd strategically placed the groceries on the floorboard of the passenger side so she had to sit in the middle like always.

She smiled slightly, looking over at him.

"I didn't know you could cook."

"I don't know if I can either," he said laughing. "I might need help."

Charlotte nodded and looked out the window at the town passing them by. She told herself to be happy, to have fun with him like always, that he'd be leaving soon and she owed it to him. All the while the nagging voice inside of her told her she didn't deserve that. That she shouldn't be able to be happy at all. But she fought it as much as she could, scooting closer to Wyatt and asking him about work, about the cattle, Garrett, whatever she could to get him talking instead of her.

When they arrived at the bunkhouse the sun was already beginning to set behind the mountains, making the skyline glow grapefruit orange. The days were already getting shorter and Wyatt almost said so but he stopped himself, not wanting to draw attention to what they both knew was coming. It was barreling at them no matter what they did. With the worst possible timing, October would arrive without fail.

Wyatt carried the groceries in, not allowing her to grab any of the bags, then had her sit at the kitchen table while he commenced cooking. He put a Corona in front of her, making small talk about the ranch, about the vaqueros and their big extended families and endless family parties. Charlotte listened intently and smiled when he told jokes, but he could tell her heart wasn't in it. She'd not mentioned her mother to him since that awful day at the lake and he had to admit to himself that he was almost grateful she hadn't. He'd laid awake almost every night since, going over her story in his head. Her blank gaze haunted him.

"How was work at the shop?" he said, wanting her to talk to him.

She shrugged. "It was ok. Getting busier. Rose had a lot of readings since we were- since you know- we were closed that whole week."

He nodded, chopping lettuce for the salad. "Has she had you sit in for anymore readings?"

She shook her head. "Naw, I've been too busy with the other stuff."

"What's she going to do without you when you go to college?" he smiled at her.

Charlotte's face fell and she quickly picked up her beer, taking a long drink. He knew immediately it was the wrong thing to say somehow, but he'd chugged his beer down, making his tongue loosen.

"I don't know. I don't know if I'm going anymore."

"But-" he said confused, "but you've done so well on your tests and everything. Why wouldn't you go?"

She looked down at the table, her hands on her beer. "I'm just not sure anymore. Of what I should do."

He nodded, trying to ignore his heart pounding in his chest. "I know how you feel," he said, smiling at her sadly. "But I do hope you go. You should- I know how bad you want it."

"Let me help you do something," she said, no longer able to sit. "You wanna bake these?" she asked holding up the potatoes.

He nodded. "I'm already messing this up, aren't I?" he said joking.

Charlotte smiled. "No, but you should put these in now rather than wait. They take awhile."

She stabbed each one with a fork repeatedly before placing them in the oven. When she turned around he was standing in front of her. He'd opened another beer for himself and he felt it go to his head. He smiled, looking down at her, moving closer. He knew she wasn't her normal self, she was fragile, almost breakable compared to normal, so he approached her softly, leaning down to kiss her gently. She kissed him back, moving her arms up around his neck. He moved his mouth away from hers and buried his face in her neck, snuggling into her.

"I miss you," he whispered.

"I'm right here, how can you miss me?" she asked, a slight smile in her voice.

"I know you are. I just- I'm sorry for how hard this is on you."

She pulled away from him gently but he kept hold around her waist.

"I'm fine, Wyatt. You don't have to worry about me. You've got enough to worry about."

He locked eyes with her then and almost let it all come out. Almost asked her what would happen to them, how they could stay together. He'd thought about it over and over. He'd marry her. He'd do whatever she wanted to do, as long as they could be together. But he said none of it, all of the words he'd practiced dead on his lips. So he kissed her instead, cracking a joke about her apron he wished she'd brought.

Dinner was delicious in its simplicity. He'd grilled the steaks on the front porch using mesquite wood that gave off a smoky, masculine scent and flavored the steak much the same. He'd pulled it off, but not without help. He'd intended for her to sit the entire time without helping, but that didn't happen. Instead, she quickly and efficiently chopped up the rest of the salad, tossing the dressing and seasoning it with salt and pepper before removing the baked potatoes from the oven and finishing them off with butter, sour cream, and steak sauce which Wyatt found surprisingly tasty.

"Thank you for dinner," she said, smiling at him across the table.

Wyatt smiled back and laughed. "Well, you pretty much made everything better than I could have, so thank you."

Her appetite had not been what it used to be but she tried hard to eat as much as possible so he wouldn't feel bad. He'd put so much thought into making something nice for her that she shoveled it down her throat even though her stomach wanted none of it. He dropped the ball on dessert, forgetting completely, so they opted for another beer instead, both of them already feeling foggy.

They sat on the front porch on metal rockers that had been on the ranch for what looked like 50 years. The night was quiet and warm but not as warm as their July nights, thick with humidity. The weather would still be hot in Tucson and the rest of the state for months to come but not here. Here, Wyatt could feel fall approaching, the slight shift in the wind welcoming in a new beginning.

"Do you want to stay over?" he asked, full of liquid courage. "I mean- I don't want you to think I brought you here just so we could- you know- but. I don't know. This'll be one of the last weekends I have before I go. So-" His words hung in the air, bringing the ticking clock front and center where it couldn't be ignored.

"Yeah, I want to stay," she said quietly, reaching for his hand.

Wyatt exhaled, relieved. "Ok, babe." He pulled her hand up to his mouth and kissed the back of it softly, looking into her face on the dark porch.

He wanted to ask her more about her mom. He wanted to ask her how she was feeling, really. He wanted to ask her if she'd write to him in basic training, and if she'd still be his even though he was gone, but he didn't want to ruin that moment with her. Her beautiful sad face looking back into his, there in that place they'd first loved each other. Sometimes, there are no words.

"Are you tired?" he said after a stretch of quiet between them.

"No," she said quietly. "But why don't we go to bed anyway."

He could hear her smiling again and he was relieved to know she was still in there. To know that girl he loved so much was still inside of this Charlotte, with her eyes so sad and her laughter gone.

"Deal," he said, leaning out of his chair to kiss her softly.

They held hands walking to the bedroom on the dusty wood floors. They entered the bedroom and walked toward the edge of the bed, standing in front of each other in that place once again. He looked down at her and smiled shyly.

"All summer and you still make me nervous," he said, honestly.

He put his hands on either side of her face and kissed her, pressing against her soft, full lips until they yielded to him entirely. She put her arms around him, moving her hands up and down his muscular back and pulling him against her.

He didn't want to be too harsh with her, but he wanted her so badly that he had to make himself be soft. It had been two weeks since they'd made love in that very room but it felt like the first time all over again. He slowly moved his hands down and pulled at the bottom of her sundress, removing it over her head and laying her on the bed. He kissed down her body, slowly placing his lips on the top of her breasts popping out of her lace trimmed bra before removing it and moving his tongue over her hard nipples.

Charlotte breathed heavily, whispering all of the things he loved, begging for him. When he pulled her panties down, he pushed his hand gently between her legs, feeling her. She sighed, moving her body against him and pulling at his bicep. She was so perfect that way, her guard down and her body free. She was so much herself in those moments that it only made him love her more intensely. When he came down on top of her he loved her slowly, pushing in and out of her, kissing her full on the mouth. She was softer than normal- almost breakable. He moved the way he knew would push her to her edge, loving her like he knew she wanted until she finished, panting into his mouth. He allowed himself release only after he knew she had what she needed.

"Charlotte," he whispered fiercely. "I love you."

But she couldn't answer back, her tears already dropping from the corner of her eyes and onto his neck where her face lay buried.

⚭❖⚭

It felt strange to be back in his hometown after the whole summer. He'd practically disappeared off of the face of the earth when he moved to Patagonia and that wasn't in the plans. He thought he would have been back up many times to see friends, his dad, his old life, if only for a couple of weekends. But then, there'd been her. She also wasn't in the plans, as the best things in life often aren't.

It was still hot even though it was September. Wyatt's shirt stuck to his back as he exited the freeway on his side of town, driving toward the Catalina mountain range stretching wide on the skyline. His whole life he'd lived in the shadow of those mountains but he still looked at them in awe. They were stunning- rocky and green after a wet monsoon season and he felt his chest ache when he looked at them. He loved this place, it was ingrained in the fabric of who he was, and yet, he knew he didn't belong there anymore. Suddenly, his puzzle piece didn't fit.

He looked up at the rocky cliffs high above him and once again wished she'd come with him. He'd asked her, practically begged her to come, but she wouldn't budge. Rose needed her at the shop, she said. She couldn't bring herself to burden her again after missing so much work. Wyatt knew if he had asked Rose she would have said yes but he didn't want to force Charlotte. She'd shown small glimpses of who she was like the night at the bunkhouse the weekend before that and he didn't want to chance ruining her progress. He had to be gentle to coax her out of the shell of grief that surrounded her.

The Marine recruiting office sat in the strip mall near his high school. It always struck him as odd that military recruiting offices were at places like that, doors down from sandwich shops and nail salons. Wyatt knew the recruiters since they frequented the high school, constantly handing out pamphlets, bumper stickers, and keychains. He'd watched them speak to other students, joke with them, creating a friendly rapport. He'd never once spoken to them until that day he decided on his own what he would do. The recruiters had been pleasantly surprised since everyone knew Wyatt was a stellar student-athlete with the ability to play ball at the next level. He wasn't even on their radar for recruitment because of that, but there he came, ready to sign his soul over to the Marine Corps that day. Just 18 and full of defiance for what the rest of the world expected him to do.

Wyatt pulled into the parking lot, throwing his truck into park. He'd worn his nice jeans, boots, and a clean t-shirt since he still felt he needed to make the right impression. The day was stiflingly hot though, and he regretted his decision to not opt for shorts instead. The air conditioning poured into his face as he opened the glass door to the office. Usually there were two or three recruiters sitting at desks when he'd come in before, but not that day. That day only his favorite recruiter was there sitting at a desk, deep in paperwork when Wyatt entered.

Sergeant Ben Waltrip was a classic Marine poster boy. His lean physique was emphasized by his khaki shirt tucked neatly into his blue slacks with red blood stripes down each side. He stood almost as tall as Wyatt and had blonde hair buzzed into a high and tight haircut that was standard issue for every Marine. Unlike Wyatt, though, he was outgoing and wildly charismatic. He could talk to a wall, and probably recruit it into the Marine Corps as well. He looked up from his paperwork when Wyatt walked through the door.

"Wyatt!" he said jovially. "Thought you might have gone AWOL before you even started!"

He stood and moved around his desk to shake Wyatt's hand firmly.

"Here have a seat. You need a drink? Water or anything?"

"No, thank you, sergeant," Wyatt said formally, still nervous around him despite knowing him for months.

"How's your summer been? Ranch work go well?" Ben closed the folder in front of him and gave Wyatt his full attention, sitting forward in his chair with his arms resting on his desk.

"It's been good. Hard work, but it's been an experience." He wondered as he said it if his voice gave him away, if Sergeant Waltrip could see that the summer had been an experience because of more than just the ranch.

"You have time for any fun on top of that work?" he said grinning, as if on cue.

Wyatt mustered a smile. "Little bit," he said even though that wasn't exactly how it felt at the moment.

Waltrip flashed him a toothy white grin. "Atta boy. It's important to get some of that out before basic. You won't be having fun for awhile but after that, it'll get easier."

He looked at Wyatt as he said it and Wyatt could see the man's eyes flash with regret. Sergeant Waltrip's words were smooth and practiced, Wyatt could tell. He could also tell that he'd been recruiting in peacetime for far too long. He'd have to change his canned speeches to reflect that but Wyatt wasn't about to call him out on that.

"Ok, so. Let's go over your itinerary, alright? Let me grab your file." He opened a drawer on his desk and removed Wyatt's file. It was strange to see his name like that, printed so formally on official looking documents. "STERLING, WYATT" popped out in dark letters.

"Looks like you leave in two weeks. Is that right?" He flipped his papers over to look at the calendar under them. "Yep. Wow, that's coming up," he said to himself. "So you'll be headed to the Marine Corps Recruiting Depot in San Diego. Weather will be great, that's the silver lining," he said, and shot Wyatt his Hollywood smile again.

He spent the next 30 minutes going over everything Wyatt could expect in basic training, although Wyatt had heard it all before. The lack of sleep, the mental exhaustion, the physical tests. Wyatt could feel his stomach churning as he spoke to him, not because he was afraid of any of that, but because it was real. He was two weeks from leaving her.

"Then after that'll be graduation. You'll get a couple of days off to be with your family, then on to Marine Combat Training and MOS school."

Wyatt nodded, thinking about the long road ahead of him. "Yes, sir."

"You're ready. I know it doesn't feel like that but you're ready. Just remember that they'll break you down to nothing only so they can build you back up their way."

He scrutinized Wyatt, looking close into the young man's face. "You didn't go and get yourself a girlfriend this summer, did you?"

Wyatt's jaw dropped a bit but he caught himself quickly and tried to look nonchalant.

"Yes, sergeant," Wyatt said quietly.

Sergeant Waltrip smiled, but looked more exasperated than happy for him. He shook his head slowly.

"I'm not surprised. You're a good looking kid," he said, and smiled sadly. "You remember what we talked about with that, though?"

Wyatt thought back to all of the times he'd spent in that office since the previous spring. How Waltrip and the other recruiters, all single or divorced, had lectured him not to get a girlfriend before basic training. Actually, it seemed they were more advocates of him never getting a girlfriend at all.

Wyatt nodded at him. "I do. I didn't plan to, but it just- it just kinda happened."

Waltrip sighed and looked out the front window of the office. Something about the look on his face made Wyatt feel bad for him. He looked sad, almost regretful with his handsome face set in a thin line.

"Just remember, Wyatt. Remember the only person you can count on is you. You and your new brothers."

⚘⚭O⚭⚘

Wyatt almost headed directly back to the freeway to go back to Patagonia, but guilt got the better of him. He drove toward his childhood home with his nerves tight and a guilty conscience. He knew he should have come home over the summer, if even for a day, but he hadn't. It had all gone by so fast with her and he couldn't ever bring himself to miss a day from their southern Arizona haven. Plus, he'd wanted out of Tucson so bad, he couldn't stand the thought of returning back to the place that his mom no longer was and where his bachelor father now stayed, all the while pretending nothing had happened. They'd all ignored it for so long that it was past the point of even being on the table for discussion.

When he reached his dirt road toward the outskirts of Tucson, he slowed down to look at the familiar desert that surrounded him. It was different desert than the type in Patagonia. Here, too, the brush was green from a wet monsoon season, the first one he'd ever missed in Tucson his whole life. But unlike down south, the Tucson desert was sprinkled with saguaros and cholla cactus, making it uninhabitable for anything that wasn't tough enough. That was why he loved it. It had a harsh beauty to it that not everyone could see. It was so much a part of him that it made his heart tighten to be back. Despite himself, he missed it.

He saw his dad's large Dodge truck as he pulled in the drive, so he would not be off the hook, he'd have to see him after all. He'd have to apologize for being gone so long and go back to their unspoken agreement of not saying anything that truly mattered. He parked his truck in his usual spot and took a deep breath before getting out to walk to the front door.

The house looked as well kept as it ever had, hedges trimmed and weeds pulled. It was an old home, built in the 80's in the popular brick style of the moment, stretched out long and flat with low ceilings. Wyatt looked around and saw that the flowerpots that once covered the front porch were noticeably absent. It was his mother's only outside chore, those flowers. Wyatt wondered what his father did with them or if his mother had taken them with her to her new life. He placed his hands on the knob but realized he couldn't just walk in unexpected, so he knocked quietly on his own front door, standing several moments before his dad answered.

Sam Sterling opened the door wearing his work wranglers and an undershirt. His dark hair was peppered with gray, more than Wyatt remembered. He looked smaller somehow, definitely thinner. He'd already removed his boots for the day and had a Coors Light in his hand, which seemed early, even for him.

"Wyatt?" he said, his face surprised. "Prodigal son returns, huh?" Sam cracked a smile and put his hand out for Wyatt to shake.

"Hi, Dad," he said awkwardly as Sam used his free hand to slap his shoulder.

"Where the hell you been, boy? Thought you might've left to the Middle East before saying goodbye."

Sam walked into the house, leaving Wyatt to follow. The place was clean but didn't have its normal smell. No fragrant candle permeating the air, nothing baking in the oven. It smelled a lot like the bunkhouse- stagnant with men. Wyatt looked around the family room and kitchen. There still hung pictures of western scenes and decor but gone were the family portraits that used to litter every wall. Only a couple of pictures of Wyatt in his little league uniform remained. He was so distracted by the house that he didn't realize he'd gone silent and not responded to his father. Sam sat himself back down in his recliner and looked up at his son.

"You filled out. Must be feeding you ok down there," he said.

"Huh?" Wyatt said distracted. "Oh yeah, there's a lot of work, so... must be why."

He tore himself away from looking around his old house and sat on the couch on the other side of the room from his father. He'd known this wouldn't be an easy visit but he didn't anticipate this. The awkwardness of it all overwhelmed him entirely.

"What you been up to? Staying outta trouble down there?" Sam asked, looking the boy up and down.

Wyatt flushed and wondered if his dad and Sergeant Waltrip had some kind of superpower that allowed them to see that he was no longer a virgin.

"Yes, sir," he said as steady as he could. "Just been workin' a lot."

Sam made small talk about the ranch work, about the cattle and the various projects he'd completed. He asked after Garrett and other ranchers he knew in the area, most of whom he'd rodeoed with at some point. Wyatt answered him, trying to ignore how wrong it felt to be there in the house without his mom. Without all of the things he'd known his whole life. It was physically uncomfortable for him to fake it- to continue putting on a show. He had no idea what that summer, or Charlotte, had done to him, but he was no longer the Wyatt who used to live there.

"Well, what finally brought you up here?" Sam said, appraising Wyatt's face.

Wyatt shifted uncomfortably again. He knew it was a sore subject. "Came up to see my recruiter today. Leave in two weeks."

Sam nodded slow and glanced back at the TV muted on the news. "Gonna have your work cut out for ya if you head over there. Them bastards are nothin' nice."

Wyatt glanced at the screen and saw the reporter in a helmet and bulletproof vest crouched down speaking into the camera intensely. Stark, dusty desert surrounded him as the camera cut to explosions in the distance. He looked away quickly, glancing out the window toward where the horses were in their backyard. He looked around, searching the seemingly empty corrals.

"Where are all of the horses?" he asked, his heart pounding.

"Sold em," he said shortly. "Kept Lacey, but had to get rid of the rest."

"But why?" Wyatt asked, forgetting their rule about not talking.

Sam shifted in his seat, growing visibly uncomfortable. He took a long drink of his beer then looked back at Wyatt. "Movin'. No need to take them all with me," he said without emotion.

Wyatt thought about his horses, some he'd had for over ten years. He'd taken care of them, they'd been his job practically his whole life. He'd loved and cared for them like they were family and now they were gone. On top of that, his dad would be gone, too. His childhood home was no longer theirs. He could feel his stomach churning and that feeling of hopelessness return, the same he'd felt when Charlotte left.

"Were you gonna tell me?" he spat out without thinking.

Sam laughed coldly. "Were you ever gonna come home? You're workin' two hours away and you haven't been home in months."

"You could've called me!" Wyatt said, growing angrier.

Sam shrugged. "Just figured you were ready to move on."

Wyatt ran a hand through his hair, trying to get his temper under control. "Where are you going?"

"Back to Alabama," he said, letting his words hang in the air. "Nothin' for me here now." He took another swig of his beer and looked back at the TV.

"So that's it? You and mom just put in your time with me and now that's it? Everyone's just gonna fucking leave?" He was shouting now, so out of control of himself he could hardly believe it was him talking, especially to his father.

Sam looked at him and puffed out his chest. "Watch your mouth in my house. You're still my son," he said sternly.

"Well, you could've fooled me. You and mom don't give a shit about me. I was your little show pony my whole life and I do one thing you don't want me to do and poof. That's it," Wyatt said as he stood abruptly and moved toward the front door.

Sam stood, moving to stand in his son's face. They stood eye level, both staring back at each other with the same crystal eyes. Sam set his jaw, his neck and face flushing through with anger.

"Don't talk about your mother like that, you hear me? We didn't raise you to talk like that to your parents, Goddamn it."

"What did you raise me for?" Wyatt shouted back. "I'm not good enough now because I wanted to join the Marine Corps? Is that it? It had to be college? Had to be your way? What the fuck do you two want from me?"

"That's enough, Wyatt. I don't know who the hell you think you're talkin' to but you know better than this."

"So you'll go back to Alabama and what? I'm just not going to see you and mom again? That's it? And neither of you have the fucking decency to tell me? We're just gonna keep ignoring it like we have everything else?"

"You wanted to be a big man and sign up to go over there and get blown up so you can make your own fuckin' choices now!" Sam screamed back at him. "You made your bed! I did my job. I raised you right, now it's on you!"

Wyatt stared back at his father, fighting the tears forming in his eyes. Red-hot anger burned inside of him and he clenched his fists to his side. He breathed heavily, trying to steady himself to no avail. His father stood glaring back at him.

"I did everything right. All these years. And this- the Marines aren't bad. I just don't understand," he said more calmly.

"And you won't. You won't until you have a son of your own. Then it'll sink it. You made a choice. So now you live with it. Maybe die with it." Sam's eyes flashed with regret as soon as he said it but he didn't apologize. He didn't take it back. He set himself in stone looking back at Wyatt who felt his father's coldness as plain as day.

"Fine," Wyatt said flatly. "This is goodbye then."

He stuck out his hand for his father to shake, willing him to stop him. Willing him to realize that this would be it. There would be no other chance for them before he left. But Sam wouldn't budge. He looked his son back squarely in the eyes and shook his hand firmly.

"Godspeed." Sam said quietly, and walked out the back door on the porch, looking out into the distance.

Wyatt looked around the empty living room, suddenly quiet. He walked toward his pictures hanging on the wall and looked closely at one. He was 12, the same age as Charlotte when she had to go through hell. He looked at the smiling boy's face in the picture, head high and baseball bat on his shoulder, face tanned with the spring sun. It was like looking at a picture of someone else. Someone he once knew. He pulled the picture off the wall, tucking it under his arm and walked out the front door, closing it quietly behind him.

"I want you to regress me," Charlotte said to Rose as they sat down for morning meditation.

Rose was taken aback. Not only had Charlotte shown little interest in the spiritual side of things in recent weeks, but she was borderline demanding in her request, which was not normal for her at all. Rose sighed heavily, looking back at Charlotte.

"Ok..." she started slowly. "Let's talk about why you feel that would be productive."

"Because I'm a fucking mess," Charlotte said shortly.

Rose looked at her niece sadly, assessing her. Charlotte's hair was down and messy around her face. She was dressed and ready for work in a tank top and jeans but her face didn't look like it normally did. Her eyes were puffy with dark rings underneath them and her cheeks looked thinner. Rose thought sadly that she knew this girl. This was the girl who had shown up on her doorstep in May. The broken little girl that she thought she'd fixed for good.

"You're not a mess, babe, you're just swimming in grief right now. It's going to get better," she said quietly, trying to coax her from the edges of herself.

Charlotte shook her head once. "No. It's more than that. It's here again. I remember how it feels. But it's worse this time."

Rose's heart pounded in her chest and she could feel her palms sweat. She'd seen clients who were in the throes of the dark night before and she'd been able to help them out easily. The difference was, they had no idea what they were up against, so they listened to Rose's every instruction, never understanding how serious their situation actually was. But not Charlotte. She knew the hopeless spiral which she'd entered. Only a couple of weeks ago, Rose had told herself she could handle it now, after their summer of building up the fortress around her soul. But that wasn't the case. Lily's death had pushed her from a cliff and sent her tumbling down to a place where she could no longer see the light. Rose knew that ultimately it would only be Charlotte who could recover herself, that all Rose could do was guide her.

"Charlotte, I can help you. I know it's hard. I know it seems dark but-"

"It feels more than dark," Charlotte said dully. "My dreams-" she started. "They're bad."

Charlotte's eyes glazed over as she thought about her nightmares. Her mother's decayed face. Wyatt with blown off limbs. She was losing the fight within herself, her mind taking her over. If she was psychic like everyone said, then the future was bleak. So bleak, that she didn't know if she wanted to see it.

"Dreams are symbolic, babe. They indicate the battles we have in our own mind. Don't let them overtake you."

"But what about when you've had dreams about something and then that happens? Nothing symbolic about that. Those are premonitions."

Rose was as patient as ever. "You're right," she said softly. "But there's a difference between a dream like that and just a regular old symbolic dream where your emotions are played out for you. You have to really feel that difference."

"I feel nothing," she said stoically. "That's why I want you to regress me. I just need to see how this all fits in. What plan I've made. Maybe then it'll make sense."

Rose sighed and looked at the beautiful girl in front of her. She knew Charlotte's life would continue to be an uphill war. She'd seen that for a long time. The girl had not cut out an easy road for herself, although Rose knew it would get better. She just didn't know when.

"Alright, babe," Rose said quietly. "We can regress you. There are some things you need to know about regression before we start, though," Rose began.

Charlotte looked back at her aunt with her eyes rimmed in black circles. She nodded at her, indicating she was paying attention, but Rose saw the glazed over look in her eye and she knew the girl wasn't grounded. She was living in the prison of her own mind instead of the present moment and for once, Rose doubted her ability to help her.

"So the first thing is that these lives are over. The point of regression is to move forward by going backward. To realize that the things we carry- the battles, the hurt, all of that- ends with that life. They're lessons for soul growth- no need to get too attached to them. Does that make sense?"

Charlotte nodded. "What about relationships? Do those end with each life?"

"Good question," Rose said, encouraged by Charlotte's participation. "That particular relationship ends but our relationships with people in our soul groups never really end. They continue on, just in a different capacity. Like you and me, for example," Rose smiled. "Right now we are this way but we've been siblings, business partners, friends, mother and daughter. We've had many lives together which means we've played many roles. It's why we are so connected now."

Charlotte had heard most of this before and she believed it. Now though, after her mom died the way she had, she wanted to know the reason. She had to know why she had it in her to turn her back on her mother, essentially killing her. Maybe there was something, some way of understanding that.

"I get it," Charlotte said shortly.

"And Charlotte-" Rose hesitated. "I know you might want to see something about your mom. You know, why this happened, but, well-" she faltered. "Sometimes the guides show us only what they think we need to know. Give yourself time to figure out everything with your mom. Something like that isn't easily understood. It's a process."

Charlotte nodded her head again, annoyed at how transparent she was in front of Rose. She was so ashamed of her heart at that moment that she didn't want anyone looking at it like Rose was prone to do.

Rose smiled sadly at her. "Why don't you lay down on the couch like a good patient and I'll sit here. Let's just say a quick prayer for protection and peace, shall we?"

Rose closed her eyes and grabbed Charlotte's hands, praying hard in her mind and asking humbly for protection and guidance. To be able to cure Charlotte of her hopelessness. Charlotte did not close her eyes, nor did she pray. She stared at the rug under her feeling nothing. Undeterred, Rose opened her eyes and situated herself in the armchair, ready to work. Charlotte lay flat on the couch with a pillow under her head, ready to follow instructions.

"Ok, this is very simple, Charlotte," she said, her voice soothingly soft. "You just listen to my voice and try not to think too much. Just go where I lead you."

Charlotte nodded and closed her eyes gently, listening to Rose's calm words instructing her to let go. For a long time Charlotte thought it didn't work, that she wasn't hypnotized at all. She felt no different than normal except maybe a little sleepier.

"It's time to go back. Go back to a life that can help you understand this one. Go back to the place that will help you move forward," Rose gently directed.

Charlotte exhaled slowly and grew quiet. Rose thought that she might have fallen asleep, that exhaustion might have gotten the better of her, until Charlotte finally spoke. Her voice was sad, barely above a whisper.

"It's Wyatt," she said, on the verge of tears. "I see Wyatt."

⸙

Wyatt planned on driving straight to Charlotte's house. He ached to fall into her, to tell her everything that had happened with his dad. How empty it all felt. He wanted to tell her about the file folder with his name written on it so permanently that it made him want to scream that he didn't want to go, right there in the middle of the office. He wanted to tell her how despite his best efforts he'd cried driving back down his dirt road, knowing it would be the last time ever he'd leave his childhood home.

He could tell her none of that though. He could have told the girl he knew a month ago, but not this girl. Not the girl who already carried the weight of the universe on her shoulders with her jaw set, trying like hell not to let anyone see how it was breaking her. He couldn't do that to her. So he drove to the lake instead, pulling his truck to the front where only a few people sat on the shoreline. Summer was over and there was no one swimming, no one picnicking, no kids playing in the sand. As much as he had enjoyed the silence on the other side of the lake all summer long, he ached for that noise to be back again. He missed the people in the sunshine, their echoed voices floating down to their place where they'd been together. The absence of it, the silence of only nature and a few birdwatchers meant that it was over indefinitely. Leaving was not months away, it was not a nightmare, it was here and it was worse than he could have imagined.

He rolled down the windows in his pickup and let the early fall air blow through the cab. Charlotte had told him that she'd prayed, that she begged God for help once and that her prayer had been heard. He believed that if anyone's prayer deserved to be heard, it was hers. He thought of her sitting on the back of the parade float, shining like a beacon for everyone to see. She was not of this earth, she was something else and he knew that the first time he saw her. Yes, Wyatt thought, her prayers deserved to be heard, but what about him? He knew nothing of God, of religion. More and more he felt as though he knew nothing of life at all. Would anyone listen? Would anyone hear him?

Wyatt ran a hand through his hair and looked out across the lake, choppy with the day's wind whipping through the valley. He'd been a different person when he came here in early June. He could never have imagined how much this place could have changed him. How much she could have changed him. He closed his eyes, listening to the wind coming through the mesquite trees. He didn't need help as much as she'd needed it and he knew he didn't deserve it like she had, but he asked anyway.

I need help. He said in his head. *Please, God. Please help me.*

⚜

He was only two weeks from leaving. Only days remained and still they hadn't made a plan. Wyatt told himself that by this time they would have a plan the way he liked to. She'd come visit him after graduation, she'd write to him and him to her. He'd come to see her wherever she was and whenever he could. All of their obstacles were passable, they just needed a plan of action. But none of that was discussed. None of it was set in stone like he wanted it to be. He couldn't even bring it up since she wasn't herself anymore. She'd lost the look in her eye, the one that said she could do anything. It felt selfish for him to make demands of her now that she was so lost, so fragile to the world.

411

He'd sat at the lake until nightfall, unable to get ahold of himself for some time. When he finally left, he didn't feel better. He felt even more lost. He was disappointed in himself that he'd felt nothing when he prayed. Nothing but the wind blowing across his face and the silence of the world around him. As much as he tried, he didn't feel that his prayers were heard.

He'd gone to her that night, ready to put his misery aside to fake it for her. To be the Wyatt she needed. But he didn't have to. Rose answered and told him Charlotte had gone to bed early, and asked him to come back the next evening instead. The way she said it, so full of remorse and sadness for him was unsettling, but he felt relieved in a way. He had nothing else to give that night and thought he might do better the next night anyway. He'd gotten into bed without eating dinner, listening to the sounds of the men sitting in the kitchen chatting in Spanish. He stared at the ceiling, trying to find a solution. He came up empty over and over again before finally drifting off to sleep hours later.

He'd gone through work the same way he had when she'd been gone- in a fog, forgetting what he was doing, he wasn't even in his body at all until someone would yell at him and bring him back to earth. He didn't know what hurt more, leaving her or the complete disintegration of his family. All of it at once was more than he'd dealt with his entire life, making him feel the terrifying feeling of under preparedness he despised.

He finished work at the ranch at 4 o'clock, an easy day in comparison to others. He took the time to shower and change before going to her, hoping she was better that day. That the shine would start to return if only a little bit. She was like a fire when she was herself, and Wyatt needed her warmth more than he could explain.

It was the first day of October. The air had changed and the weather began cooling. It was the time of year Arizona natives lived for and usually he felt the same- but not this year. He drove to her with an anxious stomach and an eager heart, still hoping against hope for a solution. When she opened the door, though, he knew she wasn't any better. She smiled at him but it didn't reach her eyes. She looked thin and pale, her tanned skin fading quickly after her weeks inside. She wore torn jeans that hung loosely from her slender hips and a t-shirt snug around her chest.

"Hey," she said quietly, opening the door for him.

Her arms didn't go around his neck instantly like they used to and it hit him like a physical punch when she didn't touch him first, but he reached for her anyway, gently so he didn't scare her. She seemed so close to breaking that he watched every move he made, dancing carefully around her feelings.

"Hi," he said, leaning to hug her softly around the waist. When he pulled back to look in her face he could tell she'd been crying. "You ok?" he asked quietly.

"I'm fine," she said walking toward the kitchen. "You want something to drink? A Coke?"

Wyatt closed the door and shook his head. "No, thanks. You got any prickly pear margaritas?" She turned and gave him that same sad smile, shaking her head back at him.

"Long day?" she asked moving to sit on the couch. He moved after her, sitting as close as he could without making her uncomfortable.

"Kinda," he said, not elaborating. "I came over last night but you were sleeping."

She nodded, looking away. "Rose told me. Sorry. I was so tired."

"It's ok. Where is Rose, anyway?" he said looking around.

"She had to go-" Charlotte hesitated, "she had to run up to Tucson and do some business I guess."

Wyatt nodded and looked in her eyes, trying to connect with her. He put a hand on her knee and smiled, just barely. She asked about work and Garrett as always, trying to get the focus off of her. He hadn't loved her since that one night in the bunkhouse and he longed to so fiercely that he was afraid it was written all over his face. It wasn't that he wanted the sex as much as he wanted to be close to her, share that secret place that no one could go except them. His heart felt tight, lonely even though she sat right next to him.

"You wanna go to dinner? Or the lake? We could go over to Sonoita to the Ranch House?" he said, reaching for something to make her remember how happy they'd been. How alive she'd been in those places with him.

She shook her head slowly. "I don't really feel up to it, Wyatt."

He nodded slowly, looking down at the ground, trying his hardest not to feel frustrated or disappointed. It was no use though, his face betrayed him as always.

"I'm sorry. I know I've been- you know- I've been a mess," she said quietly.

He looked over at her, her face tired and worn thin. She was still beautiful, there was no doubt, but she wasn't herself. A grayness washed over her, making her seem like a different person.

"It's ok. I understand," he said quietly, even though he didn't.

Despite himself, he wanted her to care about him leaving. He needed somebody to fall apart to, but there was no one. There was quiet between them for a moment until he looked at her, grabbing her hand and holding it in both of his.

"Charlotte- I-" he faltered, "I know you're going through a hard time. I mean- more than hard, I know. I just- I'm leaving, Charlotte. I'm leaving in less than two weeks. And we- we haven't talked about it, you know? What it means for us or anything."

She looked up from their hands and into his face, her green eyes cutting through him just as always. But this time they had something else behind them, something hidden.

"I know, Wyatt. I'm sorry. I haven't been any help with that. I haven't given you any support," she looked back down at their hands intertwined. "You've been nothing but good to me. You don't deserve that."

"No, Charlotte. I understand. I know you're hurting. I just- I guess I just want to know what's going to happen, you know?" he smiled sadly at her. "I just want to have a plan."

She nodded, looking anywhere but in his face. His heart dropped and his stomach churned, as he sat waiting for her to speak. Her long quiet pause made him think he might vomit right there.

"Wyatt, you have this great big, exciting change coming. I know you're nervous about it but you're going to do so well." She looked up at him finally, her eyes watering. "You remember what Aunt Rose said? That you can do anything? Well you can. I've seen it, too. You're so much stronger than you think you are."

He said nothing, his mouth going completely dry and silent. It wasn't like the pep talks she'd given him before that. It felt different. It felt like goodbye.

"I'm not ok, Wyatt," she said after pausing briefly. "It's not just my mom. I can't even explain it to you, but I'm not ok." She looked at the ground, fighting tears before taking a shaky breath and looking back at him. "I don't wanna hold you back. I want you to be able to do what you're destined to do."

His blood pumped in his veins and he could feel his heart pounding in his chest.

"How would you hold me back? You're not going to hold me back from anything," he said as patient as he could.

She shook her head slowly. "Wyatt, you're meant for more than this. You're meant for more than me. I'm not going to distract you from that. I'm not ok-you don't deserve to have to feel like you need to take care of me. You have more important things to worry about now."

"No I don't, Charlotte," he said, his voice raising now. "I love you. You're going to be ok. You're going to get better," he said, longing for her to remember the girl she was. The warrior Rose had told her she had inside.

"Wyatt, you don't understand. I've seen this happen with my mom and dozens of men. She ruined them," she said earnestly.

"You're not her!" he said dropping her hand and standing abruptly. "And I'm not them. This is us!"

"Wyatt, please don't be mad. You have to believe me. You don't want me," she said looking up at him.

"So you're gonna tell me what I want now, too?" he yelled. "Don't tell me what I fucking want, Charlotte, I want you!" His face reddened and he could feel the sweat forming on the back of his neck. "I'll marry you right now. So don't tell me I don't want you," he spat fiercely.

The tears were flowing down her face now and she stood in front of him, looking up at him with a pleading look in her eye.

"Wyatt, please. You have to believe me. I'm doing this because I love you. I only want the best for you."

"You're the best for me!" he yelled back at her, his eyes watering as he fought to keep himself under control. "If you don't want me just fucking say it-don't tell me this is because you love me. If you loved me you wouldn't do this!"

"Wyatt, I do love you. I've never loved anyone like I love you, but I- I don't want to hurt you."

"Well you are!" he said, completely out of control of himself. "Feels like someone cut me with a knife. Are you happy?" he yelled cruelly.

"No!" she yelled back, sobbing now. "I never wanted to hurt you, please," she said reaching for him as he pulled his hand away from her and walked toward the front door.

"Why are you doing this? It doesn't have to be like this!" He couldn't calm himself down, as much as he tried. His temper carried him someplace else entirely.

"There are things that you can't understand, Wyatt. You just have to believe me. Please."

He'd once told her that he'd give her whatever she wanted when she pleaded that way and he thought of it in that moment- how he'd do anything for her. But this was asking too much.

"I meant it when I said I loved you, Charlotte," he said quieter now. A tear fell from the corner of his eye and he wiped it swiftly with the back of his hand. "Remember that."

He could take no more. He couldn't be in that house with her, a place where they'd loved each other so passionately, so purely. He couldn't look at her tear-stained face another moment longer. He turned and flung open the front door, moving swiftly toward his truck.

"Wyatt, please!" she yelled from behind him. Her voice was still uneven with sobbing and he ached to hold her, to comfort her, but his pride wouldn't let him. "Don't leave like this," she pleaded from the porch as he slammed the truck door after him.

The sun was setting over the mountains in the distance, making the world glow pink and orange. He fired up his truck and looked at her standing on the porch. She was still crying, the tears flowing steadily down her distraught face. She held one hand wrapped around her thin stomach and the other raised halfway in the air, bidding him a sad farewell. The gravel kicked up under his tires as he backed out of the driveway.

"Goodbye, Wyatt," she whispered to the quiet of the porch.

⋘᠁⧉᠁⧉᠁⋙

Wyatt drove. He didn't know where he was going and he really didn't care. He just needed to be anywhere but there. He didn't cry once he was alone in the car, although it probably would have felt good to. Instead, he seethed, beyond angry and she'd decided what was best for him without considering how he would feel. That she'd changed so quickly, so violently that it'd left him reeling for an answer. For a solution that wouldn't come.

When darkness fell he found himself through wine country and almost to Tombstone, the quiet and desolation of the desert around him bringing him the solitude he sought. He pulled over on the side of the empty highway, parking his truck in a dirt pull out off of the road. He put his truck in park and rolled down the windows, letting the cold fall air blow into his face. Despite being so worked up, he fell into a fitful sleep, waking with a start throughout the night thinking of her and her vacant eyes staring back at him.

The sun was barely rising as he woke for good and he crunched the time in his head. It had to be pushing 6:30, which meant he was late for chores, but for once, he didn't care. He'd slept all night in the coldness of his old truck, parked far away from everyone and everything he knew. He rubbed his hands over his face and thought remorsefully about how he'd yelled at her crying face. The shame washed over him then to think of it. He didn't even know who the person was. That person who lost all control like that and had it in him to behave that way.

He fired up his truck and pulled back onto the highway headed toward Patagonia, feeling the emptiness in his stomach and the numbness in his head. He took a deep breath and was shocked to hear the shakiness in his breathing. He'd forgotten that he'd cried, right in front of her. He'd not only screamed at her, he'd cried, creating a more pathetic display than he thought possible.

He listened to the quiet hum of the engine, driving back in a haze. He didn't hesitate to pass the turnoff for the ranch, blowing by it without looking back. He drove straight to her, determined to talk sense into her. Determined to keep himself under control this time. Rose's car still wasn't in the drive and the curtains to the house were drawn but he knocked loudly on the front door, waiting several minutes for her to answer before walking to the backyard. She was nowhere to be found and Wyatt started to feel that familiar feeling of panic creep up on him again, only this time it was worse; this time, he was sure it was bad.

He walked all the way around the house and up the front again, circling around to the shop. She'd be working, but he'd ask to talk to her anyway. He'd beg her to reconsider. To listen to him this time. He walked up to the front door of the shop, flanked by potted flowers and wind chimes, singing softly in the fall wind. He looked up at the door and felt the world fall out from under his feet when he read the sign taped on the door.

"Closed until further notice."

Wyatt stepped backward as if he'd taken a punch to the stomach. He felt a coldness wash over him and his hands begin to shake.

"No," he whispered to himself. "Please-no." But no one responded. The tingling of the wind chimes the only sound.

❧❧❧ ❧❧❧ ❧❧❧

SNOWFALL – *Book Two*
coming soon
www.katiejdouglas.com

Acknowledgments

The first person I have to thank is Megan Hennessey, my friend, my confidant, my editor. Thank you, Megs, for encouraging me from the very first word I wrote. Thank you for your endless edits and for talking about these characters and this book as if it were real life. Thank you for telling me you felt jipped after reading the first kissing scene and making me rewrite it. You will never know what it's meant to have your support from the start. Your light, love, and positive energy have a hand in this dream coming to fruition.

To my husband Jack who is the most steadfast person in my life. Thank you for loving me and supporting this dream of mine. Thank you for taking care of us and always being my steady place to land. And thank you for loving this book. It means the world to me.

To my three beautiful children, Bailey, Cody, and Cade, you are the reason for all I do. I don't even remember who I was before I was your mama. All that you've taught me about love helped me write this.

To my mother, the best person I know, for teaching me it is never too late to pursue anything in life and for showing me that grace and goodness come in all packages. Thank you, papa, for believing in me and always rooting for me.

To my siblings, Sky, Jo, and Clay. I'm thankful we are all so close and that anytime I laugh with you guys, all is right in the world. Every bit of confidence I have comes from knowing that no matter what I do, I will never be without you guys. To my brothers-in-laws Lou and Scott and sister-in-law Jen, thank you for dealing with our family and for always supporting all of us.

Thank you to my in laws, Kathy, Jack, Kelly, and James who are so much more than the family I "married into." Thank you for being the best in laws in the whole world. I'm blessed to have you in my life.

To Kate and Brian Hope, my dear friends of so many years. Thank you for believing in me and supporting me. You are true friends and that is a rare thing in this world. Kate, your support for this book means so much to me. I'm so lucky to know you.

Thank you Mandy and Sean Osborne for being the incredible humans you are. Sean, thank you for letting me interview you about the Marine Corps after we drank a bottle of rum. I get it now- I'm in love with the Marine Corps, too.

To Vicki and Angel, thank you for being my biggest fans, always. Thank you for laughing at my jokes and for your never-ending encouragement. So thankful for your friendship.

To my soul sisters Jess, Kittrin, and Tina. Thank you for rooting me on always. Some of the best times in my life have been on a barstool next to you broads.

To my friend Shannon who is beautiful inside and out. Thank you for your vision and for telling me how much this book touched you.

To my nieces and nephews Canyon, Aspen, Tucker, Hadley, Ame, Isla, and Rhett. You make my life happier and I'm thankful for you all every day.

To my favorite band Reckless Kelly for being my muse and my inspiration for the title of this and my next two novels. Thank you for your Art.

I have to thank my photographer for this novel, Ashley Elicio. Your work, your pictures completed my vision for this book. I can't thank you enough. Thank you to my makeup artist Karen Bracamonte for transforming me for the pictures for this novel. You ladies are angels and your enthusiasm for this project made me even more excited.

Thank you to BJ Kurtz, an incredible indie author and friend. Thank you for helping me through this process.

To my dear friend Tiffany Nunn for always being there for me.

Thank you to my book cover designer Rachel Christmas for being so amazing and creating the most beautiful cover.

Thank you to Matthew Croy for the endless amount of Marine Corps information. Semper Fi!

Thank you to the angels I know I have around me every day. Dad, Grandma, uncle Groovy, Grandpa, probably countless more. Thank you for guiding me and for teaching me that we never really go away.

Lastly, I would like to thank everyone who has supported this book launching. I am beyond blessed with great friends and family and I had the courage to follow this dream thanks to that. Whether I succeed or fail, I am thankful for all of those who believed in me.